SHE WAS BEYOND SHYNESS NOW, BEYOND FEAR.

Dacey shivered like a wild animal under Quinn's caress. He poured kisses on her, plundering her lips, her neck, the softness of her throat.

"Ah, God, Dacey, you are lovely . . . a goddess." His voice was almost a groan.

And she felt beautiful before him, feeling his look like a warm touch on her full breasts. He was beautiful, too, Dacey thought feverishly. His body, everything about him, as clean and strong as any wild animal. Was this . . . this wonder . . . what it was all about? This love, this melting joy? She had never known such rapture could exist—and they soared together, two sparks exploding outward from a central fire. . . .

Kimberley Flame

JULIA GRICE grew up in Michigan and has lived in Florida and Hawaii. She has worked as a newspaper reporter, social worker, and librarian, but for the past eight years she has devoted all her energy to writing. Julia Grice now lives in Michigan, where she loves to swim, paint, play racquetball, and do original needlepoint.

SIGNET Bestsellers

KIMBERLEY FLAME

JULIA GRICE

A SIGNET BOOK

NEW AMERICAN LIBRARY

TIMES MIRROR

PUBLISHED BY
THE NEW AMERICAN LIBRARY
OF CANADA LIMITED.

PUBLISHER'S NOTE

This novel is a work of fiction. Names, characters, places, and incidents
are either the product of the author's imagination or are used fictitiously,
and any resemblance to actual persons, living or dead, events, or locales
is entirely coincidental.

Copyright © 1983 by Julia Grice

First Printing, August, 1983

2 3 4 5 6 7 8 9

 SIGNET TRADEMARK REG. U.S. PAT. OFF. AND FOREIGN COUNTRIES
REGISTERED TRADEMARK · MARCA REGISTRADA
HECHO EN WINNIPEG, CANADA

SIGNET, SIGNET CLASSIC, MENTOR, PLUME, MERIDIAN
and NAL BOOKS are published in Canada by The New American
Library of Canada, Limited, Scarborough, Ontario

PRINTED IN CANADA
COVER PRINTED IN U.S.A.

For my mother and father,
Jean and Will Haughey,
in deepest thanks.

Readers should know that the policy of apartheid, or complete separation of the races, began in South Africa in 1948. The Prohibition of Mixed Marriages Act was passed in 1949, followed by the Immorality Act a year later, which imposed severe penalties for sexual intercourse between whites and nonwhites.

But in the time of the 1870s, the period of this book, the older Dutch policy of *Baasskaap*, translated as "boss-hood," was in force. This meant white domination. In the early days of Kimberley, there were prostitutes of all colors who entertained white customers, and some men did possess dark-skinned mistresses.

I would like to thank Lee Butcher, who contributed invaluable help in the planning, writing, and editing of this manuscript; and Al Zuckerman, who was more than generous with suggestions and guidance. For their help and suggestions for research materials I am also very grateful to Margaret Duda, Pat and Sandi Scafetti, Vera Henry, Maskew Miller Publishers, Struik Publishers, South African Tourist Corporation; McGregor Museum, Kimberley; and Muriel Macey, Africana Librarian, Kimberley Public Library.

SECTION ONE

1872-1875

1

IN THE HARSH AFTERNOON LIGHT, the town of New Rush, beginning to be known as Kimberley, looked like a heat mirage. Sun flashed off its corrugated-iron roofs and white tents, making a blinding glare that hurt Dacey McKinnon's eyes.

She heard the Afrikaans curse of the wagon driver. An ox bellowed as he cracked his long whip, only a skillful inch away from the animal's flank.

Dacey caught her breath, feeling excitement kindle in her like the incandescent flame of a paraffin footlight. It was an excitement that had been slowly growing in her for the six hundred hot, dusty miles of their journey by ox cart from Cape Town.

South Africa. Mile after mile of desolate, grassless near-desert, dotted with an occasional thorn tree and strange, jutting hills called *koppies*. Herds of game: kudu, gemsbok, springbok, animals with a delicate, elusive beauty. And always the stifling heat, the dust that gritted between the teeth and coated the skin and made one dream of a real bath, in a real tub.

They'd come all this way on the basis of an excited letter from one of Papa's drinking cronies, who'd told of fabulous diamonds being found, fortunes made or broken in a single day. Miners by the thousands, aching to be entertained.

Good sense told Dacey that this would be like all their

other ventures—better in the dreaming than in the doing. Probably they'd earn only enough for their keep, their passage home, and the cleaning of their threadbare costumes, now stuffed into the collection of trunks and sets that rode in the second wagon.

Still . . . diamonds! All along, Dacey had had the feeling that Kimberley wasn't to be just another stop on the troupe's long journey to obscurity, but something more. Something fateful, that would change her life forever.

And aren't you being a fool, Dacia McKinnon? she asked herself ruefully. You're as bad as Papa, with all his schemes and omens.

Wedged in beside her father, she clung to the swaying wagon seat and craned for a glimpse of the settlement, where they were scheduled to go onstage tonight.

Papa had already warned her that here on this vast central African highveld, there was little wood or brick with which to build. Therefore, people made do with canvas or corrugated iron, and she should be prepared for . . . well, simplicity.

Still, what she saw now was a shock. Tents! Everywhere, hundreds of them, plainly being lived in. There were covered wagons by the score, some with strings of laundry hung out to dry. Rickety iron sheds bore the signs of business establishments and looked as if they might topple at any moment. There were a few one-story buildings that straggled around a huge, dusty square jammed with ox teams and crowds of men. And over everything, like a huge, inverted bowl, arched a sky so stunningly blue that it seemed to have been painted.

As the wagons rolled toward the square, the hooves of the eighteen oxen churned up choking clouds of dust. Dacey swallowed back her disappointment. What had she expected? The venerable, centuries-old buildings of London, from which they had come? Trees and gardens and civilization? This was Africa, not England, and this was 1872, a year of possibility and adventure.

The Market Square smelled of dust, cattle dung, and oxen. As the two wagons creaked into the square, filled with the seven men and four women dressed in flamboyant clothing, a few passersby stopped to gape at the wagons flying the

McKinnon pennant, which snapped and rippled in the hot breeze.

"They have noticed us." Dacey managed to say it lightly, knowing that this would please Papa, who always courted publicity, saying that it was the bread of an actor.

"They certainly have, and I trust that they will crowd into our performance tonight in large numbers. You must air out all the costumes, my dear, and make sure that our jewels glitter properly. Not that paste gems will be very impressive here, where diamonds are the main business," Papa added wryly.

Diamonds. Her spirits rising, Dacey squirmed for another good look at the square. Throngs of miners jostled each other, most of them young, their faces tanned mahogany from the fierce African sun. She saw black men in tribal gear, white men from a dozen countries. Bantu, Indians, Malays, Dutch, all rubbed shoulders. Yet, Dacey noticed, there was an aggressive strut to the way all the men walked, no matter what their color.

It was then that Dacey realized one of the men was staring at her.

For an actress, of course, being looked at wasn't unusual. Dacey had been on the stage since she was four, and it was to be expected that the entrance of a theatrical company into this out-of-the-way town would cause some notice. Still, she knew instantly that this was no ordinary curious glance. Set beneath strong, straight, black brows, these eyes burned at her as hard and blue as the African sky itself. His hair was black, too, unruly beneath the hat he wore at a jaunty angle. He had high cheekbones and a full, humorous mouth . . .

Their eyes met and held, the moment seeming to last forever. The oxen plodded into the square, but Dacey barely noticed, so pinned down, so vulnerable did she feel in the hot intensity of this man's look.

She jerked her eyes away from him. Her face hot, from both sun and embarrassment, Dacey inspected her lap. She knew all too well what *he* saw: fiery red-gold curls unsuccessfully pushed under a straw bonnet. A blue merino dress with double flounces and braid trim, her last good gown, dust-coated from traveling and stretched too tightly across her full breasts.

Dacey flushed, thinking of the way she looked. Somehow, in the weeks since she'd turned eighteen and they'd left England, her body had ripened. Where once she'd been straight and lanky, suddenly she had womanly curves. Full, taut breasts strained at the blue merino, and the corset that laced her waist only gave her body a more voluptuous definition.

"Dacia, my dear, I believe you have an admirer," Papa said. He did not sound entirely pleased.

Dacey stared at the hands twisted in her lap and wondered if the man was still staring at her. She lifted her eyes. He still was.

"I'm sure it's just the . . . . the wagons, Papa, that he looks at. And the flags we fly."

"Nonsense." Papa rubbed his left eye, reddened by dust, and then smoothed his flowing gray mustache, also tinted by dust. His voice was deep, rich, theatrical. "Ah, well, don't look so flustered, Dacia. Aren't we in the business of being looked at? And perhaps it's a good omen, my daughter, on our arrival in this godforsaken place. The McKinnon Troupe may be about to make its fortune at long last."

Barely listening—she'd heard that before—Dacey sneaked another peek from under her lashes, only to discover that her admirer was now grinning at her. His teeth were very white against the burnished suntan of his face. He was tall, ruggedly handsome, and even his well-cut suit of clothes could not conceal the aggressive thrust of his shoulders.

Her face hot, she turned away. She sagged with relief when the wagon finally turned a corner and the man with the blue eyes and black hair was lost from sight.

One of Papa's omens, indeed! Everything, to John McKinnon, had some sort of mystical significance. His dreams, she thought, were as faded and dusty as Papa's *Hamlet* costume, or the flowing wig he wore for *Othello*. Dacey had spent the last fourteen years of her life following Papa's dreams about like some tantalizing will-o'-the-wisp. Now here they were in Africa, nearly at the end of the world.

Where was there to go after this?

Abruptly some of Dacey's excitement at being in Kimberley vanished. She felt hot, grimy, and in need of a bath. She leaned back against the uncomfortable wooden seat, shaded by gritty canvas, and noticed that the wagon was passing a saloon. KING OF PRUSSIA SALOON, a sign proclaimed in handlettered splendor. Yet the building itself was no more than a tent. A knot of miners poured out of its door, laughing, jostling each other, their sun-brown faces running with sweat. Dacey smelled the malty odor of beer and knew, by the way that Papa suddenly sat up straighter, that he did, too.

"Papa . . ." she began warningly.

"I have a thirst, Dacia, and I also have a very good feeling about this place. I think our luck will soon change."

"Papa . . ."

"No, my darling Dacia, jewel of my old age, you must not worry or fret yourself—*this* time I'm going to be very careful."

Papa leaned toward Dacey and planted a reassuring kiss on her cheek. Helplessly she felt the soft, silky brush of his mustache and smelled the pungent odor of bay rum, tobacco, and beer that for her would always be her father. The man she adored and always had.

"Papa," she tried. "You promised . . . no gambling—"

"And I will keep my promise, my dearest child. Have I ever been known to break a promise made most solemnly?"

"No, Papa." But Dacey couldn't help adding, "You have bent a few promises, though."

"Not this time, and not this one." Papa's smile was dazzling, the one that had charmed a thousand women. "And now let us signal our driver and instruct him to take us to the center of town. We must find accommodations, a bath, a place to lay our heads when we have completed our performance tonight. The show where you, my dearest jewel, my Dacia, are going to shine a thousand times brighter than any diamond *they* can unearth here in the mines of Kimberley!"

The Theater Royal was the most unprepossessing theater that Dacey had ever seen. Shedlike, it was one story, its corrugated-iron front coated with the inevitable Kimberley dust. Tattered playbills clung to its walls while a cloth banner announced a group called the Dazzling Damsons. Their dates included tonight, Dacey saw in bewilderment.

Alarmed, she hurried inside the building to find the manager, a tall man named Tony Agnelli, who had a shock of curly hair and eyes that kept traveling to the front of Dacey's dress.

"I'm very sorry, Miss—ah, McKinnon, but it is quite impossible for your troupe to play tonight. I cannot imagine why you would have thought you could."

"But—"

Dismay plummeted through Dacey. Royce, Lavinia, and the others were already walking about the town, nailing up playbills wherever space could be found. Papa had disappeared, presumably to find them a hotel. And Dacey had undertaken, as she always did, the chore of arranging their performance and dressing quarters at the theater.

It was a job she hadn't considered would be difficult, since they had signed a contract with the Theater Royal before leaving London.

She informed the manager of this fact, allowing her eyes to meet his firmly. She might be only eighteen, but she'd been dealing with stage managers, lighting men, and tradesmen for years. Necessity had given her a crispness, an air of authority, that usually got her what she wanted despite her age.

"Certainly you had a contract," Agnelli informed her. "For a performance *last* month."

"But I wrote you a letter! I sent you word that our ship was delayed because of storms. We certainly arrived here as quickly as we could; it's a long journey from Cape Town, as I'm sure you know. Hot and dusty, camping on the veld every night . . ."

Dacey kept her voice level, afraid to show her alarm.

"I didn't get any letter. And tonight, the Dazzling Damsons are playing, didn't you see their banner out front? I have high hopes for them. A small revue, but good quality, from Australia. We had the devil of a time replacing you last month, I might add. I'm considering suing you for breach of contract."

Dacey drew herself up. It was a disaster to arrive in a town without a firm commitment at a theater, but not for anything would she let this man see her fear. She wondered what they were going to do now. There were eleven in the company. It was not a large group by London standards; still, it meant eleven mouths to feed, eleven people to house in hotel rooms. And if this Mr. Agnelli actually *did* sue them for breach of contract . . .

It didn't bear thinking of.

"Then it is time we arranged a new contract," she told Agnelli sweetly, giving him her most brilliant smile. "We'll go on—yes, tomorrow night. We're already distributing the posters, and I guarantee you there will be many disappointed patrons if they cannot get tickets to *Othello*. And *Hamlet*, we also do that superbly."

Agnelli seemed unimpressed. "I need to see how the Damsons do."

Dacey reddened; a variety revue was being put ahead of the McKinnons, who had played the finest theaters in London! She was glad that Papa was not here to be humiliated.

"There can be no comparison, of course," she insisted. "They are merely a revue: songs, skits. *We* offer the finest drama in the English language."

Agnelli ran a hand through his hair, his eyes dipping once more to the full curve of Dacey's bosom. "How many women are there in your company?"

Dacey stared at him. "Why, four, including myself. The others are Lavinia Curran, Mary Matson, and Eleonora Kelly, wives of two of the men."

"Ah, and is this Lavinia Curran as pretty as you are? And what of the two others, will they pass muster?"

Now Dacey was beginning to see. She straightened her spine, feeling the indignant flush of blood to her cheeks. "Are you telling me that people come to your theater merely to see . . . female flesh?"

Agnelli nodded. "This isn't prim and proper London, Miss McKinnon. This is Africa, and Kimberley is bursting at the seams with eight thousand young white men. There are ten thousand blacks, and hardly any women. Black *or* white."

"I see!"

"It's tough to make it here, Miss McKinnon. This theater has a bar that runs the entire side of the building, and you have to play to the drinkers, who'll be very glad to heckle you if they don't like you. There are plenty of fights, too. Only last month we had a brawl and five actors got bloodied noses when they joined in."

The McKinnons were going to have to play under the crudest of music-hall conditions. But Dacey swallowed her dismay. The company had to survive—and they were depending on her.

"Do you think that we McKinnons are brawlers, Mr. Agnelli? Or sluts? Well, we aren't." From somewhere she summoned the courage to give the manager a confident smile. "But we *are* talented, and we can tailor our performance for any audience, including yours. I'll be here tomorrow, promptly at noon, to sign the contract."

Dacey hurried down the street, holding up the hem of her blue dress so that it would not trail in the thick dust that was scattered with droppings from the hundreds of oxen that were outspanned here. A fly buzzed persistently at the back of her neck, diving toward her damp skin. The afternoon sun lowered itself over the iron roofs, still stiflingly hot.

Dacey was tired, irritable with the heat, and afraid.

Despite her best efforts, the most she'd been able to extract from the manager of the Royal was a half-promise. *If* the Damsons lost popularity after a night or two, and *if* some other, better attraction didn't come along . . .

The contract that she and Papa had signed in London was worthless.

She continued down the street, past the clutter of buildings and tents, one of which bore the sign: SEWING, CHEAP.

Dacey slapped at the fly and tried to calm herself. They had been in worse situations. Once, in Edinburgh, the company had nearly starved when Papa gambled their entire strongbox on the turn of the cards. Another time, Royce McKinnon, who was Papa's rakish young half-brother, had come down with smallpox. Papa insisted on leaving the troupe's meager funds with Royce until he mended. That time, they'd gone hungry, too.

But they'd always managed. Was not Papa one of the century's great tragedians? Had he not played twice before Queen Victoria, the culmination of his life's dream? Royce, too, could speak with such passion that women in the audience had been heard to sob.

Dacey also had talent, Papa insisted.

"You're so like your mother, Dacia," he would say as the curtain rang down and he scooped up some of her bouquets to hand her. "She was the finest actress in New York when I met her . . . hair like ingots of gold, a face like a nymph. Her timing was flawless. If she had not died of a miscarriage—"

He would sigh, his eyes filled with moist sorrow.

"Dacey—Dacey, stop, wait up for me!" Dacey was jerked out of her thoughts by a cry behind her. She turned to see Lavinia Curran, the only other unmarried girl in the troupe, hurrying to catch up with her.

Lavinia was a plump, pretty blonde, with the easily flushed skin of an English milkmaid. She played minor roles, handled props and lighting, and made eyes at Royce McKinnon. Everyone in the company knew that Lavinia yearned hopelessly for Royce, who would have nothing to do with her.

"What do you think of this place?" Lavinia prattled, half out of breath. "Miners everywhere, and all the nasty dust! And have you seen the *mines* yet? The hugest hole in the ground that you've ever seen, it quite takes your breath away, Dacey."

Dacey only half-listened to Lavinia's chatter. She was planning what they would do next. They'd prepare their costumes, she decided, and find somewhere to store their trunks and sets. And . . . yes, they'd boldly hang their playbills. They'd circulate them among the bars, saloons, and eating places, drumming up excitement for the company and its plays. They would force Agnelli to sign them . . .

"So, Dacey, I told him to take his hands off me or I'd slap him right in the face, and you should have seen him apologize and back away, it was really quite comical."

"Lavinia, what on earth are you talking about?"

"Haven't you been listening? I was telling about the miner who tried to accost me in front of the King of Prussia Saloon. Can you imagine such a grand name for a mere tent?"

This was the same saloon that they had passed earlier. Dacey felt a twinge of apprehension. "Was Papa there?"

"Oh, yes. As a matter of fact, I think he was playing a bit of roulette. It was very exciting, he was winning this time, and you know how generous that makes him. He has promised to buy all of the women new gowns, and for the men, new suits of clothes. And he says— Dacey? Oh, Dacey, where are you going?"

But Dacey had already picked up her skirts and was running, in the harsh diamondiferous dust, toward the King of Prussia Saloon.

By the time she reached the tent saloon, she was nearly crying with vexation. A hundred times Papa had shed tears in front of Dacey, apologizing abjectly. That was when he lost. But when he won, Papa was jubilant, flinging down bills and coins in triumphant victory. He was always wildly generous with his winnings, buying jewels and flowers and dress goods for Dacey and others in the company.

She stopped in front of the saloon and gazed at its exterior. It *was* no more than a tent, its canvas stained with dust and watermarks. Yet the saloon bulged with noise and activity, nearly bursting its seams with male laughter. She could also smell the stench of beer, whiskey, and unwashed bodies.

She edged toward the open door, trying to see into the dimness. Should she go in? As she well knew, decent women were forbidden to enter drinking saloons. If a female did venture inside, she would be hooted at, insulted, and certainly asked to leave.

She drew a sharp breath, calculating what to do. If Papa was winning, he'd be impossible to drag away. If his luck had just started to turn against him, he'd insist on staying to recoup his losses. Only if he had lost everything could she persuade him to go home.

Just then a good-looking man pushed his way out of the

door, his walk an arrogant swagger. It was Royce McKinnon, Dacey's young uncle.

"Well, hello, Dacey, are you here to spy on us?" Royce gave her a rather resentful look. He had never been able to conceal his resentment that it was Dacey, rather than himself, who actually ran the troupe.

"Spy? Of course not! I'm just wondering if Papa is inside."

"He is. He's having a good streak, too. Or at least he was, and I'm sure he'll get it back again."

Royce was only six years older than Dacey, with the flamboyant looks of the born actor. His hair was a brown mane of wavy splendor, his eyes large and flashing, his mouth full. The smallpox had left slight scars on his cheeks, a fact that did not stop him from pursuing any woman who caught his eye. There was forty years' difference in age between Royce and Papa, the result of Papa's father remarrying at age sixty-six. That made Papa more like Royce's father than his brother. Which, Dacey surmised, probably accounted for some of the rivalry that Royce felt toward her.

She started toward the door of the saloon, only to feel Royce's hand on her arm. "I wouldn't bother him if I were you, Dacey. You might disturb his luck. Those are rich men in there: to them, one diamond means nothing. You should see it, Dacey—some of them are covered in diamond rings, stickpins, and tiepins!"

"I imagine it's a sight," she said.

"Oh, indeed. This is a fabulous town! Look, why don't you go find the other women? We'll be along directly, in time for the show." Royce's shrug dismissed her.

Dacey drew herself up, giving her uncle a long look. "There won't be a show tonight. Our contract fell through, and we'll have to scramble if we want to get any work at all."

"No contract? But you should have—"

"*I* did everything I could," she flared. "And now, don't you think you'd better go into the saloon and fetch Papa out? This very minute, before it's too late?"

Royce had the grace to flush. "I will, but I hope—well, I hope it's not too late."

*   *   *

"Papa? Oh, no, Papa, not *all* of the company's money!"

The cry tore out of Dacey's throat. It was ten minutes later, and Papa, Royce, and four of the other actors had emerged from the saloon looking sheepish.

The others had started toward the square, Royce among them, and now Dacey faced her father, trying to absorb this new disaster. As she and Royce were talking, Papa, in a burst of optimism, had staked the remainder of the company's money on a number that had lost.

Everything they had was now gone, except for pocket money. Dacey remembered that time in Edinburgh, when they had been forced to raid restaurant trash bins, and felt ill.

"My darling Dacia," Papa said in his deep, theatrical voice, "I'm abject with shame at the terrible error I have made. What a fool I am, a capering, posturing, painful fool!"

"No. Papa . . . don't talk that way." Torn with love, Dacey wanted to reach out and smooth away the genuine distress from Papa's forehead, the anguish from his eyes. In this aftermath, he always loathed himself for what he had done.

"I must say it, Dacia. After all my promises to you, what can you think of me?"

"I love you. Oh, Papa—"

But John McKinnon had turned and was walking away from her, his shoulders bent, his walk suddenly unsteady, like the sixty-four-year-old man he really was.

"Papa!" Dacey ran after him, forgetting the disaster, everything except Papa's abject misery and shame. "Oh, Papa, it's all right, truly it is. We—we'll get a contract tomorrow, we'll make more money. Don't we always make money? We'll do it again."

"Spoken like a true McKinnon. My daughter, you are a brave girl, a valiant one." Papa turned, and she saw moisture in his eyes. She gulped hard, swallowing back her own sudden tears.

"Of course we will make money again," Papa went on heavily. "That is our destiny, that is why we are here in Kimberley in the first place. But for now . . . I think I wish to be alone. To walk a bit by myself, to take an inspection tour of this settlement in which we find ourselves.''

He started on ahead, leaving Dacey no choice but to drop back and allow her father to walk on by himself.

Blindly Dacey started to walk, too, in the opposite direction. She, too, needed to be alone, to think and to plan. They had no contract and now almost no money, except for what individual members of the troupe carried in purses or wallets. This would last a few days, maybe weeks, if they were careful. And then what?

They were stranded in Kimberley, a six-hundred-mile land journey and a long sea voyage from London, without even enough money to buy their return passage.

To Dacey's right, a cluster of tents was jammed together, several bearing crude signs: BED FOR RENT. Was the company going to be reduced to renting space in some tent to sleep? Could Mr. Agnelli somehow be persuaded to let them sleep in the theater? All eleven of them . . . ?

Her mind throbbed with questions and worry. Money! What a precious commodity it was. With it, an actor lived his life comfortably, buying the flamboyantly tailored clothes vital to his profession, eating in decent restaurants, patronizing good hotels.

But without money an actor was helpless. Dacey had heard terrible stories, they all had, of thespians who had run out of funds and hope, becoming dependent on the charity of relatives or strangers. Of aged actors who had fallen ill and been left stranded by their company in a foreign city . . .

She shuddered, pushing away the thought. It wasn't going to happen to them, or to Papa. She wouldn't let it; she'd fight, she'd do anything she had to. She was a McKinnon, wasn't she?

Automatically Dacey's feet had carried her farther down a road where huge mounds of whitish-yellow dirt had been heaped in an untidy array, reminding her of the slag heaps of the deserted coal pits at Wigan, in England. She heard shouts, the ringing of pick axes, the roar of machinery.

Then, walking forward, she saw it. The Kimberley Mine, the mine that Lavinia had spoken of.

It was an enormous, gaping excavation in the earth that, to Dacey's startled eyes, seemed to stretch on for a mile. Cautiously she edged forward, through a maze of windlasses and other machinery, until she was at the lip of the huge, slanting, dangerous-looking hole.

It was as if she had stepped to the edge of an enormous ant pit and looked down into its depths. Crowds of nearly naked black men swarmed at the bottom of the excavation, or on walkways of rock, swinging picks, lifting shovels, loading dirt into buckets. Dacey could hear them call to each other, their voices liquid with a dozen African tongues. More men climbed to the surface on rope ladders, or loaded buckets that were being hauled to the surface in a spiderweb network of ropes.

The buckets, she saw, were filled to the brim with more of the dry whitish earth.

Was this where the diamonds came from? And all that dust, she thought. No wonder the town was filled with it.

She stared into the pit, lost in her thoughts. Diamonds . . . All of her life Papa had told her stories of some of the world's most fabulous gems. The Koh-i-noor, the Regent, the Great Blue, known as the "cursed diamond" . . . She shook herself. The chance of finding such a huge stone here, or anywhere, was surely very remote. But she knew that plenty of ordinary diamonds were being found in the mine every day. Surely the funds belonging to one small theatrical troupe could mean little in comparison with that.

She gave a start as a troupe of chattering black workers pushed past her, apparently on their way home after a day's work, their broad faces streaked with dust and sweat. An orange-red disk of sun had begun to sink over the rim of the big hole.

A sudden thought had come to her—the glimmering of an idea. She drew a deep breath and started after the workers, in the direction of town.

Papa had lost their money—but maybe she could get it back.

2

AS DACEY MADE HER WAY through the streets back to the King of Prussia Saloon, the purplish glow of dusk settled over the town like a gaudy cloak. All around her, cookfires glowed in pinpoints of light. The air reeked of woodsmoke, roasting game, dust, and the smell of ox dung.

The night here in Kimberley seemed alive with strange sounds. Bursts of laughter. Shouts, a man's hacking cough, the bellow of an ox. There was the distant howl of some veld animal, probably a hyena or wild dog.

All at once, Dacey felt weary. She was tired of strangeness and longed for the familiar streets and chimney pots of London. Unconsciously, she began to hurry, and taking a wrong turn, she found herself in a mean, squalid area of tents that were no more than blankets flung over a rope. There was the high, metallic twang of some native musical instrument and guttural shouts in Afrikaans.

The native encampment. Here, too, was the smoke of cookfires, the smell of roasting meat. But as Dacey quickened her steps, she smelled the odor of some harshly burning weed. It was a thick, choking, acrid smell that seemed oddly malevolent.

A little thrill of fear ran through her. On the trip from Cape Town, the Boer driver had talked, in his accented English, of massacres of Boer farmers, and something terrible that he called the Kaffir Wars. Apparently, white settlers had been brutally murdered, mowed down by native assegais. The driver had spared no drama in his tale of attack, battle, bravery, and death.

But surely, Dacey assured herself, things were safe enough here in Kimberley. Weren't the black-skinned men here merely to work in the mines, hadn't she glimpsed some of them on the street today, clad in bright clothes, beads, bits of bone in their ears?

Hurrying now, she found her way through the crooked, haphazard streets, forced several times to dart into the shadows as groups of drunken miners emerged from saloons. Once she was challenged by a stray dog that braced itself in the dust, barking and growling at her menacingly.

Dacey stood still, her heart pounding in her throat as she crooned to the animal. "Good doggie . . . good doggie . . ."

Its bared teeth flashed at her.

"Rufus! Rufus, come now, you mangy old bastard!" A man called sharply to the animal, and it trotted away.

Dacey allowed herself a sigh of relief. It had been someone's ordinary dog after all. Almost, she had allowed herself to be caught in the sinister spell that Kimberley had woven around her, a spell augmented by the dusk, the strangeness, and her own exhaustion from their journey.

Calming herself, she walked quickly on until she came to the tent where, earlier in the day, Papa had lost the troupe's money. The King of Prussia Saloon. She could scarcely see the hand-lettered sign now, but she could still smell the beer and hear the loud voices of the men who crowded inside. The tent was even more crowded, she saw, the canvas actually bulging with movement from within.

She heard a tide of gleeful shouts, and then a man came staggering out of the saloon.

Hastily, Dacey withdrew to the shadows at the side of the tent. She watched in shock as the miner fumbled at his clothes and then began to urinate into the dust, his water flowing out in a full, interminably long stream that seemed to last a full five minutes.

But at last he was done, and then, humming to himself, he

began to weave off down the street. His progress was lighted by a sliver of a moon that rose over the roofs of Kimberley.

Dacey waited until he had gone. Then she crept forward to where a rent in the side of the tent revealed a yellow slit of light.

A feeling of dull defeat filled her. She had planned to walk boldly inside and shame the miners into returning the funds they had taken. With a huge diamond mine out there, she had planned to say, why did they need the money of a small, destitute theatrical company?

The words had been on her lips, ready to pour out in a passionate speech. Now she realized what a mistake that would have been. The miners, drunk on beer and whiskey, would have roared with laughter at her scolding. Then they would have tossed her back onto the street, humiliated, no better off than she had been before.

Tears stung her eyes as she bent over and put her eye to the slit in the tent. Some reckless impulse made her want to see what it would have been like if she *had* been foolish enough to go inside.

For a moment, her eye had trouble adjusting to the bright glow of light inside the tent. Paraffin lamps were strung overhead on wires, illuminating the men crowded about a large table.

From her limited view, Dacey could see only that the miners wore a variety of clothing, from black broadcloth suits to threadbare, dusty shirts, to velvet jackets. Once, when a man turned, she glimpsed a hat decorated with ostrich feathers and a tiepin that flashed with unmistakable diamond brilliance.

She caught her breath. So Royce had been right—some of these men were decked out in gems. But others, she saw, looked rough, poorer, the very set of their bodies aggressive and hungry.

Suddenly the men's voices quieted, and Dacey heard the sound of dice being shaken. As the crowd shifted, she could see part of the table about which they stood.

Diamonds. Hundreds of them, perhaps thousands, she realized in awe, were spread out on the table like pebbles carelessly dipped out of the bottom of a river. Rough, uncut stones, some were large, others smaller, their shapes rounded, or half-angular. But all were semitranslucent, as if the river water were actually caught in their depths. All possessed an eerie, icy beauty.

But why were the diamonds spread out so carelessly on the table, why did the men crowd about them so tensely?

Then, with a shock, Dacey realized. These miners weren't gambling with money as she had, naturally, assumed. *They were gambling with diamonds.*

She felt her throat close with the impact of it. Diamonds instead of money! The meaning of what she saw swept through her, carrying her away on a tide of sick excitement.

Kimberley *was* diamonds. The town lived and breathed gems, had no other reason for existence but diamonds. For what man who owned such gleaming stones could not expect to be rich, richer than Dacey had ever imagined or dreamed?

She stared hypnotically at the fabulous stones, seeing ice palaces of diamonds, glittering, flashing prisms of beauty and power. . . . Then the crowd of men shifted and closed in again, and once more their bodies hid the table from Dacey's view.

She blinked, feeling dazed. Had it all really happened? Had she really seen heaps of diamonds, piled up like gravel in their vast numbers?

"Hey, what in the bloody hell are *you* doing out here?"

It happened so quickly that Dacey did not even have time to gasp. A large hand inserted itself in the collar of her gown and dragged her toward the entrance of the saloon.

"Please! Let go of me!" Dacey squirmed angrily, but her captor merely grunted and gripped her harder, his other hand swinging around to grasp her throat so that her cries were choked off in midword.

Terror flooded her as she felt herself being yanked inside the hot, crowded tent that smelled suffocatingly of whiskey, smoke, and the perspiration of a hundred close-packed bodies. Her captor's hand was like an iron claw, gripping Dacey's windpipe and choking off her air.

The room spun, and faces wavered toward her, then re-
ceded again, going black.

Then Dacey felt herself being flung away. She spun into
air and staggered, nearly falling. The back of her dress had
been ripped, and there was throbbing agony in her neck
where the man's fingers had clawed her. But she was aware
only of the sweet rush of air into her lungs.

"A girl, by God!" someone shouted. "A girl, spying on
us!"

Dacey fell into the edge of another table and held on to it,
drawing in huge gulps of air.

"I *wasn't* spying!" she managed to croak.

"Then what were you doing? You're a stranger in town,
by the looks of you. And that's one thing we don't like much
here in Kimberley, strangers. Not even a woman."

Dacey's captor was a huge, black-bearded man whose
belly overflowed his belt and whose shoulders were enormous
and meaty. Behind him, the bodies of the others blocked off
her view of the table of diamonds, although she saw that
several of the men had drawn pistols, apparently to guard the
uncut stones from theft by their own numbers in the excitement.

"Please," she begged. "You must let me explain. I'm
Dacia McKinnon. I'm a member of the McKinnon Theatrical
Troupe, and—"

"The McKinnon Troupe? Never heard of them."

"We are . . . are famous, we've played all of England and
Scotland, we—"

The bearded miner moved closer and now Dacey saw that
he held an open knife cupped in his palm. Its stubby blade
was almost dwarfed by the size of his hand, the blade gleaming in the lamplight. He did not actually threaten her, but
merely held the knife casually, naturally, as if it were an
extension of his body.

"Please . . ." she breathed.

No one said anything. The tent was full of silent tension,
as if all the miners waited for some decision to be made.
Dacey suppressed a scream. "I didn't mean anything by
coming here, truly I didn't! This afternoon my father came
here to the saloon to gamble, and I thought—"

"You were spying on us. You were going to slip in and rob us. You're nothing but a diamond thief!"

"No—no—"

"Do you know what we used to do with diamond thieves back on the Vaal River? We'd spread-eagle 'em. Peg 'em out in the dust and leave them to the sun and the flies and the wild dogs and vultures. Ever see, miss, what vultures can do to an animal? They start eating it while it's still kicking and struggling. Eat off half the face, maybe, or start on the belly, the entrails . . ."

Dacey gagged, choking back nausea. Some of the miners had begun to laugh, now, at her fear, while others simply stared at her. Over by the table of diamonds, a man with a pistol glared at his friends.

From somewhere Dacey summoned the bravery to lift her chin and stare her tormentor in the eye. Her eyes flashed as her desperate anger grew.

"Stop it!" she snapped. "Stop scaring me! I meant no harm, no harm at all to your foolish diamonds." She whirled furiously to spit her words into the faces of the gawking men. "If you ask me, the most likely thieves for those precious uncut stones of yours are right here in this tent—yourselves!"

It was as if she had blasphemed. The tense atmosphere in the tent grew perceptibly thicker. Men eyed each other nervously, and one let out a curse. Several moved nearer, their eyes angry. Dacey knew she'd made a mistake. By telling the truth, she'd only made them angrier than ever . . .

Then she heard a pealing burst of laughter.

"What's the matter, men, can't you look the truth in the face?"

A tall man stepped into the light. As he came forward, Dacey suppressed a gasp. For it was the same man who had stared at her on the street today, whose bold eyes had captured hers in a spell of strangely exciting intimacy.

Tall, more than six feet, he moved with an easy, confident lope to the center of the tent. He was an arresting sight in his well-cut black broadcloth suit, his white shirt immaculate, his dark cravat impeccably tied. Yet for all the gentlemanly attire, there was something feral about the man. Something wild and forceful that held the eye.

Maybe, Dacey thought with pumping heart, it was because of the black hair, thick, unruly, that curled away from his temples to form long, fierce sideburns. Or the high, almost arrogant cheekbones, like those of an Aztec warrior. Or perhaps it was the blue eyes, darkened now in the lamplight almost to black, that held a glint of savage humor in their depths.

She stepped forward, remembering that this man had seen her in the wagon that flew the McKinnon pennant. He could vouch for the truth of what she said.

"Please," she begged. "Tell them. I'm Dacey McKinnon, from the McKinnon Troupe. We just arrived in town today, you were there, you saw us."

"Indeed I did." His quick grin teased her. Then, casually, he moved forward and extended an arm to Dacey. "Gentlemen." He nodded to the miners. "This lady is with me, so I'll thank you to hand her over to my custody. I assure you that thievery is the last thing on her mind."

Someone laughed, and the man with the knife muttered something. But he backed away, moving his hand so that the blade was no longer exposed to view.

Tensely, feeling as if this was some drama in which she did not know her own part, Dacey grasped the arm of her rescuer, feeling the ripple of hard, taut muscles underneath the cloth.

"This way," he murmured as he steered her toward the door. "And smile, dammit, give them the biggest, most stagy smile you've got."

Dacey did as she was told. Her heart was knocking in her throat, her knees wobbled until she thought she would collapse with her fright, but she forced open her lips and she smiled dazzlingly at the miners in the tent.

It seemed she had to hold her smile forever, as they walked the gauntlet of the staring men, who moved reluctantly aside to let them pass.

"How can I ever thank you for helping me?" she began as

soon as they had reached the street. She thought her knees would sink with her relief.

"Hush," he growled. "Not yet. Keep your back straight and walk away with me until we are around the corner and out of sight. They are all half-drunk; maybe by tomorrow they'll have forgotten who you are. That will be just as well, I can assure you."

"But—"

"Do as I tell you," he snapped. *"Walk."* Adding force to his command, he actually shook loose Dacey's hand and placed his palm in the center of her back, propelling her along with such speed that she thought she might tumble into one of the many potholes that filled the road.

"Please," she gasped, "do we have to walk so fast? You've rescued me, and I'm grateful, but you're dragging me along like a criminal! Anyway," she added indignantly, "I don't see what I've done that's so terrible. I was going to ask them to give back my father's money. Instead, I peeked into the tent. Was that such an awful sin?"

To her dismay, her rescuer scooped both arms about her, bringing her unnervingly close to the male, muscular bulk that lay beneath the suit he wore. He pulled her around a corner where a bleak little street of corrugated-iron buildings lay deserted, the metal gleaming in the moonlight.

"There," he said harshly. "There are no saloons in this block, thank God, so you're safe for a while. Or do you always roll into a town in the late afternoon and by nightfall stir up its worst hornet's nests?"

Dacey drew herself up angrily, unhappily aware that the torn cloth at the back of her gown caused its neckline to gape, revealing inches of soft flesh.

"Sir! I am Dacia McKinnon. I'm a Shakespearean actress, a decent woman, not a—a floozy or a diamond thief or whatever it is that you think I am!"

"Did *I* say you were a diamond thief?" Maddeningly, he was laughing.

"No, but they certainly did! If you hadn't come along, they probably would have torn me into little bits and fed me to the v-vultures . . ."

Dacey's anger had evaporated without warning, leaving her with the weak, stunned, jellylike feeling of disaster averted. Now, for the first time, she realized the full extent of the danger she'd been in. She could have been knifed. Raped. Or even worse.

She was shaking violently. A sob caught in her throat, pushing its way past her lips before she could stop it. Furious at herself for this weakness, she turned to hide her face.

"Go ahead," he told her. "Have a good cry. Probably you need it, and maybe it'll cause you to stop and think twice before you do such a damn-fool thing again."

"Oh! I'm not a fool, I— Oh, damn—" She whirled, her humiliation giving her a last desperate energy as she rushed toward him and began to beat at him with her fists. He was so tall she had to reach up to do it, frustration giving her a wiry strength.

"Hey . . . hey, enough. I'm not your punching bag, you know." His chuckle was low, rich. With deft ease, he grasped her hands and forced them down, pinioning her. Dacey stood rigidly, all too aware of his touch, the fact that his hands were so large that they completely covered her own.

"Are you going to stop this nonsense?" He was grinning. "If you don't, I won't let go of you."

"I—I'm sorry I hit you," she whispered. "Really I am. If you'll let go of me, I won't do it again."

"Are you sure?" Again that maddening grin flashed white in the moonlight. "You still seem pretty dangerous to me."

"Well, I'm not! Can't you accept a genuine apology, Mr.—"

"Quinn Farris," he supplied. "Formerly of Tucson, Arizona, and Virginia City, Nevada, now of Kimberley." He gave her a self-mocking little bow. "And now, come along. We'd better keep walking for a while so that you can work off that hot little temper of yours before someone else takes offense."

She felt her face grow warm; everything he said made her look like a headstrong fool. But obediently she began to walk, and soon they were at the end of the street, turning onto a footpath.

"I hope you know where you're going," she said. "Because I certainly don't. I'm hopelessly lost."

"We're going to get you a drink. I think you could use one."

"A drink? But—"

"It'll only take a minute, and a few swallows of brandy ought to take care of your shakiness. I felt your body trembling back there, you know. You're still terrified, you just won't admit it."

His guess was accurate. Dacey felt herself flush as they followed the path that wound through a ramshackle group of tents and up a slight rise, to where the leaves of a lone camel-thorn tree rattled in the slight evening breeze. Near the tree, a neat tent had been erected, with a few pieces of wooden furniture arranged around a small, dead cookfire.

"Is this where you live?" she couldn't help asking.

He smiled again. "It certainly is; I'm very proud of it, as a matter of fact. This is one of the more palatial dwellings in Kimberley. But it's only temporary. Someday I plan to have a real office, and who knows? Maybe a mansion with forty rooms."

Quinn Farris left Dacey and ducked into the tent, returning in a moment with a bottle and a metal cup. "Here. Drink this, it'll relax you."

She took the cup that was thrust into her hand. "What is it?"

"I told you, brandy. Go on, drink."

He looked expectant, and Dacey had no choice but to lift the cup to her lips. The brandy was harsh, searing her palate and throat as it went down. She coughed and choked, and Quinn patted her on the back and handed her the cup again.

"I know it's African rotgut, but right now you need this, I'm afraid, Miss McKinnon."

He went to the campfire and returned with a wooden bench, which he pulled up for Dacey to sit on. She sank onto it, exhausted, and he straddled it beside her.

"All right." He scrutinized her with blue eyes that seemed to see everything. "Now you can tell me what you were doing gazing into the King of Prussia Saloon at an array of uncut diamonds, probably about a third of them illicit?''

Dacey squirmed under the intensity of his look. She felt a tremor stir in her belly, a shiver tighten the skin of her arms as she began to explain.

"My father, John McKinnon, is a wonderful actor, and a wonderful man, but he has one failing. I'm afraid that he believes in the fortune of random chance, and he—''

"Say it bluntly. You mean, he's a gambler.''

"Well, yes . . .'' Hating the word, Dacey plunged on. "He lost everything we possessed this afternoon at the saloon, even our passage money back to London. I was going to go inside and shame the men into giving it back.''

"What?"

"I said I was going to shame them.''

Quinn threw back his head and laughed, the muscles of his strong, corded throat working. "You can't mean that!''

"I do mean it. I was going to get back our funds,'' she repeated hotly. "But when I got there and I looked into the tent and saw what they were doing, gambling with d-diamonds, I realized that there was no chance. And then the man dragged me inside and said I was a spy.''

"I see. And did it ever occur to you that what you were doing was foolish and dangerous? Miss McKinnon, you're a lovely woman—that's obvious. And you seem intelligent. But it's apparent that you don't know one damn thing about South Africa, or this boom town you've wandered into without the slightest idea of what it's all about.''

Quinn leaned forward to grasp Dacey's shoulders, turning her so that she was forced to face him. His touch was hard and seemed to burn through the fabric of her dress, searing her skin. In the darkness, shadows carved his face, outlining his cheekbones in sharp relief.

"Why,'' she said, "it's a diamond town, of course.''

He almost shook her. "Naturally! But don't you realize, you little fool, what a hotbed of intrigue and greed and passion you've stumbled into? Those men thought you were spying on them! To you, apparently, that means little. But to them—my God, Dacia, to them, diamond theft is a crime worse than murder.''

"Than . . . murder?'' She moistened dry lips.

"That's right. You see, even in their uncut state, diamonds are very small. Most are tiny enough to be swallowed, and they are ridiculously easy to steal, to buy and sell illicitly. Here in Kimberley, a man's reputation for honesty is the most precious thing he possesses. And there is nothing—*nothing*— that makes a miner angrier than the prospect that some of the stones he sweated out of the earth should fall into the hands of someone else.''

"I see. But I wasn't—''

"You made them think you were. Dacia, this isn't civilized London, this is South Africa. Dark Africa. A few years ago, diamonds were found on the Vaal River, about fifty kilometers from here. Diamond thieves were flogged, or spread-eagled, or dragged mercilessly through the river. Taxes were collected at gunpoint.''

So some of what the man with the knife had told her was true. Dacey stared at Quinn Farris, feeling chilled.

"But I don't plan to have anything to do with diamonds,'' she finally said. "We are merely going to put on our plays at the Theater Royal.''

"Ah, yes. Are you sure that's why you came here? Most people do come to Kimberley because of the diamonds, one way or another.''

Dacey couldn't understand why Quinn's blue eyes suddenly raked her coldly, why his mouth had twisted as if he were accusing her of some crime. She put down her cup onto the bench and jumped up, feeling her blood pound.

"I don't understand, Mr. Farris, why you are shouting at me like this. I haven't done anything, other than stand at a tent staring in through a crease in the canvas. That might be a foolish act, but it's certainly no crime, and I don't care how many diamond thieves have been dragged through the river!''

She glared furiously at him, then felt the tears sting again at the backs of her eyes. She turned and began to run back down the path, back toward town.

"Dacia! Miss McKinnon!'' He ran after her, calling to her.

Angrily Dacey darted over the rocks in the direction she thought they had come. He had laughed at her, had practically accused her—and she hadn't done anything. She'd wanted only to get back Papa's money, was that so wrong?

"All right, I'm sorry." He caught up to her, grabbing at one of her hands to force her to stop. "I do apologize, Miss McKinnon, for frightening you." In the darkness, Quinn looked fiercer than ever, his mouth a straight, unsmiling line. "I was merely trying to tell you that Africa is a harsh land, and Kimberley a tough town. You've stepped in way over your head, I'm afraid. Accept your father's money loss. Take passage for England and go back where you belong."

"I haven't *got* passage money!"

"Then I'll loan it to you."

Dacey pushed at the mass of curls that had slipped out of its pins, unhappily aware of the tears that streaked her face, mingling with the dust.

"I appreciate your offer, Mr. Quinn, but I don't want or need your charity. There are eleven of us in the company, and we'll earn our passage ourselves—by performing." She swallowed her pride and continued. "But there is one thing you could do for me . . ."

"What is that?"

"If you could help me locate the rest of the troupe and assist us in finding a place to stay tonight, a decent hotel, with maybe a real bathtub and lots of warm water . . ."

For a long moment the hard blue eyes searched hers, and then Quinn Farris nodded. "Very well. If you'll promise to stay out of trouble."

"I told you, I *didn't*—"

She faltered. He was looming toward her, and then she felt his arms reach around her, pulling her upward, enfolding her against the tall, lean body. With one hand Quinn tilted up her chin and then his lips searched hers, hard, demanding.

Dacey felt her heart hammer as she tasted Quinn's kiss, his sweet breath. Her body melted into his, her bones turning fluid. She was overwhelmingly aware of the strength of him, the deepness of his chest and shoulders, the urgency that transmitted itself to her like thrumming electricity. . . .

Then, as quickly as it had begun, it was over. Quinn released her, and Dacey found herself trembling again, her breath coming in quick gasps. Birds' wings seemed to beat in her chest and throat.

"I'm sorry, Miss McKinnon, I shouldn't have done that." Quinn said it hoarsely, and she sensed that he had been as affected by the kiss as she was.

"You might as well call me Dacey," she said. "Dacia is only my stage name, what Papa calls me when he's feeling very grand."

"I see."

They began to walk along the path together, their footsteps falling into harmony. Silence settled between them, heavy with a meaning that Dacey dared not interpret. He had kissed her. She had responded, wildly, totally beyond control. If he had not released her when he did . . .

What was happening to her? Why did she feel so strangely off-balance, as if what had happened tonight would forever change her?

3

AFTER SEEING DACEY BACK TO the hotel he had found for the troupe, Quinn Farris walked back through the town, thinking about the girl he had just rescued. The beautiful little minx of an actress who'd gotten herself into trouble as easily as breathing.

He smiled to himself, remembering the brilliant smile she'd given the miners, despite her fear. How lovely she was, with her mane of red-gold hair, the color of the African sun just at sunset. Her green eyes held a dozen moods, all of them tantalizing, and her skin was as flawless as English porcelain. Vividly he remembered holding her pliable body. The lithe waist, as slim as a girl's. And those full, curved breasts that had pressed against him, all woman . . .

What in the name of God was she doing here in Africa? Quinn kicked angrily at a loose rock, seeing it land several feet away, silvered by the moonlight. He hadn't lied when he told her Africa was tough. Only the strong could survive here. Could a soft, vulnerable girl like Dacey survive against all the temptations of riches and power, the men who would try to use her?

Quinn doubted it.

Again he found himself thinking of her courage. Most women of the type he had known in Virginia City would have been turned to jelly by the ugly miner who had flashed the knife. Even Janine . . .

But quickly he chopped off the thought of his wife, tamping down the harsh surge of anger that filled him whenever her name entered his thoughts. He slowed his steps and stood looking back the way he had come, toward Kimberley.

The moon had risen high now, flooding the ramshackle town with pale light. In the daytime, Kimberley always seemed ugly to him, a squat town crouched on the veld, its citizens foraging out to chop down the few trees that remained for firewood, spreading their tents and buildings, their deep, gaping mine pits.

But at night the town was different. It was softened somehow, made pure by the moonlight. In the clear light, there could be no quarrels or rivalry or striving or even triumph: there was only the silver glow and the peaceful surfaces of buildings.

And you are a fool, Quinn Farris, he told himself as he began walking again. Thinking about a girl, and the moon, like some love-struck calf. Dacia McKinnon was beautiful, but there were other women who hid their vulnerability behind flashing green eyes. There were always women, weren't there?

Love, Quinn thought bitterly. It didn't exist, not as he had imagined it once, not as he had heard it whispered. Love was a commodity, measured in material objects such as diamonds. Yes, an expensive necklace of brilliant-cut stones, gleaming on the soft throat of a lovely woman . . .

He had been born in Tucson, Arizona, the son of a Savannah planter who had gone west in search of adventure. His mother died giving birth to him, and his distraught father took the infant back to Savannah, where Quinn was raised by an aunt and uncle in the tradition of Southern gentility. Quinn was schooled by a tutor and grew up loving the soft, lush, gentle life that had been his father's birthright, and was now his.

Then one day, when Quinn was ten, his father came back for him. He took the boy to Arizona and retaught his son to ride, in the Western way. He taught Quinn to shoot, to survive in the desert, to hunt and trap in the mountains where green pines and flowing streams created a world of beauty.

When Quinn was seventeen he ran away to fight in the War Between the States. At Shiloh, his lower right calf was hit by a bullet that went through the fleshy part of his leg. Taken to a field hospital, he lay in a long row of groaning wounded— men and boys lying in filth and vomit and blood, sobbing for help, for water, for release from pain, for their mothers.

Quinn tried to help the boy next to him, who looked to be about sixteen. Struggling to sit up, he managed to tear off strips of his own shirt to bandage the boy's bleeding, bubbling chest. He waved and called out for one of the Confederate doctors to help his friend. But no doctor came. And within an hour, the boy beside him lay silently. He was dead.

When they finally came to bandage Quinn, he struck away the doctor's hands and pulled himself up. Limping, leaving a bloodied trail of red behind him, he walked out of the hospital and stole a horse. He rode it west again. This wasn't his war; he had done no good with his futile shooting, he didn't like killing and he saw no purpose in it. He had seen too many bodies, wearing blue or gray uniforms, and to him there seemed no difference between the two.

When he got home to Tucson, he learned that his father had been dead for four months, accidentally killed by a bullet while cleaning his rifle. While he had been firing bullets to kill, his father had died of carelessness. Quinn visited the arid mesa where the saguaros grew and where his father had been buried. For a long time he stared down at the crude wooden marker, tears running down his cheeks.

After a while he discovered that the desert wind had blown the tears dry from his face. He resaddled his horse and rode northwest, to Nevada.

Virginia City was a town of frame houses cupped in tilted hills, sprawled with the zigzagging trestles for oar cars, hoisting works, shaft heads, and railroad tracks. This was the center of the Comstock Lode, and this was silver mining.

Silver! The Chollar Mine was yielding millions of dollars'

worth a year when Quinn arrived, and the town simmered with excitement. Quinn took a job in an assayer's office, weighing ore. Within months, he was running the office while Arnold Poudreau, the owner, attended to other things.

Years passed and Quinn stayed in Virginia City; where else was there to go? And he liked the aura of excitement and power, even if he had to enjoy it secondhand.

Then one day the assayer invited Quinn home for dinner. There he met Janine Poudreau, his daughter, recently home from a private girls' school in the East.

"So you are a Southerner, from Savannah. You have a very gentlemanly accent, don't you?" Janine was petite and dark-haired, with eyes the color of warm amber. At school, she had acquired a flirtatious air that Quinn found very charming.

"I'm a Westerner now," he told her. He was already enchanted with her, the way she moved, her bright little laugh, her quick gestures.

"Are you going to be rich someday, Quinn Farris?"

"Of course I am. That's why I came here."

"I only want a *rich* husband," Janine told him, dimpling. "So you'd better not come around to court me unless you can promise me a diamond necklace to hang around my neck that's so heavy its weight drags my head forward."

She was so tiny—only five feet two, almost a foot shorter than he was. She was exceedingly pretty, and Quinn knew that she had dozens of other admirers. He smiled at her joke and took her arm, asking her if she'd like to walk with him in the hills, where the mining trestles and prospectors had not yet ravaged and the view was crystal-clear.

Janine declined. She hated walking and was afraid of snakes.

Eight months later, Arnold Poudreau died unexpectedly of a liver ailment. Janine, whose mother was already dead, was left alone in the world, the sole owner of the assaying office, along with a modest inheritance.

Quinn was touched by her straits—a girl of her beauty needed a protector in a rough town like Virginia City. But she had crowds of suitors, and he was busy clearing up the papers left from Poudreau's death.

A week after the funeral, he was working alone in the assaying office when he heard a knock at the door. It was Janine, wearing a blue silk dress with an enormous bell skirt that made her look like some swaying, exotically beautiful flower.

Her lashes fluttering, her smile enchanting, she got straight to the point. "I want you to marry me, Quinn Farris. Will you? I need someone to make me rich, and I've decided you're the one who can best do it. You're hard and you're tough, and there's something about you—I don't know what it is. But I want to go along on your coattails."

Quinn stared at her, unable to believe what he had just heard. Finally he concluded it was another of Janine's jokes. "Pardon?" He couldn't help grinning at her. "I thought I heard you propose to me."

Her amber-gold eyes met his. "I did. That time I talked about the diamond necklace, you thought I was flirting, didn't you? Well, I wasn't. I've been looking over the crop of men here in Virginia City and what I see are a lot of lazy slugs. None of them with grit. None with the kind of drive I suspect you have." She dimpled at him. "And besides that, none of them are very good-looking. I want a rich husband *and* a handsome one."

Quinn's heart had begun to pound thickly. He had thought of Janine so many times, had imagined her in his arms . . .

"It sounds like a business arrangement," he teased. "If so, then what do you offer me, Janine?"

"Me. And the assaying office. And my father's inheritance. It isn't big, but if you're careful, you can make it go far. I want to be rich. Richer than anybody else in this town, and I want to wear the biggest and most beautiful necklace that anyone here has ever seen. I want to *glitter*. Will you help me to do that, Quinn? Or do I have to find somebody else?"

What could Quinn say? What could he do? He was made uneasy by the bold way she had proposed marriage to him, by the odd things she said. But he had loved her for eight months now. He had never seen another girl like her, doubted if he ever would again. She was rare and enchanting, and this topsy-turvy proposal only proved that Janine had spirit.

She was looking at him, waiting for an answer.

"All right," he consented huskily. "I'll marry you. And I'll make you rich. We'll be—" He laughed. "We'll be kings here in Virginia City, we'll own it all when I'm through; why not?"

He scooped her up and hugged her and whirled her around. When he kissed her, her lips were as soft as violet petals, as kitten fur.

Two weeks later they were married and Quinn began what he thought of as "the plan." Using the assay office and the knowledge of mining that he had gained, Quinn bought some shares of the Chollar Mine and traded them for others. He staked some prospectors and took a percentage of their discoveries, bought claims, sold them, and finally began a mine of his own: the Janine.

A year later he owned a complete works, from shaft to hoisting house to loading chutes, and was taking out $800,000 a year in silver, this in an era when a million dollars was a fabulous sum.

Best of all, he was enjoying himself. He loved it all, the power plays, the rivalry, the push for control. It was his natural milieu.

That summer Quinn went to New York and returned with a necklace for Janine. It was the embodiment of every extravagant wish she'd ever voiced to Quinn. Forty diamonds were strung in a brilliant rope and a huge pear-shaped pendant stone was surrounded by ten smaller flashing gems. Before purchasing it, Quinn had lifted it carefully in his hand. Yes, he decided, it was heavy enough to weight her neck forward.

Janine flaunted the necklace. She wore it to parties attended by the wives of other mine owners, and to the theater, where everyone gaped at her. Janine glowed under their scrutiny. Quinn knew she enjoyed the picture they made, the swath they cut in the town, the personage *she* had become because of the diamonds that Quinn bought her.

But a year later, the tide of good fortune turned. The riches that Quinn had built up so easily began to tilt away from him.

No matter how desperately he scrambled, he couldn't get them back again. He learned that his enemy was Robert Kennerd, a stubby, balding man in his early forties, who'd always disliked Quinn and who had been one of Janine's suitors.

One by one, the careful bricks in the edifice that Quinn had built tumbled down. He risked the Janine mine to save himself, and suddenly found himself deeply in debt, ruined. One afternoon, while Janine was at a tea party, Quinn was forced to go into their bedroom and open the strongbox where they kept the necklace. He used it to repay his debts.

In the gracious society of Savannah, and in the harsh life of Tucson, Quinn had been taught that a man always kept his word. So, his heart aching, he discharged his last obligation, knowing that Janine would want him to keep his honor. And he'd make it up to her. They'd go away to one of the newer mining camps in the West, and he'd start over again.

"You did *what*? You sold my necklace! To satisfy your damned Southern gentleman's honor? I really can't believe you would do such a stupid, stupid thing!"

Quinn looked down at his beautiful young wife, seeing for the first time the tiny, avaricious lines that bracketed her mouth, the complexion that had turned icy-pale. Janine's eyes glowed like an angry cat's.

"I did it so that we would not be humiliated by not paying our debts," he told her gently.

"Our debts! Damn our debts!" screamed Janine. "You fool! You groveling, ridiculous fool! You handsome nothing!"

Quinn stood rigid. Every word of Janine's cut into him like the blade of a rapier. If she had been a man, he would have hit her. But she was a woman, a tiny one, she weighed half of what he did, and honor forbade him to touch her.

"I hate you, Quinn Farris," she shouted. "And do you know something?" Her face had twisted into an ugly mask, marred by fury and greed. "I never would have married you if I hadn't thought you'd make me rich—never! I don't love you, Quinn, and I never have!"

Quinn froze. Then, drawing a quick breath, he threw his leather wallet on the table; it contained every cent he still owned, enough to support Janine for several years, if she were careful. He turned sharply on his heel and left the room. He walked directly to the stable where he kept his horse, and he saddled Apache, riding him in the hills for long hours. He felt as if the underpinnings of his life had been knocked away, leaving a huge, raw, aching void.

Janine had used him. As deliberately, as calculatingly, as she used a silver brush to comb her soft hair. It was true that he had wasted her inheritance and lost her necklace, but he was a man of honor. He would still pay back his debt to his wife—pay it back twentyfold, repay it in stunning, insulting measure.

He would settle their debt far beyond what she'd ever hoped to get from him, even in her wildest dreams; he would make her regret what she had done to him. And then he would turn on his heel and leave her again.

That was why he had come to Africa. Because he had heard about the diamond discoveries, and diamonds, to him, held a terrible significance. They would be the means by which he would revenge himself on Janine. Here in Kimberley, he was going to amass diamonds. Riches, *power*.

As Quinn approached the tent, his feet crunching on gravel, he saw that the paraffin lamp had been lit, casting a yellow glow through the front flap. Suddenly, as if his arrival had signaled it, a metal plate came flying out of the tent. It spun, landing against a rock with an angry crash. A second plate followed it, hurled with even more venom.

Quinn sighed, then gave a tired grin. "All right, hold your fire." He bent and stepped into the tent.

"I saw you. I saw you, Quinn Farris, I saw you in town with that Englishwoman!"

Lying on Quinn's camp bed was a beautiful, naked woman. Her skin was the color of cinnamon mixed with cream, her hair ebony silk. The lamplight gleamed off her long, strong legs, the wide-curved hips and flat belly. Her waist was small enough so that Quinn's two hands could span it, her breasts full and pointed, quivering now with her indignation.

"You were walking all through town with her, *ai*! I followed you, I saw everything. What were you doing with her, with those people? Who were they?''

Her first name was Natala, the rest of her name something long and African, and she was what South Africa called "Cape coloured." Her ancestry was a product of the mingling of Dutch settlers with Malay slaves, Hottentots, Xhosa, and Arab.

"They are actors, Natala, people who have come from London to act on the stage at the Theater Royal."

"The theater?'' Natala stiffened, her nostrils flaring. "You never take me there."

"And you know why I can't." Quinn felt a spasm of pity for this woman who had been educated by missionaries but who, because of racial barriers in the town, was denied so much. Natala seldom mentioned these hurts and slights, but he knew that she felt them deeply.

"Then tell me why you were with them," she persisted, swinging her legs to the floor with a catlike, graceful movement.

"Dacey got into trouble at the—''

"*Dacey?*" Golden eyes focused on him, dilating like a lioness'. "You call her Dacey, then? What kind of a foreign name is that?''

"Her name is Dacia; it is an English name."

"English! It is a name of nonsense sounds; it is ugly!''

He had first seen Natala at the Vaal River diggings. Fallen ill with blood poisoning from a small cut, he was feverish, tossing and groaning in painful delirium. He had been only vaguely aware that one of the other diggers had gone for help to a nearby native encampment, where there was reputed to be a woman good with medicines.

For several days he had not known that Natala was there. He was aware only of soft hands that urged strange-tasting mixtures into his mouth, of a fire that had been built near him. Sharp, acrid roots burned in the steam she made, searing his nostrils. But the pungent smoke seemed to ease his pain.

After the infection was broken, Quinn lay ill for many days, too weak to move. He became aware of the beautiful young woman who nursed him, caring impassively for his

most intimate needs. Gradually Quinn grew stronger. One
night Natala crawled onto the pallet beside him and stripped
off his clothing. Her mouth caressed him, licked him, bringing him to full manhood. When he was ready, she positioned
herself above him, on all fours like some magnificent naked
animal. Slowly she lowered herself on him. It had been
months since Quinn had had a woman, and the fires in him
erupted in a pounding passion that spent itself quickly.

The next time she came to him, Quinn was strong enough
to take the initiative. Again the passion flared between them.
It was something so frankly physical that it seemed to Quinn
to have nothing at all to do with love, but to be more a part of
the illness, and the pungent herbs, and the dark African night
flung with a million pinpoint stars.

When the Vaal diggings dried up, Quinn came to Kimberley,
where diamonds had been found on farms at Dorstfontein and
Bulfontein, and, later, near the De Beers farmhouse. Natala
followed him, bringing with her her extended family, mostly
women, an amorphous group of sisters, grandmothers, and
cousins who appeared to hold Natala in awe because of her
medicinal abilities.

One day Natala told him that she was expecting a child.

Quinn's first reaction was dismay. A child, an obligation,
binding him to this beautiful woman who had been to him
like a plaything, nothing more? Many men, Quinn knew,
boasted of their by-blows, counted them as a badge of manhood.
He knew he could never take fatherhood so casually.

Five months later, a girl-child was born. Quinn went to see
her at once, and held the infant in his arms, a child with skin
as white as any Savannah belle, her features delicate and
perfect, even aristocratic. Holding her, he felt curiously moved.
This was his child, his blood. A tiny human being that he
could not allow to disappear with her wandering family into
the barren highveld.

Yet he knew that he could not marry Natala; social mores
in Kimberley forbade it, and men who did marry native
women became outcasts. Besides, he was still married to
Janine.

Quinn made Natala his permanent mistress. It was not a

bad life: she made few demands on him, keeping a small hut of her own on the outskirts of Kimberley. She gave the baby, whom she had named Lalah, to her people to rear in their kraal. Natala devoted herself to Quinn's needs, and to the herbs and spells that she sold in her hut.

And she never let Quinn forget that he owed her his life, that she could take the little girl, Lalah, away with her at any time.

"Never mind the sound of Dacey's name," he told Natala now. "She got into trouble at the King of Prussia Saloon and I had to help her. Otherwise, she would have been in danger."

"Danger! Pfah!" As Natala rose, a scent drifted from her, like the musk of crushed flowers. "She is a fool, that girl, as all white women are. I do not see what men find beautiful in such women. Their faces turn red from the sun and their skin grows brown spots!"

Quinn threw back his head and laughed heartily. "Those are called freckles, Natala, and the white women hate having them; that's why they always wear hats. As for you, you don't need to worry, you'll never freckle, your skin will only grow more smooth and lovely. As you well know, your beauty is matchless."

"Is it?" Her anger gone, Natala preened in front of him. "Am I beautiful enough for you, Quinn?" She said his name with a slight, delicate elongation, so that it sounded more like Queeeen.

"Very beautiful," he assured her.

And yet, Quinn wondered, was he telling the truth? Odd, how that Dacia McKinnon girl had disturbed him. And Natala, with her sharp intuitions, had sensed that.

"Quinn. Love me, please." Shamelessly, she pressed her nakedness into him, her breasts firm against his chest.

Quinn groaned as he felt himself swept into the familiar desire. With one motion, he picked her up and carried her back to the bed. He stripped off his clothes and they came together with the burning need of animals. She writhed under him, hot and moist, her softness, her lush breasts, and her pounding hips an equal match for his own desire.

For a moment Quinn let himself know only the physical.

Natala's panting gasps and cries, her fingernails clawing at his back. Then he climaxed in a sweet sharp burst of fire. Hearing Natala's abandoned moans, he knew that she did the same.

Afterward, they held each other, their skin slick with perspiration. Quinn's breathing slowed, his thoughts returning to him from their limbo of sensation. He felt a disturbing moment of emptiness. He had joined his body with this woman. Even now, he could hear Natala's satiated sighs, her soft, greedy breathing.

Yet, as ever, something was missing, something that even with Janine had been absent. Was it love? Quinn laughed to himself derisively.

He rolled away from Natala and lay still, staring up at the flickering lamp. *Was* there something more? Something that could engage the spirit and essence of a man and a woman, transcending their bodies to become as eternal as human beings could ever achieve?

"What are you thinking about?" Natala demanded.

Quinn hesitated. "Nothing."

"You are thinking about that English girl, aren't you?"

'No, I'm not. I'm thinking about something else entirely. And now, Natala, perhaps it's time for you to go. I need to be alone."

"Alone? Alone to think about *her*, you mean. *Ai*, that is what you always do when you are alone, Quinn . . . think! You think about faraway things, don't you? That country of yours, Arizona. Virginia City. That ugly white woman who you said was your wife."

Natala spat out the word *wife*. She jumped out of bed and grabbed for the saffron saronglike native dress that she had worn here. With furious motions, she fastened it around her body.

"And now," she exploded, "you're going to think about that Englishwoman. That Dacey."

Quinn felt a surge of temper, which he controlled. "Dacia McKinnon is merely an actress, Natala. Her troupe will give a few performances in Kimberley, and then they will move on, as actors always do. She is no threat to you, none at all.

Nor is my past life, or the thoughts I carry in my head. You are entirely too possessive, Natala. Do you know what possessive means?''

"Yes." She gazed at him sullenly, then dropped her eyes. "I have heard that word."

"It is not a good word. It is a word that makes a man feel restless.'' Quinn reached for his pants and pulled them on.

"Be alone, then, Quinn!'' she cried. "Have your own thoughts if you want them—I cannot stop you! But I don't want you to think about any woman but me.''

Then, swiftly, Natala ducked out of the door of the tent and disappeared into the night. Behind her she left only the musky sweet fragrance she wore, heavy with flowers.

4

DACEY STOOD BEHIND THE VELVET curtain at the Theater Royal, peering out at the audience. The miners, crowded ten deep at the bar, had already begun their drinking. She could hear their shouts and laughter, the clink of glasses. At the piano, a man pounded out showy revue tunes, winking and bowing. There was the pungent smell of beer, smoke, and perspiration.

Dacey wiped her forehead. The iron roof had caused the building to bake all day in the sun, and added to that heat was the glow of the paraffin footlights and the press of hundreds of human bodies.

"Three sheets to the wind before we even play to them!" Lavinia mopped at her own damp face and leaned forward to take her turn peeking through the curtains. "Ugh! I heard the bartenders talking, Dacey. They said there are rowdies who heckle the performers, and plenty of fights."

Dacey nodded. They were lucky to be here at all, she knew. This morning Tony Agnelli, the theater manager, had sent a message that three members of the Damsons had come down with enteric fever. Could they fill in? The engagement could last a week or more. But, the manager had added sternly, he wanted the plays to be "juiced up" for the Kimberley audience. No long, dull, wordy speeches; excitement and amusement were what was required.

Papa had been in a rage, but Dacey prevailed, and they had

worked all day, preparing a mélange of Shakespeare's fieriest scenes that Dacey hoped would enthrall this difficult audience.

She had even removed a row of ruffles from the neckline of her dress, exposing the creamy shadows of her cleavage, and now she felt nervously exposed. They *had* to be a success here. . . .

She heard a sound behind her and turned to see Royce McKinnon. As Lavinia gave up her place at the curtain, Royce leaned forward to inspect the milling, drinking crowd.

"A piece of cake," he announced. "No worse than the pit at the Globe when old Will himself had to grab his audience." He shrugged. "It'll be fine as soon as I get out there."

Dacey felt a twinge of annoyance at Royce's egotism. "*You* will charm the wild beasts, Royce? You and you alone?"

"Of course." He was airily confident. "But who cares about that now?" He leaned toward the two girls. "Do you know where we are? We're in diamond town! Diamonds by the pound out there, not more than a mile from us, maybe even beneath our feet right now, who knows?"

As he said this, Royce looked down at the planked floor. Involuntarily, Dacey and Lavinia did the same. Then Lavinia giggled. "Are you going to be rich, Royce?"

"Oh, Royce," Dacey said, stifling a laugh. "Don't tell me that you've caught diamond fever?"

"And what if I have? You needn't laugh. I plan to return to London decked out in diamonds like some of the men I've seen here in Kimberley. I've been hanging about the streets, I've seen them haggling and dealing and boasting. Fabulous stones are being found here every day."

Royce mimed cupping a huge diamond—as big as a hen's egg—in his hand. "One stone like this, one big one, and I'd retire to London. I'd buy myself a carriage and house, not just any house, mind you, but a manor house at least. Maybe even a castle. What do you think about me buying a castle?"

Lavinia giggled adoringly, but Dacey remembered the array of rough stones she'd seen spread out on the table at the King of Prussia Saloon, and gave an excited shiver.

All through the performance, as Dacey waited for her cue

to go on, Royce's words seemed to tease her: "Fabulous stones are being found every day. . . . Not just any house, mind you, but . . . maybe even a castle. . . ."

She watched from the wings as Papa stormed and emoted, his voice rising and falling tragically, lulling the drinkers at the bar into a hushed silence. Then it was her own turn. She was Lady Macbeth, she was Portia and Juliet, diamonds completely forgotten.

Time sped in a perspiring blur as the footlights blazed. At last it was over, and Dacey curtsied gracefully, sinking to the floor as Papa had taught her, her arms stretched out, her hands drooping like flower petals.

Applause rose. It roared around her, punctuated by raucous calls and whistles.

She sank into another deep curtsy, and when she looked up again, one of the miners, a man who had been standing at the bar, suddenly strode toward the stage. He paused by a foot-light to stare directly up at Dacey, a thickly built man with brown eyes and a brown beard whom she had never seen before.

Then something flew through the air. For an instant it gleamed in a dazzle of light as it arced over the footlights. Then it hit Dacey's arm and glanced off onto the boards.

Automatically, she stooped to pick it up. She opened her hand and stood staring into her palm, in which lay a small stone, its shape roughly faceted into a triangle, its color as translucent as glass.

Beside her, Lavinia let out a squeal. "Dacey! Do you realize what that is?"

It was a diamond.

There were no flowers in Kimberley, so the miner had thrown her a diamond instead.

Dacey's breath caught in her throat. When she looked up, the miner, staggering slightly, was walking away.

That week, the McKinnon Troupe put on two shows a night in the hot, crowded, noisy theater, and Dacey was the center of envy of the entire company. They clustered about her to stare in awe at the small clear diamond. Lavinia and the other women were thrilled and envious. Royce looked sullen, and more than a little angry.

"Why should such things always happen to you, Dacey my pet?" he demanded. "Isn't it enough that you run this troupe when by rights I should be the leader?"

"But Papa is the one who asked me to—"

"He should have asked *me*," Royce rejoined sharply.

Two days later, Dacey took the diamond to Christian Street and learned that its weight was slightly under one-half carat, small by Kimberley standards. But its color was Cape white, it was free of impurities, and the dealer bought it from her gladly. The price she received was, of course, a small fraction of what the cut gem would fetch later in Amsterdam or Antwerp.

Still, Dacey pocketed the cash, feeling heady with the ease of it all. One moment, she had been curtsying, the next she had watched a diamond glitter its way through the air to her. It seemed almost magic. Suppose the stone had been bigger? Five carats, or even ten? Then she could have used it to pay for their passage home. Maybe there would have been something left over, to buy a house for herself and Papa. They could live comfortably, free from the financial worry that had plagued them ever since Dacey could remember.

Dacey lay awake at night in the hotel room she shared with Lavinia, thoughts racing through her head. The diamond. The tall, handsome man with the unruly hair, Quinn Farris, who had kissed her so boldly. Even now, thinking of him caused a weak, melting feeling to spread through Dacey's belly. . . .

"Dacey!" Lavinia poked her head around the corner of the cubicle, heavy with the scent of powder, where the women of the company dressed. "Dacey, there is a man waiting outside for you."

"A man?"

"Yes. Do you suppose he's the one who threw you the diamond the other night? Maybe he's come to ask for it back." Lavinia tittered maliciously and slammed the door behind her.

Dacey stared thoughtfully at her reflection in the glass.

Since she'd caught the diamond, the other members of the
company seemed to resent her. Even the ticket-takers and
bartenders stared at her. It seemed that she had become a
small celebrity, the actress who'd been tossed a diamond
onstage.

But her benefactor, whoever he was, had not come forward
again, and Dacey privately doubted he would. He had probably thrown the stone in the excitement of the moment, maybe
even while drunk. She was sure that he regretted his impul-
sive action by now.

Anyway, what if he did return and demand his diamond
back? What could she tell him, since she'd already sold it?

Dacey sighed, examining her own image in the tiny, flawed
mirror. Her hair, freshly washed in beer shampoo, was a
burnished mass of coppery curls. Tonight her eyes looked
greenish-hazel, almost dreamy. Dacey leaned forward to scrub
at a last trace of rouge on one high cheekbone, stopping to
examine a sprinkle of freckles that had appeared across the
bridge of her nose.

Freckles! She rubbed at the offending marks and finally
made a face at herself and gave up. Men regularly got such
blemishes in the sun, didn't they, and nobody said anything.
Why should women have to labor to protect themselves from
the light with hats and parasols? This didn't seem fair to
Dacey, and privately she loved the fierce African sun. Why
couldn't she bask in it as much as she pleased?

Finally she grabbed for her bonnet and shawl, and left from
the tiny back exit of the theater, hoping to avoid the man,
whoever he was, that Lavinia had said was waiting—just in
case he *was* here to demand his gift back.

"Well, if it isn't the famous diamond girl."

It was Quinn Farris, carrying an oil lamp whose swinging
light cast shadows upward onto his face in harsh relief, giving
him a rakish, almost bandit look.

"Oh—" She gave a startled cry.

"Do your fans always give you such glittering tribute,
Dacey McKinnon?" he teased.

She felt the blood rush to her face. "Why—why, no, in
London it was always flowers, and Lavinia usually got far

more bouquets than I did. Sometimes she couldn't carry them all home, but would have to give them away to wardrobe women and ticket-takers . . .''

Her voice faltered. Quinn was smiling at her, his teeth very white against the contrast of his tan, his physical presence so dominant that she felt herself ache inside.

"Come," he said. "Let's go have some supper. I can't promise anything very glamorous here in Kimberley, not yet, but I expect that will change one day if the city grows."

He took her arm, obviously assuming that she would go with him, and Dacey felt a tide of excitement ripple up and down her arms. He was so tall . . . he made her feel very small and soft and feminine, very . . .

She felt a stab of surprise. *Happy* was the word that had jumped into her mind.

"I . . . I must be back at the hotel soon, or Lavinia will start to wonder," she blurted.

"Ah, yes, Lavinia, the one who receives vast tributes of flowers."

"Lavinia is considered to be very pretty, a true English beauty," Dacey defended her friend hotly.

"She ought to be in a dairy ladling out curd cheese," Quinn remarked. "And unless I miss my guess, in ten years she will be very bossy and plump."

They walked onto the street, Dacey hurrying her steps to keep up with Quinn's longer ones. He seemed to loom beside her, large, very male, clad in a dark suit with a cut that emphasized the easy grace of his body.

"I don't blame that smitten miner who threw the diamond to you," he said abruptly. "If I had had a stone with me tonight, I would gladly have thrown it, too."

Dacey did not know what to say. Again her cheeks grew hot, and she plucked at the folds of her blue merino dress, smoothing the fabric into little pleats. They were crossing the big Market Square now, the stalls empty, deserted of their usual confusion of pedestrians and milling ox teams.

Five minutes later they were seated in a tent restaurant, at a table spread with a checkered cloth and clean china plates. A sputtering tallow candle revealed a spread of food that looked exotically strange.

Dacey looked at Quinn, puzzled.

"This is Boer food, Dacey." He smiled at her. "The Boers are descendants of the Dutch who colonized South Africa. *Boer* itself is a word that means farmer, and that's what most of them are. A very stern and tenacious people, almost biblical. Here, try this. This is bobotie, a spiced meat casserole, very succulent. This is sosatie, which is spiced meat on skewers. And, later, there will be konfyt . . ."

Dacey tasted everything, exclaiming at the flavors so different from the bland mutton they had been eating at their own hotel. But she found that her appetite was not great. Somehow, it was hard to eat when she was sitting across the table from Quinn. How disturbingly handsome he was, with his high cheekbones, his blue eyes set beneath straight brows, the full, humorous mouth bracketed by laugh lines.

Dacey ached, remembering that she had kissed that mouth. She had been enfolded in those hard-muscled arms, she'd pressed herself shamelessly against . . .

Her heart hammering, she pushed away the thought and tried to concentrate on the conversation.

Quinn was telling her about Virginia City and silver mining. He spoke of Arizona, caves, rattlesnakes, mountains. Dacey listened, enthralled, and then she told him of her own background, spent traveling from theater to dusty theater. She even told of Papa's dream to play once more before Queen Victoria before he died.

"I suppose he has always held that up to me," she mused. "Royalty . . . recognition by the queen . . . to Papa, that has been a pinnacle of his life, something by which he has measured himself."

"And your dreams, Dacia? What are they?"

Quinn's glance held hers, warmth seeming to flow between them.

"I . . . I'm not sure," she said at last. "I suppose I, too, have dreamed of being received by the queen. But I think what I want more than anything else is just security. Freedom from money worries, a place where Papa and I can always feel safe. In fact, I've had a feeling about Kimberley . . . something is going to happen here. Something wonderful, I know it is.''

''I suppose you mean diamonds, then.'' Something in Quinn's face grew cold, and it was as if a mask had been drawn down over his features, turning him into a stranger.

What had she said?

''What's wrong with diamonds?'' she tried to joke. ''Isn't that why you're here, too? Why everyone is here?''

''Yes. It is.''

''Well, then?'' Dacey touched her napkin to her lips, then rose, feeling as if the golden mood of the night had somehow been spoiled. ''I think I should go back to my hotel room now,'' she added. ''It's late, and Papa always sits up to make sure I'm back. And Lavinia asks a million questions.''

''Then we must be sure to forestall that.'' Quinn nodded and rose, too, giving Dacey a polite smile. But she still sensed the curtain that had dropped between them, ruining the evening.

When he left her at her hotel, he was scrupulously formal, a stranger who bowed over her hand, his eyes cold and distant.

That night Dacey lay awake for hours, going over every word she had said, trying to figure out what had gone wrong. Why should the mere mention of the word *diamonds* make Quinn angry? Or had it been something else, had she unwittingly offended him in some other way?

Finally, near dawn, she fell asleep, but even her dreams were restless, full of diamonds that flew in the air like birds, and Quinn's eyes, cold with anger . . .

The next morning she crawled quickly out of bed and dressed. Lavinia was still mounded under the covers, breathing heavily, but Dacey felt an urge to be up and about. She wasn't going to let Quinn Farris bother her. Let him say what he would, she had as much right to be interested in diamonds as he did. . . .

She decided to go to the Market Square and buy some lace, if she could find any, with which to trim her blue merino.

And if there was a dressmaker, she'd order some new gowns. Two bolts of silk were in her trunk, bought months ago in London when Papa had been feeling flush.

This morning the square thronged with activity, for food had to be bought daily so that it wouldn't spoil. Ox-drawn wagons, laden with produce, jostled for position, the animals trampling the dust and bellowing. Crowds of shoppers—black, brown, and white—hurried among the stalls that were laid out with an assortment of wood from Bechuanaland, carcasses of game, poultry, fruits, and vegetables. There were even more exotic items such as antelope hides, rhinoceros horns, and elephant tusks.

Dacey strolled up and down, examining the goods and listening to the auctioneers, who shouted out their spiels, their voices competing for attention.

She stopped to examine a large, curving piece of ivory, a pale object nearly as long as she was, wondering what anyone would wish to do with such a thing. Curiously she reached out to touch its slightly ridged surface.

"An elephant had to die for you to be looking at that tusk now," a voice said beside her. "I certainly hope you're not going to buy it."

She turned to see Quinn, wearing a wide-brimmed hat tilted back at a rakish angle. Her heart gave a crazy, thumping leap.

"Oh . . ." She drew back from the tusk in dismay. "I didn't know. Of course, I wouldn't have bought it anyway. What would I ever do with it?"

"They kill animals indiscriminately here," he told her, taking her arm as he had last night, to lead her across the square through the crowds. It was as if their meeting had been planned and there never had been any cloud between them.

"Springbok," he went on. "Eland, hartebeest, impala, lion, elephant—the white men shoot them for sport, and the natives for food. The whites use rifles, and the blacks use dogs to trap their prey, or they catch them in nets or traps. Just like the buffalo in the American West, Dacey, there used to be enormous herds of game here in South Africa. But their numbers are growing smaller daily.''

Dacey hurried beside him, while throngs of miners crowded in front of auction houses, making it difficult to pass. Once, when a passing cart jostled them together, she felt his arm touch hers, and a shiver of sensation jolted through her, delicious and strange.

Quinn stopped at a tent kitchen and bought sandwiches made of sliced cold chicken and thick brown bread, some cake, and a bottle of white wine produced in Cape Town.

''We'll have a picnic, get away from all this swarming humanity. Legitimate diamond buyers, confidence men, thieves, crooks—they are all here, Dacey, and every one of them has diamonds on his mind.''

A little silence hung between them, and then Quinn grinned at her. It was an oblique apology, she knew, for what had happened last night.

They walked out of the town, skirting past the western section of the settlement, where the African workers lived in a collection of miserable tents made of odd bits of canvas strung between poles.

The men slept on the bare earth, Quinn told her. ''There are natives from a dozen tribes here, Dacey. Xhosa, Zulu, Basuto, Tswana, even a few Bushmen. There are even Griquas, descendants of white men and Hottentot women. They all want to earn money to buy rifles and their lobola.''

''*Lob*— What's that?'' Dacey stumbled over the unfamiliar word.

''Why, it's the price of a wife. Here in Africa, a black man offers a dowry of cattle to the father of his prospective bride.''

''Do you mean that he *buys* her?''

''Well, in a way, but it's not as simple as that. The offer of cattle stands as a way of saying that he can care for the girl, but also as a covenant, a binding promise between the two clans.''

For an instant, Quinn's voice grew husky. When he fell silent, Dacey was quiet, too, striding along beside him as they left the outskirts of Kimberley and found themselves on the bare veld.

Brown, dusty, dry, with almost no grass, the land seemed to stretch out limitlessly to the horizon, dotted by an occasional thorny tree or a bunch of prickly low shrubs. Overhead the sky burned harsh blue, utterly cloudless, in which a yellow eye of sun glared down.

"This is what the Bushmen call the *karoo*, or desert." Quinn took Dacey's hand to lead her over an outcropping of wind-scoured rock. "There is very little water here, but the Bushmen were hardy people and they found what there was. They have left paintings on the rocks, very strange and wonderful, I'll show you sometime. Meanwhile, like the animals, the Bushmen are also dying out. Civilization has done it to them."

They walked for about an hour. Just when Dacey was beginning to pant from the heat, they settled in the dubious shade of a scraggly camel-thorn tree, in which a long weaver-bird's nest hung. With a smile, Quinn took off his hat. He hung his suit coat on a branch in order to provide a further patch of shade for her, adjusting it with a flourish.

"There, glorious shade for milady. We must protect your complexion at all costs."

Gratefully, Dacey sank onto the ground, adjusting her bonnet so that no new freckles could plague her. She looked around. "All this dry emptiness!" she exclaimed. "It's so big, so harsh, so—"

Quinn gave her a quizzical look. "Maybe you don't find it beautiful, not yet. But you will. There is a grandeur in these huge sweeps of space, and in the endless array of harsh colors. Because of the dust, there are spectacular sunsets here on the veld when the sun seems almost to split apart the sky."

"You really love Africa, don't you?"

"Yes. I believe I do. Although there are times when—" He stopped, abruptly, as if he had said too much. "Tell me, Dacia McKinnon, do you always wear a hat?"

"What?"

"Your hat." His smile teased her. "I'm afraid you've

already got freckles—very nice ones, I noticed them this morning—and in a few weeks you'll have a ruddy suntan whether you want it or not.''

Dacey didn't know whether to smile or be annoyed. Quinn's eyes had fastened on her with a gentle, searching look that caused a soft warmth to spread through her.

''Well?''

She hesitated. ''Oh, all right.'' Flushing, she reached up and unfastened the ribbon that held the straw bonnet around her chin. She lifted off the hat, hanging it on a small, thorny bole of the tree. It seemed a very intimate act, as if she were taking away some barrier that stood between them, revealing her true self to his scrutiny.

Quinn's voice was husky. ''What lovely hair you have, Dacey. Its color is incandescent—not really red, yet not entirely gold, either. Coppery. Especially now, when the sun catches it and makes halos of your curls.''

He said it softly. A little heartbeat of silence seemed to hang between them, full of tension.

''Won't you take the pins out of your hair for me?''

The pins. Dacey's heart leaped, and she felt her mouth grow dry. Suddenly she felt frightened, and yet excited, too. To take the pins out of her hair, sending it tumbling nakedly about her shoulders; a woman did that only in the privacy of her bedroom in the presence of her husband or lover.

''Would you? It would mean so much to me to see you with your hair down, Dacey.''

Her mind spun and she moistened her lips, feeling helpless, caught in Quinn's gaze and in the tumult of the feelings that poured through her. Desire, fierce and melting. Excitement that seemed to sear her very bones. And the feeling, growing ever stronger now, that she belonged to him.

She felt her hand rise. Trembling, her fingers pulled out a pin, then another. Curls came tumbling down around her shoulders and neck, the feel of them unbearably sensual. She moved her head, tossing her hair so that the sun caught it, aware of his growing excitement.

''Beautiful.'' His voice was almost a groan. ''Oh, God, so beautiful . . .''

He extended a hand to touch her hair and Dacey sat frozen as a sensuous quiver went through her. His slow touch, the way his fingers delicately brushed her neck, making her skin ripple with pleasure . . . She shivered like a wild animal under his caress.

Then with another groan, Quinn reached out to take her in his arms. He pulled her close and held her shaking against him until her body quivered no more, but yearned toward his. His long body was hard and muscled, and he smelled, fragrantly, of the veld, of tobacco smoke, and clean, male perspiration.

They were locked in tight embrace, their bodies straining together. Quinn poured kisses on her, plundering her lips, her neck, the softness of her throat. Dacey moaned and gave herself up to him, aware of his hands at the buttons of her dress, releasing them.

She was beyond shyness now, beyond fear. Her breath quickening, her heart pounding, she helped him with the last buttons. She shrugged out of her petticoats, her camisole, and corset, until at last she was naked before him, aware of her own body as she had never been before.

She felt beautiful before him, feeling his look like a warm touch on her full breasts tipped with pink, her curves, which were taut and warm and wholly female.

"Ah, God, Dacey, you are lovely . . . a goddess . . ."

Quinn quickly stripped off his own garments and Dacey's eyes drank in the sight of the well-made body with its wide shoulders, upper arms knotted with muscle, the powerful chest. A few soft curls of dark hair on Quinn's breast followed the midline of his body to his belly and groin, and the full, urgent power of his manhood.

He was beautiful, Dacey thought feverishly. His body, everything about him, as clean and pure and strong as any wild animal, some fierce, yet gentle king of the veld. . . .

Quinn spread out their clothing for them to lie on and then lowered himself beside her, enfolding her in his arms. Dacey moaned with pleasure as his hands caressed her spine, the curves of her hips, thighs, buttocks. She urged her body even closer to his, responding totally, excitingly aware of the hard, throbbing press of Quinn's sex against her.

She was being swept up, rushed away in a torrent of desire that she was powerless to control. She felt warm, open, melting. She wanted him to touch her more, harder, in other, deeper ways. She wanted—

Quinn kissed her breasts, tonguing the nipples into sweet, erect fire. The ache in Dacey's groin grew. His kisses, more demanding, moved around the orbs of her full breasts, and he tongued their undersides, kissing a trail down the lines of her ribs to her belly.

He licked and tongued her, his kiss drawing out soft, molten fire, floods of sweetness. Dacey writhed in pleasure, her heart pounding so rapidly that she thought she would scream out. For an instant she seemed to hang on the verge of an enormous precipice. Then her body gave an enormous throb and she flew over the edge, flew into maelstroms of soaring pleasure.

Was this . . . this wonder . . . what it was all about? Was this the love that a man and a woman made between each other, this melting joy?

But before Dacey could open her mouth to murmur Quinn's name, she felt him lower himself onto her, gently parting her legs. She stiffened against him and for a moment there was pain, pressure. Then he was inside her, and blocking out the discomfort was a new growing sensation of urgency, before which her other desire had been nothing.

To lie open to receive this man—to be joined with him in naked, raw intimacy—never had she believed such rapture could exist. She sighed and cried out, barely aware of the tears that streamed from her eyes as Quinn took her from one sensation to another, filling her, pounding in her, until at last she shuddered again in a climax even more blindingly pleasurable than the one before.

And this time they soared together, two sparks exploding outward from a central fire.

After they had made love, Quinn's mood changed, seemed to grow somber and quiet. They lay naked, curled on the spread of petticoats and other garments, watching the sky where a lone hawk wheeled and circled against the blue, finally diving for prey.

Sighing, Dacey snuggled up to his nearness. She felt warmed with happiness, with utter peace and contentment. *Quinn*. He was hers now, and the knowledge sang in Dacey, a beautiful certainty that she wanted to treasure.

"Papa will want to meet you," she whispered at last. "Do you know that he saw you looking at me on that day we came into town and he said that you were an omen—of good things to happen . . ."

Her voice faltered. Quinn had drawn in his breath harshly. His face had become the grim mask of last night, his brows scowled together, a pulse beating fitfully at his temple.

"Quinn? What's wrong?"

He did not say anything. Frightened, Dacey sat up, realizing that he had gone into another black mood. But why? What had she done? Her hands shook as she reached for her clothes and began to pull them on, her fingers moving automatically.

"I shouldn't have made love to you, Dacey. Dammit, I never should have brought you out here. I should be cursed for doing it." Quinn, too, had begun to dress, pulling on his clothes with savage movements.

"What . . . what do you mean?"

"I mean that I am married, Dacey. To a woman in the United States. And worse than that, I already have a woman here in Kimberley, a mistress."

Shock hit her like a slap of frigid water. Married. A mistress. At the brutal words, Dacey felt as if he had hit her, as if he had wrenched at the beauty they had shared, destroying it. She sank down on the earth, reaching out her hands to steady herself, seeing, for an instant, the gray-yellow arid earth tilt and turn beneath her.

She heard herself say something. "I thought . . . I thought that you—"

"No, Dacey. I'm not free. Oh, God, I should have told you. I wanted to. I was going to do it last night, and then you started talking about diamonds with that light in your eyes, and I didn't. Maybe I didn't want to tell you. I'm sorry, Dacey, you can't imagine how sorry."

Every cruel word seemed to drive a spike straight through Dacey's heart. He was apologizing for the wonderful thing that had happened between them, for giving her the sharpest joy she had ever known in her life. She felt her body squeeze with a grief that could not seem to find voice, but remained frozen in her, turning her to ice.

"Tell me," she said slowly. "Tell me about it, Quinn."

In a low voice, Quinn told her about Janine Farris and Virginia City, ending with their angry parting and the mocking taunts that Janine had shrieked at him. He also told her about Natala, his lovely, jealous Kimberley mistress and the beautiful child now being cared for in a native village.

"You have . . . a baby?" Dacey thought she would collapse from the shock of it. A bitter pang stabbed at her, that some other woman had been able to give him this.

"Yes, I'm afraid so, darling. Lalah is what her mother named her, but someday I will call her Lilah. Her skin is as pretty as cream. Her hair is dark and soft, and her eyes are mine, her nose, the shape of her mouth. She is a year old now, and I visit her as often as I can. Natala is jealous of her and tries to withhold her from me. But I do go to see her, and someday I'll take Lilah back to the United States with me and show her her other heritage. Rear her as a lady."

"I . . . I see."

Quinn's face looked bleak. "There is more, Dacey. I owe Natala my life. She saved me from blood poisoning when I was at the Vaal River diggings; without her I would surely have died. There is an old belief that if someone saves the life of another, then that person belongs to him. Natala believes that . . . I do know that I am bound to her."

Quinn paused and looked at Dacey with eyes gone as hard as stone. "And even if I did not have her, there is still Janine, to whom I am legally married. So, you see . . ."

Dacey did see, all too well. Time seemed to spin around them and the sun overhead seemed glaring and cruel.

"You could divorce your wife," she whispered, knowing how hopeless it was. Divorce in her own country was rare, almost unheard of. And in the United States it was sure social stigma.

"Divorce? No, I cannot, not yet."

"But—why not? Why?" Now, at last, Dacey began to cry, racking sobs that pressed agonizingly at her throat and breastbone.

"Don't. Oh, for God's sake, don't cry. Please, just listen to me. I am . . . flawed, Dacey. There is something in me, perhaps you have already sensed it. A barrier that stands between me and any woman whom I might want to love fully. And there is Janine, something I have vowed to do before I—"

But Dacey didn't want to listen—she couldn't. She clapped her hands to her ears, shutting out Quinn's hurtful words. When he touched her, she sprang away from him as if he had been a scorpion.

"*No*! Please—don't touch me!"

"Dacey . . ." Quinn sounded as miserable as she felt, but Dacey didn't care. How could he have done this to her? He had made love to her, accepted her virginity, her trust. Now he dared to tell her that he couldn't take her as his wife, that he was flawed and could not love her.

But then, looking into Quinn's eyes, Dacey saw mirrored there her own pain. Slowly, her anger seeped away. She shivered, hugging herself, amazed at the emptiness that filled her now.

"Is it really so bad as all that, Dacey?" A sudden, tiny smile quirked the corner of Quinn's mouth.

She stared at him, amazed that he could smile. "Yes! You've hurt me, you've—"

"Dacey. My darling, there are two ways to look at life. *You* are looking at the long haul, the spread of years that stretches out to the ends of our lives. That view, for us, is indeed a bleak one. But there is another vista, the one we see around us now, at this very minute."

Quinn gave a wide gesture that took in the low line of hills that marked the horizon, a distant thorn tree, the wheeling hawk silhouetted against deep blue. "Isn't this beautiful, too?

This, the *now* that we can touch and hold in our hands at this very instant?''

Dacey had never thought of life in those terms.

''I—I suppose . . .'' she whispered. She felt her heart contract painfully, and it was as if some part of her moved, in that space of a few heartbeats, away from childhood forever. She did not want Quinn just for *now*; she wanted him for always. For the rest of her life, until they were both very, very old.

And it wasn't going to happen that way. She knew it by the saddened, drained expression on his face. Quinn had other obligations, whether she wished it or not: two other women, a child. He could not love her. There was no room in his life for her.

''Dacey?'' Quinn touched her face, his hands unbearably gentle. Then he put his hands on her shoulders and turned her to face him. ''I have done a criminal thing to you, but it has been done now, we have made love, and we can't go back, we can't change what has already happened. But if you would like, we'll go back to Kimberley and I'll leave you at your hotel, and I'll never see you again.'' His voice was harsh. ''Perhaps that would be best.''

''No.''

''Then what, Dacey? There won't be much for us. There can't be, not now, maybe not ever. Do you think that you are capable of living in the present, the now? Of enjoying what we can have today and not thinking of the future?''

She stared at him. She didn't know if she could do that. And maybe she didn't care, she thought wildly as she reached for him again, her hands touching the thick hair that felt so soft and silky under her fingers. All she knew was that she couldn't bear to let Quinn go. Not now, not yet.

Oh, tomorrow, she thought as he enfolded her in his arms. Tomorrow she would think about it again. Meanwhile, Quinn's hands burned down her body and his kisses flooded her senses, until she could no longer think clearly. . . .

5

DACEY AND PAPA STOOD AT the back of the empty theater,
watching as a lone black man swept up after the revels of the
night before. Even at ten in the morning, the building had
begun to simmer in the heat, and the cleaner moved lazily, in
no hurry to complete his task.

"Dacia." Papa said it in a tone unlike his usual stagy,
dramatic manner. "I have heard something from Lavinia that
distresses me. You are seeing a man."

"Yes."

Dacey swallowed hard and looked straight at Papa. She
had known this moment would come ever since she had
begun seeing Quinn more than a week ago. His mistress,
Natala, had gone on the veld to the Vaal River in search of
plants and roots; in her absence, Quinn and Dacey had gone
to the thorn tree every day.

Was it the knowledge that their time together was forbidden?
The emotion that burned between them like flame? Dacey
didn't know, and was past caring now. All she did know was
that she craved her hours with Quinn. He had captured her
heart and her thoughts, pushing away everything else, everything sensible and normal.

She dreamed of him. She counted the hours until she could
rush away from the hotel to meet him at the edge of town,
near the path. All along, of course, she had known that Papa
would eventually find out. But she had thought it would take

longer than this, that the expression on John McKinnon's face would not be quite so full of alarm.

"Dacia, tell me about this man," Papa said.

"Why—he is from America, Papa, a place called Virginia City. He is already acting as a diamond dealer, in addition to the two claims he owns. He hopes, one day when the two-claim restrictions are lifted, to start a small mining company . . ." Dacey spoke rapidly, parroting off some of the things that Quinn had told her on their walks together.

"Does he plan to marry you?"

Her heart sank. "Papa—"

Her father rubbed at his flowing mustache, clearing his throat. "Dacia, I have heard talk about this man, Farris. He is a womanizer. He keeps a doxy here, a brown woman he has installed in a hut at the edge of town. And there's no telling how many other women he has. He could even possess a wife, for all I know."

"He does have a wife." Dacey had never lied to Papa, and she didn't plan to start now.

"Then what are *you* to be to him, Dacia?"

"I don't know. I . . . I love him, Papa."

"Love? Then you are a fool, my girl, a damned fool!" Papa gripped Dacey and shook her. "Just because I am an old man, do you think that I don't know how you feel right now? I loved your mother, but there was a woman before I met her. I, too, agonized for love once. But it went away, Dacia, it passed, and I didn't hurt myself because of it. I did not break my heart."

Dacey could not speak. She felt herself shaking.

"Dacia, I want you to promise me you'll never see Quinn Farris again."

"I . . . I can't promise that, Papa."

"You must. There is nothing he can give you, can't you understand that? Children, love, devotion . . . he is a married man, he has a wife, a mistress, they will take it all from him." Papa shook her angrily. "Dacia, there is nothing he can give *you*, nothing!"

That night Dacey walked through her two performances in a cloud of misgiving and misery. Was Papa right? By seeing

Quinn, was she only hurting herself? Would her love for him pass away, as Papa said his own early love affair did?

No, no, she thought violently as she curtsied for the miners' tumultuous applause. I won't think about it, I'll live for now, for today, just as Quinn said.

After the last performance of the night, Dacey changed out of her costume in the crowded dressing room she shared with Lavinia, Mary Matson, and Eleonora Kelly. The room, so tiny that they had to take turns in front of the mirror, reeked with the smells of powder, perfume, spirit gum, and female perspiration. It was an odor Dacey had smelled all her life, and she barely noticed it.

"Dacey, when are we going to be paid?" Lavinia tapped her on the shoulder. "We've played six nights now, that's twelve performances, and there has to be some money. I want to buy a little gift to take home to my mother."

The two other actresses crowded close, adding their own pleas, chattering about the marketplace and the exotic items they had seen there. The company had been poor for a long time, Dacey realized with a pang. These women had endured a long voyage with its seasickness, then a grueling forty-day journey by ox wagon. And Eleonora, Dacey knew, had two small children in England, being cared for by a sister.

"We have to save for our passage, but I suppose there could be a small pay," she conceded. "I'll go to Papa and arrange it," she added, carrying out the fiction that he was still the troupe's leader.

The women squealed with pleasure, and Eleonora began to list off excitedly the things she would buy for her children.

"Are you walking back to the hotel?" Lavinia asked Dacey after a moment, her expression inquisitive and a bit spiteful. "Or do you have *other plans*, Dacey?"

Dacey reddened, suspecting that it was Lavinia who had told Papa about Quinn. "I'll walk back by myself, I think. You all can go on ahead. Or do you think you'll be meeting Royce, Lavinia?"

It was Lavinia's turn to flush. In the past week, Lavinia had renewed her campaign to charm Royce McKinnon, but had met with little success. Royce, easily bored, had spent every spare moment roaming the town. He had even ventured, it was whispered, into the section of town where a small number of black-skinned prostitutes plied their trade.

Now, as Lavinia flounced out of the dressing room with the others, Dacey grinned at herself in the mirror. Lavinia's tempers were as ephemeral as mist. By morning the other girl would be bubbling with good humor again, her spitefulness forgotten.

She left the dressing room and walked down the corridor that led to the men's dressing room. In one of the rooms, she heard voices, and knew that a few of the men lingered, removing their stage makeup. But the second room, the one that held Papa's trunks, was deserted.

Dacey went into the empty room and locked its door behind her. Then she went to the shabbiest of Papa's four trunks and opened it with a key she carried in a small bag. In England, they had utilized the services of a bank, but Dacey did not trust any of the banks here in Kimberley. She could not feel confident in any bank that had a corrugated-iron facade, and Papa had objected to wearing a thick money belt, claiming that the bulge would ruin the lines of his clothes.

She rummaged in the trunk, pulling out layers of brocade waistcoats, silk stockings, cocked hats, wigs, suspenders, and, finally, a collection of old theater programs that dated back to when Papa had first met Dacey's mother on a New York tour. When all these items were pushed aside, Dacey pulled the hidden leather thong and lifted up the trunk's false bottom.

She reached into the narrow compartment and pulled out the flat metal box where they kept the company's money. Using another key, she unlocked the strongbox and stared into its interior in shock.

The box was empty. The company's earnings for the entire week were gone.

Papa.

Dacey remembered the eager faces of Lavinia, Mary, and Eleonora. Eleonora, she knew, was desperately homesick for her children and had been counting on passage home soon. How could Papa have done this to the people who trusted him? Dacey didn't care that much for herself anymore; now that she had Quinn, the thought of returning to England no longer seemed very important.

But the others—that was different. This was *their* money Papa toyed with, and after he had promised, after he had nearly groveled with shame at what he had done, begging her forgiveness.

She didn't understand it. And, at this moment, she wasn't even sure that she wanted to. Furiously Dacey threw the empty strongbox back into its compartment and tossed the clothes in after it. She hurried out of the empty dressing room, slamming its door behind her.

A huge yellow moon leered down at her as she half-ran toward the familiar tenting of the King of Prussia Saloon, where she knew she would find Papa. Somewhere out on the veld, she heard the slavering cry of a wild jackal, the sound in keeping with her angry mood. Last week, Quinn had had to rescue her from the gamblers, but he wasn't here now, and tonight she didn't care. She was going to barge into the tent and find Papa and take any of the money that was still left away from him. After that, she would—

Then Dacey broke off the thought, shame filling her. What was she thinking of? She loved Papa. Some of her fury abated a little and tears stung her eyes. She gave an angry dash at her lashes—she wouldn't cry—and started into the saloon.

"Well, daughter, is it you? You are a beautiful sight, I must say, against the lambent splendor of the African moon."

Papa himself emerged from the tent, swaying slightly from drink, a familiar, sheepish expression on his face. Beside him was Royce, his face also flushed with liquor. In their wake stumbled several other actors in the company, their voices raised in a jovial, off-key song.

Her heart sinking, Dacey took in Papa's dejected expression. He had lost, that was as plain as the moon. And the rest were actually *singing*, as if it didn't matter that their work was gone, that they were exactly where they'd been before, a troupe stranded thousands of miles away from home.

Her temper snapped. "Papa!" She started forward. "Papa, I don't understand, how could you *do* it?"

John McKinnon's face seemed to droop even more. "I am sorry, Dacia."

"Sorry!" She was swept into a fury of love and frustration. "Being sorry isn't enough, Papa, not this time. Eleonora has been counting on going home. We all have. It isn't fair, what you do to us, to *all* of the company. You—"

Papa put up an imperious hand to stop her tirade. To her shock, she saw that he was laughing.

"Dacia, Dacia, Dacia." The rest of the men gathered about them, also roaring with laughter. Papa had puffed himself up and was looking grandly important.

"Look, Dacia, what I have for you. Just look!"

He held out something to her, and with a shock, Dacey saw that it was his money belt, so stuffed with bills that it bulged fatly.

"Papa?" She could scarcely believe her eyes.

"I won, daughter, I won! I've got a whole belt full of money, and diamonds, too—six of them! Every member of the company gets a gift, and we'll sail back to London in style!"

The others, including Royce, cheered happily.

"Papa . . . oh, Papa . . ."

"What do you think, Dacia? Can old John McKinnon still predict the turn of the wheel, the whims of Lady Luck? Aren't the McKinnons on the upward swing again?"

Dacey saw the pride that glowed from her father's face, transforming him from a tired old man into a king. She felt a spasm of love for him, for she knew that, in his way, he had done this for her. She went to him and hugged his thin frame. She clung to him, not wanting to feel the slight tremor in him, the shakiness of age.

As they turned to walk toward their hotel, the others all talking excitedly, John McKinnon bent to whisper in Dacey's ear.

"There's extra for you, Dacia. I took a chance and put in the money you got from that diamond the miner threw to you. I won twenty to one."

He had gambled *her* money, too. He had taken it out of her bag and he had risked that, as well. Dacey felt her eyes sting with tears of horror, but she choked back the cry that rose to her lips.

"You have enough to buy a claim in the Kimberley Mine if you want to," Papa gloated. "Isn't that a wonderful gift for your papa to give to you? Aren't you happy, Dacia? Aren't you pleased?"

Dacey forced a smile and continued to walk with Papa, holding on to his arm. He was her father. He loved her and she loved him, he depended on her.

How could she hurt him by scolding him?

"Darling." Dacey sighed. "Are you as happy as I am?"

"I am. God help me, Dacey, I am."

"There are times," Dacey mused, snuggling closer to Quinn's smooth, naked, sun-fragrant skin, "when I think we've already had more happiness than some people get in a lifetime."

They were at their thorn tree again, lying on the canvas cloth that Quinn had laid on the ground for their comfort. Twined in each other's arms, they stared upward at the sky that curved over them like a huge blue bubble, enclosing their love. Dacey felt lazy and happy, as satiated as a cat from drinking too much thick cream.

A black locust with red wings flew past, dipping recklessly, then buzzing away again.

As always, their lovemaking had been not just physical pleasure, but a joining of their spirits. Dacey had not known that love could be like this, satisfying dreams and desires that she had not even known she possessed. If this was living for the moment, for the *now*, then it was happiness enough for her.

Now, seeing that Quinn had fallen into a silence, Dacey spoke lightly. "Do you know what happened last night, Quinn? My father, the rogue, took all of the company's money *and* mine, and instead of losing it, as I feared, he won. Isn't that wonderful?"

"Of course, my little bird." Quinn smiled lazily into her

eyes. "And what are you going to do with your share of the winnings?"

"I'm not sure. There's passage for the troupe back to England, of course, that comes first. But I lay awake last night, thinking. Papa has always believed in omens, and I confess sometimes I made fun of him, considering him foolish, a dreamer. But now . . ."

Dacey's voice thickened with excitement. "We are here in Kimberley, and a miner tossed that diamond to me onstage. Now Papa has won six more, and a large sum of money. Surely that *has* to mean something!"

Quinn sat up abruptly, the sun reflecting on his face so that she could not read his expression. "All it means is that coincidence, which is what the gambler calls luck, worked in your father's favor."

"But what if this is an omen, just as Papa claims? What if I'm meant to buy a claim here, what if this marks a change for the McKinnons? We were poor for so long, but now maybe it can change. We could buy a house, Papa and I—"

"In Kimberley?" Quinn's laugh was harsh. "Dacey, aren't you aware that the big diamond magnates are all frantically saving their money so they can get *out* of Kimberley? They consider this place only temporary, a cross they must bear until they can go back to London or America."

"I don't care. I want a house for Papa and me. I want to be sure we'll never have to worry about money again. And I want Papa to be able to be proud of something besides his gambling winnings. To be not just an itinerant actor but somebody!"

"A person doesn't need money, Dacey, in order to be someone. You would be a wonderful woman if you never owned another penny again for the rest of your days." Quinn spoke slowly, his brows pulled together in a frown. "As for security, I've observed, most women find that in marriage."

Marriage. The word dropped between them like a stone. It seemed to confront them, to accuse.

Dacey turned to look at Quinn as he stared out over the veld, his strong jaw knotted, his mouth rigid with pain. Marriage, she thought, swallowing. She was well aware of what he had meant when he had said it. He could not marry her, but someone else could. And, someday, would.

Their idyll—their now, the moments stolen together—was going to have to end.

Her lighthearted mood of the day had seeped away, and it was with difficulty that she hid her distress as they dressed and prepared to return to town.

That afternoon, Dacey put aside her heartache about Quinn and took the money her father had given her, walking to the Kimberley Mine.

Sounds rose in a hubbub around her: the squeak of winches, bellow of oxen, the sound of picks and shovels. Men shouted to each other in a dozen languages. The air was thick with dust, and she saw two men arguing over a claim boundary, their faces red. Just as Dacey walked past, one hit the other viciously on the jaw.

Dacey edged away nervously, wondering what kind of a world this was, where miners argued amid chaotic confusion. And confusion it was. During their hours at the thorn tree, Quinn had told Dacey more about the mine. She knew that claims measured only thirty-one by thirty-one feet, hardly larger than a living room. Property was in such demand, Quinn said, that fortune seekers bought and sold claims only a few feet in area.

"But that's incredible," she had said, laughing, not knowing whether to believe him.

"It's true, though. And it makes for much rancor and hard feelings. Each man simply chooses a site and starts digging. It's quite a mess, especially when walkways have to be preserved to give access to claims in the middle of the mine. You can be sure there are plenty of disagreements."

"Still, it must be exciting to know that fabulous finds are being made, practically under your own feet!"

"Exciting, yes. But thefts by the black workers are almost impossible to prevent entirely, and it is the curse of Kimberley. Hatred for a man who is caught buying stolen diamonds from a black is virulent."

"I see." Shivering, Dacey remembered the grim, angry

faces of the miners in the King of Prussia Saloon. "It all seems—well, so savage somehow."

"Savage is exactly what it is. This isn't civilization, Dacey—this is a tough mining town. Only the strong survive here."

Now, walking through the immense, sprawling activity of the Kimberley Mine, Dacey thought of what Quinn had said, feeling her throat close with misgiving.

But she did have Papa's winnings clutched safely in her bag and she was determined not to leave Kimberley without giving his omens a chance.

Why, otherwise, would that miner have tossed a diamond to her? Why would Papa have won six more? It was luck, a signal that their fortune was changing. But, Dacey reminded herself, luck could not change if you did nothing to help it. All she wished was to find one or two medium-sized diamonds. Enough to tuck by a nice amount of cash . . .

To her left, she glimpsed a crude canvas lean-to, where about seven black men sorted gravel at a table, supervised by a fat white man who kept mopping his face and drinking from a water jug. Dacey drew a deep breath and approached the fat man, giving him her warmest smile.

"Sir? I'm wondering if you could tell me—"

The man gave Dacey a long, assessing look that started at her straw bonnet and continued down to her dusty shoes, missing nothing. His small eyes gleamed.

"Say, aren't you that there actress? Didn't I see you at the Royal in that Shakespeare show?"

"Yes, but I wanted to ask—"

"Not now, honey, I'm supervising the men here and haven't got a relief. Otherwise I'd come with you, and damn the Kaffir bastards. Look, could you come back tonight? I'm off at the east side of town, right off the Market Square, and I'd pay well. For a girl of your looks, I'd pay top dollar."

"Top dollar?" And then, in a flash of horrid comprehension, Dacey realized. The man thought her a prostitute! He thought she had come here to the mine in order to sell her body.

"Sir, I'm a respectable actress, a decent woman, and I'm not for sale—to you or to anyone!" She picked up her skirts and fled, hearing the man call after her.

But he did not chase her, and after a while Dacey resumed her walk again, vowing to be more careful next time.

Still, it took some minutes to regain her courage as she circled among the endless confusion of men, horses, ox wagons, windlasses, and carts. Several diggers paused to stare at her, and when this happened, Dacey flushed and hurried on, nervousness filling her again.

But at last she spotted a man working alone, apparently engaged in the construction of a winch. He was young, about twenty-five, Dacey guessed, and worked shirtless, his muscular chest gleaming with sweat and dust. Brown hair fell untidily into his face, and yellow dust clung to his beard, giving him a streaked look.

Boldly Dacey walked up to him. "Pardon me, but I wanted to ask—could you tell me how to buy a claim here?"

The digger looked up, startled, and she saw his eyes widen at the sight of a well-dressed, pretty young woman.

"Please," she repeated, annoyed. Was the presence of a woman *that* unusual here at the mine? "I'd like to buy a claim here at the Kimberley Mine. Could I buy one from you?"

"From me?"

"Why, yes, is there something wrong with that? I assure you, I have money, and I'll pay the going rate."

Had he, too, seen her at the Royal? Was that why his eyes were fastened on her face so insistently? Dacey could have stamped her feet in frustration.

"But you're a woman," he said at last, dismissively.

"Yes, I am, but that shouldn't make any diff—"

"You can't buy in here." He scowled at her, rubbing his beard. "Look at this place, just look around you." His gesture took in the yawning, huge excavation and all its frenetic activity. "Is this any place for a pretty woman? A woman belongs in the town, working in a laundry or a restaurant, or being a proper wife, or . . . other things. But not here. This is a man's province."

"Oh, it is?" Dacey felt her temper flare. She had been stared at and thought a prostitute, and now she was being made to feel inferior because she wore a dress instead of a pair of grimy trousers. "Well, I've worked on plenty of stage sets in my time, and I've wielded a hammer before, too, *man's* work. And I'd like to tell you something. That winch you're building is never going to hold. You need some cross braces and you need longer, heavier nails, or it will fall apart just as soon as it starts turning. And I hope it does!"

As the miner's mouth fell open, Dacey gathered her skirts and backed away. She turned and began to hurry over the cluttered, bare earth, toward the next row of sorting tables.

"Well, miss, and what did you expect? *They* think mining is a man's work and they've made it into their own private territory. They have their own ways of shutting us out, you may be sure."

Bella Garvey was a seamstress-laundress, a comfortable-looking woman of fifty whose plain black dress and corset could not conceal the bulges of her figure. She had brown hair streaked with gray and pulled back into a bun. Her brown eyes, the color of tortoiseshell, regarded Dacey warmly.

Fuming, Dacey had come here to order two gowns made of the fabric in her trunk. Now she could not help bursting out to the seamstress with her indignation.

"It's all so unfair! I have money to buy a claim, but they all stared at me as if I were a freak. I approached *five* miners, and each acted as if I had no business even being among them."

"Oh, you're no freak, not you." Bella spoke through a mouthful of pins, deftly folding, tucking, and pinning. "I saw you last night at the theater—you're a wonder. Up there on the other side of those burning lights, you take a person to another world entirely, you're that good."

"Oh! That's so kind of you." Dacey felt touched at the compliment, and a little bit cheered. She had felt so defeated after leaving the mine, and her pert words to the bearded miner had not made her feel much better. What good was money in her purse if men resisted her buying a claim? Made it plain that she didn't belong among them?

"What brought you to Kimberley, Bella?" she asked the

dressmaker, trying to take her mind off her own sagging spirits.

"Diamonds, what else?" Bella gave a dry laugh. "But the most important thing was a man. My husband, Jake, God bless him, died of dysentery two months after we got here. The water here is filthy and has to be boiled, but Jake didn't heed my advice. He insisted on using a common drinking cup over at the mine."

"Oh, I'm so sorry."

"So was I, I'll tell you. I was left with an eighth of a claim, but I couldn't make a go of it alone, so I sold it. Now I have my laundry, and a bit of a business making dresses. Someday, when this town gets bigger, I'll open a little shop. But for now"—Bella shrugged—"I manage."

Dacey flushed, thinking of her own purse well stuffed with pound notes and coins. "You said you owned part of a claim once. Why couldn't you make it go?"

"Why, without a man, there's precious little a woman can accomplish here in Kimberley. I couldn't boss the laborers— they didn't want to take orders from me. I couldn't fight the miners on either side of me, who wanted to edge in on my territory. I couldn't wield a pick or heave a shovel, and I couldn't work all day in the hot sun—heat makes me faint."

"I . . . I see." Everything Bella said seemed to confirm what Dacey had already observed, and she felt herself slump with dismay.

"Stand up, dearie, or this seam'll be crooked." Bella turned Dacey around slowly, inspecting the pinning and basting she had done. "Good, good, you're going to be stunning in this dress, you'll make the men look, I assure you. Gold silk, very stylish. Ever think of getting a partner?" she went on.

"A partner?"

"Eh, and what else? You provide the money; he provides the labor and know-how. A man is necessary here, honey— and not just for the bed." Bella chuckled.

"A man is necessary here." The seamstress' words and her suggestion that Dacey get a partner echoed in Dacey's mind as she started back to her hotel. Maybe Bella was right, she thought. Certainly the Kimberley Mine did look rough and intimidating. But if a woman had a man to stand beside her, if she could work with him equally . . .

Dacey did not realize that her footsteps had deviated from the route back to her hotel until she found herself on a side street off the Market Square, approaching the iron building that Quinn kept as his office.

QUINN FARRIS, DEALER IN DIAMONDS. FULL MARKET VALUE GIVEN FOR ALL CLASSES OF DIAMONDS. The sign was neatly lettered. Quinn, she knew, kept hours here in the late afternoon.

As she hesitated, a pair of dark-clad men shouldered their way out of the building, speaking rapidly to each other in Italian. When they had disappeared down the street, she drew a sharp breath and opened the door.

6

LILAC DUSK WAS SETTLING AS Natala crouched beside the brown, sluggish water of the Vaal River, where she had gone to collect the herbs, barks, and roots that she used for her magic. She fed another chunk of dried game dung to the small fire she had built, watching it flare up again.

The river was a sparse oasis, a line of green where birds swooped and dived in its fringe of dwarf willows, mimosas, and karee bush.

But only the riverbank was thick with trees. On all sides, the dry veld stretched to the horizon, its normal yellow-brown tinted rosy by the sinking sun. Away from the river, a three-foot acacia tree could be a landmark, visible for miles. Dark ridges of rocks, like the backbones of buried monsters, cut the plain into strips. And when the wind blew down from the Kalahari Desert, it scoured up the dust in choking, stinging storms.

Natala loved the savagery of this wild, desert land. It appealed to something dark and primitive in her, attuned to the animalistic spirits that walked the veld, along with spirits of dead ancestors.

The women of her kraal, Natala knew, were frightened of such specters. Like most Africans, they were terrified of the dark. Each night they cringed at the thought of the terrible night things that they feared might savage them if they left the protection of the fire and the others grouped around it.

Although she did have a fire, Natala was not afraid. She tossed the flames another chunk of antelope dung, watching the red flare up vividly. The missionaries had told her about their God, Jesus Christ, and had taught her that the dark was only savage because of living predators, not dead ones. Darkness itself was benign. And it could be used—if only to influence the terrors of others.

She inched closer to the fire, eyeing with satisfaction the hide bag of medicines she had already collected. Bark, roots, dagga, more than enough for months.

She had some dagga, already dried, with her now, and slowly, ceremonially, Natala twisted some of the dried plant into a tight rope and touched its end to the flames.

Almost immediately, the harsh, acrid smoke flared up. It surrounded her with a thick cloud of the substance that could quicken men's hearts, giving them desire and swirling, tumultuous dreams. Natala breathed deeply of the smoke and for the first time allowed herself to think about Dacey McKinnon.

The actress, the pale-skinned English girl, had dared to walk with Quinn through the town, to look at him from under her lashes. Did a thin-blooded English girl think that she could attract a man like Quinn Farris? That she could ensnare him with the wiles of her body?

That was the real reason that Natala had made the long journey over the veld: for the fire, for the purpling dusk now fading to black, the smoke that she now inhaled deeply into her lungs. She needed the deep, primitive emptiness of the desert in order to think.

She closed her eyes and began to sway from side to side, murmuring words that had been taught her by Teki, her mother, handed down from the long darkness of the African past. Then she felt it: the first clouding of her senses, followed by a heightened awareness.

Natala opened her eyes. The dark sky, scattered with the first bright stars, seemed to swoop toward her. The stars were tiny daggers that reached downward to stab her . . .

She sniffed deeply of the smoke, letting it reach harsh fingers deep into her mind. Then she leaned forward, focusing her eyes on the flames that burned at the base of the fire.

Ai, there they were. Tiny shapes glowing there, almost human in their lineaments. Dacey McKinnon, a quick, blue flame. Quinn, redder, richer, burning with power. And herself, Natala, a flame erratic and jumping, first waxing high, then flickering almost to nothing.

At the sight of the flame that resembled herself, Natala frowned. She passed one hand over her forehead, her belly knotting. She had looked into the fire many times since her initiation. But never had it been like this, so puzzlingly obscure. And now, she saw, the Dacey flame was mingling with the one that stood for Quinn, the two drawing together and twisting in one spiral. Red sparks snapped and jumped, flaring into the night.

Natala scowled in quick anger. Then she watched as, slowly, the two dancing flames separated from each other. They began to burn, each alone . . .

Natala breathed in the smoke from the dagga and felt it fill her lungs. She sat long into the night, pondering, while the moon moved above her and the stars flamed and time shifted like clouds in a pot of river water.

Ai! She moistened her lips and began to sway back and forth, monotonously. And the words that she muttered were a curse . . .

Dacey edged into Quinn's office, her eyes immediately drawn to the sight of Quinn seated at a makeshift desk, a bar of sunlight caught in his thick, dark hair. As always, the sight of him sent a little sensual shock thrilling through her. How handsome he was, with a physical magnetism, a strong presence about him that could cause her mouth to dry, her heartbeat to thicken.

To cover her reaction, she glanced down at the desk in front of Quinn where, also picked out in the shaft of sun, were two uncut diamonds. The light seemed to savage them, sending out knife blades of glitter.

"Oh . . ." Dacey was struck by the opulent sight. "Your diamonds . . . they are beautiful."

Quinn scowled down at the stones, regarding them contemptuously, almost as if he hated them. "Beautiful, but imperfect." He touched one with a small tweezers. "This one, Dacey, is a river diamond—that's because of its color, almost blue-white. It is twenty carats, a good size, but inside are a large group of 'feathers' that will spoil its brilliance when it is cut. As for this one, it actually has a crack. Which means that a blow to the stone, or even a change in temperature, might cause it to fracture."

Quinn sighed and put both diamonds into a small leather sack, tossing them into a small metal safe as if they were no more valuable than pebbles.

Dacey watched in awe: she knew that she would have treated *any* diamond with reverence. "Oh, but surely those are still wonderful stones," she couldn't help protesting. "Someone will want them—"

Quinn shrugged. "Someone, yes, but not me. The stones I want must be perfect . . . But enough of that. Tell me what you think of my office."

She looked around at the tiny, sparsely furnished office; it contained several tables, a wall safe, a small diamond balance scale, a paraffin lamp, and very little else.

"It's very—" She faltered.

"Spartan?" His somber humor gone, Quinn grinned at her. "Oh, I know that, but one of these days I'll send to Cape Town for some fancier furniture and some rugs." His eyes moved over her, warm with desire. "You look very pretty this afternoon. Although . . . Do I see some mine dust on the hem of your dress?"

Dacey flushed, realizing that he knew she had been to the mine.

"Yes," she admitted. She touched her purse, full of the money that Papa had won. "Oh, Quinn, I want to buy a claim!" she burst out. "Maybe even two of them. I have the money, and I know I could do something if I were given half a chance. Just because a person happens to be a woman doesn't mean that she couldn't work hard, that she couldn't find just as many diamonds as any man!"

The smile on Quinn's face instantly disappeared, leaving his expression grim, carven. He leaned back in his chair, tossing the diamond tweezers onto the table with a sharp snap. "So you have it, too."

"I have what?"

"Diamond fever, Dacey. I suppose I should have known this would happen. Diamonds are a sickness that strikes everyone here, from the lowliest Bantu worker right on up to every visitor who arrives. As for you, are all women alike? Are diamonds the first and only thing on their minds, to the exclusion of all else?"

How bitter Quinn sounded, how angry! Dacey didn't know why his voice had grown suddenly so cold. She felt chilled as she sat down in a canvas chair. She began toying with the clasp of her bag, touching the jet beads and tassels that were sewn to its sides.

"I came to ask you if you'd be my partner," she forced herself to say. "The men at the mine all laughed at me; they said I had no business at the diggings. None of them would even talk about selling to me. But, with the two of us—"

She leaned forward eagerly. "You've already told me that miners are now restricted to holding only two claims—that's to prevent one person from taking more than his share of the diamonds."

"Yes, yes," Quinn agreed impatiently. "But, Dacey—"

"We could circumvent that. You could own your two claims, and I'd own mine. Only we'd really own them together, and that would make four—"

"No."

She stared at him, hurt by the short, curt word. His dark eyebrows were knotted together and his mouth formed a straight, cold line.

"I don't work with partners, Dacey," he repeated, the sentence an unmistakable dismissal.

"But . . . I don't understand."

Heat rose to Dacey's cheeks, spreading to her neck and chest. She couldn't believe that Quinn would treat her this way. Why didn't he want to be her partner? They'd made love. They'd been as close as a man and a woman could get. Quinn had felt that closeness, too, she knew it with every bone of her body. And now he wouldn't even listen to her.

She could have been anyone, even some stranger who'd wandered in off the street to ask for a loan!

Quinn had gone to the window, where he stood with his back to her, the set of his shoulders hard, unyielding.

"Dacey, mining can be a brutal business. I learned that lesson in Virginia City, and I learned it all too well. If things went wrong, I would never want another person, especially someone like you, to be dragged down with me."

"But I wouldn't be dragged down with you! I'd bring you good luck, I'd—"

He turned, putting up an impatient hand to stop her protests. *"No*, Dacey. Besides, I don't think you realize just what it is that you are really asking me."

"What do you mean?" she faltered.

"I mean that you are asking me to be much more than your business partner. Well, aren't you? Didn't I tell you on the veld that we could not look to the long expanse of years, but must live only in the here and now? Oh, God, Dacey!"

And now Dacey saw the anguish that twisted Quinn's face, giving him a harsh look. There was no trace now of the laugh lines that bracketed his mouth or fanned out from his eyes.

"I can't do it, Dacey. You know that. It's something that I'm just not free to give."

It—meaning love. Dacey stared at him, feeling as if he had suddenly stripped her naked, revealing raw hopes, plans, dreams that she hadn't even known she possessed. And maybe he was right. Oh, God, maybe she really had been asking for more. Maybe she'd been asking for his love.

Well, it was plain that he didn't want to give it to her—oh, he'd made that very clear indeed! An aching fissure of emptiness seemed to split across her heart. Quinn didn't want her. He could not have made it clearer. Their love was never going to work; Papa had been horribly, cruelly right.

Dacey sprang to her feet, driven by a thick anger that stabbed her like a sword. Her movement was so swift that her purse fell to the floor, and she bent down and scooped it up, feeling her body shake.

"So you don't want to be my partner!" she snapped. "Well, it's very plain to me why. You've already got several—a mistress here in Kimberley and a wife in Virginia City. Why should you need any more women than that, when two are enough to keep you busy? Oh, Papa was right! He was right in everything he said. You *are* a womanizer! You don't care about me, you never did, you wanted only my b-body . . .''

Her throat ached with the desire to cry. Dimly she heard him say, "Dacey, that's not true."

"Isn't it?" she shouted. "Oh, Quinn, don't tell me that. I'm a fool, the biggest fool who ever lived. I never should have let you make love to me, and I damn well wish I hadn't!"

She was on the street again, barely aware of how she had got there, feeling only the harsh pain that seared her throat, consisting of unshed tears. She stumbled down the crude walk, avoiding groups of miners, barely seeing them.

Her mind repeated the argument with Quinn, over and over. "I don't think you realize just what it is that you are really asking me. . . . I can't do it, Dacey. You know that. . . ."

He couldn't love her. He had rejected her—not just her partnership, but all of the wonderful feelings they'd shared together, the love that had just started to grow between them, the joy they'd found under their thorn tree. To her, these things had been important, but to him they'd been only an interlude.

She'd been living in a fool's dream of love and passion. Now the dream was ripped away and she was awake again, aware of reality. Quinn Farris wasn't for her. She laughed to herself bitterly. He already had a wife. And a mistress!

Dacey wandered the streets of Kimberley, allowing her feet to take her wherever they would. She felt empty, hollowed out to the core.

"Watch it! Watch where you're going, for Christ's sake!"

Dacey felt strong arms clamp about her midsection and yank her roughly backward, out of the path of a huge wagon, its bed spilling over with Bechuanaland lumber for the mines.

Her rescuer dragged Dacey a few more feet, then released

her, propping her against the side of an iron hut. The cart driver cursed at her as he drove his team of oxen past them.

"What's the matter with you?" an angry male voice demanded.

"I . . . I guess I just didn't see them." Dacey leaned against the sun-hot building, pulling at her bonnet, which had fallen to the back of her head.

"You weren't even looking. Were you trying to kill yourself? I told you, the mines are no place for a woman!"

For the first time, Dacey looked at the miner. He had evidently just finished washing, for his hair was wet and slicked back and his brown beard was still damp. It was the same young miner who had been working on the winch earlier in the day.

The one, Dacey remembered, flushing, whom she had told that she hoped his construction would fall apart.

"I'm sorry, I was careless," she apologized. "And I do thank you for saving me."

"You shouldn't have been here at all," he told her aggressively. Then he softened. "But as long as you are . . . I'm Jed Donohue."

She forced a smile, seeing the coarse, yet good-looking features, the heavy jaw and strong nose that looked as if it had once been broken. "And I'm Dacey McKinnon."

"Since you're so interested in mining, would you like to walk around and see my claims?"

She hesitated.

"Come on, I've got two." He expanded with pride, thrusting out his burly chest and throwing out his shoulders so that he seemed to stand taller than his five feet nine inches. "Come on, and mind your step."

Dacey allowed herself to be led—what did it matter?—around the lip of the huge excavation, past horses powering winches, and over a rock walkway that extended downward into the mine.

"Watch it!" Jed Donohue commanded. "Don't slip—these rocks can be dangerous!"

Dacey didn't need any warnings. She clutched at Jed, staring dizzily downward at the black workers toiling antlike amid a confusion of boulders and cutout sections of earth. Heaps of fallen dirt and rock littered the area.

In a few minutes, they had reached Jed's claims and found seven or eight black men swinging picks. Sweat, sunlight, and dust glittered on their nearly naked bodies, and several had bits of bone thrust through their ears. One, taller and broader than the others, glanced up curiously at Dacey as they approached. He had a fine, broad forehead and dark intelligent eyes.

"Well?" Jed wanted to know. "What do you think of it?"

Dacey looked about, at the tumbled rocks, the clouds of hot dust. Picks rang against rock and men shouted; down here in the mine, the volume of noise was even more deafening than it was on the surface.

"It's . . . . incredible," she shouted over the din. Some of her anger over Quinn's rejection was retreating, to be replaced by a growing excitement. The mine—everything about it—was rough, raw, crude, no more than a confused crater of dirt and rocks, toiled in by dusty men. And yet diamonds could be found here. *Were* being found, every day.

"Damn right it is!" Jed shouted back. "Now, come on back up top and I'll show you my sorting tables."

Ten minutes later they were inspecting the makeshift tent strung over a long table to protect the workers from the worst of the sun.

"This yellow ground is easy to work," Jed told her. "All we have to do is break it apart and pick it over. Would you like to see some diamonds?" As Dacey stared in surprise, Jed reached into his pants pocket. He pulled out a grimy, grease-stained envelope. He slit it open and with a flourish tipped its contents into the palm of his hand.

Dacey felt awed. Cupped in Jed's hand were about thirty rough diamonds, gleaming like bits of ice. Some were clear, others slightly yellowish, and the shapes varied from round to angular.

"This is a week's take. And some of 'em are pretty small and only of industrial quality," Jed admitted. "But I've got one big one. Look at this fellow here, he's at least eight carats. Do you want to hold it?"

Dacey remembered the bigger stones she had seen in Quinn's office. She hesitated, torn between her strong desire to touch the diamond and her fear of somehow dropping it into the dirt and dust at their feet, where it might be forever lost.

"Go ahead," Jed urged. "Feel it. Feels great, doesn't it? Diamonds are the hardest thing in nature, and yet to me, they always feel kinda smooth and just a bit greasy."

Fascinated, Dacey hefted the tiny stone with its octahedron shape in her fingers, turning it so that it caught the sunlight with a vibrant, shimmering flash. What sort of gem would it make someday? Would an elegant lady wear this diamond on her finger or at her throat?

Jed was grinning. "I see you like it. Most people do. Diamonds sorta grow on you." He took the stone back and tipped all of the diamonds back into the envelope. "Look, would you like to go back into town and have a meal with me? I know you have your show to put on tonight—I've seen it about five times—but maybe there's time if we hurry."

Dacey thought of Quinn and suppressed a pang that cut at her throat like a rough knot of rope. "I . . . of course," she said at last. "I'll eat supper with you."

Why shouldn't she eat a meal with this man? she wondered defiantly. Why shouldn't she do anything she chose?

Jed came from a poor Boston Irish family, he told her over a meal of beef stew and dried-apricot pie. "My folks are lace-curtain Irish—that's the proud sort," he told her. "We didn't have money, but pride—that we owned in plenty. I had a cousin over at the Vaal diggings. He sent me a letter and I sailed over last year, working my passage as a deckhand. I walked from Cape Town to New Rush, as Kimberley was called then."

Dacey nodded, listening as Jed told her of his plans to grow rich. "Rich enough to keep a fine house and a pretty woman in it, and the finest, fanciest lace curtains a man can buy."

Jed paused to devote himself to his meal, scraping up the last bit of beef gravy with a chunk of bread. Finally he looked up at Dacey again.

"I was there, you know."

She looked at him, puzzled.

"In the tent, I mean, that night you got dragged into the King of Prussia Saloon. That was an awfully damn-fool thing you did, you could have got yourself killed. Diamond thievery is serious business."

"I did get that impression," Dacey said wryly, remembering the fierce man who had wielded the knife.

"Yes, well, *I* didn't think you were up to anything bad. What, a little thing like you? You're no bigger than a minute, I could lift you up with one hand."

Jed grinned, and Dacey looked uncertainly down at her plate. Jed Donohue seemed to like her, that seemed plain by the looks he had been giving her all through the meal. He was even attractive, in a rough-hewn way. Still . . . She choked back a thought of Quinn.

"—and so that's why I threw it to you," Jed was saying. "Because I thought you'd been treated poorly, and we ought to make it up to you. Besides, you're so damned pretty." Jed's face had grown red. "I meant to come backstage, but I was a little drunk that night. I don't even remember how I got home."

"Do you mean that you . . . *you* were the one who . . ." Dacey's mouth fell open with surprise. *Jed* was the miner who had tossed her the diamond! The money that she carried in her purse at this very moment derived from that diamond. The fact that she was able to purchase a claim at all, she owed to Jed!

"Yep, it was me."

"I don't know what to say." Dacey remembered Lavinia's taunt about the miner demanding his diamond back, and felt a flush burn her cheeks. It had been one thing to possess the money when it came from some unknown source. But now that she knew that it had come from Jed, that she owed it all to him—she felt different, embarrassed, as if she had no right to it.

"I sold the diamond you gave me," she admitted in a low voice. "I'd better repay you for it." She fumbled in her purse.

Jed shrugged. "No need for that. I might've been drunk that night, but I wasn't too tipsy to know what I was doing. You're a mighty pretty woman, Dacey McKinnon—just about the prettiest I've ever seen."

She did not know how to respond.

"Would you come walking with me tonight? After you're finished at the theater, I mean?"

"Why . . . yes, I suppose I could."

She owed Jed Donohue something, she supposed, for providing the basis for the money she now possessed. What harm could there be in walking with him? Still, painfully, she had to push away a thought of Quinn, his blue eyes burning into hers, his arms enfolding her in a circle of desire . . .

After the walk with Jed through the streets of town and along the walkways of the mine again, Dacey spent a sleepless night. Finally, as dawn approached, she realized that she could not let Quinn go so easily. She had lost her temper—perhaps he had lost his, too. If they were to talk, calmly and sensibly . . .

That day Dacey had called an extra rehearsal, and they also gave a matinee performance. She did not have any time to think about Quinn until that evening. Vivid purple dusk was falling as she hurried down the path to Quinn's tent. All around her rose the tantalizing smell of cookfires. Somewhere miners were singing lonely songs, of things lost and faraway, their voices rising plaintively in the dry, clear air. Hearing them, Dacey felt a sharp stab of loss.

She came over the rise and saw Quinn, seated near his fire, cooking something in an iron skillet. He was staring into the flames, scowling as if he saw something in them that he did not like.

"Quinn?"

He turned and saw her.

"Quinn?" she whispered again. He said nothing, rising and coming to her with his arms open. He crushed her to him, running his hands through her hair with the hungry caresses of a man who touches something he may never hold again. Dacey clung to him, her throat aching.

At last Quinn held her away and looked deeply into her eyes. "Dacey . . . you shouldn't have come."

"I had to. Oh, Quinn, I was so angry, I said things— things that shouldn't have been said. I'm sorry. I . . . I hoped we could talk—"

"Hush, Dacey. You don't have to be sorry." The expression in Quinn's eyes was so bleak that Dacey felt her heart twist. She watched as he went to the cookfire and reached for a spoon to stir the curry in the pan. Spicy smells arose, yet Dacey could feel no appetite; she knew, by the way Quinn stirred the pot, that he didn't either.

He put down the spoon and stared again into the fire. "I loved a woman once. Worshiped her with all of the passion and trust of which a man is capable. And then one day I learned that she had been using me, exactly as one would use a blooded racehorse, for gain, for winning. I married her, Dacey. I'm still married. But I love you even more than I loved her."

Quinn broke off, his eyes reflecting the dancing flames. "There's no future for us, Dacey, and it will only hurt worse if we don't end it now."

Dacey, too, looked into the fire, her heart aching with each word. She just didn't understand how things could grow so cruelly, unfairly twisted. She tried to speak, to protest, and found that her voice would not emerge.

"I rode out onto the veld today," Quinn went on, adding more thorny wood to the fire. "I went to the kraal to visit my daughter."

"Kraal?"

"The native encampment—Lilah is being reared by her mother's family—and I wish you could see her, Dacey, how beautiful she is."

"I imagine she is lovely." Somehow Dacey forced out the response.

"Very. But more than that, she is eager. Even at her babyish age, she is bright and intelligent, and someday she'll—" Quinn stopped, and then, thickly, he went on. "Natala knows full well how I feel about that little girl. She knows that all she has to do is take Lilah away, across the veld to the north country, the bush. They could fade away there, be lost forever, and I'd never find Lilah again."

Dacey knelt by the fire, feeling her body shake all over. She knew what Quinn was telling her. His life was already tangled in a complicated web of obligations and ties. His daughter, Lilah, was another of them, perhaps the strongest tug of all. At this moment, she could feel nothing but a poignant, grinding sense of loss. She had come into Quinn's life too late, there was no place in it for her.

"Still, if we were just partners, only business partners . . ." She said it desperately, wanting to keep some part of him, something.

"And do you think I could see you day after day without wanting you? Without you tearing at my heart, without wanting to take you in my arms and possess you? We would only be prolonging the agony. You know it as well as I do."

Dacey did. She crouched very still, struggling not to cry.

"Darling." Quinn tilted up Dacey's chin with one strong, blunt finger. "I want you to do something for me."

"Yes, oh, anything. I will." Trembling, barely aware of what she did, Dacey rose to her feet.

He had risen, too. "Forgive me," he said softly. "I'm no good for you, loving me can only destroy you and poison your life. A womanizer!" His laugh was harsh, bitter. "Perhaps your father was right. As for you, you should be married to a fine man, bear him beautiful children, work with him hand in hand—"

Dacey bowed her head, staring at an outcropping of sand-scoured rocks that jutted from the ground. She felt numbed. Later, she knew, she would experience a wild pain. But for now, there was just this frozen stillness inside her, so deep that it seemed nothing could stir it.

Quinn's voice seemed to come from very far away. "You are too young, Dacey, too lovely not to be happy. Please. Be happy . . . for me."

She could not speak.

"Go on about your life as if I had never come into it. Return to England with your troupe. Live your life, Dacey."

Was Quinn crying? Was it moisture that clung to his

eyelashes, glittering there like tiny fragments of diamonds? Or only some trick of the setting sun?

"All right," she whispered. She steadied her voice with an act of will. Go away, she was thinking. Go away forever. Forget me forever. That was what Quinn was really telling her to do.

"You'll do it, then. Good. And you won't look back. I don't want you to look back, Dacey."

Wretchedly, Dacey nodded. Then she went to him and they stood together, touching lightly, knowing that this would be the last time. Together they stared at the violet afterglow left by the sun, until at last the sky faded into black and the stars began to come out.

7

SOME MINERS HAD TROOPED BACKSTAGE to meet the actors, and Papa was entertaining them, making jovial jokes, enjoying being the center of their attention.

"Dacey, Dacey!" Lavinia came pushing her way through the crowd. "That man with the beard is waiting for you *again*." Lavinia said it half-laughing, but it was plain there was envy in her tone. "My, but you're popular these days! I suppose he is the one who threw you the diamond?"

Dacey nodded. "As a matter of fact, he is."

"What? Oh!" Lavinia clapped both hands to her cheeks. "I was just guessing, I didn't know. Dacey, you didn't tell me, you've been keeping secrets!"

"No, I only learned it when Jed showed me his claims and sorting operation."

"His sorting operation? Oh! He must be very rich, then, Dacey. Especially if he can afford to throw diamonds around as if they were flowers."

Dacey thought of Jed Donohue, his craggy, sunburned face, the curly brown beard often streaked with dust. In the two weeks that she had known Jed, he had proved himself to be singlemindedly interested in diamonds, toiling long hours on his two claims.

"Well," she told Lavinia, "perhaps he's not rich yet, but by the way he works, he soon will be."

"I know what *I* would do if I had met a rich miner who

had already thrown me a diamond for no reason at all—I would grab tight to him and I'd marry him just as fast as I could. If he's rich now, he'll grow even richer, Dacey, and you'll have half of everything he's got.''

Lavinia's remark rang in Dacey's mind as she left the theater to meet Jed in their customary spot. She remembered what Quinn had told her about his wife, Janine, how Janine had selected him like ''a blooded racehorse'' for her own ends. How crude and greedy to think of a man in that light, as a means to getting money and nothing more.

And yet . . . she felt her throat squeeze with an unexpected twist of pain. Quinn had made it plain that he expected her to marry *someone*. A man who could give her children, make her happy. Was Jed Donohue such a man? And could she ever marry anyone, after the fulfillment she had known with Quinn?

Occupied with these thoughts, she was startled to see Jed himself stride into the stage alley, dressed in a dark suit that emphasized his stocky, brawny build. Jed was inches shorter than Quinn, a broad bull to Quinn's longer, wild-tiger grace.

''Ah, you're a beauty tonight, aren't you?'' Jed eyed Dacey's new gown with appreciation. She had splurged, asking Bella to copy the design from *Godey's Lady's Book*. The gown was made of green watered silk, with seven gathered ruffles, an underskirt of delicate puffed muslin, and sleeves trimmed in matching silk ribbons. For Kimberley, it was a gown of unprecedented elegance, and now, pleased with Jed's compliment, Dacey pirouetted happily.

''Where would you like to walk tonight?'' he wanted to know as he steered her out of the alley and onto the main road. On Jed's breath was the faint, sweetish tang of whiskey. It was an odor that seemed natural enough to Dacey, reminding her of Papa.

Dacey shrugged, for the question was rhetorical; the town was small and they had covered all of its streets many times. Now they strolled slowly, past tents, covered wagons, saloons, and canvas churches. There was a small Government House, a two-windowed corrugated-iron cottage with a wooden veranda in front.

The night air, after the day's stifling heat, was refreshingly cool, and a huge silver moon hung suspended over the rooftops. The stars looked as if a giant had flung diamond dust across black velvet.

Seeing the heartbreaking beauty of the night, Dacey felt her heart lurch. It wasn't fair. Why couldn't she be with Quinn now, instead of Jed? How could fate have played with her this cruelly, giving her love, only to snatch it away again?

It had been two weeks since she and Quinn had parted. To Dacey, it seemed an eternity. Somehow she had endured the time, hiding her distress from Lavinia and Papa, parrying Bella's questions with a smile. But at night she huddled under the sheets in her bed, her face damp with tears.

"And you won't look back. I don't want you to look back, Dacey. . . ."

With an effort, she pushed back her thoughts of Quinn and tried to listen as Jed talked of Kimberley, telling of rises and falls in fortune that sounded to Dacey as incredible as a fairy tale. A man called Cecil J. Rhodes was one of those on the way up. She listened, enthralled in spite of herself. Was it possible that Jed could be among the lucky few who rose to incredible riches? That Quinn could be, or even herself?

If she stayed here, she reminded herself. Hadn't Quinn told her that she ought to go back to England?

After they had walked about forty-five minutes, Jed suddenly steered Dacey into the shadow of a building. "Please," he muttered. "Hasn't this gone on long enough? Haven't I courted you? I'm tired of being kept at arm's length."

Abruptly Jed's arms clamped about her and pressed her to him so tightly that she could feel the hard urgency of his maleness. His lips were surprisingly hard as they forced her lips open, his tongue darting into her mouth.

As Dacey's breath caught, Jed sensed her response and began to kiss her neck in quick, passionate, hard kisses that were almost like bites. Dacey moaned and struggled, trying to get away, yet she knew she was enjoying this, too, in some guilty way. She felt a flicker of desire stir within her, a desire that she had thought she could feel only with Quinn.

Confused, she stiffened her body and tried to push Jed

away, but he held her fast, his breathing hoarse. "Dacey . . . ah, God, you want me too, don't you? What a beauty you are, what a woman . . ."

"No—Jed, please . . ."

"Kiss me again."

"No!" She gave him a push and managed to struggle away from him. They stared at each other, both of them panting thickly. Dacey's hair had fallen from the pins that held it, and it straggled wantonly about her shoulders. She pushed at it with shaking fingers.

"Jed, you've got to believe me, I didn't know . . . I didn't mean to . . ."

For an instant Jed scowled at her, his face angry. Then his expression cleared and he threw back his head and laughed. "Oh, you meant what happened, all right. You wanted me just as much as I wanted you. And it looks like there's nothing for it but for us to get married. Otherwise, we'll both burn in hell for sure."

He knew. He'd sensed the traitorous physical desire that had risen in her like a tide. Dacey could not believe that she could flush so red, that the blood could pound in her face so miserably. She'd responded sexually to Jed. Something about his hard lovemaking had brought out animal impulses in her.

She liked Jed well enough, of course. He seemed nice and it had been kind of him to toss her the diamond. Perhaps that meant generosity in him; maybe it was a sign that he could be a good husband.

But she didn't love Jed Donohue, and she knew she never could. It was Quinn she adored, loving him beyond all reason and good sense. And Quinn can't be yours, she told herself angrily. He told you to forget him, and even if he did want you, he already has two women, a mistress and a wife. What could you ever be to him except one more of what he already has too much? A second mistress?

As Jed slid his arm around her, pressing her for an answer to his proposal, Dacey felt a flood of hurt and despair. Why shouldn't she marry Jed Donohue? She had to marry someone, didn't she? Jed was good-looking enough, virile, passionate, and obviously very much smitten with her. He was hard-working, already possessed two claims in a mine where other men fought over tiny slices of land.

Working hand in hand with Jed, in partnership, they could have the four claims she'd discussed with Quinn. Twice as much diamond dirt, twice as much chance of finding fabulous diamonds, of growing rich.

And if she married Jed, a voice whispered inside her, then she wouldn't have to leave Kimberley. She could stay here, she'd be within a few miles of Quinn, she could glimpse him on the streets sometimes. He wouldn't be totally gone from her life. . . .

"Dacey? I'll make you happy, I swear it," Jed promised. "I'll do everything for you, you'll never have to lift a finger again for the rest of your life."

Dacey swallowed, knowing that Jed was offering her something solid and real, not an ephemeral dream of a passion that could never be. Still, something made her hesitate.

"I don't know, Jed, I just—"

"Is there someone else, then?"

"No," she faltered.

"Then will you marry me?"

Dacey heard her voice whisper a reply, so low that Jed had to lean forward to hear it. Her heart slamming, she realized that it must have been yes, for Jed was giving her a look of incredulous delight.

"Really? You'll really do it, you'll marry me?"

"If . . . if you wish."

"Whoopeee!" Jed let out a raucous cry, leaping into the air and tossing up his hat. His voice was full of male, jubilant triumph.

Hearing it, again Dacey swallowed back her misgivings, her longing for Quinn. She'd be happy, she told herself, despite Quinn. She'd make Jed happy, too; she'd be a good wife to him, she'd have everything out of life that any woman could decently expect.

She lifted her face to Jed Donohue and gave him a tremulous smile.

*   *   *

"Eh, Dacey, I swear you are going to be the most beautiful bride in Kimberley!" Bella Garvey basted a seam of Dacey's wedding dress, made of English torchon lace and satin that had been brought over the veld in an ox wagon. Her stubby fingers worked quickly as she completed the last fitting for the gown.

"Am I?" Dacey twisted, trying to get a glimpse of herself in Bella's small mirror.

"Oh, yes, you're quite a prize, you know. I hear that Jed Donohue has been boasting about you, saying you're the prettiest woman in South Africa, and all his."

Dacey flushed, trying to stand still as Bella nearly poked her with a pin. It was heady and exciting to be thought beautiful, to have one's wedding the talk of Kimberley, to feel that her life was speeding on ahead, almost faster than she wished it to.

In three more days, she'd be Mrs. Jed Donohue. Then, as soon as they were married, she'd ask Jed to buy her two claims, and between them, they'd own four. The beginning of riches.

"You're coming to the wedding, aren't you, Bella?" she asked the middle-aged seamstress.

"Coming? Of course I'm coming, dearie, I wouldn't miss it for the world! A wedding, and a reception at the Theater Royal! I'm even making myself a new dress," Bella announced. "Dark green satin and detachable ruffles at the hem to hide the dust. Very practical, and you should have one for your trousseau, too."

Dacey nodded, thinking of all the wedding plans. Food catered by a French chef who'd arrived in Kimberley only a week ago, hoping to strike it rich in diamonds. Music and entertainment provided by the Dazzling Damsons. Drinks for everyone, champagne and Cape wine—nothing but the best, Papa insisted, for his Dacia.

"What's going to happen to the rest of your troupe, once you're married off to a Kimberley man?" Bella wanted to know.

"Well, most of them are going back to England. Except for Lavinia, Papa, and Royce."

Bella nodded knowingly. "That Lavinia seems a flighty creature—what does *she* plan to do here?"

Dacey giggled. "For years Lavinia harbored hopes of marrying Royce, Papa's half-brother. But he never gave her a second look, and now I think she's given up. After I announced my engagement, Lavinia was so envious that she went out and got herself engaged—to Tony Agnelli, the manager of the Theater Royal!"

Both women laughed, picturing the plump, fair Lavinia married to Agnelli, who was tall, gangling, and dark, more than twenty years her senior. But Lavinia had declared herself blissfully happy. On her left hand she wore a rose-cut diamond of indisputable worth. Running a theater was lucrative, too, she boasted to Dacey. Someday she and Tony intended to build a real theater of bricks and wood, and they'd import the best European actresses, stars like Helena Modjeska and Sarah Bernhardt.

Now Bella helped Dacey slip off the cumbersome wedding dress and began fitting the two other gowns that Jed had insisted on buying for her.

"You will look *so* pretty." Bella sighed. "And you're so young. You've had no mother?"

"No, my mother died when I was four."

"And that fine, posturing father of yours—I'll wager *he* has never told you any of the things a young girl should know?"

Dacey flushed, not knowing what to say. She had grown up hearing the other actresses whisper about what went on between men and women. And how could she tell Bella that she had already lost her virginity, to a man who was not to be her husband?

"I see I've embarrassed you."

"No—oh, no . . ." Yet Dacey had flushed hotly and she toyed with a flounce, uncertain where to look.

"Eh, well, then. You'll find out for yourself soon enough, won't you? But, look, Dacey, I want you to come to me if—well, if you have questions later." Bella frowned, running one hand through her brown-gray hair. "If you need a friend, I'm here. South Africa is a harsh country and there can be many trials for a woman; I should know.''

Dacey looked at Bella, touched by her offer of friendship. "You're so kind . . . and I do thank you.''

"It's nothing.'' Bella shrugged. "Men! They can give a woman all sorts of trouble, with their grand ideas about themselves and their wild ways. I have heard things—'' Abruptly she stopped. "No sense worrying your head about it, Dacey. Your Jed seems a nice, solid sort. And that's what counts.''

It was Dacey's wedding day. As dawn thrust fingers of pale light into their hotel room, Dacey heard a scraping noise in the corridor, followed by a knock on their door. She and Lavinia both sat up in their beds as Papa's voice boomed.

"Are you decent, girls? I'm coming in with breakfast for the bride-to-be—special delicacies trekked in from the Cape at exorbitant cost, all for the loveliest bride in Kimberley!''

Their door pushed open and Papa entered, bearing an enormous tray laden with a huge breakfast, everything fabulously expensive. Croissants. Hot chocolate, omelette, ham, and several pinkish mangoes grown near the coast. There was even champagne.

"Champagne!'' Lavinia squealed. "For breakfast? Oh, Dacey, you'll be tipsy all day!''

Dacey and Lavinia pulled on dressing gowns, and the three of them devoured everything, cutting the mangoes with a knife to eat the sweet, golden fruit with their fingers. Dacey drank three glasses of champagne. It was unchilled, for there was no ice in Kimberley, but it tasted heady and delicious. Tiny bubbles seemed to percolate through her veins, making everything she looked at seem faintly hazy.

"Oh, Papa.'' She sighed as she finished her third glass. "I believe Lavinia was right, you *have* made me tipsy.''

Lavinia tittered and Papa looked pleased with himself. "Isn't this your day, Dacia? Why shouldn't you be drunk with joy? I'm more than content, too. After all, your decision means that we can stay here in Kimberley, and who knows what may happen to us now? That diamond young Jed threw you—surely it has to be a good omen."

Dacey nodded, hoping that this was true.

"Well, I suppose I had better be getting along now." Papa rose, wiping off his mustache. "This will be a long day and there is still much to be done. And I've promised that I would stop at the Blue Post and say hello to the regulars there. Most of them are coming tonight."

"The Blue Post, Papa?" It was another of Kimberley's saloons, Dacey knew, more respectable than the King of Prussia, but gambling also took place there.

"Ah, daughter, you mustn't worry about me—not on your golden day. I'm not a gambler anymore. I stopped cold on the day that I won us all that money." Papa beamed. "And I have already given over to the company their entire passage money, so that they will have it in case some untoward impulse makes me forget my resolve."

"Oh, Papa . . ." Dacey reached out to hug him, swept by a flood of love. Papa, with his fallibility, his zest, his optimism—what would she ever do without him? And now she was to be married and the McKinnon Troupe was breaking up. By tonight she would be Mrs. Jed Donohue and nothing would ever be quite the same again.

During the rest of that long day, Dacey was grateful for the champagne that had blunted her senses. She concentrated on pushing Quinn from her thoughts, washing her hair in beer shampoo and brushing it in the sun until it blazed with fiery color.

By the time she stood with Jed in front of the Wesleyan minister to speak her vows, she was in a state of numbness. Like all churches in Kimberley, the Wesleyan was made of canvas, its interior filled with backless benches, on which the wedding guests sat uncomfortably. Paraffin lamps provided lighting, and the tent was stiflingly hot.

But Dacey knew that she made a dazzling entrance in her white gown lavishly trimmed with lace. She carried a bouquet of English daisies that Bella had grown from carefully hoarded seed, her veil made of the finest French gauze.

Jed wore a black formal suit, stiffly starched collar, and his beard was freshly trimmed. He stood stiffly, his expression solemn, the picture of a nervous bridegroom. But Dacey could scarcely look at him. Her eyes cast downward, she spoke her vows in a whisper that she was sure could not be heard beyond the first row.

It all seemed to become a dream as the pastor pronounced them man and wife. Dacey moistened her lips, her mind tricking her with a vivid image of Quinn. His face shaded from the African sun by a jaunty hat, his eyes smiling at her, a deep, deep blue . . .

She could feel herself gasp for air, suffering a wild, trapped moment of panic when she wanted to drop her bouquet and bolt for the door. Had she made a mistake? A terrible, permanent one?

But then somehow Jed was smiling at her, and they were all moving toward the door, and she knew that it was too late. She had spoken her vows and she was Mrs. Jed Donohue now.

From the church the wedding party moved to the Royal, where a raucous celebration began by the long bar. Actors mingled with miners, with diamond dealers and their wives, with members of Kimberley's new Mining Board. Papa lorded it over everyone, splendid in his white evening wear only slightly creased from being stored in a theatrical trunk.

Dacey felt dizzy with the sound of voices and laughter, the pop of champagne corks. A piano rippled, and there were ribald jokes, songs and skits provided by the Damsons. The smells of perfume and sweat mingled with the rich odors of food. For Dacey, it seemed like a dream, loud and noisy and not quite real. Was this really her wedding day? The day that bound her to Jed Donohue forever, until death parted them?

"Half the town is here to see us wed," Jed boasted, looking around him to make sure that everyone noticed Dacey on his arm.

"I'm sure that's true." Dacey wondered where all of the unfamiliar faces had come from. She had already met Cecil Rhodes, a gangling young man in wire-rimmed glasses. Royce McKinnon talked diamonds with a group of men, while

Lavinia hung on Tony Agnelli's arm, pretending to be fascinated by everything he said. Bella, under the influence of champagne, had hoisted her skirts to do a breathless buck-and-wing.

Then there was a stir in the room, a buzz of conversation.

"Say, there's Quinn Farris." Jed pointed toward the door, where some late arrivals had just come in. "He doesn't socialize much—I didn't think he'd come."

Quinn. Dacey's heart gave a painful lurch. All day she'd struggled to put him out of her thoughts, accomplishing this with an act of will. Now here he was, striding into the reception, wearing a dark suit with a cream brocaded waistcoat with a gold watch chain, an outfit that set off the rangy grace of his body to perfection. Dacey realized that she wasn't the only woman to stare at his dark, broodingly handsome good looks.

She stood trembling, knowing that her face must be ashen. Why, why had he to come here of all days, to torment her with his presence?

"Will you look at that?" Jed said. "Will you look what he's done? He's brought his woman with him."

Dacey blinked. Then, for the first time, she saw the woman who had entered the theater beside Quinn. She had skin the color of creamy cinnamon, and a beautiful, exotic face with high cheekbones and the flaring nostrils of a lioness. Her lips were full, her eyes so smoky, so languorous and challenging, that every man in the room turned to gape.

Natala. This was Quinn's mistress. Dacey drew in her breath, feeling as if she might choke.

All around the room, conversation had stopped at the sight of the extraordinary brown-skinned woman. Most native women in Kimberley wore native dress, Dacey knew, bright cloths wrapped loosely around their bodies, head cloths over their hair, beads and bangles. But—as if in defiance—Natala wore European dress. Her blue silk gown clung sensuously to her body, its low, scooped neckline revealing flawless breasts.

As if enjoying the excitement she caused, Natala swept into the room on Quinn's arm, her mouth curved in a half-smile as if defying anyone to object to her presence.

Jed glowered angrily. "What the hell does he think he's doing? To bring his woman here—there's a place for black doxies, I'll admit, but to bring one out in public!"

"She isn't black, she's brown," Dacey breathed, her chest feeling tight. "And she's beautiful." Quinn and Natala were approaching them now, a strikingly handsome couple.

"Oh, yes, she is that. A missionary-reared witch, that's what she is. I've heard about the hut she keeps on the edge of town where she sells all kinds of herbs and potions. And maybe a good deal more than that, by the look of her."

Quinn and Natala had reached them now. Quinn nodded to Jed, then looked at Dacey. A muscle in his jaw flickered, and his eyes seemed to burn at her, their color darkened, their mood unreadable.

"I wish you happiness, Mrs. Donohue," he said softly.

"I . . . thank you," Dacey stammered. She was all too aware of Natala beside him, assessing her with barely concealed scorn. So this stunningly beautiful brown woman was Natala. How alluring she was! Why had Quinn brought her? To show Dacey, once and for all, where his obligations lay?

But it couldn't be entirely obligation that tied Quinn to Natala, Dacey realized with a sick feeling. He *had* to desire her . . .

She realized with a start that Quinn was asking her a question. "When does your troupe return to England?"

"In—in four days, just as soon as Lavinia is married. The others decided to stay long enough to attend both weddings."

Somehow Dacey managed to make conversation, to talk of Lavinia's plans, all the while uncomfortably aware of Natala's bold stare. What was Natala thinking at this moment? Was she aware that Dacey and Quinn had been lovers?

"We have both brought gifts," Quinn was saying now. "Mine is a blanket woven in Arizona. And Natala's—well, I'll let her tell you about it."

Dacey looked at Quinn's exotic mistress, wondering what sort of gift Natala could possibly have for her.

"Yes." Natala spoke for the first time, her voice husky, with a vibrant sexual timbre. "It is some of the herbs I have collected, medical items for the home. I have also included some senna pods and jalap from Mexico which I bought from a peddler."

Dacey reached out to accept the small leather pouch that smelled of strange herbs. "I . . . I do thank you." What would she do with these plants, how would she use them?

"You may need medicinal aids," Natala said cooly. "This land is cruel to women. There are fevers, and when white women are brought to childbed, sometimes they die."

The words, spoken in a level tone, seemed to hold an odd emphasis. Dacey raised her eyes to meet Natala's smoky golden ones, seeing in them the black pupil, like jet.

"Fortunately, I'm healthy," she retorted. "I've never been sick a day in my life. But perhaps one day you will show me how to use these herbs for the good of others."

Natala's smile was secretive. "*Ai*, I will do that."

"Come, Natala." Quinn took his mistress' arm. "We must allow the bridal couple to greet their other guests. And there are some members of the Mining Board here today with whom I must conduct business." He nodded to Dacey, and then he and Natala were gone, disappeared into the throng of wedding guests.

"I wonder why he brought her," Jed remarked later as they prepared for bed in the tiny bedroom of the small, canvas-roofed house he had bought, luxurious by Kimberley standards, although it was little better than a tent.

"I don't know," Dacey murmured, although she was sure that she did.

"Well, it was very strange. He should have known that a black woman has her place and never leaves it. There are plenty of Kaffir whores in this town, and *they* certainly never come among the whites, causing trouble."

Kaffir, Dacey knew, was a term used for the blacks and had connotations of insult.

Nervously, she smoothed the fabric of her long, voluminous white nightgown, trimmed lavishly with lace at neckline, yoke, and sleeves. All along one wall of the bedroom, the wedding gifts were arranged. Quinn's splendid Navaho blanket, in shades of rust and ocher. A tusk of ivory, an amethyst necklace, several diamonds. A corkscrew aloe, a spiky plant that grew in a whorl like a seashell. A packet of seeds for the Australian blue-gum tree.

There was even an armoire made of stinkwood, a dark, heavy African wood, with silver hinges and yellowwood panels. This was a piece of furniture of rather overwhelming majesty, and Dacey wondered how it would fit in their crude little house, which had a ceiling of sagging calico and floors made of canvas laid over dirt.

Still, Jed had paid inflated Kimberley prices for a wooden bedstead with a goosedown mattress, and there was a table with four chairs. The Donohues, he had assured Dacey proudly, would live better than most residents of Kimberley. And there was even a well, only a dozen yards from the back door.

Now, as if they'd been married for years, Jed talked about the reception, listing off for Dacey those who had attended and giving his estimate of their net worth.

"As for that Quinn Farris," he finished, "he has two claims *and* a diamond office—and I hear he's been selling winches and machines to the miners. If anyone in this town will make money, it's Farris, damn his hide. And flaunting his mistress in our faces like that. What did she give you, a bag of dead plants?"

"I haven't looked in it yet."

"Well, don't. God knows what those Kaffir witches truck around with. I wouldn't be surprised to find dead tarantulas and human eyeballs in there." Jed cackled at his own joke, then reached for his cravat and began to pull it off.

Before Dacey's startled eyes, he quickly stripped off the rest of his clothes until he stood naked before her. Above the waist, his skin was sunburned red, and below the waist, where his pants had shielded him from the sun, Jed was dead white. His shoulders seemed even more massive than Dacey remembered them, knotted from hours of swinging a shovel. His body was covered with a pelt of brown, curly hair.

As he turned toward her, Dacey stood frozen, not knowing where to look or what to say.

"Well? Aren't you going to get in bed?"

"Yes—yes, of course . . ." Hastily, she slid beneath the

sheets, her heart slamming. She felt uncomfortable and nervous, her skin clammy with unease. Her wedding night. She'd imagined many things for it, but never this: Jed's assessment of the wedding feast, as if they'd been an old married couple. Then the casual way he stripped off his clothes, as if he'd done that, too, in front of her a thousand times.

She felt the mattress sink as Jed got into bed and reached for her. His breath smelled of champagne and the whiskey that had been served at the reception, and there was also the underlying odor of musky maleness.

"Ah, God, Dacey, I've waited so long—I want to see you. I want to see what I've married."

Jed lifted up the hem of the nightgown, pulling it back to expose her body. Dacey suppressed a gasp, lying naked before him, feeling exposed and vulnerable. She trembled under his scrutiny, her heart pounding so loudly that she was sure he could hear it, too.

Breathing thickly, Jed reached out one hand and covered her left breast, cupping it. Then, with his thumb and forefinger, he squeezed her nipple, hard.

"Oh!" She let out a little cry.

"Did you like that?" Jed gave a deep groan. "I have more in store for you, Dacey, I'm going to take care of you properlike. I'm going to stoke those fires in you that you didn't want me to know about, tried to hide from me. By God, yes, I am . . ."

Jed rolled on top of her, his weight heavy, smothering. His hand groped between her legs, forcing her thighs apart. Dacey could feel his urgency, the taut bulge of his maleness. Suppressing another cry, she forced herself to lie still, to allow it to happen.

"Ah . . . ah . . . that's it, that's it, oh, God, Dacey . . ."

With his knees Jed spread her legs wider still, and then, abruptly, he pushed himself into her body. Dacey, already nervous and apprehensive, was not prepared and her tissues were dry. But Jed did not seem to notice her discomfort and began to thrust inside her. He moved at first slowly, then with rapid haste, until at last he shuddered, uttering a hoarse groan.

Dacey lay beneath him, feeling his hands clutch at her as he climaxed. She hadn't felt anything, other than discomfort. Was this it? Was this all there was, this quick, animal coupling? She hadn't even felt the desire she'd experienced the night that Jed had kissed her in the shadows. Just—nothing.

In a moment Jed rolled away from her and propped himself on one elbow. "Was it good, Dacey? Was it good for you? I'm sorry . . . I got carried away. You're so pretty I just couldn't stop myself."

He sounded genuinely sorry. And he was her husband. Dacey drew a deep breath and nodded. "It's all right," she lied. "I did like it. It was wonderful."

That night he made love to her three times. By the third time, the discomfort was gone, the friction as Jed moved inside her, mildly pleasurable. Finally as they lay together, their bodies sheened with perspiration, Dacey began to nod sleepily. An intense wave of drowsiness crept over her, as powerful as a drug.

She was married now. Her husband had taken her, marked his possession of her. It had been strange and new, but she had survived it. Tomorrow, perhaps, the lovemaking would be better. But no matter how often she made love to Jed, she knew that there would always be something missing.

For an instant she thought of the way Quinn's eyes had searched hers as he had congratulated them. If it had been Quinn loving her tonight . . . She felt a flood of weakness, of helpless desire, a pang of anguish so strong that it seemed to sear her like a flame.

Finally, with Jed's arm still draped heavily over her hip, she fell into a restless sleep.

8

DACEY STOOD IN THE DOORWAY, gazing moodily out at the street. This morning, she had supervised Makema, their Bantu maid, in the sweeping and dusting of the two-room house. She had shopped in the Market Square, then shown the black girl how to press her petticoats with a sadiron that had been heated red-hot in the fire.

She had even practiced singing for an hour, so that when Jed came home tonight from the mine and wished to relax, she could entertain him with songs from the London stage. She had a clear, sweet, true voice and a natural memory for music.

Now Dacey sighed, breathing in the thick stench of cattle droppings, dust, and bad drainage that permeated the town. She was bored. In spite of all that she had accomplished today, it was still only one o'clock in the afternoon. The rest of the day stretched before her, an arid desert in which there was not one interesting thing to do.

Jed had allowed her to buy the two claims, but to her dismay, he had forbidden her to go near them, insisting that it was too dangerous for a woman in the mine area. He also forbade her to go to the Theater Royal, saying that the stage was no place for a respectably married woman to hang about.

She watched idly as three Bantu women rounded the corner and walked up the street, chattering to each other in their tribal language. They were barefoot, their feet large and splayed, the soles covered with a hard, horny substance that served them like shoes. They had hard, tight bodies, and their faces, with slightly aquiline features, were animated. But by the way they walked, and the sleazy colors of their hipwraps, Dacey knew them for what they were: prostitutes. Black women bought or stolen away from their tribes, to be sold in tiny cribs in the town, as if they were cabbages or vegetables, a commodity.

The women disappeared behind the far corner, their laughter ringing out. Flushing, Dacey stepped back within the house. Almost . . . yes, almost she had envied those Bantu women for their happy, natural joy.

What was wrong with her? Why did she feel such lassitude, why couldn't she find satisfaction in anything these days? Her body even felt wrong, awkward, and big. Her breasts were oddly sore, the nipples tender.

Stop feeling sorry for yourself, she ordered herself. Just because you are married now . . .

She walked into the tiny bedroom and took her straw bonnet from its hook, carefully putting it on. It was even more important to guard her skin from freckles, now that she was married to Jed. Jed admired women with porcelain skin. He had already praised Lavinia's complexion, telling Dacey that she should emulate her friend's caution with the sun and perhaps borrow some of the lemon paste that Lavinia used on her fair skin.

Oh, *verdamdt*, Dacey muttered to herself, borrowing one of the curses she had heard the ox drivers use. *Verdamdt* the sun, *verdamdt* freckles . . . and everything!

As if the swear word had released something in her, she whirled out of the small house, caught in a sudden excess of energy that spun her like a top. Outdoors, the sun was high, glaring off the corrugated-iron shop fronts. It was February, the height of the summer, for here in Africa, south of the equator, the seasons were reversed, and June, July, and August were the winter months.

She hurried down the street, feeling suddenly impelled by urgency, although she couldn't imagine why. Where was there for her to go? What to do? She had fallen in the habit of visiting Bella almost every day, but today Bella was busy with a big sewing project for Mrs. Oskar Van Reenen, the resident magistrate's wife. Less often, she visited Lavinia, but Lavinia, now that she was married to Tony Agnelli, had begun to put on airs. As assistant stage manager, she was bustlingly important, full of schemes, plans, and projects.

When she was with Lavinia, Dacey felt envious. It was an emotion that was unfamiliar to her, one that made her feel small and nasty and horrid. Lavinia seemed genuinely happy, both with her life and with her husband, her pleasure glowing from her like a candelabra. How, Dacey had wondered, could it have happened that way? Dacey had been so sure that Lavinia married Tony Agnelli for spite, because Royce didn't want her.

Now, apparently, Lavinia was *happy*.

No, Dacey decided rapidly, she didn't want to go see Lavinia today; she'd do something else, something different and new.

But what?

She walked down Christian Street, where Quinn Farris kept his office. As she passed his sign, her heart gave its familiar, squeezing pang. But the office was closed; she knew that Quinn kept hours in the late afternoon only. During the day, he had other projects, and, according to Jed, was fast becoming one of the richest men in Kimberley.

"The man has golden luck . . . everything he touches, everything!" Jed had said it half-angrily, smacking a fist into the palm of his hand.

"I imagine he works very hard," Dacey ventured, wondering how much Jed knew of her relationship with Quinn.

"Hard? Oh, hell, yes, he never stops, that man. He's obsessed, he works twelve hours a day, thirteen, even more." Jed gave a self-deprecatory laugh. "Works almost as hard as me, eh? Well, we'll see. We'll just see who goes the farthest, won't we?"

Dacey had given Jed a sharp look, wondering if he suspected how violently her heart always lurched when she heard Quinn's name. But apparently he did not. Jealous, competitive, he talked that way about all the diamond men in town. Cecil

Rhodes, Barney Barnato, J. B. Robinson, they were all his rivals, and he was intensely interested in their doings, driving himself hard at the mine, returning home each night coated with a sticky film of dust and sweat that had to be soaked out of his hair and beard.

Now Dacey found that she had veered toward the native section of Kimberley. It was a sprawling warren of narrow roads crammed with makeshift tents, cookfires, and native grog and gun shops. At night, she knew, the African section came alive with voices, laughter, and music. But at this hour, most of the men were at the mines. The ones who were not, snoozed in the heat of the day or played a desultory gambling game with pebbles on a board.

Dacey kept on walking. Somewhere a woman was singing, the high clear notes rising mockingly into the still air.

At last the tents began to thin out. The road narrowed and split into paths, some wandering off into the veld, others circling toward the Kimberley and De Beers mines, shortcuts for the workers.

Dacey chose one of the paths, deciding to walk for a while longer and then return home to bake a pie for Jed's supper. She was not a good cook; actresses, who ate mostly in hotels, seldom were. But Jed insisted on good food, and several times had staged full-scale rages when the meal was not to his liking.

She skirted a bare outcropping of rock, where lizards sunned themselves. Then, to her left, she saw it. A conical hut built in the African manner of mud and daub, its sides traced with an elaborate, pleasing design, its roof thatched. There was a dooryard garden, carefully cultivated, strange plants growing in profusion. The singing she had heard, Dacey realized, must have come from this hut.

She approached it, nothing that the path to its door was well-trodden and small items had been left in the dirt: bits of colored rock that glistened, a few dried flowers, some small, dark carvings.

"*Ai*, so you have come. I knew you would."

A woman appeared in the door of the hut. She was half in shadow, so that all Dacey could see was the mass of dark hair, the curved line of hip and body. But the husky voice was one that she had heard before; it belonged to Natala.

She had come to Quinn's mistress' hut.

"You said you would show me how to use the herbs you gave me as a wedding gift," Dacey blurted to cover her shock and embarrassment. "But perhaps you are busy . . ."

"No. Come inside. I would talk with you."

Dacey had blundered along the path without thinking; Natala had not been on her mind at all. But now the other woman's eyes were fixed on her like golden, brooding pools that seemed to look within Dacey's skull, reading every thought in her head.

She swallowed her misgivings and went inside. The hut was larger than it looked, its floor made of some dark substance that had been waxed to a shiny, hard finish. Its walls and roof were festooned with plants, some hanging in great clusters, others hung individually on thongs to dry. There were bark, branches, dried flowers, bulbs, roots, all emitting a deep, aromatic smell. There was also a large clay bed, on which were spread blankets and tanned animal hides, and two ornate European chests.

Dacey allowed her eyes to lift to Natala. At Dacey's wedding, the other had worn European dress flamboyantly and well. But today she was clad in a saronglike cloth of orange-dyed material that revealed the sinuous lines of her body and her splendid, bare breasts.

Natala's feet were also bare, and around her neck she wore a necklace of what appeared to be lion claws. Dacey stared, fascinated. Even Natala's odor was exotic, a scent like crushed flowers mingling with something dark and female.

Quinn has made love to this woman, came the quick thought, which she immediately pushed away. She felt uncomfortable and wanted to leave.

"Have you brought the herbs with you?" Natala wanted to know.

"No, I . . . I forgot."

"I have others that I can show you, then." Natala glided to

one of the trunks and opened the lid. She took out a large hide bag and pulled from it a mass of dark bark and roots.

"This," she said, holding up a twisted root, "is good for childbed. You must make an infusion by boiling this in water for four days, adding liquid so it does not go dry. Strain it through cloth, then put the mixture in a covered pot for another four days. It will hasten contractions and make birthing easier."

"I . . . I see." Something about the way that Natala looked at her, some hot emotion that flared in the smoky eyes, made Dacey uneasy.

"I hear," Natala went on, "that you white women give birth in a bed, lying on your backs, attended by men. Is this true?"

"Why, yes, in some cases . . ."

"Black women do it the natural way, squatting so that the child is pushed easily through the birth opening." Natala paused. Again something flickered in her eyes. "When is your baby to come?"

"My baby?"

Natala's eyes swept professionally up and down Dacey's figure, lingering on her waistline, then moving to her breasts. "You are to give birth to a child, I see it plainly."

Dacey felt a wave of shock and dismay. "But—but I'm not pregnant!"

"*Ai*, but you are. Your breasts are sore, are they not? And you have missed . . . yes, two months' bleeding now."

"Yes, but I didn't think—"

Dacey's face burned. She had always had irregular menses and she had thought that the cessation of her monthly bleeding might be due to the violence of the sex that Jed took from her. He took her repeatedly each night, often without gentleness or care, and sometimes, afterward, she had bled.

"You did not think that when your bleeding stopped that you might bear a child?" Natala chuckled. "*Ai*, you English-women do not listen to your bodies. But I will give you this herb—and this, for the childbed fever, if you should get it. Make a tea and drink it hot, four times a day. You found the leaves in the sack I gave you?"

Dacey didn't want to admit she hadn't looked in the sack, so she merely nodded, edging toward the door. A baby! She was going to have a baby! How could she have been fool enough not to have noticed it herself? Waves of shock poured over her, suffusing her with heat. She had been married to Jed for two months. Yet she had missed two menses, and that meant—

My God, was it possible that her baby was Quinn's?

She could feel her mind screaming, beating at the barriers of emotion. Quinn's baby . . . *No*. No, it couldn't be. Life could not be that cruel.

"I . . . I think I'd better go back to my house now," she managed to tell Natala thickly. "There is much that needs to be done."

"*Ai*, yes, you will be busy. There is your husband, to whom you must give this news, your *man*." Natala emphasized this word curiously. "Do you think that he is at the mine today?"

"Of course he is," Dacey answered the question, feeling dazed.

"All day?"

"Yes, of course!"

Natala seemed to find this funny. She tilted her head back and laughed, the notes emerging richly. "Maybe you need a potion, too, Dacey Donohue. Something with which to keep your husband satisfied and at home."

Dacey stared. "What do you mean?"

"*Ai*, there are many potions I could give you if I wished." Natala gestured toward the festooned plants. "There is almost nothing I do not know. Poisons and cures, spells and curses. I know the heart of a man almost before he knows it himself . . . and I know what is in the heart of *your* man."

Dacey edged away, sensing the malice in the other woman's tone. "I . . . I don't want to hear."

"But you will hear. Black women—*he* calls them Kaffir whores—are what he desires. *Ai*, yes, black meat is sweeter than any other kind, many men find it so, and your husband is one of them."

Dacey gasped .She lifted her skirts and turned, hearing Natala's laughter drift down the path as she ran, panting, from the thatched hut.

Pregnant! *Was* Natala a witch to know such things, or had she merely observed the physical facts of Dacey's body? And to accuse Jed of seeking out black prostitutes! How could she possibly know such a thing, how could she dare to say it?

As Dacey ran home, her mind struggled to deal with the double shock that Natala had dealt her. *Pregnant* . . . And Jed . . . Her thoughts ran on, Oh, surely Jed had not done that thing. Not after only two months of marriage, after promising to love and to cherish . . .

Natala was a jealous woman and she had lied, that was the only possible explanation.

By the time she had reached home, Dacey had passed beyond anger into a state of numbness. She felt exhausted, but she could not rest. Dully she moved about the house, tidying it so that it would look presentable when her husband came home. She had forgotten all about the pie she'd wanted to bake, so she started a pudding from a recipe that Bella had given her.

Pregnant, pregnant . . . The word pounded over and over in her mind, tormenting her. "*Ai*, yes, black meat is sweeter than any other kind, many men find it so, and your husband is one of them. . . ."

She held on to the edge of the table, her eyes blurring with tears.

At sundown, Jed walked in the door, his eyes reddened from sand and blowing grit.

"Hello, Dacey, you look fresh and cool." He grinned at her through the coat of dust that streaked his face. "What's for supper? Anything good? And then, afterward, I want you to sing. I heard that a load of pianos is being shipped in by wagon from the Cape, and I mean to get us one . . ."

Dacey stared at her husband, unable to believe that he could talk of singing and pianos when she was so upset that her thoughts felt as if they had been split into a hundred painful pieces. But then, she reminded herself, Jed didn't know that she had gone to Natala's hut. And by the cheerful way he grinned at her— Oh, surely Natala *had* lied.

Feeling calmer, she listened to Jed's talk of his day at the mine. A miner had been accused of illicit diamond theft, and—the latest Kimberley gossip—another man had threatened him with a horsewhipping. At last Jed said, "What's wrong with you, Dacey? Cat got your tongue? Usually you're as full of chatter as a magpie."

"I . . . I walked through the town today." Dacey bit her lip.

"Alone?" Jed frowned. "I told you to take someone with you—your father, or that Kaffir maid, or Lavinia. It isn't safe here on the streets for a lone white woman, you know that. Where's my bath?" he went on. "Haven't you told Makema to get it ready yet? You know I want it as soon as I get home."

"I'm sorry." Hastily Dacey ran to find the black girl, and between them they lugged the metal container to the common well, where they paid for their brackish water and then carried it home carefully.

No, Jed couldn't have done it, Dacey assured herself for the dozenth time as the two women poured water into the tin tub. Everything Jed said and did seemed so ordinary, no different from any other night. Surely she'd know, there would be something different about him. And besides, Jed worked so hard at the mine that there wasn't time for him to find other women. . . .

But Natala said he left the claim during the day, a little voice nagged inside her. So he could have found time, if he went into the native sector with dust still on him . . . and how long would it all take? Perhaps less than half an hour . . . She shuddered.

After they had filled the tub, Jed went into the bedroom to wash, and Dacey could hear him splashing and humming. In a while, he emerged, wearing a fresh shirt and trousers, his hair damp, his beard combed into soft curls.

"Mutton," he exclaimed in distaste as they sat down at the supper table. "Isn't there anything else you can think of to serve, Dacey? And carrots! I detest carrots, I always have. I hope you've made dessert. I could really put my teeth around a thick piece of apple pie.''

"I made apricot pudding.''

"Well, you've accomplished something today, then.''

Dacey gazed at Jed, wondering what he wanted of her. He had forbidden her to do anything that interested her; she couldn't even walk through town by herself. He had got her a maid, telling her he didn't want her to lift a finger. Yet he criticised her if everything wasn't done, and accused her of doing nothing . . . She drew a deep breath, biting back sudden anger.

"Jed, I've heard that you've been seen in the native sector, that you go there to—to find women. Prostitutes.''

There. She had said it.

Jed continued to fork bites of mutton into his mouth. "Who told you that?''

"I . . . I just heard it, that's all.'' Dacey stared down at her own untouched plate, thinking of the three Bantu prostitutes she had seen earlier in the day, with their exaggerated walk and hard-soled feet. Their laughter.

"Well, you shouldn't listen to every bit of gossip you hear.''

"But did you, Jed? Did you go to those women?''

He looked up impatiently. "And what if I did? What's it to you, Dacey? A man is a man, he has needs—needs that *you* certainly haven't been fulfilling.''

Dacey sat stunned as the meaning of her husband's words sank in. She felt herself shudder with anger and revulsion, an anger all the more hot because she knew she didn't have any right to feel it. Jed had gone to prostitutes. But wasn't Dacey carrying in her belly a child whose paternity was not definitely known, who might belong to another man?

She lifted her chin, looking at her husband levelly. "We have only been married two months, Jed. After the vows you made in church—''

"Vows I have kept. Haven't I paid for every morsel of food that goes into your mouth? Aren't I sending to Cape Town for a real piano for you? Don't we live in a real house with walls and a roof? Haven't I bought you more dresses and bonnets than any other woman in Kimberley? And invested your money for you, besides?''

All of this was true. Dacey sat silent, fuming.

''I am a *man*,'' Jed emphasized. He reached for the platter of meat and speared himself another serving. ''Yes, I've got Kaffir whores, all right—all I want of 'em, and they please me like you never could. You're a cold stick in bed, Dacey. You lie there and you open your legs for me, and you do your wifely *duty*.'' The last word was a sneer.

Through a haze, she heard Jed's voice go on. ''You're a lady, Dacey. That's the trouble with you. You haven't got a drop of hot blood, there's nothing in your veins but ice water.''

Dacey stared down at the tabletop, where bits of food had been spilled, thinking she would be sick. She hadn't loved Jed when she married him . . . but she had liked him and she had expected to be happy. She had tried. Now she felt dirtied by his words, as if their life together, the very structure of their days, had been inalterably sullied.

''If I'm cold in bed, Jed, it's because you made me that way. You never gave me a chance to be anything else. A woman needs tenderness, she needs loving, she—''

''I do as a man does,'' Jed interrupted. ''You're lucky to have someone to support you, Dacey. Your fine actor father certainly can't do it, hanging about the saloons as he does. And some of the other men in this town would have you right out there at the mine, sorting diamond dirt.''

Which was exactly where she'd like to be, Dacey thought suddenly. She tightened her lips, feeling as if her head was swimming. Jed actually felt justified in what he did—he felt that *she* was the one who had done wrong! The injustice of it whirled in her mind, together with the knowledge that the child she carried might not be Jed's.

She felt herself shaking as she rose from the table. She pushed back her chair, hearing the angry swish of her skirts as she moved.

''Oh, yes, Jed, you *do* support me . . . and I'm very grateful. I appreciate every mouthful of food you've given me! But now that you've found your women and are appar-

ently so happy with them, you can have them. It's fine with
me. But you won't have *me* anymore—not in your bed.''

She hadn't meant to say it, yet now that she heard the
words emerge from her mouth, she knew that she meant
them. Perhaps Jed was right, perhaps she had been cold to
him, perhaps sleeping with him had been only a duty. It
would be a relief not to have him groping for her in the
darkness, forcing apart her legs, imposing his will on her.

Jed looked up, his mouth falling open with surprise. ''But,
Dacey, you can't just—''

''I can put you out of my bed if I wish,'' she snapped.
''And I do wish it. Haven't I done my *duty* by you, haven't I
provided you with a child?''

''A child?''

She faced him defiantly. ''I'm going to have a baby, Jed.
Does that make you happy? A child born of our union, our
'love.' ''

''But—but that's wonderful!'' Jed pushed his chair back
from the table and came toward her, joy written on his face.
''A baby . . . I'm going to have a son!''

''Or a daughter.''

''No, it's a boy, Dacey, I know it is.'' Oblivious to the
argument they had just had, Jed picked Dacey up in his arms
and whirled her about so violently that her feet lifted from the
floor. ''A boy! A son, Dacey! We're going to have a boy!
Oh, what a princess you are, what a princess!''

A princess? Or a cheater, a woman who had betrayed her
husband, in one way, as badly as he had betrayed her? Dacey
made up a pallet in the living room that night and lay there
miserably, unable to sleep or to relax.

Jed had rushed out immediately to celebrate his news with
his drinking companions at the King of Prussia Saloon. Or,
Dacey tormented herself, maybe he had gone instead to one
of his native women. ''You haven't got a drop of hot blood,''
he had accused her. Was it true? *Was* it her fault that he
sought such diversions? If Quinn had not been always in her
thoughts, would it have been easier for Dacey to respond to
her husband?

She would never know.

She lay rigidly, bleak thoughts tumbling in her head. Her baby. Was it Quinn's or Jed's? Because of her irregular menstrual periods, she realized, she would never know for sure. But as she stared at the dim shadows of the canvas ceiling, she knew one thing: she didn't want her baby to be Jed's.

She hoped that it *was* from Quinn's seed, that she could own at least that much of their love, the joy, the wonder that they had shared.

Distantly in the town, she heard the sound of shouts, the wild tinkling of a piano, perhaps Jed himself, celebrating. She retreated again into her thoughts. There was one more thing she wanted, too, she realized, She had grown up with the wrenching ups and downs of the actor's life, the constant travel from town to town. One day eating in fine hotels, the next day going hungry. There had never been roots, or a real home, and always she had worried that Papa's weakness would cause what little money they did have to slip away from them.

Security. Stability. She wanted her child to have those things, along with the love that Papa had always poured on her in lavish abundance. Now if Jed was already seeking out prostitutes, if she herself, under the sting of anger and shame, had already forbidden him her bed, then what kind of marriage did they have? Could Jed be depended upon to keep their child safe and provided for?

Dacey sat up on the pallet, and then she flung back the sheet and got up, lighting a candle. She began to pace the room, stopping to examine copies of the *Diamond News* that Jed had brought home, full of accounts of miner disputes, politics, and meetings of the mining boards of the Kimberley, Dutoitspan, De Beers, and Bulfontein mines. Quinn Farris' name was mentioned several times.

Up until now, Dacey knew, she had been an obedient wife, staying at home and allowing Jed to take care of all their business, including the two claims she'd bought with Papa's winnings.

Now, she decided reckessly, that was going to change. She

had her baby to think of—her child's welfare. From now on, she would go to the mine every day, she'd help with the sorting, and she would begin to learn the mining business. Whether Jed liked it or not.

At last, as dawn tinted the sky with faint pearl, Dacey blew out the candle and got back into bed. She felt soothed and released, as if she'd finally stopped being helpless and had taken charge of her life again.

9

"WHAT ARE YOU DOING HERE?" Jed looked at Dacey in annoyed surprise. It was the following morning, and although the sun had barely risen, already thousands of men, both black and white, labored in the mine. The air rang with the noise of picks, the whinnying of horses and mules.

"I'm here to work, of course." She faced him stubbornly.

"What?"

"I said that I came here to help, to learn the mining business."

"To learn the— Are you insane, Dacey? You're going to be a mother, not a miner. Please stop your little jokes and turn around and go back home before you get hurt here."

Jed grasped Dacey by both arms and turned her, giving her a firm little push back toward town.

She dug her shoes into the rocky ground. "*No.* I'm going to stay here, Jed. I have just as much right to be here at the mines as you do. Don't I own two claims, too?"

They glared at each other. After his night of carousing, Jed's skin had a yellowish cast under his deep sunburn and there were circles under his eyes. His breath smelled rankly of whiskey. Dacey knew that she did not look her best, either. She had slept restlessly. Then, rising at the first light of dawn, she had dressed in her oldest clothes. She had known Jed would not want her here, and she had come prepared to face his opposition.

"Yes, you own them," Jed conceded now. "But I don't want you working. You belong at home with our baby."

She laughed. "At home with it? Jed, right now our baby has to go wherever I do."

"Don't be funny, Dacey. You need naps, good food—hell, *I* don't know what you need, but I mean to give you whatever it takes. I want my son, a good, healthy boy."

"And you'll get a healthy *child*," Dacey retorted. "Actresses are a hardy breed. We continue to work right up until childbirth and then we go back to work again a few weeks later—it was what my mother did when she had me. I've never been sick a day in my life and I will happily go to a doctor so that he can assure you of my good health. But I intend to take my place here at the mine."

"But you can't. A woman has no— I need you at home to—"

"To prepare your bath? We have a tiny house, Jed, only two rooms. Makema will have our supper ready for us when we get home, and our baths will be ready."

"*Our* baths?" Jed sputtered.

"Why not? I expect to get dirty, too."

"But, my God, the men won't obey you, Dacey. Africans don't like to work for women. And you don't know a damn thing about mining."

"Then you can show me." Sensing victory, Dacey smiled, adjusting the brim of her bonnet against the sun. "All right, I'm ready to begin. If you'll be kind enough to explain to me about the sorting process?"

"Dacey." Jed said it warningly. "It's much harder than it looks. You won't even last two hours here."

"I'm going to last all day. And the day after that, and the day after *that*." She lifted her chin and smiled at him, feeling oddly calm. "And now, please, I want to get to work."

Mining, as Dacey soon discovered, *was* grueling work. The day was spent under the blast of the hot sun, with only flimsy canvas for shade. Perpetual clouds of dust blew up from the excavation, to sting the eyes and coat the skin. Sand gritted between her teeth and mingled with the perspiration on her body, to trickle between her breasts, itching maddeningly.

By ten o'clock the first day, Dacey was ravenous with thirst. Her mouth felt as dry and parched as leather, and she cursed her lack of foresight in not bringing water with her. But Jed, down in the excavation, apparently was not aware of her discomfort—or didn't care. Finally it was one of the black men who observed her thirst and pointed to a communal water jug.

"There, missy, there is water for you. I boil it, I boil it real good so we don't get sick. There is sickness, much fever in this mining camp. You always have to boil water or mebbe you die, eh?"

Gratefully, Dacey poured some of the precious fluid into the palm of her hand and managed to drink it. She was afraid to use the tin cup for fear of disease. Hadn't Bella said that her husband had used a community drinking cup?

Greedily she slaked her thirst. When she was through, she glanced at the black man, now sorting through the rocks, breaking up small clods of earth with a mallet. He was the same man she had noticed before, with a broad forehead and deep-set, kind eyes.

"What is your name?" she asked.

"I am Chaka. I am named for a Zulu king. He ruled three hundred clans and his men numbered thousands, his kingdom marching from the Kei River to the Zambezi." Chaka shrugged. "Like others, I earn lobola for my marriage price. It is hard work, but I won't do it forever. Mebbe I buy a claim of my own. Then I get rich for sure."

After talking with Chaka for a few more moments, Dacey went thoughtfully back to her work. Everyone, it seemed, even the Africans, was here to get rich.

The day inched by, marked off by the movement of the sun that scorched over the sorting tables. Several times they found tiny stones with the peculiarly clear, limpid color of raw diamonds. Dacey wiped the stones off carefully with a rag, marveling at their luster, even uncut. Diamonds. Tiny, smaller than a quarter-carat, but indisputably real.

A swirling dust dervish spun across the excavation, causing

men to blink, rub their eyes, and curse. The men broke off to eat the food they had brought with them, and Chaka offered food to Dacey, for Jed was still below in the pit, apparently determined to let his wife suffer out her day alone.

Jed wanted her to give in, Dacey knew as she chewed on the dried strips of antelope that Chaka gave her. But she was determined to stick it out—for pride, if for no other reason.

By sundown, her mouth was dry and full of grit. Her body was coated with a heavy, pasty mixture of sweat and dust, and when she touched her bonnet, sand sprinkled off its rim. But she had found two more diamonds, one of them as large as half her little fingernail.

"Jed! Jed!" She raced off toward the rim of the mine, scrambling down the levels and across the precarious walkway where he had once taken her. She met him coming up, his back bowed from weariness, his face and clothes soaked with perspiration.

"What is it, Dacey? You're not hurt, are you?" But Jed said it sourly, and she saw that he was not pleased to see her still here. Obviously he had hoped that she would grow discouraged and quit.

"No, I'm not hurt. Look! Look what we found, Jed! Isn't this a big diamond? What do you think it will weigh?"

Excited with her find, she rushed up to him, only to feel his hands go harshly around her, pushing her up the hill again. "You little fool, have you left those Kaffirs all alone up there? Didn't I tell you to watch them, to guard them?"

"Yes, but Chaka is there—"

"Chaka! He's a Kaffir! You can't trust one, Dacey, or he'll rob you blind. Where do you think that illicit stones come from? They come from the blacks in the mines, woman, they come from our own workers stealing from us."

"Oh—" Chagrined, angry—he had brushed aside the diamond she tried to show him as if it were an ordinary pebble—Dacey scrambled after Jed, hurrying to keep up with his longer steps.

"You don't belong here, Dacey. I'm amazed you lasted the whole day." Jed panted as they climbed uphill to where the sorting tables were. "But you'll soon see what you're up against. I want you to do the night search."

"The what?"

"The night search." Jed grinned at her, his triumph open. "I told you, thievery is a terrible problem here. It's ruinous. So we solve it by searching the men before they leave at night. You'd be amazed at the places diamonds can be hidden." Jed gave a coarse laugh. "Sometimes the men swallow them, and then . . . well, you can imagine what we have to do to get the stones back *then*."

Dacey could. She shuddered, staring at her husband. "Are you saying that I have to . . . to strip those men naked and look— You can't mean it, Jed."

He grinned. "I do mean it. What's the matter, Dacey, isn't your stomach strong enough for the real work? I didn't think it was. Well, I'll do the search for you then. You just run along home, and why don't you take your bath before I get there? Then you'll be all clean and pretty when I make love to you. Yes, tonight I think you'll be willing enough, eh?"

They had reached the sorting tables. The black men were already lined up in a row, shuffling their feet expectantly. Jed meant his threat about searching them, Dacey realized with a horrid race of her heart. And this, she knew, was how he expected to defeat her. Faced with a degrading body search, he was sure she'd back down and run meekly home, to prepare herself for his lovemaking.

Never had she felt so coldly furious. How dare he? To assault the dignity of these black workers, and her own—her emotions simmered at the very idea. Yet, if she backed down, Jed would interpret it as failure.

What was she going to do?

Dacey hesitated, drawing a deep breath. She decided she'd have to call Jed's bluff. Surely he would stop the search before it went too far.

"Very well," she said boldly, hiding her trepidation. "I'll do it, then, Jed, if you insist."

She was satisfied to see a startled expression cross her husband's face. She went on, forcing her voice into firmness. "Please tell the men to move before me one at a time. They must hand me each item of their clothing so I can shake it out.'' She moistened her lips, her confidence eroding. ''And then they must crouch before me and show me that they—they cannot be carrying diamonds in any of their—their bodily parts . . .''

She could barely force the words out. She could not believe that Jed, so protective of her on the streets of Kimberley, would really permit her to go through with this charade.

''Fine,'' he said, gazing stonily at her. ''Bokembi is first.''

Dacey looked at the first African. Bokembi was a youth of about seventeen, tall, with a lithe, deeply muscled body, bulges rippling from under his shiny blue-black skin.

Dacey gestured to him.

The young Bantu understood what was expected of him. Impassively he stepped out of the brief loincloth he wore. Beneath it he was naked, a young, black, healthy male.

Dacey swallowed and averted her eyes, reaching for the dusty loincloth. She picked it up and shook it, all too aware of Jed's fury. His face had gone an ugly red and a pulse beat angrily in his neck.

''Go ahead, Dacey,'' Jed taunted. ''You won't be able to carry this through.''

''I'll do it,'' she snapped. She heard the Bantus giggle as Bokembi approached Dacey and opened his mouth for her to look inside. She forced herself to inspect his teeth and gums, then peered into his ears, ran her fingers over the soft, kinky hair of his head. As she did this, Jed glowered at her furiously.

He should have stopped her, she thought in anger. This ugly search degraded both herself and the men. Worse, she saw that other miners, passing by on their way home from work, had stopped to stare. If she finished this search, she would be notorious here in Kimberley. Tongues would wag viciously . . . Yet, if she gave it up, she would be admitting failure to Jed.

She finished the head search, taking as long as she dared, wondering what to do next. How was she going to get out of this? She had to think of something . . .

''Ah, Donohue, putting the little woman to work?'' Shouts and catcalls were beginning to come from the gathering crowd.

"It's only to put her in her place, let her see where she doesn't belong," Jed called back.

Someone laughed and someone else made a ribald joke. Then the crowd shifted as a man shouldered his way through. It was Quinn Farris, his eyes flashing with anger.

"What is the meaning of this display, Donohue?"

"Why, I'm just showing her—" Jed began, sneering.

Quinn's face was a dark, tight mask of anger as he strode up to the startled Bokembi, picked up his loincloth, and handed it to him. Then Quinn walked up to Jed and smacked him across the face with the flat of his hand. The slap made an ugly sound against Jed's perspiration-damp skin.

"That's for you, Donohue," Quinn snapped. "And there will be more coming if you ever force your wife to participate in such a degrading search again. If Dacey wants to work here at the mine, let her. But don't ever let me see you treat her—or *any* woman—this way again."

Dacey didn't know how she managed to get away from the stares of the diggers or the two furious men who glared at each other until Jed finally backed away, his countenance bright red with rage. Guffaws rose, filling the air with amusement at her expense.

If Quinn hadn't come to her rescue . . . Oh, she didn't even want to think about it. She hurried blindly through the mining camp, wanting only to get home, away from staring faces, whispers, and male laughter.

"Dacey!" She heard Quinn call behind her, but she didn't stop. Humiliation filled her like a tide. She was going to be the laughingstock of Kimberley. The woman who had stripped her workers naked.

"Dacey, don't be so damned proud!" Quinn caught up to her and jerked her to a halt, pulling her around to face him.

"Please, please!" She struggled against him. "Please, just let me go home!"

"No, not yet, not until I talk to you." He pulled her along one of the paths used by the Africans to and from the mines, leaving her little choice but to go with him, unless she wished to make a further spectacle of herself.

"I came along just in time to see you searching a naked man. I must say, I was rather surprised. How did that amazing scene happen to come about?" Quinn demanded.

"It was because I wished to work my claims, and Jed didn't want me to. He hoped to force me to admit I couldn't do it. I . . . I didn't think he would carry it so far."

Quinn's laugh was harsh. "Well, I must say I have to admire your courage. Not every woman would have refused to allow her bluff to be called."

She choked back an angry sob. "Maybe. But now I'm going to be notorious in Kimberley, everyone will look at me and laugh, they'll call me the woman who searched her workers. They'll gossip, they'll—"

"And what if they do gossip? Aren't you strong enough to face a little talk?"

"But—" Her eyes stung. "But they are going to say—"

"Let them say whatever they wish. In a few days, all of the excitement will die down, and after that, people will simply remember that you stood up to your husband."

Dacey nodded, beginning to feel a bit better. For a moment they walked in silence, with the setting sun to their left, an enormous red ball sinking into the horizon against a backdrop of masses of purple and lilac clouds—a sunset the likes of which Dacey had never seen in England.

"Are you happy, Dacey?" he asked her at last, his voice low.

"I . . . of course I am."

"Are you? Married to that aggressive bull of a man? Jed Donohue is all talk and no courage. No real man would have permitted you to go through that charade at the mine today, whether he agreed with your views or not. Nor would he have allowed me to slap his face."

"He is my husband now," Dacey said quietly. "And I am . . . expecting his child."

There was a silence, and Dacey sensed the tremor that went through Quinn's body.

"I see," he said.

"He is overjoyed at the news," she forced herself to go on. "He was in town last night celebrating the fact that he is to have a son." She forced a smile, aware of how hollow it was. "It hadn't even occurred to him that we might have a daughter instead."

"We. You speak of *we*, you and Jed . . . And you are to have a baby. Oh, Dacey, Dacey . . ."

Silhouetted against the spectacular sunset, Quinn's profile looked harsh, his jaw grim. "I suppose I had better get you back home, then. Back to your *husband*."

"Yes," she said miserably. She yearned to say more, to fling herself into Quinn's arms, to blurt out her belief that the baby she carried was his. But how could she? She didn't know this for a fact, and to raise Quinn's hopes and emotions would be cruel. Besides, there was Jed. . . .

"Dacey," Quinn said as the path diverged and she must turn toward her own house. "Dacey, if you ever need me. For anything, anything at all . . ."

"Yes," she whispered. She turned and ran up the path. Her head was throbbing, and there was a fierce, intractable ache, like shards of broken glass, inside her heart.

"Eh, Dacey, the whole town's talking about how you stood up to Jed—and him trying to force you to strip those black men naked and all."

Bella Garvey was letting out some of Dacey's dresses and had begun work on a layette for the baby, cutting soft garments from a bolt of cambric that had just arrived from Port Elizabeth.

Dacey bit her lip. "It wasn't exactly like that, Bella. He didn't force me, I was the one who insisted on proving—"

"Pshaw." Bella shrugged. "It doesn't matter why it happened now. What's important is that people are on your side. Sure, they've talked, but they have sympathy for you, too. Of course, I heard that Jed is going around grumbling against Quinn Farris, but I imagine that will pass. Men like him talk more than they act—not that I'd say anything against your husband, of course," Bella added hastily.

Dacey sighed, staring down at the tiny, cutout baby garments. She couldn't help thinking of the moment that she had arrived home after the incident in the mine. Jed had already been in the house and was in the act of stripping off his dusty clothing. He had stared at her, his expression hard.

"So you showed me up in front of them all, eh, Dacey?"

"I'm sorry it had to happen that way," she managed to say, made uneasy by something rigid in the corded muscles of Jed's neck, a flick of a muscle in his jaw.

"You're *sorry*!" He had laughed, the sound ugly. "Why should you be, when you got what you wanted? You got your independence, didn't you? And now I'm the joke of Kimberley, the man who couldn't control his own wife. Well, let me tell you something." He lunged forward, to grip her arm. "At home, you're still my wife."

"Jed . . ."

"You belong to me, and you'll do what *I* tell you to do, is that clear?"

Dacey had looked into the angry brown eyes of her husband, feeling a twist of fear. He needed desperately to retrieve his pride after his public humiliation, she knew. But she could not give in to him completely—not now, not after what she had been through.

"I will still be your wife at home, of course," she told him, looking him in the eye. "But I meant what I said about denying you my bed. I won't share you with prostitutes."

His face congested, Jed approached her, his fists clenching and opening. Dacey backed away, frightened by something in her husband's face. "You won't, eh? Well, nobody denies Jed Donohue what he wants—nobody! Take off your clothes, Dacey."

"No, Jed, please . . ."

"Take them off now."

"Please, Jed, the baby . . . a woman should not lie with a man when she is pregnant, it may damage the child . . ."

Dacey did not know if this was true, but it stopped Jed, and he stood watching her, his chest heaving, his mouth thinned into a line.

"All right, then," he told her heavily. "You can get away with it, Dacey—for now. But after my son comes, then you are mine again. I'll sleep with you ten times a night if I wish, and I'll see to it that your belly is kept full of children. Soon you'll be so busy you won't have *time* to stand around a sorting table."

He seemed pleased with this thought, some of his black mood disappearing. Dacey forced a smile, allowing herself to relax a little. "Yes, Jed," she agreed.

Seven months? It seemed a long time away. She had managed to deflect Jed's wrath for now, and she had won her victory at the mine. She would worry about tomorrow when it came.

Now, as they finished their tea, and she submitted to Bella's basting and tucking, Dacey hoped that the seamstress didn't notice the bruise on her arm from Jed's ironlike grip. Dacey was proud and didn't want people to know how he treated her, or the fact that he was hardly ever at home these days. Did he go to saloons, or to prostitutes? Or did he simply walk the streets of the town alone? Dacey didn't know and felt too relieved at his absence from her bed to care.

"You hardly show at all," Bella gloated, turning her. "Do you really like working at the mine?"

"Oh, yes." Dacey couldn't help smiling. "To work all day over that gravel and then to find a stone and pick it out of the dirt and realize it's a diamond—it's an incredible thrill, Bella. If only we were allowed to own more than two claims! I think I'd start my own mining company."

There had been time, in the long nights alone in her pallet in the living room, to dream.

"I believe you would. Turn again, dearie, I want to do this arm seam. Eh, a woman has to look out for her own interests in this world of diamond-hungry men. We have to work harder and be hungrier than they are—it's the only way."

After she had finished her fittings, Dacey hurried back to the mine. Jed still objected to her working, but since their confrontation she had insisted on managing her own claims. Chaka was her overseer, managing the black workers, conducting the searches, and spelling Dacey when her pregnancy forced her to rest. Dacey trusted Chaka. She had promised him a percentage of her discoveries, and knew that, like a small number of the Africans, he dreamed of buying a claim for himself.

Now, as she approached the sorting tables, the Zulu smiled at her. His teeth were white, large, and perfect. "We have good luck today, missy. We found one pretty big green stone. Here, look at it."

Dacey examined the rough diamond. She had learned that diamonds came not only in white, but in a range of colors, from bronze and yellows, to greens, blues, pinks, even black. This stone was a deep, yellowish-green, about four to five carats in weight.

"Oh, Chaka, it's so pretty! I wonder what it will fetch on the market."

"I see you have found a rare one." Dacey heard a voice behind her and turned, startled, to see the man who had been pointed out to her as Cecil Rhodes. Although only twenty, Rhodes was already on his way to becoming one of Kimberley's richest men, and some said that he would go even further than that.

"Yes, isn't it nice?" Dacey smiled at the lanky-looking man who, Jed had told her scornfully, was a lone wolf with no interest in women. She handed the stone to Rhodes. "How would you judge it?"

Rhodes took her question seriously. He frowned at the diamond, then pulled out a jeweler's loupe from his vest pocket to peer at it more closely. "Its shape is that of a macle, or twinned crystal, which will make it more difficult to cut. But it is at least five carats, and the color saturation is strong. And there are only a few small inclusions, very difficult to see with a ten x lens."

Dacey flushed, for she didn't understand everything that he had said. "I am afraid that I still have a great deal to learn about diamonds."

"Well, you needn't fear. This stone is very marketable. Unfortunately South African diamonds are causing a glut on the European market. Prices in Amsterdam and Antwerp are dropping, and will continue to drop unless we can exert control over the industry."

Dacey nodded, flattered that Rhodes was speaking to her as if she was a real part of this exhilarating world.

"I heard about your confrontation with your husband last

month at the Kimberley Mine,'' Rhodes continued in his dry, flat voice. ''Personally, I don't care for the idea of women in the mines. I find that women are generally foolish creatures, far too interested in fripperies and socializing. But I believe his treatment of you was crass, and certainly you do seem to be a person who isn't afraid of hard work.''

Coming from Rhodes, Dacey felt sure this was a high compliment. She flushed with pleasure.

''You may do very well here, girl. You may just,'' Rhodes added in his clipped British accent. Then he turned on his heel and walked away, leaving Dacey to stare after him.

Quinn Farris walked beside the rumbling Cape wagon, hearing the bellow of the oxen and the shouts of his driver, who called each animal by name as he flicked his long whip only inches away from their backs.

Summer was ending, and the season had been marked by some of Africa's spectacular thunderstorms, cataclysms of thunder and lightning as violent as the continent itself. During a rain, inches of water could pour onto the dry earth. Only a few hours after a storm had hit the faraway range of mountains, water could rush down a dry streambed, smashing anything that lay in its path.

But today, the sky stretched overhead, deep blue, lit by a harsh sun. Quinn narrowed his eyes against the sunglare and stared ahead. Just beyond the jut of one of the strange, flat-topped hills that the Boers called *koppies* were the thatched farmhouse, outbuildings, and kraals of Piet Van Der Berg. This was a Boer farmer who, Quinn had learned, possessed a fine coal-driven water pump.

Quinn wanted very badly to buy the pump. The Kimberley and De Beers mines, the Dutoitspan as well, had been flooded by the summer rains. Water had collected in the lower levels, eroding walkways, causing mudslides and rockfalls. Quinn planned to lease out his pump to the beleaguered miners. He had ordered more pumps from London, and when these arrived, he planned to start a leasing company.

Even if the claims limit was only two, there were still many ways to wrest money from the diamond earth. . . .

A man on a shaggy Boer horse came galloping up to meet him.

"What brings you here to my farm, *rooinek?*" The Boer had the pale-blue eyes and white beard of a patriarch, and spoke to Quinn with scorn, calling him a redneck, a term of insult. The Boers hated the British, whom they blamed for abolishing the native slavery they had depended on, and for taxing them.

Quinn nodded to the hostile farmer. "I am not British, but American. And I come with an offer to buy your water pump, *mijnheer.*"

"I will not sell my pump, but you may feed and water your animals and share a meal with us. Your driver may eat with my servants. Then, in the morning, you will return to wherever you came from."

Undaunted, Quinn tipped his hat. "I come from Kimberley. It is a city of diamonds—and I have brought both diamonds and gold with which to trade. But we will talk of that later. I accept your kind hospitality, *mijnheer*, and I will do my best to persuade you that we can do business together."

Five days later, Quinn lay in the lee of his wagon beside a small fire, now burned down to embers, and stared up at the night sky. His driver, Frikkie, was off in the farmer's native compound, flirting with a pair of giggly Cape Coloured girls.

Five days, Quinn thought in exasperation. It had taken him that long—and a whole envelope of rough diamonds—to complete his transaction. He had had to scheme and cajole, smile at the farmer's enormously fat wife, admire his cattle and sheep, and consume vast quantities of heavy Boer cooking and Cape wine.

But now he had his pump. It was in perfect running order, would pump vast quantities of water, and make him a fortune. Yet now, as Quinn stared up at the Milky Way, he felt anything but triumphant. He was owner of two profitable claims, his diamond business grew daily, and his water pumps would soon make him the most powerful man in Kimberley.

Yet, with each passing day, his triumphs seemed to matter less and less. Dacey Donohue. How she haunted him! Her face, the variable moods of those flashing green eyes . . . On the day of her wedding, her face had looked as set and still as a painting, her beauty carved of palest porcelain. But at the mine, when Jed Donohue had tried to force her to search the men, her eyes had blazed.

When Dacey had told him that she was pregnant, Quinn had wanted to shout and rage with the cruel shock of it. To wish to take Dacey into his arms, to crush her to him, to hold her and love her and take care of her for the rest of his life, and know that he could not—

Instead he had remained silent, hidden his deep anguish, and told her to go back to her husband, the hardest thing that he had ever done.

Quinn twisted and groaned, watching as a star fell out of the Milky Way, leaving a flaring trail across blackness before it died. Why couldn't she have gone back to England as he had asked her to do? If she had, he would not have known about her pregnancy. He would not have to suffer, knowing that every night another man took her into his arms and loved her. . . .

Quinn threw an arm over his face and tried to sleep.

He was dreaming . . . dreaming that he and Dacey were under the thorn tree again, wrapped in each other's arms. Their bodies were bared to the sun and to the light desert breeze that played across their skin. Against his chest Quinn felt the full, voluptuous breasts push against him.

Feverishly he stroked the skin that was as soft as silk, lithe and firm and strong. He bent his mouth to those small, perfect, exquisitely pink nipples and began to tongue them, drawing soft little cries of ecstasy from her, cries that only drove him to greater passion. . . .

He thrust within the hot core of her, where her womanhood took him and surrounded him with sensations of throbbing pleasure. They rocked together, lost in each other. Then, subtly, the dream changed. Quinn smelled flowers and felt her legs lock around him, her fingernails rake into his back.

But he did not feel pain, for he was riding his desire, plunging on a limitless journey, dreamlike, unbearably sensual.

"Dacey!" he cried out at the moment of passion, and felt the rivers of pleasure burst again and again. "Ah, God, Dacey . . . love . . ."

"Dacey? You call out *her* name?"

The soft, cool voice was female, but it was not Dacey's. The love-moist, smooth body that wrapped itself around Quinn was not Dacey's, either. Abruptly Quinn wrenched awake. He pulled away, smelling the rich, crushed-flower scent of the oils that Natala used to anoint herself.

Natala. He had dreamed of Dacey, but it was Natala to whom he had actually made love; somehow she had followed the track of his wagon and found him here, had crawled onto his blankets with him.

"What are you doing here?" He raised himself on one elbow to look at her, naked and beautiful beside him.

"What are *you* doing, speaking of Dacey Donohue in your sleep?"

There was a sudden flash of silver in the moonlight, the movement as quick as a cat's pounce. Quinn froze. Natala held an assegai firmly at his throat, one of the short swords that the Zulu used for killing. Her face, sheened with moisture, looked feral, angry; her nostrils flared.

He was only a millimeter away from death.

Quinn lay very still. He did not even allow his heart to pump with the beginning of fear. Once, on the Vaal River, a roving group of Xhosas, intent on rape and slaughter, had raided their camp. Natala had thrust her assegai into the heart of a snarling black man and pulled it out again, her face frozen into a mask of passion, her eyes glittering.

Their group had overcome the marauders, and Quinn had managed to forget his mistress' face as it had looked that night. Now he remembered again.

Calmly, he looked Natala in the eye, aware of the edge of the blade touching his jugular vein. If she plunged it forward, it would slice directly into his throat, pouring his blood onto the ground.

Would she kill him? What would she do? Natala was a mystery to him, the lusts and desires that drove her alien to his thinking. But he could not lie here with his neck exposed to her blade as if he were a sheep.

Slowly, carefully, Quinn sat up. As he did so, Natala moved the sword with him, so that when he was fully upright, the gleaming metal still bit at his throat.

"You were gone five days," she whispered. "I did not think it would take that long, I feared you might be in danger. I followed your wagon tracks."

"You didn't need to; as you can see, I'm perfectly safe. The bargaining took longer than I expected."

Their eyes remained locked.

"*I* am your woman!" Natala cried. "I and no other! I am more beautiful than she, am I not? Tell me, Quinn. Tell me that I am."

He looked at her savage face; in the moonlight, it did indeed possess a wild, fierce beauty. But it was a beauty utterly without warmth. She was like a night spirit or an elemental, a force of nature.

"You are beautiful, Natala. No man could deny that."

"And desirable?"

Anger twisted in Quinn, thinning his voice. "Yes, you are desirable. You know that, you have always known it. I think you were born knowing it."

Cautiously he lifted his hand and pushed away the assegai, feeling her give up her resistance. When it was safely away from his body, he reached for the handle and wrenched it out of Natala's grasp. He tossed the sword into the darkness, hearing her sharp intake of breath.

"If you ever . . . *ever* . . . raise a knife blade to me again, or cause harm to Dacey, I'll never lie with you again, Natala. You will be finished to me, as used up as an ear of corn after the corn is consumed."

For an instant Quinn thought she was going to spring at him. Then she tightened her full-carved lips and looked downward.

"I can make spells," she whispered slyly. "I could bewitch her, Quinn, I could even poison her if I chose. I am well-versed in the arts of poison."

Quinn felt a spurt of horror. Was she saying that she would

kill Dacey? His arm snaked out and he gripped Natala's chin, forcing it upward. He stared into her rebellious eyes.

"If you ever do that, Natala, if you dare to touch one hair of Dacey's head, or her child's, I will hunt you down and kill you like an animal, like a wild dog."

Her mouth twisted. "*Ai*, you would never kill me, your heart is too soft, in the white man's way."

"Is it? Don't test my resolve, Natala."

"But you are only a man, you are not—"

"Be still," he gritted. "Or I will kill you now."

Anger hung between them, an actual, physical thing, as real as the veld around them, or the star-dusted sky, or the jackal that howled and slavered a mile or so away. Quinn bored his eyes into Natala's, giving her no quarter, until at last he saw fear grow there, alive and naked.

Satisfied, he released her. She crouched, huddled sullenly.

"Very well!" Her head was bowed, her lower lip quivering. "As you wish, Quinn. I will not hurt her. But I only ask this: that you make love to me again . . . to *me*, not to that English actress! I can take her man—I can have any man she possesses, anytime I want!"

Quinn supposed that this boast was a feminine way of saving face. "I imagine you can," he said, thinking that she was like a savage little cat, totally feline in her jealousies.

"I know I can." Sinuously Natala rose to her feet. She was totally naked, moonlight glittering from her silken skin. Taking his hand, she drew it to the flatness of her belly, the silky fur between her legs. Musk emanated from her like a sensuous perfume.

"Come," Natala whispered. She turned and threw something onto the fire, some dried root that quickly ignited, sending up an acrid smoke. "Come and lie with me again."

"No," Quinn groaned, with a last thought of Dacey, of her beautiful, poignant face. "No . . ."

But the dagga smoke had reached his nostrils now. His head felt oddly light, swimming with strange, thick desire. When Natala pulled him down onto the ground, he sank beside her without volition. She caressed him, smiling.

As if this were still a dream, as if he could not stop

himself, Quinn lowered himself onto her body. He slipped into the hot, animal moistness of her. He felt her soft wetness envelop him, and then she began to move under him. She moved wildly, thrusting forward, drawing him deep, deeper into her spell.

When at last he exploded, it was with a cry almost of pain. The spasm rocked through his mind and body, crashing through all the barriers of his spirit. *Dacey . . . Dacey . . .* But he did not know if he called her name aloud or if it was something that he only wept.

10

IT WAS NIGHT, A WEEK later, the stars overhead so large and clear that Natala felt as if she could reach upward and pluck one to string on the glass-bead necklace that she wore about her throat.

About her body she had draped an orange cloth, with another head cloth tied about her hair to conceal it. In the dark, she knew she looked like any ordinary African woman, and would be taken as such.

Yet she was more beautiful than any of them, she assured herself, touching the bracelet of lioness claws that she wore around her left wrist, her talisman. Beautiful enough to possess any man she wished. And tonight the man she wanted was Jed Donohue, Dacey's husband.

Why shouldn't she take Jed? Defiantly, Natala hastened her stride along the path toward streets already noisy with laughter and the notes of a raucous piano. She had already shown her power by possessing Quinn, by showing him arts of love that she was sure were unknown to a white woman like Dacey Donohue. Now, to clinch her victory, she had to have Jed, Dacey's man.

She would take him, too, on a wild journey of sexual gratification. After that, she would own him utterly, and forever spoil him for Dacey. Her power, her beauty, would be supreme.

Natala scowled, feeling her heart pump with the anger that

she had to keep in check since she and Quinn had arrived back in Kimberley. How dare Quinn cry out Dacey's name when he made love to *her*? How dare he threaten to hunt her down like a dog?

Staring into Quinn's eyes, seeing the threat there, Natala had been afraid. She had insulted him by telling him that his heart was soft like a white man's, but all along she had known that it was not. She could not have loved him if he had been weak. He was strong, his heart was powerful as a lion's. What he said, he meant.

Natala shuddered, picturing a future without Quinn, as bleak and empty as the veld after a ten-year drought. She needed Quinn. Required him, just as she craved the fiery dagga or her lone walks into the desert. Love? She tossed her head scornfully. Those were white men's words, having nothing to do with what she felt.

And tonight, Natala was going to have revenge. If she could not strike a direct blow at Dacey Donohue, then she would strike an indirect one. Once and for all, Dacey would learn which woman was the strongest, which held the real power over men . . .

Jed Donohue, Natala knew, frequented the King of Prussia Saloon. He usually spent the night drinking, or gambling a little. When she reached the saloon, she paused outside in the road to listen to the sounds of revelry that came blasting from within. Even from the street, she could smell the pungent odor of beer and the scent of many crowded male bodies.

A night breeze suddenly nudged at the back of Natala's neck, lifting the ends of her head cloth and causing her to shiver. For an instant apprehension filled her, a premonition of disaster. Then she gave an impatient gesture, brushing the mood away. She withdrew into a shadow and settled herself to wait. Sooner or later, Jed would appear. If not tonight, then another night.

There was plenty of time.

Three hours later, Jed Donohue did stride out of the saloon. He was a broad, stocky man with the aggressive shoulders of the bull buffalo, but with none of that animal's courage.

There was a weak look to the set of his mouth over the curly brown beard. Natala was pleased to see that he was alone. He would be easy to accost. And once he saw her, he would be hers. There were things about which Natala held doubts, but her own seductiveness was not one of them.

As the miner started down the dusty street, Natala glided out of the shadows. Imitating a street woman, she sauntered toward Jed, swinging her hips provocatively.

"Well, hello! What have we here?" Jed saw her at once and stopped. His voice was thick with whiskey and desire.

Natala smiled, but said nothing. She posed for him, moistening her lips in a way that she had learned made men's lust rise. Jed Donohue, she saw, was no exception.

"Come . . . come with me," he mumbled. "I know a hotel . . . Do you speak any English at all? Never mind. We'll go there and I'll show her . . . show Dacey . . . just who's the boss . . . ."

The hotel to which he took her was one of Kimberley's few two-story buildings, a crib that had been built for the sole purpose of selling women in tiny little rooms. Natala, who had intended to take Jed to the veld, stopped at the front door, wanting to object. But Jed, already breathing hoarsely, would brook no opposition. He threw a bill to the desk clerk and pulled her through the tiny lobby and up a narrow wooden staircase.

The hotel stank of perfume, African body oils, sweat, and candle tallow. A few of the doors were open, and Natala glimpsed the interior of the cribs—a crude cot, a single chair, a candle guttering in a metal holder, a black girl naked or wearing only the briefest of cloths. In one cubicle, a man took a woman in full view of passersby, heaving and grunting over her body, while she stared up at the ceiling, her expression blank.

The sight was animalistic, curiously horrible. Natala shuddered, averting her eyes, some of her confidence deserting her. She shouldn't have come here.

Jed pulled her into a room at the far end of the upstairs hall. There was a candle in this room, too, and Jed lit it from a match he carried. An opened window looked out on a back alley, a night breeze causing the flame to waver. Natala swallowed back her misgivings and reached inside her garment for a bit of the dried plant she carried with her. She tossed the dagga into the candle flame.

Instantly an acrid smoke billowed forth.

"What's that stuff?" Jed demanded in a slurred voice. "It smells . . . smells funny . . ."

Natala smiled. She touched the fastening of her wrap and let it drop from her body. She was pleased to see Jed's eyes widen at the sight of her full, bare breasts tipped with dark nipples, the voluptuous hips and narrow waist. Before she left, Natala had anointed her skin with oil. Now she knew that her skin gleamed in the lamplight, that she was alluring. Jed's hoarse groan, his roughened breathing, proved it.

Smiling, preening for him, she added more dagga to the flame. Then she glided toward him.

"Ah . . . ah . . . ah . . ." Jed Donohue pumped over Natala, driving himself deep within her. Natala's thighs were wrapped around his back, her fingernails digging into his skin like cat claws. She was in control now; she owned him, every reaction, every shudder of his body. She could cause him to climax now, or she could stretch out his ecstasy for hours, toying with him, bending him to her will.

Squeezing her inner muscles tightly, Natala caused Jed to groan deeply. Satisfied, she repeated the action, playing him as if he were an instrument. At last she relented. She heard his hoarse cry as he convulsed, spurting his seed into her.

Satiated, Jed collapsed over her. But when Natala rolled out from underneath him, abruptly filled with revulsion for what she had done, Jed reached for her.

"Hey, not so fast. I want you again, I'm not finished with you yet."

Natala had intended to leave, hurrying quickly into the night. She had demonstrated her power, she had consumed him, now she was finished and wanted only to get away.

"No," she whispered.

"Oh, ho! Who do you think you are? Did you think that

you could shake it in front of me, tease me, then not expect me to take all I want? I want my fill and I intend to get it.''

Naked, as broad and massive as a bull, Jed lunged to his feet and started drunkenly toward the wool pants that he had flung on a chair. He began fumbling in a back pocket.

Money, Natala realized with a sudden, cold clench of her belly. He intended to pay her, just as he would have paid any other woman he brought to this place.

She sprang up off the cot, the dagga smoke still reeling through her lungs. Jed's movements, as he peeled out some bills, seemed exaggeratedly slow. He was going to pay her! She, the most desirable woman in Kimberley, who could command any man she chose, was being treated as a prostitute.

Anger twisted in Natala, along with a deep, confused fear. If a man could pay for her body, then maybe she wasn't so desirable after all. Maybe . . . Old teachings, lectures from the straitlaced female missionary, whirled in her head. The flickering candle, almost at the end of its wick, sent shadows leaping across the room.

"No!" Natala cried out as Jed came toward her with the pound notes.

"Go on. Take it. Are you scared of a little money? Or should I pay you in beads or mirrors or pretty stones? Is that what you want, Kaffir girl?''

At the insult, Natala froze. She was Natala, and she was beautiful, and she could not bear the word that came out of Jed's mouth, cutting her down to a status against which she had fought all of her life. Involuntarily, she screamed out, pushing at the hands that thrust the money toward her.

It all happened quickly. Jed stumbled backward. He was drunk, and the hallucinatory smoke from the dagga had left him disoriented. His arms flailed, windmilling in circles as he staggered backward.

Natala could only watch as Jed stumbled, clutching at the windowsill for support. Then his knees buckled. Loosely, fluidly, Jed's body bent double at the waist, and he fell out the window.

Natala heard a strangled cry and then . . . nothing.

She ran to the window and looked down, seeing a dark

form sprawled in the dust, moving slightly. He was alive. Choking back a gasp of fear, she grabbed for her garment and flung it on, leaving the necklace scattered on the floor. Something made her pause to blow out the guttering candle, and then she rushed out of the room and down the hall to the staircase.

Jed was drunk and tomorrow he would remember little, she assured herself as she hurried past the dozing desk clerk and into the night. And even if he did, the fall had not been great, from only one story up. He would live.

She would say nothing to anyone.

Dacey yawned and lifted her head, wondering why she felt so stiff and tired, why every muscle in her body ached. She yawned again, enormously, and looked around her. She was in the living room, seated at the wooden table. Apparently she had fallen asleep last night over her account books. Yes, the page was bent where she had lain on it, and the table was scattered with the bodies of the moths who had dived too close to the flames of her oil lamp.

She rose and stretched and rubbed her tingling arms and legs, trying to work the circulation back into them. Her mouth tasted sour and her dress was untidy, her hair straggling out of its pins to fall on her shoulders in confusion.

She was annoyed at Jed for not waking her when he had come in last night. Apparently he had not thought it worthwhile to bother.

They lived like strangers these days, she and Jed, barely speaking to each other. Jed plainly hated her for refusing him her bed, for her independence, her work at the mine. He resented that she was actually making a profit, that her claims, in fact, were proving more fruitful than his own. She was sure that the only reason he tolerated her at all was because of the child she carried.

"Dacia! Dacia, are you up yet? Child, it's long past nine o'clock!" A knock at the door aroused her from these thoughts, and she hurried to open it, admitting her father.

"Why, Papa, good morning!" In spite of her grumpy mood, Dacey couldn't help smiling at her father. In the months they had been in Kimberley, John McKinnon had acquired the look of a prosperous diamond dealer. He wore their ostentatious garb: velvet jacket, gaudy cravat, white waistcoat, leather breeches, polished boots, and, fastened to his belt, a canvas bag supposed to contain a fortune.

This was what the "big" dealers wore, Papa insisted, and he would do the same. Who was to know what the bag contained? And if he chose to spend his afternoons at the Blue Post, lifting a few glasses with the regulars who had become his friends, that was fine, too. He did sell a diamond now and again, and his good luck was bound to begin soon.

Dacey was glad that Papa was happy here in Kimberley. He was sixty-four, and why should he not take it easy now, enjoying the days that were left to him? As long as she had money, her father would never want.

"Daughter, did you oversleep?" John McKinnon wanted to know. "You look as rumpled as if you just rose from bed about two seconds ago. I thought you were always at the mine by this hour. In fact, I've just come from there. I was looking for you."

For the first time, Dacey noticed that Papa was out of breath. Perspiration glistened on his high Shakespearean forehead.

"I did just get up," she admitted. "I fell asleep over the accounts. Papa, is anything wrong?"

"I hope not." Still, Papa hesitated. "But I suppose— Well, Dacia, the truth is, you had better wash your face and drink a cup of coffee and then come along with me to the Kimberley hospital."

"The hospital!"

"It is surely nothing to worry about, I've heard that cases like this sometimes recover spontaneously, it is a matter of muscular exercises . . ."

"What is? Papa, what are you talking about?"

Dacey's heart had lurched sickeningly, and her first panicky thought was of Quinn. Something had happened to him. He was hurt, lying near death in the hospital. That was why Papa had come . . . She felt the room sway around her, her insides turning to ice. Quinn, oh, my darling . . .

"Is he . . . is he all right?" she whispered.

"He will live, anyway." Again Papa hesitated. "Such a freak accident it was. He appears to have fallen, Dacey."

Dacey uttered a high, strangled laugh. "But how could Quinn have fallen, Papa, in this town? There are only one or two buildings that are more than one story high. Unless— unless it was the mine—"

She thought of the deep excavation of the Kimberley Mine, the walkways and pits, and felt a wave of nausea.

"Quinn?" Papa stared at her. "Who said anything about Quinn Farris? I'm talking about Jed. Your husband, Jed. Somehow he managed to fall out of a window. He is in a hospital bed and he can't move his legs."

Papa went with her to the hospital. On the street, several miners turned to stare at them curiously, and Dacey realized that word of Jed's accident had already spread.

Why couldn't Jed move his legs? How could he have fallen out of a window? Had he been drunk? A thousand questions flew through her mind as Papa led her up to the low, corrugated-iron building that served as the town's makeshift hospital.

They stepped inside, breathing in the smell of disinfectant and ether. A nursing sister stopped them from going to the ward, explaining that Dr. Sowers wished to speak with Dacey in private.

"In private?"

"Come, Mrs. Donohue, the doctor is very busy today and he is waiting for you in the operating room. It's best that you talk with him first."

Dacey faltered, swallowing. All the way over to the hospital, she had had to fight a hideous relief that it was Jed who was hurt, rather than Quinn. She hated herself but couldn't stop, and now, seeing the nurse's serious face, guilt plummeted through her. Jed *was* her husband. He had been injured, might even be dying. Of course it was a terrible tragedy.

Dr. Sowers was a tall, thin Englishman with very fair skin and sandy, receding hair. He waited for her in a small operating room furnished starkly with a wooden table and equipment cabinets. Through the glass doors, she could see a collection of scalpels, knives, forceps, and saws. Shuddering, Dacey averted her eyes.

"I hope you plan to come to me for a prenatal examination," the doctor remarked, inspecting Dacey's rounded figure. "Most women are not aware that an examination before the infant is born can save lives. I am also skilled in the use of forceps," he added with satisfaction.

Dacey stared at him, unable to believe that he could talk of childbirth now. "But my husband—please, I understand that Jed is in hospital. What happened? Is he all right? Will he live?"

"Oh, he'll live. Your husband, unfortunately, has suffered a spinal-cord injury."

"Spinal cord? Does that mean that his back is broken?"

"I am afraid so. Mrs. Donohue, your husband is paralyzed from the waist down and will probably never walk again. The air in Kimberley, the heat, and the dust are going to be very bad for him, and if I were you, I would take him back to England at once."

Dacey felt a wave of shock, lifting her like one of the huge combers that swept the Atlantic Ocean. Words, inane ones, popped out of her mouth. "But he . . . he isn't British, he's American."

"Oh, American, is he? I didn't realize . . . Well, then, take him to America." The doctor nodded and started toward the door, plainly relieved that his news had been delivered and wanting to get on to other things. "If you need a sedative, Mrs. Donohue, I'll prescribe one. Of course, there will be laudanum for your husband. He will be in no pain, but his mental state is sure to deteriorate."

With this word of cheer, Dr. Sowers strode briskly out of the room, leaving Dacey to sink against the operating table, the strength flowing out of her body. Jed, paralyzed? Unable to walk? Advised to leave Kimberley? Her mind struggled to absorb the news.

"Dacia, so he's told you. My child, my child . . ." Papa pushed open the door, his arms outstretched to her.

"Papa—oh, God, I can't believe it." She went to him.

"This . . . this hardly seems real to me. It seems like a dream, an ugly dream."

"Of course it does. You are in shock, my darling daughter. There will be time enough later to absorb this—it will be all right, my Dacia, truly it will . . ." Papa held her, and Dacey burrowed into the shelter of his arms as blindly as a mole seeking shelter in the ground.

Papa patted her and murmured words of comfort. Finally he said, "And now you must calm yourself, Dacia, and try not to look so upset. We must go to see your husband now, and you must not frighten him with the expression on your face, Dacia. You must not let him see how hopeless his situation really is."

"*Papa!*" She buried her face against Papa's waistcoat, feeling sick with guilt. She had been relieved. *Relieved* that it had been Jed instead of Quinn, and Jed must never find out.

The ward was a long, narrow room full of beds. In some, miners groaned with enteric fever. Several had been injured in the mines and were swathed in bandages. One man's face was scarred with burns, probably from an overturned paraffin lamp, and several, victims of miners' ophthalmia, had compresses laid over both eyes.

Many of the patients turned to stare as Dacey and Papa walked down the row to the end of the room, and Dacey had the odd feeling that they knew more than she did about what had happened.

"So you came to see the damage," Jed said sourly. He looked up at her from a bed, wearing a cotton gown that barely covered the bulging muscles of his arms and chest. At first glance, he seemed normal, save for the pallor beneath his sunburn. Then Dacey saw the dark bruise on one side of his jaw, and the fact that, although he gestured with an arm for her to come closer, his legs did not move an inch.

Stretched out beneath a sheet, they lay so still that they might have been molded out of plaster.

"How . . . how are you?" Dacey whispered.

"Oh, just *fine*. I can't move my legs, I'm going to have to be attended by a male nurse for the rest of my life, and that idiot of a doctor wants to send me back home because he doesn't think the air here is any good." Jed said it brutally. "Well, I'm not going, Dacey. I came to Kimberley to mine diamonds and that is exactly what I plan to do. Whether Dr. Sowers likes it or not."

"Oh, Jed." Dacey was swept with pity for the man who spoke with such anger. Instantly she forgave him for the strip search, the prostitutes, everything else that had happened between them. Jed had been so large, so full of blustering life. Now that life seemed frighteningly diminished.

She started forward, intending to embrace him.

"Stop it! Don't touch me!"

"But, Jed . . ." She stopped, rebuffed.

"Now, Dacia, you'd better give Jed some time to get used to things," Papa remonstrated.

"Yes, Dacey, I have to get 'used' to not having any legs."

"Jed, oh, Jed," Dacey whispered. "I am so sorry. How could it have happened? To have fallen—"

"I don't want to talk about it," Jed snapped.

"I'm sure that Jed is tired," Papa put in. "We'll come back tonight, and you will have to begin making plans to go to Cape Town, where you can get a ship to—"

"I'm not getting a ship to anywhere. I said I'm not leaving Kimberley, didn't you hear me, old man?" Jed's eyes flashed, yet Dacey thought she saw pleading in them. Again she felt the spasm of pity.

"Of course it's too soon for any decisions yet," she said quickly. "And if Jed wants to stay here, I think that would be fine. I'll see to the claims. I've already been managing mine, and now I'll simply do Jed's, too. It will all work out very well, and—"

"No." Jed said it flatly. "I'll do my own claims." There was a wild, glazed look in his eyes, as if he were about to weep. "No woman looks after me—and no woman does my work, not now and not ever!"

So that was how it began, the new time in Dacey's life that ever afterward she would divide into two periods: before Jed's accident, and after.

Before, Jed had been a vitally active man, a constant presence at the mine, harrying the workers, boasting of their finds, an obsessively hard worker himself who labored from first light to sunset.

Jed was still that man, but now his legs would not carry him unaided to the mine site. He raged at finding himself in this situation, insisting that no one touch his claims but himself.

"But someone has to be there," Dacey protested, visiting him in the hospital. "How can the men work without an overseer? They'll stay in the native section, gambling and playing music and eating if someone isn't there to supervise them."

Jed scowled, clenching his fists, the muscles of his forearms rippling. "I know that, dammit! But they won't loaf for long—I'll see to them. I'm going home from this damned hospital tomorrow morning."

"But the doctor said—"

"*Tomorrow*, Dacey. I want you to get me an invalid chair, a chair with wheels."

"But you know how rough and rocky the ground is, how can wheels maneuver? The danger—"

Then Dacey bit off her words, swallowing her concern. She hated having to tell Jed how dangerous the mine was, when once he had said the same thing to her. Her heart ached for his helplessness. She had had another talk with Dr. Sowers, learning what must be done to care for her husband. Even his bodily functions must now be managed by someone else, an unbearable humiliation for a man as proud as Jed.

She had decided to train Bokembi as Jed's male nurse. Bokembi was young, agile, strong, and good-tempered, suiting him ideally for this task. The only problem, Dacey knew, was getting Jed to accept such help. But since he did not wish Dacey's assistance in these intimate matters, Jed had little other choice.

"I'm helpless, so damned helpless!" he raged. "To have to be cared for like a baby—it revolts me! And it's all the fault of that accursed Kaffir bitch."

Dacey stared at him. Jed had not mentioned a woman before. "What did you say?"

He reddened. "Never mind."

"But I thought you said—"

"I said never mind! What is the matter with you, Dacey? Must you be a busybody, poking your nose in everywhere? It's bad enough that you stand back and gloat over my predicament."

"I gloat over what happened to you?" She could scarcely believe her ears.

"Yes, you love having me like this, Dacey, don't you? Helpless, at your mercy! You can't fool me, I know the way you think, you want to take over my mine. Well, I won't let you. I might have a problem with my legs but my head is as strong as ever, and so are my arms."

Saying that, Jed suddenly snaked out a hand and gripped Dacey's forearm, squeezing it so tightly that she cried out. Several patients, in beds along the row, turned to gape at them.

"Jed," she whispered. "Please . . . the other men are staring . . ."

Jed flung her away from him as if her flesh scorched him. "Get away, then, Dacey. Go on home and get my chair ready for me, you can find one somewhere. You have two legs, you can go anywhere you please . . . but you won't get *my* claims. That's one thing you won't grab."

Shaken, Dacey left the hospital. How could Jed possibly think she could be *glad* this had happened to him? Of course, she reassured herself, he was distraught over being helpless. This made him lash out at her, at everyone around him, in futile rage. In a few weeks he would adjust to his condition. Meanwhile, she must do what she could to help him.

Her first task was to get the invalid chair he had requested, not an easy job in Kimberley, where everything had to be shipped in from Cape Town or Port Elizabeth.

"I know exactly what to do," Papa said. "See if you can buy an invalid chair from the hospital. If they won't sell you one, then maybe Royce has one. That auction house of his is stuffed full of goods being sold on consignment."

When the hospital refused to part with any of their precious chairs, Dacey went at once to visit Royce McKinnon. Since the troupe had disbanded, Royce, by dint of fast talking, had ingratiated himself with the owner of a small auction house. A quick study, he had learned auctioneering, and now he could be found on market mornings, rattling off his rapid spiel.

Dacey prayed that there would be something suitable at the auction house. She dreaded having to tell Jed that she had been able to do nothing, that they would have to wait months for a chair to be shipped.

To her relief, she found Royce at the back of the huge, sagging tent, recording lot items in a small notebook, looking bored with this duty. He hurried forward to greet Dacey and to commiserate over Jed's accident.

"Too bad." He shook his head. "A man's excesses certainly do catch up with him, don't they?"

Was there a look of malice in Royce's eyes?

"What do you mean?" Dacey asked sharply.

"Oh, nothing, just talk . . . Jed was out making the rounds of the saloons, everyone knows that. When a man gets too much whiskey in him . . ."

Dacey regarded her young uncle, struck by an evasiveness in the way he spoke. "There's more to it than just Jed drinking, isn't there, Royce? Today he said something about a woman. A Kaffir, as he called her."

Royce looked uncomfortable. "Well, people will always talk, won't they? Come on, Dacey, let's look back through the tent. I think I have a wheeled chair somewhere about this mess . . ."

He turned and began threading his way through the recesses of the tent, which was crammed with everything a miner might need, from picks and shovels, to wheelbarrows, carts, saddlery, lumber, buckets, even a stack of precious and highly expensive clay bricks.

"Royce!" Dacey hurried after him. "Royce, you didn't answer my question. Why did Jed mention a Kaffir woman? I want to know. When Papa and I walked to the hospital, people kept staring at us. And in hospital, the patients stared, too. It was as if they all knew something I don't. What do they know, Royce? What really happened to my husband?''

''Look.'' Royce pointed to a shadowy corner of the tent. ''Here is an invalid chair, shipped out last month for a man who died. We were going to put it on the block, but instead I'll give it to you. It should be just right for Jed.''

''Thank you for the chair, but, Royce, I have to know . . .''

''You *don't* have to know, Dacey. What good would it do you? He's crippled, isn't he? Nothing can change that.''

Fuming, Dacey wheeled the cumbersome wooden chair, with its huge side wheels, home over the rutted, dusty roads. What had Royce meant to imply with his hints and innuendos? That Jed had been seeking out some black woman for the night? Well, she wasn't stupid, she'd already guessed that. Hadn't Jed made it plain to her that he preferred such women?

But the mystery, whatever it was, would have to be cleared up later, she decided, yanking the chair around a particularly large pothole. For now, she had to bring Jed home, and that was going to require all of her fortitude.

Dacey planned an elaborate dinner to welcome her husband home. Pink roast beef, candied sweet potatoes, cabbage salad, and apple and raisin pie, all Jed's favorites. As a special treat, she added some of the Boer konfyt, fruits preserved in a sweet syrup.

The meal, however, was less than successful. Jed drank glass after glass of wine, saying little, while Dacey tried to entertain him with light gossip about the mines and what had been going on in his absence.

At last Jed threw down his fork with a loud clatter. ''Let's not pretend, Dacey! You prattle about the Kimberley Mine and the Dutoitspan, of politics and rivalries, just as if nothing had happened! Who are you trying to fool? I'm a cripple. Come on, say the word. *Cripple!*''

''No, Jed, please . . .''

''*Say the word, dammit!*'' Jed pounded the table until the wine bottle toppled to its side and leaked red fluid, like blood, onto the table. ''Bokembi!'' he shouted. ''Call him, call the Kaffir, Dacey, and tell him I want to go to bed.''

''But it's only seven o'clock. I thought I would . . . sing

for you tonight. I know you like to hear it, and I had planned a program of songs for you . . ."

"A program of songs!" Jed glowered. "Why? Because you feel sorry for me? That's what this huge meal is all about, isn't it? Because your little heart bleeds for your poor, handicapped husband. Well, you can stop that right now. I'm going to be just as good as ever."

That night, however, when Dacey had slipped beneath the sheets of her cot in the living room, she heard sounds coming from the bedroom where Jed was. They were the racking noises of a man's muffled sobs.

Days, weeks. They passed for Dacey in a haze of work and exhaustion, as summer moved into fall and Africa's winter neared. She had not seen Quinn for several months; it was as if he had deserted Kimberley and everyone in it, including herself.

Grimly, she struggled to do what must be done. To see to Jed's comfort and run their small house, to go to the mine every day. Jed, too, went to the excavation, shouting and railing at Bokembi if his chair slid into a pothole.

But the chair could not be wheeled into the deep excavation, so Jed insisted on being carried on Bokembi's back along the walkways, where he was lowered by ropes to his claims. One day, Bokembi nearly slipped, and after that the black youth refused to carry him any longer.

"I do not want to go to Land of the Dead, I do not want to fall," Bokembi insisted.

Reluctantly, Jed had to accept his position as onlooker, confined to his chair, unable to go to the depths of the mine to inspect his holdings.

"I feel impotent!" he raged one night as he and Dacey arrived home after a day at the mine, both of them coated with the usual film of fine dust. "Helpless, so damned helpless!"

"You need an overseer." Dacey sighed. She was too tired to feel her usual spasm of pity. Her pregnancy was now obvious, and she had suffered some swelling in her ankles. At this moment she felt so weary that she wanted to lie down on her cot and close her eyes. She felt as if she could drift forever, on a river of exhaustion.

"An overseer? You mean a white one, I trust. And who do you suggest I get? Some *kopje* walloper?" A *kopje* walloper was a small-time opportunist who, lacking claims or capital, toured the diamond-sorting tables in hope of picking up or fiddling a bargain. Royce McKinnon, Dacey felt sure, fitted into this category.

"No, I'm sure I could find someone suitable for you, Jed. If you'd let me place an ad in the *Diamond News* or the *Mining Gazette*, we could interview—"

"No! I don't want some idiot coming in and ordering around my Kaffirs and stealing my diamonds. I'm capable of doing that myself."

"What? Of stealing your own diamonds?" Dacey said it dryly. She was growing fed up with Jed's rages and complaints, the drinking that had grown steadily worse since his accident. Then too, if Jed had only known it, she had had to shield him more than once from news that would have driven him into a fury. One by one, other miners had been approaching her with offers to buy their holdings "now that your husband is a cripple."

The first time that this had happened, Dacey had stared at the miner in surprise. "But my husband doesn't want to sell."

"He ought to, ma'am." The man, an Australian, rubbed a grizzled mustache. "A man without legs can't run them blacks, and a pregnant woman can't take a man's place."

Dacey, who had already put in a full day's work, straightened up wearily, feeling the pull of her back muscles. "I certainly can take a man's place; I've been doing it for months now, or perhaps the news has slipped your notice." She glared at the middle-aged miner. "As for my husband, he doesn't need legs in order to supervise his workers."

The Australian smirked at her. "What *I* heard, he yells at 'em and hits out at 'em with a stick. That's if he's in a bellowing mood, which he usually is. Me, I'd be afraid my men were stealing from me."

Dacey swallowed, for this last point had struck home. The

diamonds gleaned from Jed's claims *had* markedly decreased, while her own claims, under Chaka's leadership, were yielding higher than ever. But Jed violently refused to allow Chaka near his claims, claiming that he didn't want any "black Kaffir" getting control of his holdings.

"Are you sure you don't want to change your mind, Mrs. Donohue?" the Australian urged now.

"Yes, I'm very sure."

"Well, you'll change your mind soon enough. Everyone here is taking bets on how long you'll last. Expecting a baby and tied to a cripple . . . When you're ready to sell, I'll be back."

"Don't count on it!" Dacey had snapped. She had turned away, feeling bitter.

She had not told Jed of this incident, or of others equally offensive. But the truth was, they *were* having troubles with Jed's claims. Jed knew his yield was falling off, and this only made him angrier, more despairing.

Where would it all end? When would Jed accept the fact that he had limitations, that life could not go on as it had before?

One chilly morning she was at the sorting tables, wrapped in a loose woolen shawl that hid the new, heavy lines of her figure. Around her the Africans laughed and joked in a mixture of languages. Suddenly Dacey looked up to see Quinn Farris stride over the hill.

He moved easily, confidently, like a man who owns the world and knows it. Seeing him, her heart gave a painful twist. Hungrily, her eyes took in every detail of his appearance. Today he wore a pair of dark, form-fitting trousers that revealed the clean, muscular line of thighs and long legs. His wide shoulders pushed at the seams of a beautifully cut jacket made of supple antelope hide. It was attire that made him seem big and relaxed, somehow at one with wilderness and open spaces.

Dacey's eyes rose to Quinn's face. His skin was still burnished to a dark tan, his features arrogantly carved, the laugh lines around his mouth giving him a look of humor. His black hair curled away from his temples to form an unruly forelock.

She felt her heart give a painful twist. How handsome he is, she thought. And how much I have missed him.

"Where . . . where have you been?" she heard herself blurt out. "I thought perhaps you had left town for good." Then she flushed bright red in confusion.

His eyes, the color of the harsh blue winter sky, examined hers intently. "I've been traveling. To Cape Town, Beaufort West, and such out-of-the-way spots as Grootjongensfontein, Witsand, and Askraal, in search of more water pumps for my leasing company." Quinn's mouth gave a wry twist. "All of it to accomplish my main goal in Kimberley, which I suppose is the same as yours: to get as rich as possible, as fast as possible."

Was he mocking her? Dacey smoothed the fabric of her old merino dress, uncomfortably aware that it was streaked with dust and stretched far too tightly over her abdomen. She felt pregnant, awkward and untidy, and it did not help to have Quinn's eyes on her, so intent.

"You have heard about Jed's accident, of course?" she asked him.

"Yes, I did, and I'm very sorry, Dacey. For you as well as for Jed."

"Jed gets along very well in his invalid chair now," she said defiantly.

"I am sure he does. I have also heard that he is having trouble with his claims."

"Who told you that?" Dacey said angrily. Then she reddened. "I . . . I'm sorry. It's just that Jed won't accept my help, he won't use Chaka, and he doesn't want an overseer. He can't even go into the excavation, Quinn, nor can I, in my present condition."

She stopped, not wanting to sound self-pitying.

"It must be rather difficult. Since I heard the news, I've been thinking about you and what I could do to help. I came here today, Dacey, to offer to—"

"To buy our claims? You, too?" She stared at Quinn, feeling betrayed. Furiously she threw her mallet on the ground, where it rattled among chunks of fallen gravel. "I'm sick and tired of people coming here to try and capitalize on Jed's misfortune! Yes, he's lost the use of his legs, but his feelings are still there, and he suffers, Quinn! He loves the mine, he is desperate to work his claim, he is so sick and angry and confused . . ."

She stopped, too overwrought to go on. Tears burned out of her eyes and slid down her cheeks, making trails in the dust that coated her skin.

"You poor baby." Quinn said it softly. "No, Dacey, I didn't come to buy your husband's claims away from him, I only came to offer my help. You are a loyal wife—and very courageous."

Courageous. She felt her lower lip quiver and bit down on it to stop its trembling. She wanted to break down at the kind words, to fling herself into Quinn's arms and sob on his shoulder. The past months had been searingly difficult, taxing her courage. There had been many offers of help: from Papa, from Bella, Lavinia, and others. But never had it been so tempting simply to throw herself into another's arms and give up.

"I'm not very brave," she admitted in a low voice.

"Of course you are. You are brave beyond all measure. But there are times when courage just isn't enough, Dacey. You need more than that."

Again her temper flared. "What *do* I need? A new pair of legs for Jed? That would help immensely, and if you can provide that, we will both be very grateful!"

She hadn't meant to sound so prickly, but somehow the words flew out anyway. Damn Quinn, she thought. Damn him for making her feel so soft and vulnerable, for making her want to crawl into his arms and give up.

Jed was her husband, her responsibility. He suffered, too, he needed her. She must remember that.

"No," Quinn said. "I wasn't thinking about a new pair of legs. Although if I had the ability to give them, I'd do so happily. I'm talking about know-how, Dacey. You work hard, but maybe there is more you could learn about the mining process that would help you. And more you should know about handling your workers, getting the best work you can out of them.''

"Oh—''

"I would be glad to help you, Dacey, to teach you. Show you how you can shore up your claims, use horses more effectively, guard your areas from falling rock. And I will allow you the free use of my pumps.''

"Your water pumps?" Dacey lifted her head eagerly. Standing water had been a real problem, forcing the abandonment of part of one of her claims and one of Jed's as well. "Oh, Quinn, would you?''

"You know I will. You know I'll do anything for you.''

His voice was husky.

11

THUS IT WAS BORN, THE strange friendship between Quinn and herself that was based strictly on mining and diamonds. They were instructor and pupil, diamond dealer and apprentice.

Quinn visited Dacey's claims daily, sometimes bringing others with him, men who told her about judging raw stones, building winches, handling her workers. Hungrily, Dacey listened, and tried to learn as much as she could. Quinn's coal-driven water pump was the envy of the diggers of surrounding claims, who gathered in crowds to watch the water being sucked away.

Dacey felt grateful for the seemingly magical power of the pump, and Jed was cheered to watch it work.

"At least one thing is going right for us," he gloated. Dacey was amused to note that he had put away his dislike for Quinn to permit the pump, and allowed herself to feel a burgeoning of hope. Maybe life was getting better for them. And if it was, she knew it was all due to Quinn.

One day Cecil Rhodes, who operated a rival pumping business, stopped by the claim to watch the operation.

"I see that your child is due to come soon," he said to Dacey, and gave her his dry smile.

"Yes, it is." Long ago, Dacey had lost her shyness over her pregnancy. Here under the open blue sky, Victorian prudery seemed irrelevant.

"I assume you plan to return to England for your lying-in? Or at least to Cape Town, where there are competent doctors?"

"No, I plan to give birth right here in Kimberley. Dr. Sowers at the hospital will deliver me."

Rhodes raised an eyebrow. "But, Kimberley . . . Not that I'm saying anything against Dr. Sowers, of course . . ."

Dacey caught her breath. It had never occurred to her to go anywhere else for her lying-in. She gazed toward the huge, yawning mine pit, over which a deep sky stretched a canopy of blue. Overhead a hawk soared and dipped, riding a current of air. A few wispy clouds floated at the horizon, looking light and insubstantial.

"It is so beautiful here," she said at last. "I don't want to go—I can't. Jed needs me, and my mine is here, and—and other things which are dear to me. Besides, why shouldn't my baby be born in South Africa? The country is growing. Soon there will be a railway in Kimberley, and our diamonds will be famous all over the world."

Rhodes eyed her sharply. "Yes. I agree." Suddenly he reached out to shake her hand. His palm was dry and smooth, like that of an old man. "If there is ever any assistance I can give you, Mrs. Donohue, don't hesitate to call on me. I have few friends, but I value every one of them."

Dacey felt a resurgence of energy as she entered the final month of her pregnancy. It was a time when she felt refreshed by the cooler air of winter and filled with new enthusiasm. Each week, she held in her hand a heap of raw diamonds, stones that glistened with translucent light, holding in their depths the fascination of the ages.

Diamonds were worn by queens, princesses, and kings, by rajahs and sultans. . . .

She took the stones and sold them to Quinn, or occasionally to Papa. With the money, she paid off her workers and ran her small household, saving the bulk of her earnings to buy more claims once the two-claim restriction was lifted.

One morning she awakened at dawn with a nagging, throbbing ache that centered in the small of her back. Ignoring it, she rose and breakfasted with Jed, averting her eyes from her husband's usual haggard morning look, the faint odor of whiskey that remained on his breath. By mutual consent, neither of them talked much in the mornings; this was a time for Dacey to plan her day, to go over in her mind the instructions she would give her workers.

Usually, she looked forward to going to the mine. Today, however, she felt heavy and cumbersome. It was an effort even to call for Bokembi to push Jed. But finally they were ready, and she walked alongside the bumping chair, listening to Jed's complaints that the yield of diamonds in the mine was growing smaller by the week. The diamonds were running out, he insisted. Beneath the yellow ground where the stones were being found, was only sterile, bluish earth.

Jed was only making excuses, Dacey thought. "Jed, if you would let me put Chaka over your men, I'm sure your claims would do better."

"No! How many times must I tell you, Dacey?"

"But I only thought—"

"Then don't think. Isn't it enough that you must accompany me to the mine every day, like my nanny? I'm a laughingstock among the men."

Dacey felt sure he was anything but that, but she tightened her lips, saying nothing. By the time they reached the excavation, weariness had settled over her like a familiar cloak. Soon, she realized reluctantly, she would have to give in to the demands of her body and allow Chaka to supervise the work while she stayed at home.

The day inched by. A harsh, sand-laden wind blew in from the Kalahari Desert, scouring the mine. Stinging bits of dust rattled canvas and eddied around Dacey's feet as she sat trying to sort the diamond dirt. Her backache grew steadily worse. Jed spent his time wheeling his chair back and forth near the sorting tables, shouting at the men when they did not work fast enough to suit him. Twice he slapped Bokembi's legs with the thin, flexible stick he now carried.

Bokembi, usually sunny-tempered, glowered sullenly.

The wind picked up, its irritation affecting all of their moods. By four o'clock, the Africans were muttering among themselves, and Bokembi scowled at Jed, his arms crossed over his chest.

Dacey's heart sank. The nightly search was coming up, a ritual that made Jed unpleasant. Tonight, she was sure it would be worse than ever, and they could not afford to antagonize their laborers. In the past months, several had quit, and Dacey worried that more of them would do so.

"Missy, I want to ask if you buy more horses for the winch," Chaka began, approaching Dacey. "Two have died with horse disease, and—"

"What do *you* know about horses, Kaffir?" Jed demanded unpleasantly. "I thought cattle was all you blacks knew—that and trying to get yourselves claims in a white man's mine."

As Chaka drew himself up, Dacey spoke warningly. "Jed, I believe we've had enough here at the mine for one day—at least I think you have. You're tired and angry, and that isn't good for the men. I'm going to have Bokembi take you home."

"The hell you are. There are two more hours of daylight."

"That may be so. But the wind is making everyone irritable, and there is no sense making the tension worse." Dacey tried to smile. "I'm sure you'll feel better after your bath and dinner . . ."

Jed began to double up his fists, but today Dacey was in no mood for his temper. She was tired, her backache gnawed at her with steady pain, and if they lost their workers, they'd be forced to close down. Word of Jed's temper had spread throughout the native sector.

She edged around the front of Jed's invalid chair, staying out of reach of the long, muscular arms that could snake out and grab her with lightning strength.

"Jed, you have lost the use of your legs, and my heart aches for you." She said it firmly. "But you don't have the right to antagonize our men. We need them. If they all quit, how will we get the diamonds out of the earth? That's why I'm wheeling you home right now. And you are going to stay at home until you can treat our people with decency."

She faced him defiantly, too tired now to care what Jed—or anyone else—thought.

Jed rubbed a hand through his unkempt beard. He glowered at her. "Dacey . . . damn you, I'll get you for this."

"No, Jed. You won't do anything to me at all, because if you do, I . . . I'll have Bokembi and Chaka strap you to your chair with bedsheets, and that is how you will spend your day, imprisoned in a straitjacket as if you were a lunatic."

She could not believe that she had really said such a terrible thing, but in this moment, she knew that she meant it. She saw Jed's face pale, then slowly turn an ugly brick red.

"What did you say, Dacey?"

"You heard me. I've had enough of your tempers and rages. I'm tired and I'm pregnant, and if I were to quit work here at the mine, it would all go. *I'm* the one who is keeping both of us afloat, Jed!"

She had said too much; Dacey knew it the moment the angry words flew out of her mouth. She was sickened to see Jed recoil as if she had slapped him. Yet both of them knew that she had spoken the truth.

Jed started to say something, then choked back the words. Slowly the color drained again out of his face, leaving it a sickly white. He bowed his head and grunted something that Dacey took to be assent. Then he motioned to Bokembi to come to take the chair.

Jed permitted Bokembi to wheel him home. His head was sunk down on his chest, as if all of the fight had been leached from his body. Walking beside him, Dacey felt worse than ever. She had threatened a helpless man, had used that helplessness against him. She felt sick with shame and vowed to herself that she would make it up to Jed somehow.

But he had to stop hitting and insulting the men . . .

When Jed was settled at home, Dacey walked back to the mine, intending to pay off the workers and give Chaka his percentage of the week's take. As she walked toward the sorting tables, she noticed that the mine site seemed oddly deserted for this time of day. Horses were tethered; picks, shovels, and barrows stood where they had been abandoned.

Something, she supposed, had happened. But Dacey felt too weary, too heartsick at the scene with Jed, to speculate on what it could have been. She walked heavily to the sorting tables and sat down in a camp chair to count out money for the workers.

Chaka came from around the long line of winches. "Mista Jed is safe at home, then?"

"Yes, he is trying to rest."

"He has the sickness that comes from anger, missy. He wants to strike out at the spirits that hurt him, but he does not know how to find them."

Dacey nodded, sorting the money into piles for each man. What were the spirits that haunted Jed? she wondered. Surely it was not only the accident that had brought them out. His anger had been in him, waiting, long before he had been hurt . . .

Abruptly her thoughts scattered as she was seized by a paroxysm of pain that clutched at her belly like an iron band. It seemed to last interminably, as if some huge, driving force was trying to split her body apart.

"Missy?" Chaka looked anxious.

The pain gripped her, carrying her with it. Then it faded away, as quickly as it had arrived, and Dacey slumped in the chair, her body soaked with perspiration. "It's . . . it's all right, Chaka."

"Your child," the African said. "It is coming, missy."

"Yes, perhaps. But many women have gone through this before, and it will go easy with me, Dr. Sowers said—"

But her words of reassurance, meant more for herself than for Chaka, were lost in the depths of another contraction, even harder and stronger than the last. Pain clawed at her abdomen, hardening it to rock. Dacey twisted and writhed, aware that a gush of liquid was now pouring down her legs.

"*Ai*, missy, the water. You will have that baby soon. Soon!"

"Yes," she panted, beyond all shame now. "Yes, I think I will. You must run to the hospital and get Dr. Sowers. Bring him here at once. And meanwhile, Chaka—drape the canvas around me in a small tent so that I will have privacy. I don't want to have my baby out in the open, like an animal."

Chaka's dark, kind face twisted. "Yes, missy, I make a tent. But it is not a good time to give birth. There has been a big cave-in at the Dutoitspan Mine. All the men are there. The doctors, missy, the nurses, they be there, too.''

"No, Chaka, no. There must be someone . . .'' She spoke with difficulty. ''A nurse . . . someone who could help me . . .''

"I go, then, missy. I go and see.'' Swiftly Chaka rearranged the canvas that shielded the sorting tables, making a crude enclosure. But by the time the canvas was safely around her, Dacey was beyond caring about it. She was impaled on a sharp sword of agony that twisted at her viciously.

Dacey did not know how long she lay twisting and moaning in the canvas lean-to, on the bare earth. The desert wind whipped particles of sand into the tent and into her eyes and hair. But she barely felt their sting; she was only aware of the pain, the contractions that gripped her, one after the other.

Earlier, she had talked to Bella about the birth, and the seamstress had assured her that her first labor would probably be long, that her pangs would begin as much as ten or fifteen minutes apart. There would be ample time for her to get to the hospital so that Dr. Sowers could attend her.

Apparently, Bella had been wrong. Her labor had begun hard and strong—even Dacey, novice as she was to motherhood, knew that. She needed help now. She rolled from side to side, choking back harsh cries. Would Chaka arrive in time with Dr. Sowers? What would she do if he did not?

But after a time, even that did not seem important. As Dacey uttered hoarse, panting screams, she felt her civilized veneer fall away. She was only a female animal, suffering something that she did not understand.

Time passed. Half an hour, perhaps longer. Suddenly there was a flare of sunlight inside the enclosure and Dacey became aware of a hand holding back the canvas.

"Dr. Sowers is at Dutoitspan Mine, missy. He is busy, all the nurses, too. But I brought help for you, I brought good help.''

Dacey could not move or reply. A huge fist of pain was crushing her down, splitting apart her bowels. For endless seconds it bent her to its power. Then, within seconds, it abated. Dacey moaned and looked toward the opening of the makeshift tent, where a woman crouched, silhouetted against the late sun. She had skin the color of cinnamon, hair that was a cloud of silky black.

Natala.

"You are birthing," Quinn's mistress said calmly.

"Yes . . . yes . . . oh, God, another one is coming . . ." Dacey stiffened, her eyes fastened on Natala's in appeal. For once she did not care that this was Quinn's woman, the mother of his child, her rival. At this moment they were only two women, and the fierce strength of the contraction would not allow Dacey any pride.

"Please," she whispered. "Please, Natala, help me."

Something flickered deep within Natala's smoky eyes. Then swiftly she knelt beside Dacey, supporting her to a sitting position.

"You must squat, Dacey—squat like an animal. Then the child will slide out easily with your next pain—and I will help by pushing it."

Dacey was too weak to rise by herself, so Natala helped her, pushing a chair near Dacey so she could clutch at it for support.

"*Ai*, you are not in hospital now; you are giving birth as black women do. Just do as I tell you."

Dacey groaned and bit down on her lip as another pang seized her. Finally she could not hold back a scream and she almost blacked out, half aware of Natala's hand on her belly, pressing downward.

The pain changed, became a flowing, a delivering. Dacey forgot about Natala and concentrated on the fiercely satisfying act of expelling the child from her womb. She gasped, she panted, she sobbed.

And then she heard a baby squall. Its cry rang out, lusty and strong.

"My baby? Is that my baby, Natala?" Dacey could scarcely believe it, how all the pain could slide away to be replaced with this wonder, this sense of joy and powerful accomplishment. Looking downward over the mound of her own body, Dacey saw Natala's hands move and then Natala lifted the child, holding it high.

"You have birthed a girl-child."

"Oh . . . a little girl . . ." Dacey felt soft, weak, suffused with happiness. "My baby, oh, Natala, please, let me hold her."

Natala glanced down at the child she held, a curious expression, almost of hatred, crossing her face. Instead of handing the infant to Dacey, she continued to hold it, rocking back and forth.

"*You.*" The beam of sunlight that streamed into the lean-to caught Natala across the cheek and temple, glowing against her skin. "You are a white woman, weak and pale. Women like you do not belong in Africa. The air is not right for you, nor do the spirits like you."

What was Natala saying? Why didn't she hand her the baby? Dacey felt woozy, floating on a soft cloud of relief that her torment was finally over. She yearned to cradle her child, to hold it close to her breast. Odd, how the sun seemed to pick out the exotic features of Natala's face, turning her eyes into gold, her demeanor into that of a priestess.

"I would like to hold my little girl, Natala. Please . . . give her to me."

Still Natala did not relinquish the infant. Her golden eyes blazed. "You should leave Africa. *Ai*, if you do not, then a curse will fall on you. Your life will be as barren as the veld after many months without rain, as dry as a rock that has been scoured clean by the wind . . ."

Was it a dream, the strange, curselike words that Natala uttered? Dacey stirred groggily. "*Please.* I want my baby."

At last she felt the infant being laid gently on her belly.

"She is healthy." Natala's voice was brisk and it seemed to come from very far away. "You must make the infusion I gave you if the fever comes—do not forget. I will wait for the afterbirth, and then I will go."

"But—"

"I will go soon."

Dacey drifted into a fitful sleep, lulled by the erratic sound of the wind that flapped at the canvas. She cradled the infant close to her body, shielding it as best she could from the blowing sand.

When she opened her eyes, Natala had gone and dusk had fallen. It was hot and close inside the tent. Where was Chaka? Had she been left alone here, at the deserted mine site?

"You should leave Africa. . . . If you do not, then a curse will fall on you. . . ." Had Natala really said such an incredible thing to her? Or had it only been a dream, the product of stress and pain? Already Dacey's memory was blurring over the birth itself and all that had happened.

As she struggled to sit up, balancing the infant carefully, she heard the crunch of feet on gravel and the soft chatter of African voices.

"Missy." Chaka pulled open the lean-to flap. "I brought men to carry you back to your house. You ride on long piece of canvas rolled over wood. Soft journey for Missy."

"Chaka. Oh, Chaka." Tears spilled out of Dacey's eyes, easy, ridiculous tears of relief that she wasn't alone here, that it was finally over. Beside her, the infant made soft noises.

"You lie still, missy. I do all the work, we have you home quick."

Beside Dacey, the baby stirred, waving its tiny hands, tinted pink. Dacey touched the miniature fingers in wonderment, marveling at the perfection of her child. Already, she thought, the infant was pretty, her nose uptilted and perfect, her eyes large.

"I'm going to name you Elizabeth," she whispered. "After my mother. Would you like that name? Do you think it suits you?"

The baby cooed, as if in response.

But before Chaka, Bokembi, and the others could get the stretcher out of the lean-to, Dacey heard more voices and looked up to see Quinn push aside the canvas.

"Dacey . . . My God, are you all right?"

Her heart gave a joyous leap. "I had the baby, Quinn . . . I had a little girl!"

"I see you did." His voice broke. "I came as soon as I could, as soon as Natala told me."

Dacey held up the tiny girl for inspection, and there was a moment of silence while Quinn's eyes drank in the oval face, the rosebud mouth and tiny nose, the slate-colored eyes and wispy dark hair.

"She is beautiful, Dacey, just like you." Quinn's voice sounded thick. "Her nose is a perfect little bud. Her hair . . . her eyes . . ."

While the Africans readied the stretcher, Quinn and Dacey gazed at each other, their glances intense. Dacey felt as if she were swimming in the love that flowed between them, a love so warm, so rich, that it was like a living thing. Was the child Quinn's daughter? Dacey felt sure that she was, she knew it, believed it now, with every instinct of her body. And she sensed that Quinn felt the same. They did not have to say it, the knowledge sang between them.

Quinn leaned forward to touch her, and they murmured to each other, soft words, little ones that made no sense, yet meant everything. Dacey had to blink back stinging tears. She knew that if she lived to be ninety years old, there would never be a moment of greater joy for her than this. To be encircled in Quinn's arms, to hold their daughter, the child they had made together, of their love . . .

Quinn's smile was soft. He leaned forward and planted a gentle kiss on Dacey's cheek, the brush of his lips sweet. "Hey, no tears. This is supposed to be a happy moment, Dacey."

"It is, oh, it is. If only . . ." But she could not allow herself to mar their moment with regrets.

"Darling Dacey, you were very brave to give birth like this, alone here at the mine. I don't know why Natala left you here as she did—I apologize deeply for her behavior. I'll see to it that the men get you home safely. Then I'll go and find Bella Garvey. I'm sure you'll want a nurse, and I think she'd be just the one."

"Yes. Oh, thank you . . ."

Abruptly Dacey felt weak again. Some of the joy seeped from her as Chaka and Quinn carefully moved her onto the makeshift stretcher.

She had to go home now, to Jed, her husband, the legal father of the child to whom she had just given birth. Would Jed be disappointed that he did not have a son?

But she felt too tired to care. They had a beautiful daughter. And she wanted only to hang on to this moment, the few brief minutes when Quinn would be with her, walking alongside the stretcher.

Quinn Farris had to tear himself away from Dacey, from the pale, yet incredibly lovely face that gazed up at him from the stretcher, the tears dried now on her cheeks.

Regret, anger, and love filled him as he turned and strode down the path that led to his mistress' hut. How beautiful Dacey was in her motherhood, how vulnerable. More than anything on earth, he wanted to go with her, take care of her, see that she lacked for nothing.

But he could not do that. She was not his woman, she belonged to another man.

Quinn slammed a fist into the palm of his hand, almost rejoicing at the savage pain this gave him. The infant that Dacey cradled in his arms was his. Something about the way Dacey had looked at him, some tender set of her mouth, convinced him that this was true. So now he had two daughters, Lilah, and this child, this new baby with her delicate beauty.

The sun had already set, but there remained a faint afterglow, splashes of purple and lilac fading into gray. Quinn narrowed his eyes at the sky, fighting back a surge of anger. Fate had played a bitter prank on him. Given him Dacey, taught him to love her when he had not believed that such love was possible, bequeathed him another child. But, in giving those things, it had also mockingly taken them away again.

For he already had a wife to whom he was legally bound, whose taunts still rang in his head, spurring him on to work. A mistress to whom he was morally obligated, another daughter who, by her very existence, pulled at his heart.

And Dacey had Jed, a helpless man dependent on her . . .

He had reached Natala's thatched hut. Through the open door he saw the glow of an oil lamp, the blaze of a cookfire. She saw him at once and turned.

"Where have you been?" she demanded, her face distorted with anger.

"Where do you think? You delivered Dacey's baby, then

left her alone, with none but Africans to help her." Fury thickened Quinn's voice.

"She did not need any further help. I did what I could. Did you not tell me never to harm her? I obeyed you, Quinn."

With a swift, seductive gesture, Natala released the clasp of her dashiki, allowing it to fall to the floor. Beneath it she was naked. Her body was pagan, flawless.

Quinn stared at the smooth, lush skin. He felt no desire, nothing but a dulled pain.

"No, Natala. Put your clothes back on. I will not make love to you tonight."

He saw shock fill her face. But instantly she covered the emotion and drew herself up, her eyes blazing at him. "Is it her? Is it that pale Englishwoman you think about, who drives you away from me? She is ugly, ugly!"

But Quinn, thinking of Dacey, could not respond. He felt sickened by Natala's jealousy. He turned on his heel and left, striding quickly down the path.

"You will be back!" Natala screamed after him. "I will make a spell, a potion . . . you'll see, Quinn! My magic is strong!"

12

THE NEW BABY REIGNED IN the small house like a queen, surrounded by the gifts she had been given. Among them was an elaborate pram from London, shipped in by Papa at fabulous expense.

Lavinia brought a doll, larger than Elizabeth herself, whose china eyes stared at the world with calm contemplation. Chaka gave the baby a delicate ivory carving of a springbok. With smiles and much shrugging, Chaka admitted that he had done the carving himself.

Other gifts poured in: from miners on adjoining claims, from Royce McKinnon, who sent a bolt of fine cambric. Quinn gave Elizabeth a tiny diamond pendant.

The days slid by, one after another, as Dacey struggled to cope with the demands of her new life. Elizabeth, although healthy, was colicky. For the first five weeks of her existence, it seemed to Dacey that she did little but scream, jerking her little body and glaring at Dacey as if this were all her fault.

Dacey walked the floor with her. She patted the baby's little belly, rubbed her back, cooed, and sang, all to no avail.

"Eh, dearie, it's nothing to worry about," Bella consoled. She came every day to cheer Dacey, and to instruct Makema in the art of laundering diapers and infant gowns. "Babes sense tension in the air, that's all. God knows there is plenty of that around here."

"Oh—" Dacey flushed. Elizabeth was napping and Jed was off at the mine, so she and Bella were alone.

"Dacey, you have lost ten pounds since that child was born, ten pounds you couldn't afford to lose, and you look as pale as milk pudding," Bella scolded. "I know she keeps you up at night, but I suspect that isn't all, is it?"

Dacey hesitated, saying nothing.

"Is it that husband of yours? I know he wanted a boy, but surely he's over that by now."

Dacey mustered a smile. "Oh, he did complain at first and talked about wanting a son to take over the mine someday. Then I discovered him holding Elizabeth while she cried. Telling her that as soon as she was old enough, he'd show her the sorting tables and let her find a diamond as big as her hand."

Bella grinned. "Eh, then, he's coming around, most men do." Still, the dressmaker gave Dacey a shrewd look. "Is it what Jed *cannot* do that is bothering him?"

Dacey went red. "Oh, Bella! Before the accident, I refused Jed my bed because of—well, because of certain reasons I can't talk about. He swore to me then that after the baby came, he would fill my belly with children and keep me home, too busy to work at the mine."

Bella looked angry. "I see. And now, because of his condition, he is unable to carry out his 'threat,' and he blames you."

Shamefacedly, Dacey ducked her head.

"Eh, men! What problems do they not give us? But at least you will be spared having a dozen children clinging to your skirts and sapping your strength. . . . You must try to find a blessing in this, Dacey. There is always one, if you look for it."

The days continued to pass, marked off by Elizabeth's growth from a newborn to a sturdy four-month-old who had begun to smile, whose wispy hair now formed an adorable dark curl on the top of her head. The screaming spells had stopped. Now Elizabeth was cooing and happy, and Dacey doted on her, begrudging every moment that she had to leave her baby with Bella while she went to work at the Kimberley Mine.

One day Lavinia came to visit, bringing theater gossip. In the months since her own marriage, Lavinia had become a smooth young matron. She wore dark gowns trimmed with layers of braid and flounce and had gained at least fifteen pounds. Her eyes seemed sharp, bright, and determined.

"Oh, Dacey, you are so *out* of what has been happening in town," she chattered. "There was another diamond-theft scandal, with two men sent to prison in Cape Town for life . . . *life*, Dacey, can you imagine it, and they kept swearing their innocence, only no one would believe them. And then, at the Royal we have had several hits, and there was a scandal when a girl we brought in for a revue ran off to marry a digger. Tony was so angry I thought he would burst a vein. I had to fill in for her," Lavinia added complacently. "I did very well, too."

Dacey smiled, suppressing a pang. Her own days on the stage seemed very far away now.

"But I am a solidly married woman now," Lavinia went on. "And I am insisting that we remodel the theater. We plan to import enough bricks to build a facade in front of the building. They are costly, but the town is changing, Dacey. Some of us intend to live in style someday. Don't you agree that we should?"

As Lavinia paused for breath, Dacey served a slice of yellow pound cake, heaped with whipped cream and slices of mango. Lavinia attacked the cake with gusto, dabbing at her mouth with a napkin.

"Are you aware, Dacey," she remarked after a moment, "that your husband is causing gossip in town these days, too?"

Dacey, in the act of pouring tea, paused, startled. "Jed? Causing gossip?"

"Why, yes. Don't you ever *hear* anything? Don't you even know what your own husband is doing? That's really why I came here today, to make sure that you did know."

"I see." Dacey lowered the teapot and gazed at her friend. "I think you had better tell me, Lavinia."

"Well. Everyone knows, of course, what he's like at the mines. Shouting at the men, hitting their legs with his stick—why *does* he insist on carrying it, Dacey? But this is different."

"How is it different? Please, Lavinia, will you tell me what this is all about?"

Lavinia pushed away her empty plate. "It's very simple, Dacey. Everyone knows there was a native woman involved in Jed's accident. Now he has sworn revenge against her. There are whispers that he's been forcing that servant of his to take him into the native sector while he searches for her."

"I . . . I see." Dacey sat, stunned. It was true that Jed sometimes was gone from the house in the evenings for long stretches of time, with Bokembi to push his chair. Dacey had assumed that he was frequenting the saloons again. She could not begrudge him this small pleasure, so she had said nothing.

"But there's more, Dacey! Last night, he actually found a girl. And he beat her, beat her within an inch of her life, they say."

"*What?*"

Lavinia's eyes glistened with the pleasure of being the first to deliver this news. "Dr. Sowers treated her at the hospital. He said it is amazing that Jed could do so much damage with a stick. Fortunately, Bokembi managed to stop him before he killed her. But here is the terrible part. She says she wasn't even in town when Jed was hurt. She says she was with her tribe in . . . oh, in Tswana or someplace like that."

The gossip network in Kimberley was intricate and detailed, surprisingly accurate.

"My God," Dacey whispered. She felt nausea well up inside her, along with a dreadful, gripping fear.

"Dacey? Dacey, are you all right? You look so pale. Did I say the wrong thing?"

"No . . . no, I'm all right, Lavinia. I'm glad you came to me with this." Dacey rose to her feet, steadying herself. In the other room, she could hear Elizabeth babble to herself as she awakened from her nap. "But, please, Lavinia, I have to know. What is the black woman's name?"

"Now, really, Dacey . . ."

"I must know her name."

"It is Setenga, then, I think that's what they say. She is Zulu, I think, and not even a prostitute, but a wife. She came here to be with her—"

But Dacey was not listening anymore. She made her excuses and waved Lavinia out of the door. Then quickly she scooped up Elizabeth to deliver into the care of Bella. Finally, her heart slamming fiercely in her throat, she ran to the Kimberley hospital.

A nursing sister told her that Setenga had been treated and released. Native patients were not kept in the hospital.

"But where? Where is she now?" Dacey demanded to know.

The woman shrugged. "Who knows? These people come and go, they shift and move about. It is quite hopeless to keep track of them, they are as ignorant as children."

"They are not children, they are people," Dacey snapped.

But the nurse's face had gone blank, and Dacey did not want to waste time arguing. She turned on her heel and left, hurrying into the native streets. Already there was talk of building compounds to house the native workers. These would be vast enclosures surrounded by a double barrier of corrugated iron, with a horizontal grating running outward several yards to prevent objects from being thrown out of the compound. Workers would spend their entire lives in the compound, when they were not working. This, Dacey knew, was an angry reaction against the illicit diamond thefts and against the blacks who dared to try to buy claims in the mines.

Now she shivered as she hurried past the beginnings of one compound, thinking that the construction was only one more symbol of the white man's contempt for the black.

Asking directions, she was at last directed to a shabby lean-to made of tattered canvas, little better than a hovel. Inside, two women tended a girl who lay prostrate on a blanket, her body a mass of welts.

Dacey gasped, staring down at the prone girl. Jed had done this. All along, she had been hoping that Lavinia had exaggerated, that town gossip had woven a fabric of half-truth.

But these bruises were real. And in their shape, Dacey could actually see the contours of Jed's stick, the discolorations exactly its width.

She struggled to contain her anger, searching for something to say.

"I . . . I am Mrs. Jed Donohue. I have come to see if you are all right, to see if you need anything."

Setenga's eyes did not register comprehension. Two tears trickled down her cheeks, among the bruises. Once, she had been a pretty girl, with the clean, almost Semitic features that some Africans possessed, the result of inbreeding with Arab slave traders generations ago. Probably when the bruises faded, Setenga would again be pretty. But for now she was beaten and battered, and Dacey felt sick that Jed could have done this.

"Do you speak English?" she asked when Setenga continued to stare at her blankly. "Do any of you?"

"I speak," said one of the other women. She was middle-aged, with the long, pendulous breasts of a woman who has suckled ten or more children.

Dacey moistened her lips. "Will you ask Setenga, then, what happened? Why did he do this to her?"

The woman spoke to the injured girl, who responded in a high, clear voice. The middle-aged woman translated laboriously.

"She say she saw white man in chair with wheels. He pulled at her clothes, then he began to hit her with stick. She cried and tried to run, but fell. The boy who push the chair, he pull the man off Setenga. The man say Setenga push him out of a window. But this is not true. She was not even here then. She has only been in this place—" The woman counted on her fingers. "Seven suns. Seven suns, no more."

The story was confused, but its import was clear enough to Dacey. Jed had struck out at an innocent girl, one who had nothing to do with his accident. She felt a sharp, corroding anger as she reached into her money purse for a roll of pound notes.

"Here, this is for you." She pressed the bills into the Zulu girl's hands. "I know it's not enough—nothing can be. But please use it to buy food, or poultices for your bruises, whatever you need.''

Leaving the native area, Dacey walked directly to the Kimberley Mine. She found Jed in his chair, sweat running freely from his face as he labored over chunks of diamond earth. Beside him the Africans worked in silent concentration, a marked contrast to the other sorting areas, where the men joked, laughed, and talked in their native tongues.

"Jed!" Dacey could scarcely control her fury. "I must talk to you at once."

He looked up. "Can't it wait, Dacey? I'm busy now, we have just brought a good load of dirt to the tables, maybe the best we've seen in months. I want this to be done right."

Dacey stepped forward, grasping the bar at the back of Jed's chair. Furiously she shoved the chair over the rutted ground until they were alone.

"Jed, I have just come from the native streets where I saw a girl named Setenga. She is covered with bruises from head to toe—bruises that you gave to her."

Jed scowled. "Yes, and I only wish I'd done more, the Kaffir bitch! I'll get her for doing this to me, for leaving me without legs. I'll fix her."

"Jed, she isn't the one who did it. She wasn't even *in* Kimberley when you were hurt, she . . ." Abruptly Dacey's anger flowed out of her, to be replaced by sick despair. "Oh, Jed. Jed . . . I don't know what really happened to you that night. I'll probably never know. But you must stop thinking about it now. Stop brooding—and *let it go*, Jed."

He stared up at her, his eyes reddened by the mine dust and perhaps by tears. "I can't."

"You've got to! Oh, Jed, what if you'd killed that girl? If she'd been white and you'd done that to her, someone would have horsewhipped you, or you'd have been sent to prison in Cape Town to work on the breakwater. But because she is a native, you got away with it."

To Dacey, this fact seemed wrenchingly shameful. She watched Jed gaze down at his lap, where his still hugely muscled arms lay lax, his thick fingers twisting together. He said nothing.

"Jed," she began, "I'm going to give Bokembi strict orders that he's never to take you to the native sector again."

"All right."

"I'm sorry, I really am. But I swear it: if you ever hurt another woman again, I . . . I'll do something awful to you, Jed. I mean it!"

"You'd threaten a crippled man in a chair, wouldn't you, Dacey?" Jed's voice cracked. "You'd humiliate me, you'd—"

"Stop it. I'm going to find Bokembi now, Jed, I'm going to give him his orders. And that will be the end of the matter. Do you understand me?"

She waited, shaking, for his answer.

"Yes," he muttered at last. "I understand you, all right."

After her ultimatum to Jed, Dacey felt sickened to the core—both at Jed for the dreadful thing he had done, and at herself for again using his helplessness to threaten and control him.

But what else, she asked herself in anguish, could she have done? If Jed could beat a woman, then he *wasn't* entirely helpless. And he could not be allowed to hurt innocent people, no matter how much he himself suffered.

And Dacey knew that Jed did suffer. His moods ranged from petulant rage to dull apathy. Some days he did not go to the mine at all, but would sit on the veranda, playing with Elizabeth or talking to her in a monotone. At night Dacey often heard him sob or mutter to himself. What did he say when he thought that no one else could hear him? What was happening to her husband?

She went to the hospital and got laudanum for him. Although Jed at first refused the dosage, eventually he consented to take it three times daily. The sedative calmed him, blunting his rage and giving his eyes a curiously blank expression. Jed's burnished sunburn began to fade, and his curly beard showed a few gray hairs. But he was quieter. The sound of sobbing came from the bedroom less often now.

In this respite, Dacey made up her mind to build a larger house. She and Jed needed more privacy, and Elizabeth badly needed room to play. She began sketching her ideas, deciding

on a facade constructed of brick. She also wanted a big
veranda, with pillars and pediments, where climbing roses could
cast shadows of bloom.

Outside, she would plant the Australian blue-gum trees that
they had received as a wedding gift. There would even be a
playhouse for Elizabeth, a miniature Victorian mansion complete in every detail. It would be the sort of toy house that
Dacey herself had always dreamed of owning.

She threw herself into the house plans, using them as an
escape from her private anguish, the thoughts of Quinn that
still came to torment her.

Quinn. How he haunted her! Yet, since Elizabeth's birth,
she had seen almost nothing of him, and when she did, it was
strictly on a business basis. Grimly she forced her feelings for
him into the darkest, most faraway corner of her mind,
knowing that this was her only choice. To dwell on her love
for him, to bring out her memories, her regrets, was too
painful.

He had been a brief part of her life, the best part, he had
made her happy, he had shown her a joy that she had not
known was possible.

But now she was married to Jed. The responsibility of her
husband weighed heavily, and Dacey knew she could not
afford to think of what was finished. Didn't Quinn have his
own obligations, his own life? She must not interfere with
that. And she knew that he was busier than ever as he
amassed his own riches, rapidly becoming one of the most
powerful men in Kimberley.

Each of them, it seemed, had gone separate ways. And
maybe, Dacey assured herself with choking pain, it was all
for the best.

Life went on. Dacey had sent Natala a bolt of Japanese silk
in a deep rose-pink color, in thanks for her help in delivering
Elizabeth. For long months, she heard nothing. Then one day
she glimpsed Quinn's mistress in the Market Square, her
dark, sultry beauty the focus of many stares.

The two women regarded each other, Natala in a native
cloth of dark orange that pointed up the lush cinnamon of her

skin. Dacey had Elizabeth with her, in the pram that Papa had given her, and Natala looked sharply at the little girl.

"Her hair is very black. She does not look like you."

Dacey felt uncomfortable. "Yes, I believe that Elizabeth will be a brunette."

"*Brunette*. I do not know that word." Natala's eyes flashed as again she stared at Elizabeth. "*Ai*, her skin is too pale, see how it reddens in the sun."

All too aware of the bridge of freckles across her own nose, Dacey adjusted the child's bonnet, and then her own. Hostility seemed to come from Natala like a cloud. Dacey managed a response, relieved when Natala finally nodded to her and disappeared into the throng of shoppers again.

More days and weeks passed. One Sunday, Dacey and Jed had just come from church. Made sleepy by the long service in the stiflingly hot tent, Jed napped in the bedroom, while Dacey sat at the table pouring over detailed sketches for their home. Elizabeth crawled on the floor, and a trio of the persistent African flies buzzed near the ceiling.

Patting away a yawn, Dacey heard a rap at the door. Reluctantly she put the sketches aside and got up to admit her caller.

It was Natala, striding regally into the room clad in a gown made of the silk that Dacey had given her. The deep pink was stunning against the dark beauty of Natala's skin. Rows of flounces were trimmed with glass beads, giving the dress a glittering effect that would have been at home in any *salon* in Europe. And Dacey did not miss the diamond bracelet that shimmered at Natala's wrist, prisms of gems catching the light.

"Do you like it?" Natala preened herself, turning so that Dacey could see the back demitrain, lavishly trimmed with more beads. She was like a child, totally enthralled with what she wore. "I sewed it myself; it took much, much time."

"You did it *yourself*?" Dacey thought of the endless hours of hand sewing and tried in vain to imagine the sultry Natala at such a task.

"Missionaries taught me to sew, and this is a European dress fit for the theater or anywhere else," Natala explained proudly. "When I wear it, everyone will look at me. That is why I sewed on the beads. They have much magic, and I have sewed more magic into the hem."

Magic, in a dress? Dacey stared at her visitor and finally remembered her manners. "Could I offer you some cakes or tea?"

"I do not eat cakes. But I will drink some tea."

In a moment Dacey returned with the tea, and they sat down for an uneasy talk. Why had Natala come here? Dacey wondered. To show off the gown, to gloat over possession of the diamond bracelet, which Quinn had probably given her? Despite her arresting beauty, Natala seemed to possess a kind of primitive directness.

They chatted, of a fever that had been going about the town, of a measles epidemic that had killed several local children. Then Natala fished inside a small, beaded bag and brought out a root that she handed to Dacey. She instructed her to boil it into a tea for Elizabeth.

But still Dacey sensed that the purpose of the visit had not yet been accomplished.

At last Natala rose. "I must go, there is work to do in my herb garden." She held up her glittering wrist. "Did you see my bracelet? Quinn gave it to me."

Yes, Natala had come to gloat. Dacey forced herself to look at the diamonds cooly. "They are lovely," she murmured.

"Yes." Then, to her surprise, anger distorted Natala's features. "But not as lovely as the ones he is saving for *her*."

"For her?"

"*Ai*, I have seen them in the safe at his office. Many, many more diamonds, large ones, each more than twenty carats in weight. Each stone is perfect."

As Dacey caught her breath, Natala walked sullenly to the door, the silken folds of her gown making soft noises. "He is collecting those diamonds for his *wife*. He is going to give her a necklace. It will be so heavy that it sags off her neck, he says, so beautiful that kings and queens will envy it."

Dacey struggled to contain her shock. She felt her heart pound in thick, uneven beats, the blood throbbing in her temples. A necklace made of large, rare, beautiful stones . . . and Quinn planned to give it to Janine, his wife.

Why?

She knew there could be only one reason: Quinn still loved his wife. Hoped to use the necklace to win back her love.

That was why Natala was so angry now, why she had come here—because she, too, was jealous, and she wished Dacey to suffer along with her.

"I suppose he has worked very hard to find those diamonds," she heard herself say.

"*Ai,* indeed. He works from the rising of the sun to its setting, and thinks of nothing else."

"I can imagine." Dacey hardened her heart. If Quinn wanted his American wife, or Natala, or any other woman, then he could have them, she thought furiously. She'd been a fool—a fool ever to love him.

As Natala turned to leave, they heard a sound from the bedroom, and then Jed wheeled his chair into the room.

"Dacey, have you someone here?" He said it pettishly, his voice thickened with sleep.

"Why, yes, Jed, I have . . ." Dacey turned to introduce Natala and was surprised to see that the other was already halfway down the front path, gliding away from the house in a silken swish of fabric.

Jed scowled, staring after her. He blinked his eyes, as if to put them in focus. "Funny. But she looks familiar to me . . . and that voice . . ." Then he shook his head. "No, she can't be the one."

"What are you talking about, Jed?"

"Why, the whore, the Kaffir whore. For a minute I almost thought—"

Then Jed smacked his hands down on the wheels of his chair and turned it, rolling it back into the bedroom. Numbly, Dacey turned away. Quinn was saving diamonds to make into a necklace for his wife. Someday he would take it to Janine and use it to win her back. What other explanation could there possibly be?

She sank down at the table, the lines of the house plans blurring before her eyes.

SECTION TWO

1876

13

"MAMA, ARE WE GOING TO buy me a new dress? With lace, like yours?"

Beside Dacey, small Elizabeth danced up and down, in anticipation of their shopping trip.

"Of course, darling. First we will buy the bolt of material. Would you like a nice, checked gingham? Pink . . . yes, that would look very nice with your dark hair."

Dacey had to bend down to talk to her daughter, now a grown-up three years old, with masses of black, curly hair like Quinn's. Elizabeth's eyes, as well, had turned the exact deep blue of Quinn's.

It seemed obvious to Dacey, if not to Jed, that Quinn was the little girl's father. In a hundred ways, the child resembled him, from her slightly cleft chin, to her delicately straight brows. And it was plain, even to a casual onlooker, that when Elizabeth reached womanhood she was going to be very beautiful. Her fair, translucent skin, her perfectly formed features, all were exquisite.

Now, as they trotted along to Bella's, Elizabeth chattered happily about the visit. "Will Bella give us cakes?"

"Why, I imagine so. But, darling, you mustn't *ask* for them—"

"I want sponge cake, Mama! Sponge cake with strawberry preserves!"

"We'll have to see what Bella has planned." Dacey was

unable to help smiling at the pretty, vivacious child who hopped and skipped beside her.

It was a day of clear blue sky and fitful breezes. As they started down the walk, Dacey turned to look back at the house, now two years old, that she had built at the edge of Kimberley. A facade of clay brick hid the corrugated iron, and fast-growing blue-gums and beefwood trees had already begun to shoot up, providing shade. Elizabeth's playhouse stood in the back garden by an Aleppo pine. Here the child played with Kathryn, the doll that Lavinia had given her when she was born.

As they walked, Dacey thought about the years that had passed. They had been bittersweet ones, full of joy and pain. The joy was Elizabeth, the always-deep pleasure that she found with her daughter.

And the pain had been Quinn, her knowledge that the love she had for him was hopeless, doomed. There were many nights when Dacey had slept restlessly, caught in a traitorous dream of being held in Quinn's arms. Days when, walking to the mine, she saw a man who looked like him, freezing her heart. How strange and bitter that a pair of blue eyes, a confident easy way of walking, a pair of broad shoulders, a smile, could still haunt her so persistently. . . .

Another source of great pain for her had been Chaka's death. By 1874, the Kimberley Mine had contained 430 claims. As the crater was dug ever deeper, the softer rocks on the edge of the volcanic pipe crumbled. The walkways that separated the claims began to collapse. Chaka was killed late one winter afternoon when a rockfall slid down the west face of the excavation. It took four hours to dig his body out of the debris.

Dacey was distraught. She had grown to depend on Chaka—not only as an employee, but as a friend. It was Chaka who had offered her food and water on her first day at the mine. Chaka who helped when Elizabeth was born, who had taken abuse from Jed cheerfully, who had been scrupulously honest, enabling Dacey to earn thousands of pounds from her claims and Jed's.

It was Chaka who had dreamed of owning his own claim, of sharing equally in the diamond riches.

How could she ever pay him back for all that he had done? After much thought, Dacey finally hired an ox wagon and made the long trek over the veld to Chaka's family village in Namaqualand. With her she brought a small herd of cattle to give to his family, who, she knew, considered cattle the greatest riches of all.

That year, the winter rains had been profuse. Dacey was stunned to see the dry veld transformed into a spectacular carpet of flowers, stretching out as far as she could see. There was the orange Namaqualand daisy, and splashes of white, yellow, purple, and red, a display so awe-inspiring that it brought tears to Dacey's eyes.

The blooming of the veld, she had been told, was rare. Yet it had happened now, just when she was feeling most heartsick. Did God somehow wish to show her the beauty of life, to ease some of the ache in her heart?

She didn't know. She could only walk through the vast, scented fields of flowers, allowing them to lift up her spirits. If such beauty could exist, without apparent reason, then maybe her life, too, could hold happiness.

She returned home from Namaqualand feeling cleansed and heartened, ready to work harder than ever. And she knew that hard work was going to be necessary. It was going to be difficult, if not impossible, to replace Chaka. Then, too, the friable, yellow diamond earth was at last petering out. Beneath it was a layer of dark blue rock that the miners considered barren.

That year, an angry depression had settled over Kimberley as diggers gathered on corners and in the Market Square to argue. Was the blue ground sterile? Was the diamond boom nearly over?

To make matters worse, the steady flow of diamonds from Kimberley had affected the world market. Prices were dropping steadily. Men like Quinn Farris and Cecil Rhodes claimed that the miners had to band together and control the output of stones, or diamonds would become as common as eggs, their price nearly as low.

It was a controversial topic. The individualistic miners—who already hated the idea of blacks owning claims—bristled at the idea of *any* group getting control of the mines. Rhodes's ideas were stubbornly resisted.

Jed was among those discouraged. "It's no use, Dacey," he told her. "We can't pull diamonds out of that blue ground! It's so hard and dense that you can't work it by hand, and there aren't any diamonds in it anyway."

"But, Jed, the geologists say—"

"I don't care what the geologists say. I know I'm right. Letting the black Kaffirs work the claims alongside us was a jinx. They never should have been allowed in—not as owners. *They* are the cause of our bad luck!"

"Oh, Jed, you know that's nonsense. Chaka wanted to own a claim, and he was a fine man. You know that."

"He was killed by a rockfall, wasn't he? Along with six other men, white ones? Who's to say he didn't bring them bad luck? The men are angry. Some of them are going home, and I'm beginning to wonder," Jed added heavily, "if we shouldn't be among them."

Shock had rippled through Dacey. This wasn't like Jed, to sit passively in his chair, telling her that he wanted to give up. *She* had no intention of quitting—not now, not after all they had been through.

"Jed, I think you're very wrong," she began. "I was in the Market Square yesterday, and I heard Cecil Rhodes talking—"

"Rhodes! That college boy, traveling back and forth to Oxford, reading books, talking world politics. What would he know? Who'd listen to him?"

"I would. He says that the blue ground is going to prove even richer than the yellow, and I believe him."

"Don't be a fool. Better think about selling the house while we still can, and getting out of here."

Dacey lifted her chin. "Get out? But where, Jed? Where would we go?"

"Farther north. We'll look for diamonds somewhere else. Namaqualand, maybe. Or Botswana, the Transvaal. Or maybe we'll go back to Boston. We'll start up a shop, maybe a haberdashery. I always wanted to run a store, we can call the place Cripple Jed's.''

"*Jed*!'' Dacey hated the whining self-pity that Jed could assume sometimes.

Her husband wheeled his chair close to her, bringing it to a stop just a fraction of an inch away from Dacey's skirt. He glared at her. ''I'll say what I damn well want, Dacey. I was fool enough to let you and that Kaffir work my claims. Now look what's happened. The diamond days are over, why won't you admit it?''

''I won't admit it, Jed, because I don't think they are. And I'm going to prove it to you.''

The next day, Dacey dressed carefully in a stylish dress of toast-colored poplin with a matching bonnet and went to pay a call on Cecil Rhodes.

The young diamond magnate received her in his office on Natal Street. The room was utterly spartan, its furniture made of native woods, the lighting consisting of candles thrust into beer bottles. Dacey smelled the odor of curry and wondered if Rhodes slept here too. He had the reputation of being extremely frugal.

''Hello, Mrs. Donohue, what brings you here to my office? Do you have a sight of diamonds to show me?''

A ''sight'' was a large bag of mixed stones sold as a group.

''No, that's not the reason I've come. You see, I overheard you talking the other day in the square, and—well, I want to talk about the blue ground.''

Rhodes gave her his dry smile. ''Do you mean the so-called barren earth? If you heard me, then you know my opinion already. That ground is anything but barren. It's full of riches.''

''Yes, and I agree with you.'' Dacey's voice rose excitedly. ''I *know* there are diamonds in there, Mr. Rhodes, I've gone to look at that earth, I feel it. The only trouble is,'' she went on, more to herself than to him, ''I have to figure out what to do next. The diggers are discouraged, they are beginning to sell their claims at a loss . . .'' She looked up at the diamond man. ''Mr. Rhodes, would you advance me a loan?''

"A loan?"

"Yes, the two-claim restriction has already been abolished, and soon, I think, even the ten-claim limit will go. I want to be ready. I'm going to buy up to the limit. I want to form my own mining company."

Rhodes lifted an eyebrow. "Indeed?"

"Yes, I'll call it the Elizabeth Mining Company, after my daughter. I need the loan because I want to send to England now for some heavy equipment."

"What sort of equipment?" Rhodes's eyes regarded her sharply.

"Crushers, agitators, big machines to work the earth. Once, when I was friends with Quinn Farris"—Dacey flushed and hurried on—"he told me about silver mining in Nevada. Always, it was the same way in the American West. First the small miners would come in, working the claims by hand. Gradually they were bought out by bigger operators, who installed heavy mechanical equipment. *They* made the real money, not the small diggers."

"I see. And is this what you have in mind for yourself, Mrs. Donohue?"

"Yes." Boldly Dacey looked Rhodes in the eye. "Can you help me?"

"Perhaps. But there will be certain, ah, strings attached. I am working for political power in Kimberley, and eventually in the Cape Province as well, perhaps even farther than that. I will need allies, people to stand by me, on whom I can depend."

"I will be your ally," Dacey said slowly.

"Good. Then it is agreed." Rhodes reached out and shook her hand, his grip firm and dry.

With the loan began a period of intense work for Dacey. She was on her own now—flung into a world of hostile men, miners who cursed her as she bought out their holdings, telling her that she was being a fool.

"It's over, girl, can't you see that? Diamonds in Kimberley are finished; that blue ground is as dry as the Kalahari Desert," one man told her, spitting on the ground in a gesture of contempt. "Me, I'm going back to Chicago. Never should have come here anyway."

Dacey watched him walk away with her money in his pocket, feeling a stab of self-doubt. Were Jed and the others right? Was she doing the right thing, risking everything they owned by buying up claims?

Dacey was realist enough to know that if the mines really did run dry here, then Kimberley would become a ghost town within weeks. Flooded with water, buffeted by the desert winds, only the huge mine pits would remain as a monument to man's greed.

But that blue ground *is* going to be profitable, she assured herself fiercely. It will be, it has to be!

Now, as she and Elizabeth started across the square, Dacey noticed that there were more people than usual on the streets and that they seemed to move with harried purpose. Kimberley had grown, she reflected, since the day she had arrived. Then, it had been a sprawling, ugly tent town. It was still that, but civilization had begun to creep in.

A new kind of citizen had come to Kimberley. Foreign investors, businessmen, men who wore dark suits instead of dusty trousers and sweat-covered singlets. All of these new arrivals demanded amenities and comforts. To please them, a haberdasher had opened a shop selling hats and other fine clothing for gentlemen. There was now a stationery shop, a shoemaker, a club called The Craven. A chemist sold drugs and medicines, and a dentist had set up his office with the familiar drawing of a large tooth. The Blue Post, Papa's favorite, now boasted an elegant wood front.

Even Bella had branched out her dressmaking business, and now ran a small ladies' wear shop.

As they approached Bella's shop, with its modest facade, two miners jostled them. Roughly they elbowed Elizabeth aside, so that Dacey had to grab her daughter to prevent her from falling.

Dacey glared at the men, but they hurried on past without even noticing her, involved in some heated political argument.

Dacey sighed and pulled open Bella's door, hearing the cheerful bell.

"Hello, both of you!" Bella greeted them warmly. "How are you, Lizzie-bet?" It was her nickname for Elizabeth. "Do you want to guess what sort of cake I have for you today?"

Elizabeth squealed, delighted with this game. "Almond cake?"

"No . . ."

"Scotch bread?"

"No . . ."

"Seed cake? Gingerbread? Oh, Bella, is it chocolate?"

Bella beamed. "Queen cake today, my love, beaten with eight eggs and a pound of butter, what do you think of that? And you may be the first to taste."

As Elizabeth rushed off to the kitchen, Bella and Dacey smiled at each other. "Come and sit down, dearie," Bella said comfortably. "And tell me, how is that father of yours?"

"As well as ever. As long as the Blue Post doesn't close its doors and he has his friends, he's content." But Dacey suppressed a pang as she said this. In the past three years, Papa had grown visibly older. A bout with enteric fever had left him with a tremor, and now only the flowing mustache and booming Shakespearean voice remained of the old John McKinnon. She had invited Papa to move in with her and Jed, but he had adamantly refused. He liked the hotel where he lived, he insisted.

"Even an old man needs his freedom," he had told her, winking slyly.

As the two women settled down for a chat, the shop door opened again, bringing in a rush of noises from the street, and the sound of a horse's galloping hoofbeats.

"Bella! I need a new hat! Don't you think that this one tilts over my face at an unbecoming angle?"

It was Lavinia Agnelli, panting from the exertion of her walk. She poked her head around the corner. "Oh, Dacey, it's you. My, but your nose is covered with freckles! Don't you *ever* wear a bonnet? You really shouldn't go to the mine so much, it will ruin your complexion."

Dacey made a face. "Lavinia, you'll never change, will you?"

"I *have* changed, if you'll notice, but Tony says it's all for the better, he likes me to look substantial." Lavinia smoothed the fabric of her elegant green taffeta shot silk, the seams of which strained at her bodice. Lavinia, once hovering on the verge of plump, now had crossed over that border. She was now a large, pink-faced, perspiring matron.

"How is the theater faring these days?" Dacey asked politely.

"Oh, better than ever! We are getting a new class of crowd these days, much more refined than in the old days. Why, we haven't had a real fight in weeks, only one horsewhipping in the street, and that barely counts." Lavinia giggled, pleased with her joke. "Oh, I hear that you have hired Royce McKinnon as your overseer."

"Yes, I did."

"You and Royce never got on too well, did you? You never understood him, Dacey; he is a very sensitive person."

Dacey did not know whether to laugh or be annoyed at Lavinia's comment. She had had doubts about hiring her young uncle. But Jed, who had picked fights with overseer after overseer, liked Royce. Maybe this was because the two were drinking cronies or because Royce treated Jed breezily, as if they were physical equals.

But whatever the reason, Dacey was thankful to have an employee that Jed could tolerate, and Royce *had* done a good job. Under his direction, their new claims had already made back her original investment.

Now more shouts came from the street, punctuated by the sound of a whip cracking. A crowd had begun to gather.

"What *is* going on?" Lavinia moved her bulk to the window to peer out. "Another fight? Or a horsewhipping? I declare, these men are always in a bother about something. If it isn't black men owning claims, it's the diamond dirt running out."

The three women gathered at the window. Now men wearing the uniform of British soldiers had appeared in the hurrying crowd. Their faces looked sunburned and grim.

"Do you suppose they are here because of that Black Flag Rebellion they wrote of in the paper?" Bella asked at last in a hushed voice.

All three women shivered. In the past months, the miners' anger at declining mining conditions and the drops in prices had flared up against the Africans who owned shares of the mines. On April 12, there had been a furious confrontation at the jail. Tempers still ran hot.

"I think I'd better take Elizabeth home," Dacey decided quickly. "The British may be here to calm down the situation, but it could get worse, and I don't want her to be frightened."

"No, Dacey, you'd better stay here," Bella warned.

"Oh, is it going to be dangerous? Tony would be furious if he knew I had put myself in any danger," Lavinia fluttered.

Dacey hurried toward Bella's kitchen, where, under the eye of a Bantu cook, Elizabeth was devouring a thick yellow slice of cake. As Dacey entered, the little girl looked up, crumbs smeared around her mouth.

"Come, darling, I think we had better hurry home now. There is a commotion in the street, and I think it's best if we leave."

"No, I don't want to." Elizabeth resisted, bracing her sturdy legs against the rungs of the chair on which she was perched. "We haven't bought my dress with the lace! And then I have to have another piece of cake. Bella always lets me have two."

"I'll give you some cake to take home, Lizzie-bet." A worried Bella appeared in the doorway behind Dacey. "Dacey, surely this is nothing, just another display like we had before at the jail, a few men letting off their tempers."

Dacey hesitated, hoping that Bella was right. But Jed had been outspoken against the black claim-holders, and on the day of the jail riot he had been injured by a thrown rock. What if he were in the thick of this today? She felt impelled by an anxiety to get home and make sure that Jed was safely behind doors.

"Mama . . ." Elizabeth was whining now, made anxious by the tension she sensed in the air, the ugly street noises that had grown louder. "Mama, I want my *cake*. You promised . . ."

"So I did. We'll take it home with us, just as Bella suggested." Dacey hastily cut a thick slice of cake and wrapped it in her handkerchief, tucking it inside her bag. "See, Elizabeth? Your cake is safe and sound. And we'll come back for your new dress tomorrow. Come along, then, we'll walk very quickly. Can you do that? You're a very big girl now, aren't you?"

Elizabeth hesitated. Then, mollified by the flattery and by possession of the cake, she slid down and walked with Dacey back through the shop.

"Can I walk along with you?" Lavinia asked anxiously. "Oh, dear, I knew I shouldn't have come shopping today. I *knew* today was going to be a bad day from the time I got up this morning!" She twisted her hands together.

Dacey wished that Lavinia would keep the high, nervous quaver out of her voice. "Of course you can walk with us."

The three of them ventured onto the street. But even in the half-hour that Dacey and Elizabeth had been in the shop, the situation had worsened. Now throngs of men ran in all directions, shouting or waving placards. A few even brandished ox whips, a common weapon in Kimberley. A group of British soldiers was trying vainly to restrain a small, cursing man who struggled in their grip. Dogs barked and oxen bellowed, adding to the confusion.

"Let's hurry," Lavinia begged. "Oh, I *wish* I'd stayed home. Dacey, do you think any of these men have pistols? Bullets can ricochet, you know. Tony told me that once. It would be dreadful to be shot when we are just—"

"*Hush,*" Dacey hissed. She gestured toward Elizabeth, whose lower lip had begun to tremble. The child clung anxiously to Dacey's skirt.

"Oh, oh," Lavinia moaned as three men on horseback came galloping down the road, whipping up clouds of gray-yellow dust. "Oh, Dacey . . ."

"Just walk along, Lavinia, and be still. No one is interested in us. Why should they be? We're not black miners, thank heavens."

They hurried on, their route taking them across the Market Square, now a shifting, jostling mass of men. There were no black faces to be seen today, a fact that Dacey found sinister. Men shouted and pushed, and the air reeked of sweaty bodies and anger.

"Mama!" Elizabeth clutched at Dacey's hands. "Mama, look, there's Uncle Royce!"

Dacey whirled to look. Standing in front of the Blue Post Saloon, haranguing the crowd, was Royce McKinnon. With his flashing eyes and dramatic actor's voice, he held their rapt attention.

"Black interlopers, Kaffir bastards, they think they can take our mines away from us! They steal our diamonds, snatch the very profits out from under us, and we allow it!"

"Ohhhhh, listen to him." Lavinia slowed her steps.

"He talks as if *he* owns a claim. He is nothing but a fool, Lavinia," Dacey snapped. She picked up Elizabeth and began carrying her, yanking at Lavinia with her free hand. She was furious—at Lavinia, and at Royce, too. She never should have let Jed pressure her into hiring him. Royce was a dilettante, easily bored, always wishing to stir up excitement, whether or not it actually existed. She would fire him, she decided, as soon as this was over. Meanwhile, she must get Lavinia and Elizabeth safely out of this.

They fought their way down the street. The miners, excited and angry, whipped into a frenzy by Royce and others, were in no mood to step aside for two women and a child. Crowds poured through the streets, shoving all who were in their way. Pushed, buffeted, Dacey clung to her child, praying that Elizabeth would not be swept away from her.

After much pushing and shoving, they finally managed to reach the far side of the square. Then Lavinia stumbled, and when Dacey turned to help her, another horseman came galloping into the crowd.

The women were pushed apart. Someone's shoulder banged into Dacey's chin, snapping her head back painfully.

"Dacey!" Lavinia screamed. "Oh, Dacey, I've lost my pocketbook!"

Lavinia staggered to her feet again and was swept into the vortex of men headed for the jail, where a huge crowd had begun to gather. Dacey shouted after her, but Lavinia was already lost to sight.

"So you are brave enough to venture out in this, Dacey? Or should I say, foolish enough?"

She turned, experiencing a fire-shock of feeling that swept over her like oil being ignited. "Quinn!"

He looked down at her, his face sundarkened, the high cheekbones giving his features a savage sweep. The creases around Quinn's eyes and bracketing his mouth were so achingly familiar that Dacey felt her heart turn over. Quinn's eyes, as blue as she had remembered, bored into hers.

"What the hell do you think you are doing, taking Elizabeth out today? The British are in town to restore order, and they don't much care who gets hurt. Come on—" He took Elizabeth from her, lifting the little girl high in his arms. "Come with me before you're both trampled."

"But there's Lavinia, she's in the crowd, she's just been swept away . . ."

"Lavinia Agnelli is as tough as nails, and she's just going to have to take care of herself. Come on, Dacey. Follow me."

Quinn was already shouldering his way through the crowd, Elizabeth shielded protectively in his arms, and Dacey had no choice but to hurry after him.

Quinn's old office was a few blocks down, on the street reserved for diamond buyers. Quinn battled a path toward it, pushing and shoving mercilessly, until at last he had Dacey and Elizabeth safely inside the door.

Dacey gasped with relief as he slammed and locked the door behind them. "I've never seen anything like it—that mob! I thought they were going to push us over and crush us, and never even notice they'd done so!"

Quinn nodded, putting Elizabeth down. "They could have. Mobs are not kind, Dacey. And the streets are not going to be safe for a while yet. The British have come in to quell rebellion, and they can be very determined. So you might as well make yourself comfortable. I'm afraid that you and your daughter are going to be stuck here for a couple of hours."

Dacey nodded, feeling her heart slam uncomfortably at the thought. To be near Quinn . . . To cover her feelings, she looked around his office. In the early days, Quinn's office had been makeshift, like most other offices in Kimberley.

Now, she saw, that had changed. On the floor were Oriental rugs, their deep jewel colors vivid. The walls were mud-and-clay whitewashed to a rich patina. There was old Dutch furniture, an antique Gobelin tapestry, a shelf that held copper, brass, and African curiosities.

"Why, this is lovely!" Dacey exclaimed. "Quinn, it's stunning."

"Thank you, ma'am." He gave her a pleased, mock bow. "A few years ago, I gave up tent living in favor of comfort. Now I have small living quarters at the back, and I live very well."

Elizabeth, quickly recovering from her fear, darted across the room to examine a wooden ceremonial mask, its expression ferocious.

"Mama! Oooh, look at his face, that bad face!"

"He is Zulu, Elizabeth, and he is supposed to look bad." Quinn smiled at the little girl, then turned to look at Dacey, his eyes very blue and intent. "She is beautiful," he murmured.

"Yes, I . . . we think so." Dacey was suddenly unsure of where to look or what to do with her hands. Her heart was still hammering from their wild run. Or was it just being with Quinn again that made all the blood sing in her body? They were alone here in this beautiful office, while on the street a mob raged.

"Sit down," Quinn commanded. "We might as well be comfortable here, and maybe I can get both of you something to eat."

Food was the last thing on Dacey's mind as she made some reply and lifted her eyes to examine Quinn's face. How many times had she imagined touching the crisp black hair that curled at Quinn's temple and fell over his forehead in an unruly lock? Or touching her fingers to his lips, feeling the humorous sweep of the upper lip, the full, sensuous lower one . . .

With a start, Dacey realized where her thoughts were

leading. She yanked her fantasy to a halt and quickly looked down at her hands, barely hearing the polite conversation that Quinn made, about the mines, a new edict of the Kimberley Mining Board, a new theater in town.

For years she had fought to keep Quinn out of her thoughts, and she had thought she had succeeded—at least, she had convinced herself that she had. Now her desire for him was welling up stronger than ever. She felt weak, shaky, actually trembling under the force of the feelings that burned through her. With all of her heart, she wanted to touch him, to feel his arms close about her, to taste his sweet, tender mouth . . .

"Mama, Mama!" Elizabeth had lost interest in the fierce Zulu mask and ran to Dacey, tugging at her. "I'm hungry! Can we have Bella's cake now? We could cut it into tiny pieces, one for each of us," she wheedled. "We could all share."

Dacey saw amusement in Quinn's look.

"Elizabeth," she managed to say, "sharing is a wonderful thought, but we are in Mr. Farris's home now, and—"

"Nonsense, Dacey, let's not stand on manners today. Cake sounds like a fine idea to me, along with something a bit more substantial. Come, I'll see what I can rustle up."

"Rustle?" The term was unfamiliar to Dacey.

Quinn grinned. "In Arizona, when thieves steal a rancher's cattle, they are called rustlers."

"What is Arizona?" Elizabeth asked.

"Oh, it is a very faraway place, Elizabeth, where there are Indians and cactus and beautiful mesas and buttes; perhaps you will go there sometime and see it for yourself."

They entered the living area, three rooms furnished with more Cape Dutch furniture as imposing as that Dacey had seen in the office.

"Do you like couscous?" Quinn wanted to know.

"I don't even know what it is." Dacey felt as if all of her senses were on edge, her blood flowing like a warm river through her veins.

"Well, it's a North African dish; I learned it from a Moroccan cook at the Vaal diggings. Chicken and vegetables and chick peas and raisins, served on a bed of farina. There is a spicy sauce, and the dish is very light and tasty. I'm sure Elizabeth will like it. Shall I prepare some?''

The child stared up at Quinn, her blue eyes wide. "Do *you* cook?''

Quinn laughed. "Of course I cook, my pretty. Do you think that privilege is reserved only for women? You may even help me, if you wish. This dish calls for raisins, and I need a raisin-taster, someone who can tell me if they are quite up to snuff.''

Elizabeth gave a silvery giggle. "I like raisins.''

"I thought you would.''

"I like cake, too.''

"Ah.'' Quinn nodded solemnly. "I suspected that, too. Maybe you can give me your favorite recipe sometime. And I will give you mine.''

As Quinn and Elizabeth moved about the small, clean kitchen, apparently totally happy in each other's company, Dacey withdrew to the sitting room. Idly she walked about, feeling warmed just to be in the presence of the objects and furniture that Quinn owned. On the wall hung a tinted lithograph showing a woman wearing the latest fashion and a heavy necklace laden with diamonds. It was a reprint from *Godey's*. Was this the sort of necklace that Quinn intended to give to Janine, his wife?

Flushing, some of her mood spoiled, Dacey turned away from the picture.

A bookshelf sagged with books and with old issues of Kimberley newspapers. Looking over the spines of the books, Dacey saw everything from treatises on Africa, to history, philosophy, and novels. So Quinn was a reader, she thought with an odd pang. She had not known this about him—but how could she have? During their meetings on the veld, they had spent most of their time making love. Later, they had talked only business.

Passionately she had loved him, yet there was still so much of him that she did not know, of which she had been cheated . . .

On a desk she spotted a stack of notes in Quinn's sprawling, decisive handwriting.

"Do you find that interesting?''

She jumped guiltily, feeling as if she had been caught prying. He had come up behind her so quietly that she had not known.

"Oh, I'm sorry, I shouldn't have been looking—"

"No, I understand. You just wanted to know more about me, and I was rude enough to leave you to your own devices while Elizabeth and I cooked." He paused. "I'm writing a book, Dacey, about Kimberley. All the politics, the forces that have built this town and could very well, someday, destroy it."

Dacey nodded, experiencing a strange pang, a hurtful feeling of being left out. Quinn was writing a book and she had not known of it. What other parts of his life were utterly separate from her, of which she could never be a part?

Apparently Quinn had been thinking much the same thing, for he gave a rueful smile. "It's strange, isn't it?" he mused. "We feel that we know each other, and we do, very deeply. Yet in another way, we don't. Your life, for instance. It's been a mystery to me, Dacey. You seem to be so utterly determined to succeed at mining. And you are managing to do so, despite being saddled with a child and a dependent husband."

A hard muscle flickered at the corner of Quinn's mouth. "How do you do it, Dacey? What drives you? Is there some hungry desire in you, some ambition that will not deny itself?"

Dacey looked at him, feeling chilled. Why had he asked her such a question? What had he meant, why did he look so grim?

"Are you saying that I might be *too* ambitious?"

He merely looked at her, not replying.

"Well, I'm not!" she responded indignantly. "All my life I lived the life of a roving actor. Shabby hotels, damp theaters, never being sure where the money was coming from. Sometimes we were rich, but most often we were poor. We never could depend on anything. And now I have a chance to change that, to build some stability for my daughter, and for my father."

"Security." Quinn's eyes flashed at her, their earlier hu-

mor and gentleness gone. "That female desire to build and
furnish a nest—it all sounds very nice, Dacey. But surely it's
not only that which drives you. Don't you want power, too?"

Power. Dacey flushed, sensing a deep anger in him—yet,
why? What had she done? She wasn't power-hungry, not in
the way that Quinn's set face implied.

"If anyone has a lust for power," she flared, remembering
the lithograph she had seen that showed the woman wearing
the diamond necklace, "then it's you, Quinn, not me.
Diamonds! Large-carat stones, dozen upon dozens of them
. . . Oh, *I* know what you are doing here in Kimberley, it's
common knowledge. You are collecting diamonds to take
back to your wife!"

There was an instant of silence. Their eyes met and locked,
Quinn's eyes blazing at her like daggers. Furiously Dacey
challenged his look, refusing to glance away first. How dare
he castigate her for what he did himself? Were there two sets
of standards, one for men and the other for women? She had
just as much right to try her luck in the mines as he did!

Then Quinn broke the simmering tension between them
with a sudden, easy grin. "Peace, Dacey. Shall we call a
truce? Unless you plan to spend the afternoon not speaking to
me, I suggest that we try to be cordial to each other. Can you
smell the couscous cooking? Elizabeth helped me chop up the
chicken, and, I assure you, it will be well worth the wait."

Dacey drew a sharp breath. They were apparently stuck
here for some time; what else was there for her to do but to
forget her anger?

"Let me help to set the table for the meal," she said at
last.

The couscous was hot and delicious, redolent of spices, the
fluffy farina so light that Dacey found she had consumed a
huge plateful before she had even realized it.

"Moroccans pile all the couscous in a big plate in the
middle of the table and eat it with their fingers—of the right
hand only. The left hand is considered unclean," Quinn told
them, his earlier anger at Dacey apparently forgotten. "But
I've made a concession to our culture by using separate
plates, knives, and forks. Do you need help, little one?" he

added, turning to help Elizabeth with an unwieldy piece of chicken.

"*I* can do it—I can cut it myself." Elizabeth grinned at him, sauce running down her chin. "I like this, even if we do have to eat it with forks."

Watching the two, father and daughter, Dacey felt a twist of her heart. They were so much alike in their looks, each so full of energy and life. Yet Elizabeth thought only that Quinn was an interesting friend, with the fascinating accomplishment of being able to cook. The child had no idea that she had met her real father.

It was a thought that filled Dacey with a heavy, pensive sadness . . .

After the meal, which they finished with small slices of Bella's cake, Elizabeth grew drowsy. She crawled onto a soft couch, where she fell instantly into a deep sleep, her thumb tucked into her mouth.

Quinn and Dacey washed the dishes together, working companionably. Then they sat down at the small table. Noises from the street had quieted, then burst out with new violence, and Dacey was glad that Quinn had barred the doors and locked all the windows.

"We're safe here," he reassured her. "And now, tell me how your life has been going, what has been happening to you. I hear rumors from time to time about Jed—and I don't like what I hear."

Dacey looked down at the well-scrubbed table, tracing with her fingers the grain of the wood. "He is as fine as can be expected," she said at last. "He was injured slightly in April when the miners rioted at the jail. He is fine now, of course, although I have been uneasy about him today. I hope he isn't on the streets somewhere."

"Didn't you tell his servant to watch out for him? To keep him out of harm's way?"

"Of course. But Jed is capable of wheeling his own chair when he wishes. The ruts and potholes are deep, but Jed has always been strong."

Quinn nodded, frowning, the sharp look he gave her seem-

ing to look through to her very soul, leaving her nowhere to
hide.

"Well, if Jed is rioting today with the others, then he must
take his chances," Quinn said at last. "Maybe it would be
best for all concerned if he *were* to come to some bad end."

"What?" Dacey was shocked. "How can you say that?
Jed is a sick man!"

"Sick? He isn't sick, Dacey, he's twisted. He's also
dangerous, you little fool. Evidently you aren't aware of what
he did on the day of the jail riot."

"What he . . . did?"

"He was caught in the act of beating a black woman,
someone he found on the street and just grabbed. Admittedly,
his was not the only act of violence that day. But one of the
auctioneers was angry at seeing a woman treated that way and
pulled Jed off her. *That* was how he hurt himself, not with a
rock in the forehead, as he told people."

"I see." Dacey felt a wave of nausea and had to grip the
edge of the table for support. Jed had beaten another black
woman.

"I didn't want to interfere in your life, Dacey, I hardly
have the right to do that. But I did take steps at the time to
protect you. There is a group of diggers who live across the
road from you, men from Belfast. I hired them to watch out
for you."

"You did what?"

"They are your protectors, Dacey. If they ever hear sounds
coming from your house, noises that indicate you are in
trouble, they will help. You can depend on them."

Dacey stared at Quinn, remembering now a man who *had*
seemed to be watching her, another digger who had pulled
Elizabeth out of the path of a passing Cape cart. She didn't
know whether to feel angry at Quinn's interference or warmed
that he had done such a thing.

"I don't need any bodyguards," she managed to say. "I'm
sure that Jed isn't dangerous to me or to Elizabeth. He loves
her, he spends much time with her."

"That may be. But he is not a stable man, Dacey, he's a
walking mass of resentments and brooding. And if he were to

touch you—to harm you . . .'' Quinn's eyes narrowed. "I
would have a hard time remembering that he is confined to an
invalid chair. I think I would kill him.''

"I think I would kill him." The incredible words spun in
the room. Dacey felt her throat squeeze tightly, a soft melting
begin deep within her. Involuntarily, her hand went out to
touch Quinn's. The shock of their touching was electric, and
she knew by Quinn's light, indrawn breath that he felt it too.

"Dacey?" He looked at her, his eyes searching hers. She
could not speak. She felt herself tremble, desire washing
through her like warm water.

"Dacey? My God . . ." he said again. He rose, pulling her
with him, and Dacey allowed herself to be drawn into his
embrace, helpless to resist. For long moments they pressed
their bodies together, swaying under the impact of the fierce
emotions that gripped them both. Quinn's mouth opened
hers, took hers, his kisses so tender and yet so demanding
that Dacey grew dizzy. She arched herself close to him, slid
her arms under his shoulders, and molded her body to his,
feeling as if they were sealed together. It was an excitement
so intense that she could barely breathe, barely think.

How long, how long had it been since a man touched her
like this? Since Quinn . . .

"Elizabeth," she managed to whisper with the last vestiges
of her common sense. "She is in the other room . . ."

"She's sleeping like a granny in church," Quinn said
thickly. He kissed the hollow of her throat, his breath sending
shivers of fire through her. "But to be on the safe side, I'll
lock the door. Oh, Dacey, oh, my God . . ."

Quinn turned the lock on the door, assuring that they
would have privacy. The windows were curtained with heavy
drapes against the heat, and the room was full of shadows.
Dacey felt as if he had taken her into a dark, secure cave, a
place sheltered from all demands of the world, meant only
for them.

They embraced again, hungrily, unable to get close enough,
to kiss deeply enough, to love enough. Quinn began to
unfasten the jet buttons at the back of Dacey's gown, undoing
each one slowly, planting soft kisses on her neck, throat, and

breasts. Dacey arched and moaned, moving under his caresses, totally lost in him.

Feverishly, Quinn lifted the dress away from her, kissing each part of her skin as he removed its covering. At last Dacey was naked, her full breasts and rich curves open to him.

Quinn lifted her easily and swung her onto the bed, where he lowered her to the coverlet. He pressed his long body to hers, and they clasped each other so hungrily that Dacey thought her heart would explode.

"Beautiful," Quinn groaned. "You are beautiful . . ." He caressed her breasts, kneading the nipples until they hardened and became taut with desire. Then he kissed each one, swirling his tongue around the aureole until she gasped, feeling as if she would drown in this ecstasy.

Unable to help herself or to stop the tumultuous rush of her feelings, Dacey began to unfasten Quinn's shirt. Slowly she undid each button, kissing the skin that was revealed to her, the crisp, spiky curls of dark hair that adorned his chest.

With her fingers and mouth, she explored the line of taut muscles, following the scented curls of hair downward to the hard belly and the urgent sex. She held Quinn in her hands, feeling his throbbing urgency and her own hungry desire, dammed up for years.

A frenzy came upon them. They tangled in fierce embrace, arms and legs tight around each other, their demands almost violent now, totally beyond control. Quinn's questing mouth, the feel of his satiny skin, the fragrance of his body, these were like wild aphrodisiacs for Dacey, driving her to a passion she had not believed possible. She was lost, lost to him forever . . .

Finally she guided him inside her, almost crying out as he took his first long, deep thrust. He drove deep within her, and Dacey's whole body quivered under the impact of this possession. He began the rhythmic movements of love, slowly at first, then with greater urgency, until at last they pounded together, each taking from the other, each giving, moisture running from their bodies, their breath coming in rough gasps.

Then, almost before Dacey was ready, she exploded. She

arched her hips against Quinn and cried out with the joy that was so much more than joy, that was everything on earth that would ever be.

Afterward, they held each other, Quinn resting his body lightly on hers. Dacey licked the skin of his shoulder, tasted salt, and felt herself shiver with happiness. She felt as if she had become a part of Quinn, and he of her.

"Darling, oh, Dacey . . ." Quinn murmured soft words with no meaning, yet with all meaning. "All these years. All this time, so long . . ."

"Yes, so long," she whispered back. "Hold me, Quinn. Hold me. Please, just for a while longer . . ."

They lay wrapped in each other's arms, floating in contentment, until at last it was time to rise and dress. When they came out of the bedroom, they found Elizabeth just awakening from her nap. Sleepily, she stirred on the couch, her face flushed, her dark hair in tangles.

"Are the bad men gone now, Mama? Can we go home?"

"Yes, darling, we can go home." Dacey felt a stab of pain at the thought of this afternoon—this secret, perfect day that now had to end.

"I'll carry her for you," Quinn said. "I think the streets are safe enough now; I haven't heard any commotion for several hours. In fact, we could have left earlier if we had wanted to."

But they hadn't wanted to. A heavy, aching silence fell between them, and Dacey felt the smile fade from her lips, to be replaced by the most profound emptiness that she had ever known. A knot of sadness thickened in her throat, making it difficult for her to breathe.

"Quinn? When—when will I see you again?"

Quinn said nothing. She saw pain written on his features, apparent in the tightening of his mouth, the darkening of his eyes. What had she been thinking of? she asked herself in agony. Had she been mad, forgetting her duty to Jed, and Quinn's obligations, his life, so separate from hers?

"Never mind." She steadied her voice with an act of will, for never must Quinn suspect the pain that seared her now, the aching hurt. She forced a smile back onto her lips and kept it there, feeling as if her face was cracking in two like a plaster mask. "Today—what we had today—was enough. It will have to be, won't it?"

A catch in her throat betrayed her.

"Ah, *God* . . . Dacey, I'm sorry . . .". Fiercely Quinn pulled her to him and they clung together, heedless of Elizabeth's presence or of anything else, aware only of their own need for each other, a need that was not going to be fulfilled.

Dacey buried her face against Quinn's chest, hearing the steady beat of his heart. Her eyes burned with tears. To find Quinn again, and then to lose him. How could she let him go now, how could she ever do it?

But she had to. There was Jed, and the mine, and her life in Kimberley that waited for her outside these doors. She must find the strength to accept that life and not to look back on what had only been a dream. A bittersweet, poignant dream. . . .

In a black mood, Quinn Farris rode the hired gelding along the well-worn path that led to the kraal of Natala's family. The trail wound past rocks and around a huge, knobbed *koppie* where a camel-thorn tree grew, an elongated weaver bird's nest hanging from its sparse branches. In the tree, the birds chattered as they wove their nest from shreds of leaves and bits of dried grass.

Quinn eyed the birds dully. His encounter with Dacey had left him feeling hollowed, damaged, his emotions battered and painfully raw. He felt torn with regret and a feeling of angry futility.

They should not have made love. It had been foolhardy, an unforgivable act on his part. He could still see Dacey's face as they had parted, her skin pale, her lips trembling as she tried to hold her smile. Their love was doomed. Forbidden, made impossible by all the other lives and needs that impinged on their own.

The kraal lay at the edge of a slight depression in the land. It was a group of conical brown-thatched huts, with small square windows and walls of dried mud that had been worked by hand into beautiful and complicated patterns. The village was surrounded by hedges of thorn, so that cattle could be driven inside it at night to keep them safe from predators. In the distance, Quinn could see the grazing animals and the bright garb of herders.

Women herders, at that. Oddly, Natala's kraal was a settlement consisting mostly of women and children, set apart from others. Quinn had never grown to understand the convoluted family relationships; he only knew that here were Natala's sisters, her cousins, her mother. Most of the women were darker than Natala, their features coarser. But a few possessed her delicate, cinnamon-colored skin and a lithe way of walking that was at once beautiful and utterly natural.

Dogs and small children came running to meet him as he passed the barrier of thorns. He breathed in the familiar odors of the village. Dust. Cookfires, roasting game, the smell of mealies and *mas*, a milk curd; the sour odor of African beer. Somewhere someone played an instrument made of pieces of metal of varying sizes, the sound dissonant, tentative.

A small naked boy ran forward to take Quinn's horse, one of the native dogs trotting after him. It growled and bared its teeth at Quinn. He cursed at the animal and it backed away, slavering.

By now, the village was alive with news of his coming. He heard the soft voices of women, punctuated by bursts of laughter. In the window of one hut, a girl peered out at him, giggling. As always, Quinn had the sensation that there were many eyes on him, assessing him.

He strode between the huts until he came to the one at the end, the one occupied by the old woman he knew only as Teki. To Quinn, she seemed ancient, with her skinny, wrinkled, brown body and frizzy white hair. Her long breasts hung like flat sacks from her chest. Was Teki Natala's mother? Her grandmother? Or no relation at all?

Natala only smiled secretively at him when he asked such questions. But it was clear that Natala had learned her herbal lore from Teki, for her hut was a duplicate of Teki's, with its dried leaves and roots that hung in bunches from the roof, the tiny dooryard where plants, most of them gnarled and unlovely, grew in profusion.

Now, as he approached, he saw Teki peering out of the door at him. Her eyes were flat brown and held no welcome.

"Quinn! Quinn!" Suddenly Lilah appeared beside the old woman, a tall, six-year-old girl with a slender body and perfectly chiseled features.

Quinn caught his breath, struck, as ever, by the child's regal beauty. In a village of comely women, she was a princess. He watched as his daughter walked toward him, her movements graceful. She had large, dark eyes that at times were pools of calm contemplation, and at other times could flash with fire. Her skin was as warm and smooth as alabaster, its texture flawless, seeming almost to glow from within.

In Savannah, in ten years, she would have been heralded as a famous beauty. In France, she could have married royalty or been a famed actress, adored by millions. She would have been a prize, to be fought over and coveted. Yet Quinn knew that Lilah had far more potential than being merely the object of a man's desire.

She was intelligent in her own right. Some women in the mid-1870s were entering medicine, law, scholarly fields. Lilah could have taken her place among them, vital, strong, influential. Instead, she lived here in this tiny, primitive settlement and was being schooled by Teki, Quinn felt sure, in healing and witchcraft.

Someday she would take her place as a diviner, like Natala . . .

He pushed away a spurt of anger and knelt down to take his child in his arms. She clung to him, her odor sweet in his nostrils, for she had been taught to anoint herself with the flower scent also.

"You came again—and did you bring me another book?" Lilah demanded eagerly.

"Yes, I've brought you two. Both of them were carried by ship over the Atlantic Ocean from England. One is called *Little Women* and the other is *Hans Brinker and His Silver Skates*. That one takes place in Holland; perhaps someday I will take you there, my Lilah. We will both learn to skate on the ice, would you like that?"

"What is ice?"

"It is frozen water, very hard and very, very cold. Have you ever seen snow?"

She looked puzzled.

Quinn laughed. "Well, someday you will. Now, come with me and we'll start the book and I'll tell you all about it."

"Oh, yes, yes." She laughed and came running along beside him, the small, bright garment she wore fluttering after her. Thanks to Quinn's tutelage, Lilah was already reading aloud. She was lightning-quick, grasping each letter or word with only one explanation. Someday, Quinn vowed to himself, Lilah would be allowed to use that wonderful mind of hers. He would see to it . . .

The afternoon passed quickly. They went to their customary spot, an odd formation of rocks covered with Bushman paintings, lines of rust and ocher etched into primeval sketches of animals and hunters. Here they sat in a natural seat formed by the stone. Lilah read aloud to him in her softly accented English, and Quinn helped her with some new words. Then he told her stories of Arizona, of silver-mining camps, rattlesnakes and Indians, Johnny Appleseed and Paul Bunyan.

Lilah listened, her dark eyes fixed on his. "Will I ever see this tall man, this Paul Bunyan and his blue ox?" she asked at last.

Quinn smiled. "No, my Lilah, you won't, because I'm afraid that Paul and Babe are just a story. But there are other things, wonderful things, that I can show you. Huge red rocks and cactus taller than two men, with thorny arms that reach up to the sky. There is a wonderful, huge canyon, scooped out of the earth as if by God's hand, so big, so long and deep that it would steal your breath away to see it—"

"But I will not see it." Lilah pulled away, to gaze at him with her calm eyes.

"Why, honey, I will take you myself one day—"

"You will not, Quinn. Teki has said it. The words that you teach me, the magic in these books you bring, they are only

for the white man's world. They do not belong *here*." She
gestured around her, indicating the veld.

Quinn felt a stifling pang. "Words and books are wonderful things, Lilah. Don't you know that by now? Haven't I
taught you that much? They belong anywhere, they are the
doors that can open our minds and hearts—"

But it was as if a curtain had dropped over the child's eyes,
removing their eagerness. She rose and tucked the two books
that he had given her under her arm. "I will go now, Quinn."

"Lilah—"

But she had already turned and was loping back toward the
small, thatched village. After a few paces, she lifted the
books to her head and carried them there as African women
did, deftly balanced.

Quinn watched his daughter until she had disappeared behind the thorned wall of the kraal. Then, his heart heavy, he
walked back to his horse, which had been fed and watered
and was now tethered to a post. Lilah . . . Was it already too
late for her? He should have taken her away earlier. But he
had had business in Kimberley, ambitions, things to accomplish . . .

He swallowed hard against an onslaught of guilt and despair.

He was reaching for the horse's bridle, about to mount,
when he saw a figure approaching over the rise. By the
swaying, sinuous grace of her walk, he recognized Natala.

Calmly he waited for his mistress, knowing that Natala
bitterly resented his visits to the village, preferring to keep
Lilah locked away from him, a weapon she could use at will.

She continued toward him, a blue-dyed cloth wrapped
around her body, its looseness revealing the strong thrust of
her breasts, her full hips. Against the vibrant blue, her skin
glowed deeply.

She spat out the words. "You are here again to see Lilah!"

"Yes, I am." Slow anger churned in Quinn, an anger
directed at himself as well as at her. "You know that I see
her regularly, Natala, and that I will continue to do so. She is
my daughter, and I pay well for her support here, or had you
conveniently forgotten? The food these people eat—the cattle

that they herd—all of these were bought with my money, as you well know."

"*Ai*, your diamond money." Natala's eyes flashed. "You are like all men, Quinn, you think your money will buy you anything you want."

"On the contrary, I know it will not."

They gazed at each other, old emotions simmering between them. Then Natala lifted her chin and adjusted the folds of her garment, her mood abruptly changing.

"Do you think that Lilah is beautiful?"

He was startled at the question. "Of course I do. She is a lovely child."

"Lovely enough to go in the world as white?"

"Yes. If she wished it, she could do that. She could be accepted by society anywhere, in Savannah, in London, or even New York."

"New York." For an instant Natala's eyes betrayed her with a dreamy expression. Then quickly her features hardened. "I have never been to that city; I do not think I would like it. Nor would Lilah."

"How do you know what she would like?"

"*Ai*, you think you know everything, don't you? You think that you are going to make Lilah into a white woman. You want to take her away with you!" Natala accused.

"She is beautiful and gifted. Surely you would not object to—"

"Oh! Oh, you are a fool! Such a fool! Lilah is a child of the veld. She will stay here where she belongs, learning the powers, the herbs, and the spells. She will have abilities not granted to other women, common women, ordinary women like your Dacey!"

Always, it seemed, their arguments came back to Dacey. Quinn turned to leave, an act that seemed to madden Natala, who continued to taut him.

"Dacey! So small, so red-faced and ugly! With her mining company, her machines that come from England. Does she think that she can succeed in a man's world? She cannot. She is a fool, just as you are, Quinn—"

"Enough." Quinn gripped his mistress' arm firmly. "Dacey Donohue is not your concern, Natala—nor is she mine."

"No? *I* made her misfortune, Quinn, but I will never tell you how. Oh, you men have eyes, but you never open them to see—"

"What are you talking about?"

"I did not touch her. I did not harm one hair of her head, did I not promise it? Didn't I swear it? *Ai*," Natala mocked. "Perhaps I only *wished* bad for her, and that husband of hers, the man with legs of stone."

"Natala—"

"Wishes are powerful, Quinn. Do you not agree?"

Quinn shrugged, swinging onto the horse and spurring it to a gallop. He rode down the path the way he had come, his brow furrowed. Wishes. What had Natala meant when she hinted that she had "made" Dacey's misfortune?

Surely it was just talk, meaning nothing. Natala had grown too absorbed in her spell-making, he decided uneasily. When had it happened? When had she begun to use her spells and magic to control others? Or had she always done it and he just not realized?

He rode back to Kimberley, barely seeing the huge blue sky that arched overhead like an overturned delft bowl, or the hawk that rode an updraft, its movements soaring and beautiful.

14

"WELL, DACIA, MY DAUGHTER, YOU have quite an operation here, don't you?" Papa had to raise his voice to be heard over the noise of machinery and winches, the rattle of Scotch carts and the shouts of men.

"Thank you, Papa."

Dacey flushed with pleasure, for John McKinnon seldom came to the mine, preferring instead to remain at the Blue Post, where he could gamble occasionally and drink all he wished. But today Elizabeth had begged Grandpapa to come. She was delighted that a mining company had been named after her and took an eager pride in its doings, wishing to show them off.

"Grandpapa! Grandpapa! Do you want to see our Elizabeth office?" The child danced up and down beside her grandfather, tugging at his arm.

"Your Elizabeth office?"

"Why, yes, Grandpapa—it's where Mama has her account books and her big safe and her little glass that she uses to look inside the diamonds. She let me look once and I saw feathery things inside one diamond, and Mama frowned and said that it wasn't a very good stone, that it wouldn't sell for much . . ."

The child chattered, tugging at John McKinnon's arm as she pulled him toward the iron building that Dacey had made into an office.

Dacey watched them go, the old man's shoulders stooped, the child skipping with energy. She sighed, thinking of the time that had passed since the afternoon she had shared with Quinn.

Leaving Quinn, knowing that they could not be intimate again, could not even converse, save on matters of business, had been one of the hardest things that Dacey had ever done. For weeks she had been plunged into black depression. Even the simplest tasks had seemed impossibly difficult. She had walked around feeling as if she were encased in a glass shell, inches thick, that insulated her from all emotion. She could not have Quinn; nothing else seemed to matter.

Because of her depression and because Jed objected, she did not fire Royce McKinnon for his part in the Black Flag Rebellion. Instead, it seemed easier to keep him on, knowing that the alternative was a further succession of overseers whom Jed would fire.

The ten-claim restriction was lifted, and the Elizabeth Mining Company grew bigger. Quinn's business, Dacey knew, had mushroomed as well.

From a distance, she watched his meteoric rise in Kimberley. He had put out word that he was interested in looking at all large stones over thirty carats and would pay premium prices for them. Several times Dacey saw Quinn on the street. Once, she had sensed his eyes burning into her, and she had turned away, a knot of tears caught in her throat.

To look at him now was only torture . . .

As the slow weeks and months rolled by, Jed became even more dependent on Dacey. Subtly, the leadership of the mining company passed to her. With doses of laudanum, Jed had calmed down, and now he spent hours with Elizabeth, talking to her of Boston or of his early days at the river diggings.

To Dacey the friendship between the two seemed a great boon. Perhaps, beneath the torment of his spirit, Jed still possessed human love. If this was the case, then she must not give up hope for her husband.

But each day seemed to separate her even further from Quinn. Even her memories of him began to dim. Sometimes at night she would lie in her bed, listening to Jed's heavy breathing from the other room and trying to relive the hours with Quinn in her thoughts. The way their bodies had clung, each merged in the other . . .

But there was so much that had faded, blurring in her mind. What words had Quinn murmured to her? What had she said in return? Sometimes Dacey wept, for she could not recall these things perfectly. Her memories were all she had of Quinn now, infinitely precious to her. If she were to lose them . . .

But then, the next day, as she was walking to the mine or hurrying to the Market Square to buy the day's supply of meat, she would suddenly recall the lost words. Gladness would surge through her, suffusing her with a joy as strong as it was irrational.

To feel happiness over remembering a few love words spoken two long years ago? A few scraps of memory carefully hoarded like jewels?

Yet ashamedly, Dacey knew that she could never forget Quinn—and that she didn't want to.

Now, jolting her from her bittersweet thoughts, she watched Elizabeth tug her grandfather out of the mine office, the child's face alight with pride.

"He liked it, Mama!" Elizabeth shouted, running to Dacey. "I showed him everything, I even showed him how to use the scales. And the tweezers, and the typewriting machine—"

"Ah, Dacia, you are very modern, aren't you?" John McKinnon wiped dust from his mustache. "What will they think of next? A machine that prints letters on a piece of paper!"

Dacey laughed. "I'll have to admit it was Royce's idea to order the typewriter, not mine. He is always enthralled by something new. But it is pleasant to use and saves hours of writing by hand. We have a clerk who comes in to help us now."

"A clerk." Papa looked proud. "Dacia, do you remember that day when we first arrived in Kimberley? And the man who stared at you so boldly?"

"I . . . yes, Papa," Dacey managed to respond. It had

been Quinn who had looked at her that day. Didn't Papa remember?

"Well, I told you then that he was an omen of good luck, and he was. Our fortune has certainly changed, hasn't it? Or at least, yours has."

"Yours, too, Papa. Doesn't everything I have belong to you?" Dacey hugged her father, aware of tears stinging her eyes, for it was true that Papa's luck was now only at the gambling table.

"Of course, of course, Dacia. Say, where is the child going?"

For Elizabeth had scampered off in the direction of the sorting tables, her white dress flying. Its hem was already smudged with yellowish mine dust.

"Grandpapa! Grandpapa!" Elizabeth called over her shoulder. "Come and see the sorting. I want to show you. This is a baby rocker. Have you ever seen such a thing?" She pointed to a device loaded with dirt that was being sieved.

"No, my dear, I don't believe I have."

Elizabeth giggled. "*I* see it—every day, when Mama will let me come here. Sometimes when she doesn't let me, I sneak away anyway."

"And get spanked for it, you little scamp." Dacey said it sharply, although she felt her heart melt at the eagerness of the little girl, with her mass of dark curls, her blue eyes so like Quinn's. "The mine site is dangerous, Papa," she went on. "I've told Elizabeth so, over and over. The horses, the winches, all this machinery. And what if she were to slip over the edge? The hole has grown frighteningly deep. Sometimes I wonder if we are ever going to stop digging, or if we will eventually have to tunnel under the earth like moles."

John McKinnon mopped his face. "Moles? That may be. But for now, I wish to sit down, my Dacia. Can you find an old man a chair? And a cool glass of beer? That sun up there glares down at us like a brass monkey."

"*I'll* get the chair." Elizabeth raced to do her grandfather's bidding, returning with a chair and a container beaded with moisture. "We haven't any beer, Grandpapa, but there is plenty of lemonade. Will that quench your thirst? I'm going to go over to the sorting tables, you can watch me if you want. I'll look for a nice diamond for you to wear on your cravat. Would you like that?''

She was off, trotting toward the tables, elbowing her way between two Bantu workers, to plunge both hands into the crumbly diamond dirt with the ease of long practice.

Dacey and her father watched the pretty child laboring beside the black men, with their shining dark skin, under which muscles rippled.

''What an amazing child.'' Gingerly, John McKinnon sipped the lemonade. ''She loves all of this, doesn't she? Ah, she reminds me so much of you when you were her age . . .'' He paused. ''Often I wonder how Jed Donohue could have fathered a sprite like her. Heredity is strange, is it not?''

Dacey looked down at her lap, twisting her hands together. Did Papa suspect? Or, again, was this merely a careless remark with no hidden meaning?

I . . . I suppose it is,'' she agreed at last.

They sat sipping the lemonade, and Dacey ordered extra containers of the drink to be distributed among the men. Just as her father was beginning to shift restlessly, ready to return to the familiar comfort of the Blue Post, Elizabeth came flying back toward them.

''Mama, Grandpapa, look what I've found! I've found something very big and red!''

''Red? Then it can't be a diamond. There aren't any such things as red diamonds, child,'' John McKinnon said.

''Oh, yes, there are. Daddy Jed told me. He said—''

''Let me see it.'' The old man took the object the child handed him and carefully dusted it off with a handkerchief. Then he hefted the stone in his palm. It was large, about the size of a ripe plum, and shaped roughly like a triangle, parts of it smooth, other parts slightly knobby. Its color was a deep ruby-rose that caught the light, reflecting the sunlight back out again in warm fire.

''Pshaw, this isn't a diamond at all, it's too big,'' John McKinnon pronounced. ''It's just a pretty stone, that's all, my poppet.'' He handed it back to Elizabeth.

The child took the stone, gazing down at it with disappointment. "But I thought—" She looked appealingly at Dacey. "Mama, didn't Daddy say that some diamonds are in different colors? Some are green, and some are yellow, and some are brown and amber and pink, and—"

Dacey laughed. "Yes, darling, you are right about that." She reached to take the stone from her daughter. "Papa, we have found some tinted diamonds ourselves, but they are very rare. Still . . . Oh, this one *is* big, isn't it?"

A little shiver touched the back of her neck, skittering down her back. She turned the stone, struck by the fiery way it caught the light. If this *was* a diamond . . . She knew that large, fabulous diamonds did exist, the famous gems of legend. The Koh-i-noor, called the Mountain of Light, had weighed more than six hundred carats when it was found centuries ago in India. The Orlov diamond, Sun of the Sea, had been discovered in a statue of the Indian god Sri Ranga, whose eyes were made of diamonds. Blue-green in hue, it was about as large as half a hen's egg.

But wonderful stones had been found in Africa, too. The Star of South Africa had been found on the Zandfontein farm, near the Orange River, and weighed 83.5 carats. The Tiffany, a yellow diamond that was much bigger, 287.42 carats, had been found right here in Kimberley, in the De Beers Mine, just months ago. It had been bought by Charles Tiffany, the famous New York jeweler, and was now being cut in Paris.

These thoughts ran through Dacey's head in a flash, dazzling her. What if . . .

"I . . . I think we should take this stone into the office and examine it with the loupe," she said, concealing her excitement. The chances of this big, reddish stone being a diamond were remote. She knew that. Still, it wouldn't hurt to look, would it?

"Oh, Mama!" Elizabeth clapped her hands together. "Can I look through the loupe, too? Do you think it's really a diamond? A red diamond?"

Jed, who was seated at a farther sorting table, had turned to stare, attracted by the excitement in Elizabeth's demeanor. But after a moment he shrugged and went back to his work. Elizabeth's enthusiasms were always hectic.

Dacey took the loupe, put it to her eye, and stared into the depths of the stone. But the configurations of the crystal made it difficult to see clearly. Finally she went to her scales, taking the weights out of the little carved box where a space had been hollowed out for each separate designation. Her hand trembled as she placed the red stone in the basket and began adding weights to strike a balance.

"Child, child," Papa muttered behind her, "if this thing is really a diamond, then it's the biggest one that's ever been found in Kimberley. Look, it's as large as a peach."

"Or an apple," piped up Elizabeth.

Hardly daring to breathe, Dacey added another weight, watching as the scales tilted. Slowly she added another, smaller weight, then a second one and a third. "Two hundred and twenty-three carats, Papa," she breathed at last.

Dacey and her father looked at each other. The stone was not as large as the Tiffany. Still . . . Papa was flushed, and Dacey, too, felt her own excitement kindle. Beside them, Elizabeth danced up and down, barely able to contain herself.

"It is," she chanted. "Oh, it is, it is a diamond, Mama, oh, Grandpapa, and I found it . . . I found it . . ."

"Weighing the stone doesn't make it a diamond," Dacey said sharply. "And I couldn't see enough by looking into it with the loupe. It must be tested by a geologist . . ." She sank into a chair, staring at the enormous red stone that still sat in the scale. Even in the enclosed office, the triangular facets caught the light and refracted it, filled with an eery red majesty.

According to the geologist, the red stone was indeed a diamond. Its tint, he told Dacey, was slightly darker than that of the Condé, a rose-pink, pear-shaped stone acquired in 1643 by agents of Louis XIII and given by the king to the Prince de Condé for his services in the Thirty Years' War.

"Do you mean— You can't mean that it's *real*." Dacey stared at the geologist, feeling her heart begin to thump in slow, thick beats.

"I certainly do. It's quite a fine stone, Mrs. Donohue.

Very, very rare, quite a prize, I assure you. It will be the making of your fortune.''

"But what will I do with it?''

The geologist, middle-aged and grizzled, gave her a crooked smile. ''I suggest that you sell it, of course—and believe me, you can sell this anywhere . . . to anyone who has the money to pay for it, that is.''

Dacey sat silently, still trying to take in the magnitude of the news. Louis XIII, the Prince de Condé . . . fabulous names whirled in her head. Queen Victoria. Yes. Would such a beautiful stone be suitable for the Crown Jewels? My God, she thought.

She rushed out of the geologist's office on a floodtide of excitement and found herself hurrying down the street to Cecil Rhodes's office.

Solemnly, the diamond magnate examined the gem, much as the geologist had done, taking more than half an hour to inspect it.

"As no doubt you've been told, the color saturation of this gem is exceptionally strong, Mrs. Donohue,'' he told her at last in his dry voice. He wore a sober suit that covered his lanky form with a minimum of fuss, and his cravat was stiffly starched, giving him a young-old look that Dacey always found striking.

"The ruby-pink tint is caused by slight traces of manganese, making this a gem of exceptional rarity. And you are most fortunate, for this is a loupe-clean diamond, displaying no inclusions or internal blemishes. But of course, you have seen this for yourself.''

Dacey was ashamed to admit she had seen little with the loupe. ''Yes, but I never thought— I mean, men have worked in the mines of Kimberley for years and they've never found anything like this.''

"If you don't mind taking some advice from me, Mrs. Donohue—''

"I'd be glad to have some. This doesn't seem very real to me yet. I thought I would name it the Kimberley Flame. And, of course, I'll have to decide what to do with it . . .'' She realized that she was chattering nervously.

"That's what I want to talk to you about. You must guard this stone carefully. Unlike the American West, Kimberley is a law-abiding settlement. Coaches carrying parcels of diamonds to the coast are seldom robbed, nor are the banks. Still, there is no sense in tempting the greedy. You must keep this diamond a secret, think carefully, and work quickly."

"I . . . I see." Dacey tried to quell her elation. The Kimberley Flame would be the making of her fortune, of Elizabeth's, Jed's, and Papa's. It would mean the changing of all their lives. She must go back and swear the geologist to secrecy. She must not make any mistakes.

"Where should I have it cut?" she asked.

"I would suggest Amsterdam. It is a city, as you know, devoted to the diamond industry, and there are thousands of skilled cutters there. I recommend a family called Asscher. They have workshops on the Tolstraat and are very reputable. I think they can help you."

"All right."

"And I would suggest that you go yourself to have this stone cut, Mrs. Donohue. The process is risky and should not be entrusted to underlings."

Daydreams lifted Dacey on a river of excitement. Herself, being admitted to the royal chambers, to curtsy low and hand over a cut diamond of stunning beauty to the queen herself.

"We will be forever grateful to you, Dacey Donohue, for providing us with this perfect gem," the queen said in a low, throaty, royal voice. "In token of our regard, we wish to present you with a badge of our esteem . . ."

Taking Cecil Rhodes's advice, she made plans to leave. She decided to take Elizabeth with her, leaving Jed at home to supervise the mining company, with Royce continuing as overseer. She would be gone, Dacey knew, for more than a year, depending on how long it took to cut the big diamond.

She also decided to take her father with her. There were friends in London that John McKinnon wanted to see again before he died, and Dacey couldn't bear the prospect of leaving him alone for a year. If anything happened to him while she was gone, she knew she would never forgive herself.

She packed in a flurry of excitement, swearing Elizabeth and Papa to secrecy, telling Bella and others only that she wished a change of scenery.

Packing late one night, lost in dreams of being received at court, Dacey was startled to hear a knock on the door. Thinking it was Bella, she hurried to answer it.

"Hello, Dacey."

Quinn. Dacey's hands flew to her breast and she felt her heart twist and thump as if it were about to break through her chest cavity. Unlike other diamond men, who dressed flamboyantly and loaded themselves with diamonds, Quinn was elegantly tailored. His well-cut suit emphasized the breadth of his shoulders, the rangy grace of his body. He stood gazing down at her, some trick of the evening light making his eyes seem dark, almost black.

"Well, aren't you going to invite me in? Or must we conduct our business on the doorstep?" He regarded her with amusement.

Dacey managed a reply, feeling little electrical shivers ripple up and down her skin. She led him into her newly furnished sitting room. She had filled the room with antiques from England, lamp fixtures of Waterford crystal, painted screens from Japan, making it an elegant little oasis in the dusty world of Kimberley.

Now she tried to quiet her breathing as they sat down. Why had Quinn come? What did he want? Nervously she remembered that Elizabeth was asleep in her bedroom, that Jed was out drinking, the servants in their own compound at the back of the house. She was alone here with Quinn . . . Her thoughts fluttered like birds, unable to alight.

"Dacey, you seem flushed. Are you that upset to see me?"

"No! No, I . . . of course I'm not." Yet she felt her blush deepen, and she swallowed hard, hating the physical response of her body to this man. He made her feel lost, out of control, *vulnerable.*

He seemed to enjoy her discomfiture. "I have flustered you, haven't I? Well, I don't mean to disturb you, but I know that you are leaving for Amsterdam to have your red diamond cut, and I wanted to talk with you.''

''The diamond—how did you know about it? I thought I had kept it a secret.''

He grinned. ''Maybe *you* kept it a secret, but your daughter did not. Yesterday I encountered Elizabeth on the path to the mine, and she couldn't help bursting out with her news. The huge, flame-colored diamond she found, your trip to Europe to have it cut, the fact that she is going with you— this is a big event in her life, Dacey, and I'm afraid she couldn't keep quiet.''

Dacey sank backward into the cushions of the couch. ''But I told her not to tell—''

''She is still a child, and this is incredibly exciting for her.'' Quinn's smile was gentle. ''But it does mean that your secret is out. Rumors are already flying in town about the huge diamond Elizabeth found. You both have been the subject of much discussion and envy, I assure you.''

''Oh!'' Dacey tried to push away her irritation at Elizabeth, her feeling of uneasy exposure before the town.

''Soon, no doubt, men will be pounding on your door demanding to see this fabulous gem. And the newspapers, too. Not that you can blame people for their curiosity, I suppose. Still, that's one reason I've come.''

''Oh?''

''My two men from Belfast will accompany you to Cape Town and see you safely on your ship for the Netherlands.''

Dacey remembered the bodyguards Quinn had once hired for her—guards never used. ''But I don't need them,'' she protested. ''I'm sure we will be perfectly fine. We're going in one of the Gibson Brothers' coaches. There will be a driver and other passengers, we will all be very safe—''

''You'll be much safer with Rory and Seamus O'Leary. I insist, Dacey. Odds are that nothing will happen, but I want to be sure.''

How dare Quinn think that he could manage her life from afar, making decisions without even consulting her? Yet along with her anger, Dacey felt a curious warmth. Quinn cared about her. That was why he had done it.

She smoothed her fingers down the flounces of the dark-blue silk she wore, wishing that it was one of her newer dresses. Still, she knew the deep color showed off the fiery luster of her hair and accented her green eyes. Did Quinn notice the way she looked? Did he still love her? Was that why he had really come?

She felt dizzy with all the emotions boiling through her, the questions that could have no answers.

"There is another reason that I wanted you to have bodyguards," Quinn went on. "I'm hoping that you'll be carrying something else besides the Kimberley Flame."

"Something else? What would that be?"

"These." Quinn reached into his jacket coat and pulled out a leather bag that tied with a drawstring. With a swift gesture, he opened the bag and tipped its contents onto a small side table.

Dacey gasped. Before her lay spread out at least one hundred large, uncut white diamonds. Lush, glittering, it was a fabulous display of wealth, a queen's treasure trove shining in the lamplight.

"Why . . ." Dacey felt her throat close. "These are the diamonds you have been collecting, aren't they?"

"Yes. Each one of them is flawless. It took years to accumulate them."

Dacey nodded numbly, knowing that these were the stones for Janine's necklace, the symbol of Quinn's commitment to another woman. What a fool she'd been, what a dreaming, softheaded, idiotic fool, to think that Quinn Farris ever could have loved her.

He didn't, he never had. Even as she had been thinking of him, dreaming of him, he had been collecting these diamonds. The memories that she treasured had been, for him, no more than a fleeting moment of pleasure.

She felt sullied, dirtied beyond measure.

"You want me to take these diamonds to Amsterdam with me, don't you?" she heard herself say in a strange, flat voice.

"Yes, if you would. Dacey, I know that this is an imposition, but there is no one else in town that I can trust with this, and business won't permit me to go myself. We are friends and I know I can depend on you.''

She was silent as she heard him go on. "Will you have these diamonds cut for me? I want the large stones cut into a pear shape. The smaller ones will be brilliant-cut, and they will surround the pendant larger stones. I have already sketched out a rough version of the necklace; the jeweler will have to design the final version.''

Dacey was trembling, her blood rushing alternately hot and cold. How dare Quinn ask this of her? Ask her to see to a diamond necklace for his *wife*? And when the necklace was completed, her thoughts rushed on in an angry torrent, when it was splendid, glittering in its glory, then would Quinn take it back to America and use it to win back his wife's love?

Of course he would. The necklace had been intended for Janine from the start.

For an instant she had the urge to slam her hand across the tabletop, sending the hateful diamonds spinning onto the floor. Then, with effort, she controlled the impulse. No, she wouldn't give Quinn the satisfaction of seeing her lose her temper like a thwarted fishwife, a jealous lover. Why reveal to him her weakness and anguish?

"Very well," she said coolly. She reached out to pick up one of the stones, balancing it on her palm as if it were only a glass bauble, barely worthy of scrutiny. "I'll carry out your request, then, Quinn, just as you ask.''

He looked at her sharply. She thought she saw pain flicker deep in his eyes. Then his face became a smooth, polite mask like her own.

"I will be forever grateful for the favor, Dacey. And for your trouble, I have reserved two of the stones for you. I thought you would like to have them made up into a pendant or maybe a bracelet.''

A bracelet? Like the one Natala owned? Dacey thought she would not be able to hang on to the wild fury that surged through her now. It took all her effort to steady her voice.

"No, I don't want your diamonds, Quinn, I won't accept pay." She raised her eyes to his, putting all her anger, her fury, into one scorching look. "For old time's sake, I'll do you this favor. After that, all obligations are finished between us."

She was pleased to see a dull red flush spread up from Quinn's neck, to stain his cheekbones.

Dry-eyed, accompanied by Elizabeth, her father, and the two bodyguards, Dacey left Kimberley the following morning. She rode through the outskirts of town without a backward glance, so angry at Quinn that she didn't care if she ever saw him, or Kimberley, again. How could Quinn have done such a cruel thing to her? To ask her to see to the cutting and design of his wife's necklace!

Fuming, she gazed out of the dusty window of the coach as the tents and iron buildings of Kimberley grew smaller, pinned under a huge blue sky.

Very well, she thought. She'd do what he asked of her— and she would do it superbly. She'd see to it that he got the most stunning necklace possible, something gorgeous and rare. But when she returned to Kimberley, she'd toss the necklace into Quinn's face. She could picture herself, hurling it, the satisfaction of watching the rope of diamonds spin through the air, his surprise as it hit him. Oh, she'd never speak to him again, not if she lived to be a hundred years old. She'd forbid Elizabeth to talk to him, too. She'd . . .

Miserably, she sank back into her seat in the jouncing coach, her anger a choking knot in her throat. Maybe going away would help, she told herself. Amsterdam was far away from hot blue skies and burning sun and dusty diamond earth. Maybe there, she could forget Quinn and all that he had meant to her.

She certainly intended to try.

15

GRACIOUS VISTAS OF CANALS LINED with elm trees. Cobbled streets, bright patches of flowers, church spires, ornate old gates and tall, narrow houses embellished with a thousand intricate varieties of gables. Jewish streets, full of men in spit curls and yarmulkes, dressed in black. And everywhere, the canals, bisecting the Dutch seaport city, reflecting back the gentle sky.

Dacey rented a house on Amsterdam's fashionable Keizersgracht canal. A small garden at the back contained statues, a pergola, a summerhouse, sundial, even a grapevine, its stem thickened with age.

Elizabeth adored the garden and spent hours playing there or being tutored in her schoolwork. Papa quickly found an old thespian crony and made plans to visit London on his own.

"Yours is the pleasure of seeing to your wonderful red diamond," he told Dacey. "I have friends to see. Who knows? Maybe even a play or two left in my blood. Ah, to appear again on the London stage, child. Can an old man be blamed for dreaming?"

Willem Asscher, the diamond-cutter that Cecil Rhodes had recommended, was a small man with a round face and bright black eyes. He spoke to her in fluent, although accented English.

"Your stone is quite, quite exceptional," he told Dacey

after taking three days to study the Flame and make elaborate drawings of it. "It displays a natural cleavage line on its largest face, and therefore appears to be a fragment of an even larger stone."

Dacey was startled. "A second stone?"

"Ah, yes, more's the pity. Perhaps the other half will be found someday, who knows? The odds are, however, that it is lost in the dim mists of time. But at any rate, we are going to have to study *this* diamond for several months before we can even begin work."

"But I thought—"

The diamond-cutter laughed. "You thought it would be simply a matter of taking a few slices with a saw, and it would be finished? Mrs. Donohue, cutting a gem of this magnitude is a matter fraught with great risk. All crystals have tensions and places of natural cleavage. In the old days, the ancients tried to test diamonds by smashing at them with a mallet. If a stone did not crush, it was thought to be a diamond. The truth was"—Asscher shrugged—"many real gems were also destroyed in the process."

"I see." Dacey looked down at the large, triangular-shaped rough gem that sat in front of them in a vise, its red luster soft and gleaming today. If it were to shatter . . .

She forced away the unpleasant thought.

"Tell me of your plans for the stone, Mr. Asscher," she said at last.

"First I would like to polish a small facet, cutting a little window that will give me a view of the gem's interior. This is most important, as it will help me determine where any lines of cleavage or flaws might be."

After he had finished explaining the cutting procedure, Asscher took Dacey on a tour of his workrooms. Workers bent over wooden tables, some wearing odd, wire-rimmed glasses that projected inches from the ends of their noses. Some worked near globes of blue liquid, apparently for a more even source of light.

One man was marking a stone with India ink to show a cleavage point. Others faceted diamonds with saws made of fine iron wire that had diamond powder pressed into the blade to give it bite. Still others polished stones on a wheel.

There was a metal grid on the floor, Dacey noticed, to allow any chips or bits of diamond powder dropped on the floor to be recovered at the end of the day.

"Well, Mrs. Donohue, do you think you can trust us?" Willem Asscher asked as he ushered her out of the work area and into a tiny, neat office.

Dacey smiled. Everything in the workshop had spoken of caution and delicate, painstaking work.

"I'm going to have to, aren't I? Mr. Asscher, this stone is very important to me. I have great hopes for it, I would like to try to sell it to Queen Victoria." She extended her hand to the cutter. "So, please, start your study at once. And I will also need the stones cut for the necklace of white diamonds, as we discussed."

Asscher nodded. "Very well. I will keep you informed of our progress. Meanwhile, you must enjoy our beautiful city. There is no such thing as haste in the cutting of diamonds . . ."

So Dacey immersed herself in an impatient period of waiting. She waited for the Kimberley Flame to be studied, Quinn's diamonds to be cut. She sent a letter to Queen Victoria, telling her of the fabulous gem now in the Asscher workshops and asking if the queen would be interested in seeing the diamond when finished. Then she waited—weeks, months—for the reply.

Yes, Victoria would be interested in a viewing. The response came on beautifully rich vellum with the royal seal, penned in a secretary's precise handwriting.

Dacey and Elizabeth journeyed to Paris, where Dacey ordered complete new wardrobes for both of them, and they waited more long weeks for fittings. But, illogically, Dacey also waited for something else that she knew would never come: a letter from Quinn telling her that he had changed his mind, that he did not wish a necklace made for his wife after all.

Quinn sent no such letter.

At night, Dacey tossed and turned, caught in vivid dreams.

Quinn's face, dappled by shade from the thorn tree, his eyes fastened on hers with tender longing . . . Once she dreamed that Quinn wore a glittering mask of ruby diamonds set in encrusted rows. He smiled at her. Then he turned away and walked down a long tunnel, into the arms of another woman. The woman, beautiful and hard-faced, wore a small diamond mask of her own . . .

Dacey awakened from this dream covered with perspiration. She sat up in bed, wiping moisture from her hairline and temples, her body shivering. *Quinn.* What was wrong with her, what kind of insanity had taken over her mind to torment her? Why couldn't she forget this man? Had he bewitched her?

Go away, Quinn, she thought in desperation. Please, get out of my thoughts, I don't want you in my mind anymore, I don't want you. And she knew it was a lie.

One day she was called back to the Asscher workshops. They were going to start the first cleaving, the most important, and Asscher wondered if Dacey wished to be there.

Transported with excitement, Dacey dressed herself and Elizabeth in their finest clothes for this event. Dacey wore a gown of toast-colored cashmere and skirts of bronze satin. Cut in the new cuirass style, it clung closely to her body, emphasizing the flowing lines of hip and back. Inspecting herself in a full-length mirror, Dacey decided that she looked curved and lush, very feminine.

She dressed Elizabeth in delicate mousseline de laine trimmed with ruching, ribbons, and lace, brushing back the child's glossy dark curls and fastening them with a matched bow.

Elizabeth was wild with excitement as they boarded a canal boat to take them to the diamond district. She was barely able to restrain herself from telling the boatman all about their errand.

Dacey smiled, but she, too, felt tense from nervousness. Despite all planning, the first cleavage of a stone like the Kimberley Flame was fraught with risk. In a second, it could smash apart forever, and a rarity of nature, a stone of dreams, would be totally destroyed.

But she tried to push away her apprehension. Hadn't she

consulted one of the best diamond-cutting families in the world? She could not believe that luck could lead them to such a wonderful stone only to see it ruined before their very eyes.

Willem Asscher frowned when he saw Elizabeth. "This is a delicate moment, Mrs. Donohue, and the presence of a noisy child . . ."

Dacey drew herself up. "Mr. Asscher, Elizabeth found the Kimberley Flame and she has a right to be here to see it cleaved. I swear to you that she will be absolutely still. If she is not, I will take her away at once. You may trust me in that."

"Very well." Reluctantly, the diamond-cutter nodded. Dacey saw that perspiration beaded his forehead and upper lip. She realized that he, too, was nervous.

The work was to be done on a table in the center of the workshop, exactly as if this was any other diamond. Elizabeth clutched Dacey's hand, grown solemn at the importance of the occasion. A few other cutters had gathered to watch, but most of them remained at their benches. The Flame, fastened in its clamps, glowed before them.

It had taken three days, Asscher explained, to make the tiny, V-shaped incision in the gem for the cutting blade. Now, with painstaking care, he inserted a steel blade in the cleft he had made. With a mallet he tapped it.

Dacey's heart slammed and she felt Elizabeth grip her hand tightly. Then, with a stinging crack, the cleaving blade broke. The intact Kimberley Flame, still in its clamps, seemed to glint at them mockingly.

Two red spots stained Willem Asscher's cheeks as he gazed down at the broken blade.

"I have followed all rules and my calculations of the planes of cleavage are accurate; I have studied them most diligently." He drew a deep breath. "I will try again."

Dacey tensed, holding her breath. Beside her she was aware of Elizabeth doing the same. The whole workroom seemed to vibrate with tension, and all the wheels and lathes had stopped. In the silence, Willem Asscher picked up the small mallet and inserted another blade in the cleft. Again he tapped the blade firmly.

Again the blade broke.

Elizabeth's eyes were wide, but the little girl held herself very still and said not a word. Dacey felt as if every muscle in her own body was wound as tightly as a spring. The diamond was huge, immensely valuable, incredibly rare. But the cleaving was not going well: the blade had broken twice. What if, on a third try, the stone shattered? It could happen. And then what?

"Mrs. Donohue? I still believe in my calculations. But now it is up to you. What do you wish me to do?"

Dacey hesitated, looking at the ruby-colored diamond. How beautiful it was, even in its raw form. She thought of the letter from Queen Victoria, a thousand daydreams of security for herself and Elizabeth, for her family. All of this could be destroyed in an instant. And yet . . . It was luck that had led Elizabeth to the Kimberley Flame in the first place, perhaps the very luck and omens that Papa worshiped. Could she deny that luck now?

She swallowed, gathering her courage. "Go ahead. I want you to try again, of course."

"Are you sure?"

"Yes. Please go ahead."

This time, the diamond-cutter took twice as long to place a third blade in the kerf. When he had done so, he walked around the table, examining the stone from every angle, totally absorbed in his inspection. The ring of observers around the table had grown; almost all the workmen had now focused their attention on the huge raw diamond.

But Asscher seemed to take no notice of them. He frowned at the gem, checked a page of calculations, readjusted the diamond in its clamps, until Dacey thought she would explode with her tension.

But at last he was ready. Swiftly he tapped the blade with the mallet, and this time the Kimberley Flame split perfectly, one face sliding away.

"He did it, he did it!" Elizabeth squealed, unable to contain herself any longer. She hugged Dacey and they whirled around in a little dance of joy, while the cutters jabbered together in Dutch and Yiddish, and even Asscher looked smug.

"We will celebrate in my office with some wine," he announced. "Then I must get back to work. Unfortunately, this was only the beginning of my labors, Mrs. Donohue. You must wait many more months before I am finished."

For Dacey, those months inched by, but at last the day came when she held the completed Kimberley Flame in her hand. Cutting had reduced its weight by more than one hundred carats, and four smaller diamonds, also to be sold, had been cut from the leavings.

"What do you think of it, Mrs. Donohue?" Asscher asked. His eyes, too, were riveted on the flame-colored diamond that blazed in the palm of Dacey's hand, its depths fascinating in their fierce play of light. It had been cut in what jewelers called pear-shaped brilliant, and it had seventy-four shimmering facets, each perfect.

Dacey moistened her lips, stunned by the flashing beauty of the diamond. "It—it's gorgeous. I had no idea . . ."

"You should have it set simply," the cutter advised. "I myself will recommend a jeweler, Piet Du Plessis. You can trust him implicitly with this gem, as well as with the other diamonds that we have cut for you."

The other diamonds. By that he meant the diamonds for Janine's necklace, the stones that Dacey had forced out of her mind these long weeks and months, refusing to think about them.

She went to the address Asscher gave her and then waited another long eight weeks while the jeweler did his work. Papa arrived back from London, where he had appeared briefly at the Adelphi Theatre. He was full of renewed life and juicy theater gossip. Dacey took him to the house of Du Plessis, the jewelers, and showed him the Kimberley Flame, now being fashioned into a pendant that would hang from a simple gold necklace.

John McKinnon gave a low, awed whistle. Then he reached out to take the large gem in his hand. For long moments he stared down at it, turning the diamond over and over in his hands.

He frowned. "This diamond . . . it has a mysterious depth to it, Dacey, as if at its core it burns with the fire of the gods . . ." Papa gave an odd shiver. Quickly he put the gem down on a table, as if it had scorched him. "Perhaps that isn't so good, Dacia."

"I don't understand."

"There are some diamonds whose history has been written in blood." John McKinnon's deep, theatrical voice gave these words emphasis. "A man was tortured and blinded in order to gain possession of the Koh-i-noor. Tavernier, who stole the Great Blue Diamond from a statue of the god Rama Sita, met an atrocious death, Dacey, devoured by wild animals. Louis XIV wore the diamond only once and died shortly afterward. Marie Antoinette wore it, and you know what happened to her. . . . I don't mean to alarm you, Dacia, but this stone gives me feelings . . . it stirs things in me . . . I cannot fully explain."

"Oh, Papa—"

Yet Dacey, too, stared down at the red diamond. It seemed like a separate entity, she thought slowly, having nothing to do with her or with those who would later own it. Good? Evil? It belonged to itself, and if blood were shed over it, that would not be its fault.

She felt her body quiver, a chill prickling the surface of her skin.

"Papa . . ." She tried to laugh. "It is a beautiful diamond and I wish you hadn't said that. I have high hopes of selling it to the queen. It will be the making of our fortune, I know it will."

"Perhaps. But I wish you would have a duplicate made of the thing, Dacia. In the hands of an expert, paste jewelry can be fashioned into something surprisingly realistic."

"Oh, but, Papa, surely—"

"I insist, Dacia. I have said little to you in the past about some things, but this is one time when I want you to listen to me."

*   *   *

Reluctantly, Dacey did as Papa requested. It cost her an extra ten weeks. But the duplicate, when completed, was an eerie replica of the Kimberley Flame, down to the last detail of clasp and gold necklace. Only the blazing flash of light refraction could not be matched, but in dim light, Dacey assured herself, the two stones looked exactly alike. She instructed Du Plessis to scratch a tiny mark in the back of the replica, so that she would know which one it was.

Still, Papa's remarks about the diamonds whose history had been written in blood cast a shadow over these preparations, and she was relieved when it was time to make a last call at the Du Plessis workrooms to pick up the necklace that had been fashioned for Janine Farris.

The jeweler was effusive, insisting on praise for his work. "What do you think, Mrs. Donohue? Do you not think that this creation is beyond compare?"

Dacey gazed at the heavy, ornate necklace, displayed on a jewelers' bust that had lines drawn into the clay so that the balance and fall of the piece could be checked. The necklace consisted of one hundred marquise-cut stones and ninety-three round brilliants, the ten largest gems hanging pendant, surrounded by smaller ones. The total effect, Dacey thought, was stunning, flashy, ostentatious. The necklace would hang heavily on a woman's neck, tiring her muscles.

"It is—stunning, I'm sure," Dacey managed to reply to the jeweler, barely able to look at the glittering creation that would adorn another woman. She fantasized hurling it at Quinn, seeing it smash at his feet. "Would you please wrap it up so that I may take it with me?"

"Do you mean that you don't wish to try it on yourself?"

"No."

The jeweler, annoyed at Dacey's reaction, sniffed as he wrapped the heavy necklace in tissue and then laid it in a velvet-lined box. "Whoever wears it will certainly turn heads, Mrs. Donohue. But perhaps that does not appeal to you, eh?"

Dacey did not reply.

As soon as she arrived back at the house on the Keizersgracht, she thrust the box that held Janine's necklace into a deep-set pocket of her traveling trunk and refused to look at it again, or to show it to Papa or Elizabeth. She hated the necklace. Loathed it. And despised what it meant. . . .

They packed for London and left the following morning. Dacey felt weary and forced herself to travel, thinking of the hot sun and blue skies of Kimberley, so far away. London seemed chilly, drab, and sooty, and Elizabeth had caught a cold. She coughed and dragged about listlessly, begging constantly for cakes or for Dacey to read aloud to her.

Dacey had expected to be given an audience with the queen and was searingly disappointed to be shown, instead, into a room filled with a corps of elderly advisers. These men poked and prodded at the ruby diamond, held it under the light, and examined it with loupes and microscopes, whispering among themselves. Finally they conferred and asked Dacey to bring it back again in a week's time.

Dacey left, filled with hope. Victoria herself wished to see the Flame! That was why she had been asked to come back. But the following week, the queen did not appear and Dacey was greeted by a second set of advisers. Again she was forced to wait impatiently while they examined the stone.

"It is most unfortunate," an elderly gentleman told her at last. He wore the ribbons of some order on his lapel and had fussy, precise mannerisms. "Her Majesty has expressed interest in another stone called the Idol's Eye. It is much larger than this one and was found in India."

Dacey's mouth fell open: the queen did not want the Kimberley Flame. She was too shocked to be angry or to do anything but stare at this fussy old gentleman who, evidently, could not recognize true beauty when he saw it.

"You will surely be able to dispose of this gem elsewhere," the retainer added kindly. "Perhaps to lesser royalty. Diamonds of this sort can always find a home."

"Diamonds of this sort." And "lesser royalty"? When she had dreamed of the queen? Dacey nodded and fled the royal anterooms. A choking disappointment flooded her. Back in her two-wheeled hansom cab, she sank against the leather seat, feeling the energy and hope drain out of her. She had been in Europe nearly a year and a half. All of that time, she had left her mining company to Jed and Royce.

Now, abruptly, she was tired of Europe, with its soft blue skies, its tiled roofs and gables and chimney pots, its houses crammed in, one upon the other. She longed for sun, for a sky so blue that it hurt the eyes.

She wanted to go home.

The trip from Southampton to the Cape was a rough one, with stormy seas. They saw land only at Madeira, and later they had a superb view of the Peak of Tenerife. Afterward, they saw very few other ships until, approaching Cape Town, they saw at last the unmistakable profile of Table Mountain, which dominated the seaport.

Elizabeth had developed another cold aboard ship, and during the long, dusty coach ride to Kimberley, Dacey tried to nurse her. Fever, cough, listlessness—there were few remedies along the trail, other than the small supply of medicines that Dacey carried in her trunk.

Finally, they pulled into Kimberley. The streets seemed as rutted, as dusty, noisy, and hot as Dacey remembered. There seemed to be more ox teams than ever, the animals bellowing and jostling in the square. Men crowded the streets, hurrying back and forth on important errands. After Amsterdam, Kimberley seemed incredibly raw and alive.

"This child has nothing more than a troublesome upper-respiratory bronchitis," Dr. Sowers told Dacey later that day while Elizabeth waited in an examining room. "I am sure that rest and our dry Kimberley air will cure her quickly. It is your husband whom I am more concerned about."

"My husband?" Dacey's heart sank as she remembered the sullen way that Jed had greeted her on their arrival.

"Your long absence has not been good for the man." Dr. Sowers regarded her accusingly. "All of his old habits are back. The drinking, the melancholia, the apathy, the anger. Last month I treated a native woman who had been brought here. She claimed to have been beaten by a man in an invalid chair. With a stick."

"No." Dacey felt as if she would be sick.

"I tried to talk with Jed about this, but he would not listen. He is obsessed, Mrs. Donohue, with this native woman who he thinks caused his paralysis."

"But . . . what can we do?"

"We? It is *you* who are going to have to do something, Mrs. Donohue. There are people in this town who disapproved of your long absence, and I must say I agree with them. Jed Donohue is an ill man, and you had no right to shift away your burden with a feckless trip to Europe."

Dr. Sowers's eyes flicked up and down Dacey's new, fashionable, Paris-made gown. "Where, I see, you availed yourself of the pleasures of the *couturier*."

"Yes, I did buy some new dresses," Dacey snapped. "But what does that have to do with Jed . . . or with anything else?"

Angrily she walked home, Elizabeth at her side, still coughing. She had been in Kimberley less than a day, yet already problems waited for her.

At home, she put her daughter to bed, rubbing her chest with the salve that Dr. Sowers had given her and giving her some cough mixture.

"I want to go see Bella," the child begged, holding out her arms fitfully. "I want to show her the Kimberley Flame!"

"But, my darling, remember what I told you on board the ship? We must keep the Flame a secret. Only you and I, and Grandpapa, and Daddy Jed must know."

"No, no, I want to tell Bella. And Bokembi, and Makema, and Myra, and Susan-Anne, and—" The last two names, Dacey knew, belonged to small playmates, daughters of diamond-men.

She sighed, remembering how Elizabeth had blurted news of the uncut Flame to Quinn just before they had left. Quinn, who also knew of the Flame and whom she must arrange to see about the necklace for his wife . . .

She gave in to the inevitable. "Very well, Elizabeth, this is one secret that we won't keep, after all. Instead, we'll give a party, an unveiling for the Kimberley Flame, the diamond that you found. But you must promise me that you will stay quietly in bed until you are well.''

"Oh, yes, yes, Mama!'' Elizabeth's blue eyes danced with excitement. "But I want to have the''—she stumbled over the unfamiliar word—"the unveiling soon.''

"As soon as you are better,'' Dacey promised. "Then we'll show Kimberley our diamond.''

That week, Dacey had a severe talk with Bokembi, threatening him with firing, and worse, if Jed ever attacked another young woman. Over Jed's objections, she added another servant, Mubuto, to their employ. Both men were to accompany Jed whenever he made forays into the saloons of Kimberley.

"You want to keep me like a lapdog,'' Jed muttered rebelliously. "While you were gone, it wasn't like this. Royce never treated me so high-handedly—''

"Royce isn't responsible for you,'' Dacey flared. "I am. Anyway, I notice that he was far too busy while I was gone, buying himself new clothes and diamond studs for his tie, to pay much attention to you. I saw him today at the mine office. He looked like the gaudiest of the diamond buyers.''

"Royce has been very useful.'' Jed defended the overseer.

"Maybe he has. And maybe that's why you were so displeased to see me arrive home. But now that I am back, things must change, Jed. There can be no more violence against women.''

"I won't be a prisoner,'' Jed muttered. But he sat quietly in his invalid chair, looking down at his hands, until Dacey left the room. She went into her own bedroom, feeling thwarted and dissatisfied. It was as if she had never left. Everything had been here waiting for her, nothing was changed or solved.

A week later they held the unveiling, an event that was wildly successful. Men and women thronged through the big house, admiring the expensive furnishings and fingering the silk damask drapes that had to be shaken every day to remove the dust that blew in from the mines. Dacey had invited most of the town's prominent citizens. These included members of the Kimberley and Dutoitspan mining boards, a few actors,

Cecil Rhodes, some of Papa's more respectable drinking friends, Lavinia and Tony Agnelli, and, of course, Bella.

The women eyed Dacey's Parisian frock, of ecru silk, with its lush, draped style and beaded embroidery. The men talked to Jed or Papa, or crowded about the small bar, boasting of their diamond finds or discussing the latest illicit diamond scandal.

Bella swept among the ladies in a bottle-green satin ballgown, totally at home among the women for whom she sewed bonnets and gowns. Even Lavinia, fatter than ever, wore one of Bella's creations, diamonds glittering at her plump throat.

Every other woman wore diamonds, too, and most of the men. This was a diamond town: every person in the room was here because of diamonds, and here in Kimberley it was the one sure way to show off one's worth.

"Well, when are we going to see *it*?" Lavinia demanded. "This fabulous diamond that everyone is talking about! Look at your daughter, Dacey, she is positively dancing up and down, waiting for the big moment."

Dacey glanced at Elizabeth. She certainly was doing just that, unbearably keyed up with pride and the tension of the evening. If the Flame was not revealed soon, surely Elizabeth would burst.

"Very well." Dacey smiled. "I'll be back in a moment, then. We certainly must not keep Elizabeth in suspense any longer."

Excusing herself, she went to the wall safe hidden in her bedroom, where she removed the box that held the Kimberley Flame. She took out the gem, its weight heavy in her hands. As it caught the lamplight, living flames leaped within its depths.

For an instant, Dacey hesitated, remembering the Koh-i-noor, the Great Blue Diamond. Then, slowly, she placed the pendant around her neck and fastened its clasp. The huge stone felt cool for a moment against her skin, until her body heat warmed it.

Dacey moved in front of the bureau mirror to stare at her reflection. In the glass she saw a woman with masses of red-gold hair piled on her head in soft ringlets. Her slanting green eyes were soft, dreamy. The Parisian gown clung to her figure, revealing the full curves of her breasts, the lithe, slim waist.

Yet the Kimberley Flame, blazing at her throat, dominated her appearance. It gave her a look of regal bearing, like a queen. No woman could wear the Flame without looking magnificent, Dacey realized with an indrawn catch of her breath. The gem was so stunning, so blazingly beautiful, that it almost wore *her*, Dacey told herself with a nervous little laugh.

She turned away from the mirror.

An hour later, Elizabeth at her side, she had circulated through the house, satisfied with the shock waves of excitement that the stone generated wherever she went. Some of the guests seemed overwhelmed, begging to touch the stone. Others, like Royce McKinnon, flashing with diamonds himself on two finger rings and a huge cravat pin, were openly envious.

"Some people have all the luck, don't they, Dacey?" Royce murmured, his eyes fastened on the Kimberley Flame. "And to think that I knew you when there were patches in your petticoats."

"Don't forget, Uncle, I knew *you* when there were patches in your pants," Dacey retorted, moving on to the next group. She tried to stifle her annoyance at Royce. He had always envied everything she had and apparently the Kimberley Flame was going to be no exception.

At last, it was Elizabeth's turn. As the culmination of the little girl's evening, Dacey allowed her daughter to wear the Flame around her own neck. Elizabeth was nearly speechless with rapture. To the amusement of the guests, she paraded around the house, sweeping her sprigged muslin skirts as if she were a grand court lady.

"I'm the queen, the queen," she chanted happily. "Oh, Mama, isn't this wonderful? And now *everyone* knows about our diamond, how beautiful it is, how wonderful. I think we are the most famous people in Kimberley now!"

Some of the guests had already left when Makema came

hurrying up to tell Dacey that another guest had arrived, a man who was waiting for Dacey on the veranda.

"But who . . . ?" She had put the Flame back in the safe and had begun to relax a little. A glass of champagne had left her feeling pleasantly light-headed.

"I don't know who he be, missy. He just say I call you, tell you come see him there. He not want to bother your company."

"I see." It was probably just a party-crasher, Dacey decided, a miner who hoped for a free glimpse of the diamond. If so, she would quickly send him on his way.

It was only as she stepped onto the veranda, fragrant with the spicy odor of climbing roses and gardenias grown in pots, that it occurred to her that her caller might be Quinn. She had sent him a letter on her arrival, telling him that she had Janine's necklace to deliver to him, but had received no response.

But now it was too late to step back into the house. She was forced to continue forward, to where a dark shape stood at the end of the long porch. He had turned partly away from her, staring out at the bright spill of moonlight that touched the blue gums and eucalyptus. Yet, unmistakably outlined in the silver light, Dacey saw the rugged lines of Quinn's profile.

"I understand that the Kimberley Flame is fabulous, a gem without peer." His voice came evenly out of the darkness. "A pity I wasn't invited to view it."

Dacey didn't know what to say. Her heart was thumping horribly in her throat and a pang raked across the fibers of her heart like a knife blade. She remembered her fantasy of throwing Janine's necklace into Quinn's face.

She didn't have the necklace with her. But even if she did, she knew that she could not have flung it. Her body seemed filled with a tight, shaking weakness.

"I'm sorry," she managed. "I did send you a letter."

"I know. I received it," he told her, "and I'm sorry for not answering it, but I was engrossed in business. I also apologize for the intrusion tonight, but I have made arrangements for passage to San Francisco and I wanted to pick up the necklace. I assume that you have it with you and that it is as specified?"

How level his voice was, how carefully laundered of emotion. They could have been two strangers discussing a business deal. Dacey fought back tears. All those months in Amsterdam, she had hated Quinn on account of that necklace. Now, suddenly, she didn't hate him anymore. Instead she felt . . . empty. Yes, that was it, she felt hollowed out of all her love, emptied of all feelings.

Quinn wanted his necklace so badly that he couldn't wait for her to deliver it to him, but had come here to get it. He had already made travel arrangements, was apparently chafing to leave.

Well, she certainly would not delay him.

"Yes, I have it for you," she told him coldly. "If you'll wait here for a moment, I'll go and get it. You can inspect the necklace at your leisure, but I'm sure you'll find it perfect in every detail."

"I'm certain that I will, too."

Her heart in her throat, Dacey ran to the safe and got the necklace, bringing it to Quinn still in its box. As she handed the box to him, their fingers accidentally brushed.

Dacey thought she would cry out at his touch.

"You may inspect it now, if you wish," she told him, keeping her voice under control.

"No, if you say that the necklace is perfect, I'm sure that it is."

They stood silently, heaviness between them. For a moment Dacey thought that Quinn would say something else, that he was about to start forward, to take her in his arms. And perhaps she would have gone into them, forgetting everything.

Then she realized that Quinn had started toward the veranda steps. "I will be in Virginia City," he told her harshly. "Perhaps for a very long time."

"Yes."

There seemed nothing else to say, nothing that could hold them together now. Janine Farris seemed to stand between them, an insistent ghost. Dacey stood on the veranda, watching as Quinn descended the steps and disappeared into the shadows of the dark street. She wondered if she would ever see him again. And knew, by the tears choking at the back of her throat, that she still cared.

16

NATALA HURRIED DOWN THE PATH that led to the kraal of her family, a small bag of herbs and medicines slung over her shoulder. Overhead, the sun burned a hole through harsh blue. The air hummed with insect sounds and a dry breeze pushed at clumps of sand, swirling dust in tiny, vicious whirlwinds.

Her heart simmered with anger.

Two days ago, Quinn Farris had left for Virginia City, but before he departed, they had quarreled bitterly over the diamond necklace that Dacey had brought back from Amsterdam.

It had begun when Natala saw Quinn open a box lined with soft, dark cloth. From it he had taken a magnificent necklace, diamonds dripping from between his fingers like flashing droplets of dew. Natala had caught her breath, mesmerized by the heavy opulence, the white fire, of the diamonds. But Quinn had scowled at the necklace, turning the gems over in his fingers as if he hated them.

"What are you staring at?" he had asked her savagely.

"Why, that." She pointed to the necklace. "It is beautiful."

"No. It is as ugly as sin, as hatred. It is everything vulgar and glittering, Natala, and it is a weapon of revenge."

Never had Natala seen Quinn's face so dark and brooding. She watched his fingers clench on the clasp of the necklace until she feared it would break.

"Revenge?"

259

A muscle worked in Quinn's jawline and his mouth was a hard, tight slash. "I have made a mess of my life, Natala, everything I have done has forced me into choices I did not know that I would have to make."

Natala felt a spurt of fear; was she herself one of the choices he had not wished for? Slowly, she spoke her fears aloud. "You love *her*, don't you? That Englishwoman, Dacey Donohue. She is the one you still want. You have always wanted her."

For a brief heartbeat of time, Natala thought that Quinn might strike her, so tormented did he look. His eyes blazed at her. Then—she could see the effort it took—he tamped down the flame that burned in him, a flame for another woman.

"It's ironic, isn't it?" He spoke almost to himself, as if he had forgotten that she was in the room. "I wanted to take her in my arms—desperately I wanted it. Yet I could not. Her husband was nearby, her family, all the good citizens of Kimberley, and even if they had not been there, it wouldn't have mattered, because she didn't want me. She stood so straight, so cold, so rigid . . . I believe that she hates me now, Natala."

Then, before Natala could explode into the anger she felt, Quinn had turned away. And now he had left for Cape Town and soon he would be on the Atlantic Ocean in a ship, headed for the impossibly faraway country of the United States.

Dacey and Quinn . . . Dacey and Quinn . . . Hatred surged in Natala at both, for the thing they possessed between them, a thing apparently not entirely of the body, but of the mind, too, the spirit, the soul. Against their love, *she* might as well not exist. She herself was of as little value as an ant crawling up the side of an anthill, a stone kicked carelessly under a thorn tree.

She had promised Quinn that she would not hurt the Englishwoman. But she had not sworn to guard her thoughts, nor had she made any promises about guile or trickery. There were many ways in which fate could be changed: subtle, delicate ways. A word here, a small action there . . .

Quinn would soon be on the high seas, far away from

Kimberley. By the time he returned, events would have happened and there would be no way to prove that it was she, Natala, who had begun them.

Over the rise, the kraal lay spread before her, as drowsy and peaceful as always. Children and dogs came racing to meet her, but Natala waved them away, going immediately to Teki's hut. The old woman began at once with a torrent of complaints, but stopped at once when she saw Natala's face.

"Where is my daughter?" Natala demanded.

"She is by the fire, drying meat."

Natala turned and walked behind the hut, where she found Lilah tending strips of game that had been hung to dry slowly over a cookfire.

Lilah said the Zulu word for mother, and Natala nodded curtly. She sat down by the fire and gazed intently into its flames, her body motionless. Seeing that Natala did not wish to be disturbed, Lilah returned to her fire, pausing to turn pages in the book that she was reading. Natala gazed stonily at the book—it was *Hans Brinker and His Silver Skates*, well dog-eared. After a moment, Lilah flushed and put it away.

As she watched the deep glow of the coals, Natala turned her thoughts to Dacey. As part of her payment for spells and cures, Natala often extracted information from her customers. Makema, Dacey's maidservant, was in love with Bokembi, Jed's servant, who had little interest in her. Makema had come to Natala begging for a love spell.

Natala gave the girl a heavy, tallowy ointment to spread on her body and between her breasts. She also gave Makema words to say and certain other instructions to follow. In exchange she asked only for word of Dacey Donohue's activities.

What she learned was a muddle of gossip and unrelated events. Dacey had scolded her husband for refusing to take the new servant with him when he went out. She had quarreled several times with Royce McKinnon about the running of the mining company. She had given Makema a bolt of red satin from Paris.

Natala questioned the girl in detail about the Kimberley

Flame. The black maid smiled and shrugged. Missy Dacey had hidden the diamond somewhere about the house, she said. But thieves had been trying to find it. Twice the house had been ransacked, and even the office of the Elizabeth Mining Company had been searched, but nothing had been found.

Dacey had also been writing many letters, Makema revealed. She herself had mailed two of them at the post office. But she did not know what was in the letters, nor could Natala guess from the facts she had been able to glean. She decided that she must find out more.

After a time, sitting by the low fire, Natala cleansed her mind of all thoughts. She made of her mind a perfect dark space, concentrating inward. For long moments that stretched into nearly an hour, she sat utterly still, engrossed in her trance.

Gradually she became aware that Lilah, bored with watching the fire, had begun to play with a handful of pebbles. The girl tossed the stones into the air and caught them deftly, some of them shining lustrously as they flew in the sunlight.

Stones . . . diamonds . . . Natala's thoughts clicked into place again. She jumped up, grabbing the rest of the stones away from the surprised girl, every muscle of her body tightening with her discovery.

She had found it. Her plan, the way that she could get rid of Dacey Donohue, driving her from Kimberley forever.

Ai, yes, as everything else in Kimberley revolved around diamonds, so would Natala's plan. *Illicit* diamonds, and Royce McKinnon, the cocky overseer who swaggered down the street with jewels glittering from his fingers, with whom Dacey had quarreled. Wasn't Royce a man? And didn't Natala know how to twist men around her fingers, bending them to her will?

And there was also the Kimberley Flame, the fabulous large red gem that Dacey Donohue hid somewhere about her house. Would not that diamond look stunning around Natala's own neck? Would it not contain powerful magic, a powerful force?

Pleased with herself, Natala leaned forward to stare into the fire again, where a pinpoint of flame curled upon itself like a tiny red devil.

Sunlight pricked through a nail hole in the corrugated-iron roof of Dacey's office, sending a pencil shaft of light onto the casing of Dacey's new typewriting machine. In the ray of light, dust motes danced.

Dacey leaned forward and frowned at the letter she was picking out, one painstaking letter at a time. She was writing to the Empress Eugénie, of France.

Several months ago, the twenty-three-year-old son of Eugénie and Napoleon III had been killed fighting the Zulu near the Ityotyozi River. Total panic had spread among the cavalrymen, and Lieutenant Napoleon was trying to master his rearing mount when a saddle girth broke. He was overwhelmed by waves of screaming Zulu. Later, the Prince Imperial's mutilated body was found, stripped of his clothes. All that remained was a thin gold chain around his neck, with a medal of the Virgin Mary and a replica of the Emperor Napoleon's seal.

All of Europe, Dacey knew, mourned the death. Now she struggled over her letter to the prince's mother, trying to express her grief and at the same time plant the idea that perhaps the empress might wish to acquire the Kimberley Flame as a memorial to her son.

"I am sure that in this time of your sorrow. . . . A fitting tribute . . ." She stared at what she had written, then ripped the paper out of the typewriter and flung it to the floor. Her sympathy for the young prince's death was genuine, yet she felt like a hypocrite, a vulture, trying to sell the empress something in her bereavement. Yet, she knew well, royalty often did make such extravagant gestures. And Eugénie already had worn the famous Regent diamond, first as a Greek-style coronet, then as a pin for her hair.

Surely the Kimberley Flame would make a glorious addition to the French Crown Jewels . . .

Daydreams suffused Dacey, and for a moment she was lost in them, being received at court, sweeping forward in a gorgeous long-trained gown to curtsy before the empress. Then Eugénie would extend a gracious hand to her and ask her to join her for an intimate gathering . . .

A knock at the door jolted Dacey out of her reverie. She sat up guiltily, wondering if it were Royce again, here to complain or argue. Her uncle, Dacey knew, was rapidly growing bored with the mining company. He had been devoting less and less time to his job and more time to the fleshpots of Kimberley. Women, drink, gambling, boxing, theater, parties, and soirees, there was no pleasure in town that Royce had not sampled.

The knock sounded again sharply.

"Oh, do come *in*, Royce!" Dacey called. "And if you see Jed out there, I want you to tell him—"

She stopped. Her caller was not Royce, but Oskar Van Reenen, the town's resident magistrate, or chief of police.

"Good afternoon, Dacey." Van Reenen stepped into her office, a tall, heavy man with wide shoulders and a belly thickened by wine and good Boer cooking. He had been a guest at the unveiling of the Kimberley Flame, one of the ones who had admired the diamond with unabashed envy.

Now he regarded Dacey with an uneasy expression.

"Why, Oskar," she said, "what brings you here today? Would you like me to brew you some tea? I believe there is a teapot somewhere about, if I can find it—"

"No. No tea today. I have men waiting outside for me." A guilty look crossed Van Reenen's face. "I have come here about something else: a ten-carat stone with a distinctive macle shape that was stolen from another claim and hasn't been seen in two weeks."

"What?" Dacey held her smile, but felt a twinge of alarm. Oh, surely he could not think—

He leaned toward her, his face reddening. "I received an anonymous tip this morning that this illicit diamond, distinctive in marking, is to be found in your possession."

"In *my* possession? But, Oskar, this must be a joke. You know that there's never been a whiff of scandal about my name, or Jed's. We've always been scrupulously honest."

"I'm not talking about Jed's honesty."

Van Reenen said this in such a strange, clipped manner that Dacey's smile froze. Her hand closed on the casing of her typewriter, perspiration making her skin clammy. Illicit stones! Even the phrase struck terror into her heart. Illicit diamond buying was the most explosive crime in Kimberley, a constant topic of newspaper articles, a dark, underlying thread to its gossip. Those caught were sentenced to long terms of labor on the breakwater at Cape Town. The accused included every strata of Kimberley society—and it was up to the accused to prove his or her own innocence.

"But this is all nonsense, of course," she managed to say steadily, over her fear.

"Is it? According to my informant, that stone is to be found here in your office, and it isn't registered in your book. And who knows, maybe we'll find others, too." Van Reenen shook his head, his heavy jowls wagging back and forth in a way that Dacey would have found comical if she had not been so frightened. They could put her in prison. Take her away from Elizabeth . . .

She rose to her feet, aware that the blood had drained from her face, that she must look haggard and frightened.

"I've never seen that stone, Oskar! I know nothing about it. I've faithfully recorded every diamond we've found, everything I've sold. I've been very busy here at the office, there's been so much to do since I returned from Europe—"

"Europe! Ah, yes, I imagine that you could turn a trip like that to your advantage. Selling in London and Paris the stones that you managed to smuggle out of Kimberley."

"I did no such thing!"

"Didn't you? Well, we'll just see. We'll conduct a little search of the premises here, and of your books, and we'll see what we can come up with." Van Reenen stepped outside the office and gestured to two uniformed men, who entered the room without looking at her.

Was this a nightmare? Van Reenen was a man whom Dacey had entertained in her home, who had held Elizabeth on his knee, who had treated both her and Jed with respect. Dacey held herself rigidly.

"No." She said it in a low, clear voice, looking straight at the police chief. "No, you won't search my office without a warrant."

"You demand a warrant? In my opinion, that alone is virtually an admission of guilt." But the police chief fumbled in his rumpled suit coat and finally produced a folded piece of paper. "Here, will this satisfy you? It has been signed by the attorney general and is quite legal."

He motioned to the guards, who moved forward to a shelf where Dacey kept account books and wooden boxes containing records. "Go ahead, men, get started. Seize all the books, every letter, every file, and open the safe, too. I expect it won't take us long to find a certain missing stone."

The Arizona sun was hot and fierce. The stagecoach jerked and wobbled over a pothole, then strained on uphill, into the town of Virginia City. Quinn leaned forward to stare out of the dust-pocked window.

Years ago, when he had left it, Virginia City had been a rough, wild, ramshackle mining town. Now there were four- and five-story brick buildings, turreted mansions, rows of frame homes and saloons.

The coach swayed going up the steep incline of the street, over which towered the slopes of Six-Mile Canyon and Mount Davidson. They drove past the splendid new Fourth Ward school, the loading chutes of the Chollar Mine, the hoisting works of Hale & Norcross. Smoke hung in the air, a dirty pall of gray steam. Quinn watched it with a feeling of strange alienation. Had he ever been a part of all this?

To his left, he glimpsed a new mine, a jumble of roofs and smokestacks. A battered sign announced its name: THE JANINE. He stared at it, at the zigzagging trestles for ore cars that filigreed the slope of the mountain, the smokestacks that clawed the air.

The Janine Mine . . . strange, that it should possess that name. Was it hers? Had she somehow managed to make a comeback after his disastrous financial losses here, had she managed to salvage something? Above all, she had craved riches . . .

Involuntarily, for the hundredth time since he had begun

this journey, Quinn's hand went to his inside jacket pocket where he touched the box that held the diamond necklace.

In a somber mood, he jumped out of the coach at the stage stop and went into a saloon, feeling oddly reluctant to begin the mission on which he had come so far.

"Help you?" A bartender leaned toward him over the gleaming mahogany bartop. Rows of glasses and printed brewery advertisements were pasted to the mirror behind him, and patrons were crowded around a gambling table. Beer, cigar smoke, and perspiration thickened the air.

Quinn ordered beer and helped himself to the saloon's free luncheon spread, consisting of ham, turkey, cheeses, breads, pickles, onions, and various spreads. Finally, he asked the bartender where he could find Janine Farris.

"Janine Farris?" The man looked blank.

"Yes, she used to live here, was married to a wealthy mine owner," Quinn forced himself to explain. Janine's name seemed strange, uncomfortable on his lips. Maybe the mine he had seen on entering town had been a fluke, a coincidence. Perhaps Janine had left Virginia City years ago and his entire trip had been wasted.

"Oh, you must mean Janine Kennerd. She remarried, you know, after her divorce. She and her new husband, they lord it over the town now." The bartender stroked his long mustache, which had pointed, waxed tips. "What do you want with Janine Kennerd?"

"I need to see her."

"Well, she and her husband, they live up there." The man gave a vague wave that indicated the top of the mountain that dominated the town. "They like to look down on the rest of us mortal humans, you know what I mean? Besides, up there, there ain't so much smoke and soot."

Asking directions again, Quinn finally found his way to the Kennerd House, a two-story brick mansion with decorative balustrades, ornamental gingerbread, and the look of some ornate, tasteless wedding cake.

A uniformed butler showed him into a parlor crammed with objects, everything from a gilt-encrusted pianoforte to statues, claw-legged benches, looped satin drapes, and pots of ferns. An enormous polar-bear rug was stretched out on the floor, its grinning mouth revealing huge, yellowish fangs.

Quinn thought of Dacey's sitting room, furnished in tasteful elegance. He waited impatiently, pacing the room, feeling less and less at home here. The place smacked of *nouveau riche,* the conspicuous consumption of money.

Whose money? Janine's or Kennerd's? Janine had divorced him years ago, and he had not known it. Life had gone by here in Virginia City and he, thousands of miles away in Africa, had been foolish enough to blind himself to that fact.

He heard a sound at the door.

"Well, hello, Quinn. Imagine seeing you again, after all these years."

Janine swept into the room, wearing an aggressively fashionable gown of sapphire-blue faille. It was a harsh color that obliterated the soft lines of her face, emphasizing the avarice and discontent that was now carved deeply into her features.

"Hello, Janine."

They were two strangers, eyeing each other cautiously. Janine glided forward to plant a small, cool kiss on his cheek. Quinn fought the urge to wipe it away. He felt nothing for her now, not even curiosity.

"What are you doing in Virginia City, of all places?" Janine asked. She looked him up and down, raising her eyebrows as if surprised to see him in a well-tailored suit.

Quinn flushed. "I came to see you, of course. I gather that you divorced me."

"Yes, years ago, on the grounds of desertion. Did you think that I would cling forever to your name?" Her laugh was tight. "If you did, then you were an even bigger fool than I thought. Thank God for Robert, who saved me from the humiliation *you* caused me."

"Robert?"

"My husband."

Silence sank between them, leaden. Janine had not asked Quinn to sit down or offered any refreshments, and Quinn knew that she did not expect him to stay. To spite her, he strode deeper into the room, touching the top of the pianoforte, which was crammed with statuary, plants, photographs, and flowers, in the Victorian style. He was pleased to see Janine frown with annoyance.

"Is it Robert who owns the Janine Mine, then?" he asked her.

"Robert? Oh, no, *I* own it." Janine's dimple flashed, reminding him of the young girl he had married. Then her mouth tightened. "Did you really think that you left me here in Virginia City virtually penniless, except for that tiny purse you gave me? Were you that naïve? I'm a survivor, dear ex-husband. When you left, I had kept one claim back—the one that I thought would prove most profitable. I was right. I used that to stake me to other claims and then I struck a new vein of silver. Now I own the Janine, and do you know how much silver we pull out of it in a year? A million dollars' worth! And more."

Silver-mining seemed very far away now to Quinn. He stared at his former wife, hearing the strident voice that had haunted his thoughts, his dreams, his ambitions, for years.

"I'm a millionaire on my own, Quinn. I never needed you for that at all; I could have saved myself so much trouble if I'd just done it by myself in the first place." Janine's laughter rang harshly. "You *are* a fool, aren't you? And now I suppose you've come here today to beg."

At first Quinn didn't understand. "To beg?"

"Why, yes, why else would you come here? Of course, you're dressed well enough . . ." Her eyes raked him. "But you can't fool me, I know you need something, don't you? A loan? Well, I'm not prepared to give out handouts. I never spend money on fools."

She was calling him a beggar, a ne'er-do-well. Quinn reddened, feeling a spurt of rage. If a man had spoken these words, he would have dragged him into the street and horse-whipped him. But this was a woman, a tiny one at that, and one whom he had once loved.

In his breast pocket, the diamond necklace seemed a heavy burden, dragging at him, almost burning a hole through his clothes. Why, why had he done it? His feverish climb to power in Kimberley, his determination to have revenge—had it all been for this cold woman with the cruel lines on her face? He had spent years trying to prove something to a woman of little value, a woman not worth Dacey's little finger.

"No." He said it coldly, the word coming easily, as if it had been waiting in him for a very long time. "No, I didn't come here for a loan, Janine, I'm sorry to disappoint you. I don't know why I did come."

"But, then, why—"

She stared at him, puzzled. But it was finished, all of it. Quinn did not stop to respond to her question. Nor did he give her the necklace.

He turned on his heel and walked out of the room, brushing the butler aside.

17

DACEY SAT ON HER BUNK IN the Kimberley Jail, shivering despite the day's heat, which had turned the iron jail into an oven. Around her, flies buzzed and the air reeked of disinfectant, perspiration, food, and a leaky latrine.

Last night, she had heard screams as some new occupant was taken to her cell. The shrieks had continued all night, high-pitched, incoherent, mad.

But this morning there had been only muffled sobs, punctuated by a few cries. Dacey wondered if the new prisoner was a lunatic; perhaps there had been no other place to put her. Her heart ached for the torment of her fellow prisoner; yet, dully, she knew she could not allow it to ache too much. Her own predicament was extremely serious.

She had been here for five days now. Twice daily, she had been ushered into the prison yard with the other women prisoners for exercise. Several were imprisoned for diamond stealing, she had learned—and speculated gloomily over their fate.

"They don't give you a chance!" one woman wailed. "They don't care, they just stick you away and tell you to prove you're innocent—if you can."

"If you can." This was a frightening thought, one that kept Dacey awake at night on her narrow bunk, tossing restlessly, her body damp with sweat.

On her first day, she had been interrogated by Van Reenen.

According to him, there had been no entry in her books for the receipt of a ten-carat stone and four smaller gems of less than two carats each. All Kimberley dealers were required to keep careful records of their stones, and to fail to do so was serious.

In vain, Dacey tried to defend herself.

"Who was your anonymous informant?" she demanded. "Why doesn't he come forward? I think the answer to that is plain enough; he doesn't dare to reveal himself because he's lying!"

"I have trust in his statement."

"But it's a lie, it has to be!" She had lost her temper. "My God, Oskar, I have a child, a husband to care for. You've been in my home, you know my responsibilities. Why would I risk all that to steal a diamond? What am I to do about those who depend on me?"

The police chief had reddened, looking away from her. "It is a pity, of course. But I will permit you to send a message— one message, mind you, that should be sufficient. It will be to your husband, of course?"

To Jed? Dacey shook her head, feeling as if Van Reenen spoke to her through a long, echoing tunnel. Her very thoughts seemed thick, clogged with her fright.

"No, I don't wish to notify my husband."

Van Reenen raised an eyebrow. "Then who?"

"I . . . I don't know." Dacey's mind seemed to spin in short, choppy circles, her thoughts fragmented. She could call Papa, she supposed. But John McKinnon was an old man now, inclined to bluster when he was angry. Papa was not good in crises, that was why she had had to handle them when they had run the McKinnon Troupe.

Then, Quinn. Her thoughts spun. No, Quinn was far away in America, and even if he were not, why should he respond to her plea? They had quarreled, she had been cold to him . . . Perspiration began to run down Dacey's forehead, dampening the flesh between her breasts.

"Well, then? Must I assume that you wish to send *no* message?"

"No! I . . . I'll send one. To Bella Garvey. Yes, Bella. She'll take Elizabeth and see to it that Jed is cared for, too."

"And get you some kind of legal defense?" Van Reenen smirked. "Because you are going to need one. The affidavit has detailed two offenses for you: stealing an illegal ten-carat stone and being in possession of four other unregistered diamonds. Your case is being remanded to Special Court for trial."

"Trial?" Dacey felt her heart wrench.

"Why, yes. Did you not think you would go to court? I assure you, you will. And sentencing will be swift."

That nightmarish interview had taken place five long days ago. Bella had been permitted to call at the jail to leave Dacey some clothing and personal items, but she had not been allowed to talk to her. There was only a note, slipped in among some underclothing. "Elizabeth is fine and I am going to get you out."

At first, Dacey had raged at the injustice of her imprisonment. She had paced her cell, holding back tears of frustration and fear. Finally, a dull despair settled over her. Someone had done this to her deliberately. What other explanation could there possibly be? She hadn't stolen any diamonds. Why would she need to, when she already owned a prosperous mining company and a rare, fabulous diamond?

The Kimberley Flame! Did that have something to do with this predicament in which she found herself? Dacey searched her mind feverishly. Twice thieves had broken into her house to search for it, and they had even tried her office. Had someone wanted to get Dacey out of the way so that they could look for it in peace?

But, she reminded herself, Jed was still at home as well as Elizabeth and the servants, and no one in the household, not even Elizabeth, knew where the gem was. Dacey had buried it in the ground underneath the doorway of Elizabeth's playhouse.

Jed, her thoughts hurried on. Could he have done this to her? Resented her enough, wished her out of the way badly enough, to plant false evidence in her office?

Or maybe it was Royce. Royce had harbored ambitions of

running the Elizabeth Mining Company himself. Certainly, he had chafed under her leadership. And he was bedecked in too many diamonds these days, far more than he could have legitimately earned through work.

And then Dacey sagged back on her bunk, expelling her breath in a long, flat sigh. What good were all of these conjectures? Even if she were out of jail and able to work long hours in her own defense, there was nothing that she could prove. Jed and Royce both had a perfect right to go in and out of the mining office as they pleased.

And a diamond was tiny, so small that it could easily be concealed in any body cavity. Smuggling it was childishly simple, for it could be carried in the mouth, or taped behind an ear, or in the navel. It could be . . .

Stop it! Dacey ordered herself violently. Stop. Haven't you sent a message to Bella? Isn't she on the outside? Won't she think of a way?

She leaned against the iron wall and closed her eyes, wondering how long her prison term would be. She had heard of people being given twenty years, even life. Who would care for Elizabeth? What of Jed? Papa? What if Elizabeth were to fall sick again with the fever?

Dacey gave a wrenching shudder and stopped the thought. In the corridor, she heard the rattle of metal tins and pails and knew that it was the food cart. She swallowed, feeling a dry, hard knot of nausea. She knew that she would not be able to eat.

Bella Garvey finished combing Elizabeth's hair, brushing the child's glossy black curls until electricity sparked from them. The little girl sat patiently, docilely under the brush, not even struggling when the bristles encountered a tangle.

Since Dacey had been taken to jail, Elizabeth had spent long hours alone in her playhouse, playing with her doll, Kathryn.

"Why did they take my mama?" she asked Bella again and again. "My mama wouldn't steal. She would *never*."

"Of course she wouldn't, Lizzie-bet."

But apparently Oskar Van Reenen believed that Dacey had

done exactly that. Bella had stormed to the jail, she had argued and railed, pleaded and shamed. She had done everything but offer a bribe, and the only reason she had not done that was that Oskar Van Reenen had a reputation for honesty. That was what was so terrifyingly ominous about all this. Van Reenen was doing what he considered to be his duty. He believed Dacey to be guilty.

So did the newspapers. Dacey's imprisonment had been front-page material in all four papers, with editorials and long articles quoting members of the Mining Board.

"Illicit diamond traffic is a political issue, and has to be stopped," insisted one member. "Dacey Donohue apparently thinks she can flout the rules of this town. If we allow her to get away with it because she is a woman, then what sort of anarchy will be loosed on the diamond community?"

Bella had marched down to the *Diamond Times* office, elbowing her way past knots of men gathered on street corners to talk angrily about this latest diamond scandal. She glared at them, then beat on the door with her parasol until the editor let her in.

"Well, Mrs. Garvey." William Curry, a thin, balding man with perpetual ink stains on his fingers, had flirted with Bella at more than one party. Now he grinned at her lazily.

"I'm here about Dacey Donohue," Bella snapped. "Didn't anyone ever stop to consider that this woman might be innocent? That the charges might be trumped-up, fit for nothing more than dirty dishwater?"

Curry sighed. "If she is innocent, she will be allowed to prove it in court."

"William, you know as well as I do what is to be said for *that*. Those diamonds were found in her office. She didn't put them there, I'll stake my life on it. But how can she prove it? You know she can't, nobody could."

"Then she'll go to prison, won't she? She's lived here long enough to be aware of how this town works, the hatred for illicit diamond selling. It may prove to be the death of us. It brings down the prices of stones and makes a man's work useless. It—"

"Oh, stop! I've heard all that before, the Mining Board has

made it very plain what they think." Bella smacked the tip of her parasol into the floor, hearing it give a satisfying thwack. "What am I going to *do*, William?"

"Do? Why, tell her to call on her friends, if she has any. The only way to escape a diamond charge is through political clout. And in this case, even that is going to be damned hard." The newspaperman cleared his throat. "And now, Mrs. Garvey, I have been wanting to ask you . . . Would you like to take supper with me sometime? There is a new restaurant, they have a very good cook from Bombay . . ."

Leaving the newspaper office, pushing her way through the crowds again, Bella racked her brain for a solution. Politically strong friends? She knew that Quinn Farris had watched out for Dacey's interests for years, was one of the most powerful men in town. Bella had long suspected that Quinn's interest in Dacey lay far deeper than friendship. Quinn was a fine man, she thought, a bonny one, and if he were in town, Bella knew full well that he would spring to Dacey's defense.

But he was not here. He was in America.

Then, who? she wondered. Desperately she culled her mind for names, faces she had seen at the unveiling of the Kimberley Flame. But many of those people were on the Mining Board or had already expressed their hostility toward Dacey, already believed she was a thief.

Then she remembered Cecil Rhodes. He had stayed out of the controversy. And that was why Bella was now combing Elizabeth's hair and had dressed her in one of her prettiest Parisian frocks, a dress that pointed up her startling beauty. Maybe Rhodes would take pity on a pretty child whose mother was going to be taken away from her.

Elizabeth was a weapon, and Bella intended to use her. She was going to use every weapon she had.

"But, Mr. Rhodes!" An hour later, Elizabeth at her side, Bella stared at the prominent diamond man, her mouth falling open in shock. "What do you mean, there's nothing you can do? Of course there's something you can do! You can get Dacey out of jail!"

Rhodes frowned, a still-gangling young man who looked,

to Bella, as if he still ought to be at Oxford University, bent over his books. "Mrs. Garvey, I cannot. I appreciate your concern, but you must see that this matter is far more complicated than simply getting Mrs. Donohue out of her imprisonment."

"Why? Why is it?"

Rhodes got up from his chair to pace his sparse office. "As you know, the Mining Board has been bringing pressure to bear on this case. They are angry, Mrs. Garvey. That big red diamond of Mrs. Donohue's, the Kimberley Flame, has created much envy. It's a diamond of legend, of dreams. She has also built her mining company into one of the biggest in town. In short, she is one of the most envied and talked-about citizens in Kimberley. Now she is involved in illicit diamonds, and—"

Bella could stand it no longer. "But she *isn't* involved, Mr. Rhodes! That's the whole point!"

"Madam, please let me finish. The town thinks she is, and they feel betrayed. If a leading citizen can be involved in cheating, then the code of honesty in this town has no foundation and everything that Kimberley stands for is threatened."

"I . . . I see," Bella muttered, although she didn't. Beside her, Elizabeth stood rigid, her blue eyes enormous.

"I really wish I could help, Mrs. Garvey. But under the circumstances, my hands are tied. This has become a political issue. More than that, a moral issue."

"They are mad at Mama," Elizabeth interrupted suddenly.

"Why, yes." Rhodes looked startled; it was the first word the little girl had said since they had entered his office.

"But if we make them not mad, then they will let Mama out, won't they?"

"Hush, darling," Bella said at the childish logic. "Mr. Rhodes is a very busy man with much to occupy him—"

"We must make them want to let Mama out!" Elizabeth persisted. She darted to the side of Rhodes's desk to fix her eyes on his, the look curiously adult and flashing. "Mr. Rhodes, what could Mama do that would make them like her again?"

"Why . . ." The diamond man seemed startled. "I suppose she could show penitence."

"Penitence?"

"*Proof* of pentinence would be more to the point."

"What kind of proof?" Bella suddenly demanded.

"What other proof is there in Kimberley but diamonds?" Rhodes sighed and shrugged. "So, you see, Mrs. Garvey, there is little hope. We can only wait now for the trial and hope that the júry will be lenient."

"But they won't be lenient, you have just implied so yourself, Mr. Rhodes. Dacey is going to be locked away in a prison in Cape Town for the rest of her life! And don't deny it, because it's true!"

Rhodes said nothing, his silence assent. Elizabeth gave a tiny whimper, and Bella pulled the girl to her fiercely. An idea had come, to glimmer in her mind.

"I know what we can do," she said heavily. "It will hurt—oh, will it hurt—but I think I know exactly what those men on the Mining Board would take to let Dacey off."

"And what is that, Mrs. Garvey?" Rhodes's eyes met Bella's. In them, Bella read shame and a deep pity for Dacey.

Lying on her bunk in the small, darkened cell, Dacey clung to a thread of hope. Bella knew of her plight. Bella was her good friend, she would think of something. Surely, oh, surely it could not happen that she would be taken away from her child, her husband, her father, everything that meant so much to her.

She twisted restlessly, unable to find a comfortable position on the narrow mattress. In the next cell, the crazed woman muttered to herself. Dacey drew a deep breath, fighting back tears. She was afraid of going to prison. Afraid of the life that stretched before her, the emptiness.

Elizabeth, she thought raggedly. Quinn . . . Will I ever see them again?

"Mrs. Donohue! Mrs. Donohue!" The wardress, a plump, rather kindly woman who had brought Dacey extra portions of food, came hurrying down the hall, keys rattling from a chain around her waist. "They are out there, they have come for you."

"Who has?" Dacey sat up.

"Why . . . *they*. I don't know who, I was just told to bring you. You're being released."

"Released?" Dacey's first feeling was disbelief. Why should they let her out now, after nearly eight days, for no apparent reason? But the woman's simple face, openmouthed with excitement, told her that this was true. Something had happened. Bella had been able to help her, to prove her innocence!

Dacey felt a tide of relief flow over her with loose, heady joy. For a moment she gave herself up to it. Then she recovered her senses.

"Well, aren't you coming? What are you waiting for?" the wardress demanded.

Dacey managed, as she was being escorted down the corridor, to smooth the tangled red-gold curls that flowed down to her shoulders. She bit down on her lips to bring color to them and pinched her cheeks until they glowed. If she had to face Van Reenen again or a committee of some sort, she did not wish them to see any evidence of her suffering.

But to her shock, it was Bella and Cecil Rhodes who waited for her in the small lobby of the jail. Bella looked grim, and Rhodes, too, was frowning.

Dacey's heart sank. She was free—but both of her friends looked so stricken that she felt sure her release must be only temporary. She was out on bail only for a short time until her trial—of course, that was what it was. She'd been foolish to expect anything else. Disappointment bit through her, but she managed to smile as she walked toward Bella.

"Bella, dear Bella. It's so good to see you . . ."

They embraced, and Dacey felt the soft, motherly warmth of Bella enfold her. Hiding her face against her friend's shoulder, Dacey blinked back hot tears. This was not Bella's fault. Bella must not be made to feel guilty on her account.

Rhodes cleared his throat. "Good day, Mrs. Donohue. I trust they treated you well here?"

"They— Yes, of course," Dacey said proudly.

"Well, Dacey, we must get you home to that little girl of yours," Bella burst out. "Elizabeth has insisted on baking a cake for you, Dacey. I helped her with it. It is a bit lopsided and the icing slightly sticky, but I assure you it is edible."

Bella was chattering too much. Dacey looked at her friend, then at Rhodes, who glanced uncomfortably away from her.

She fought alarm. "Please . . . both of you! Tell me, what is it? Why do you both look so grim when I have just been released and am going to have a chance to fight for my innocence? Surely that's good news, not bad. It's an occasion for me to thank you for all that you have done for me."

"Of course . . ." Yet still Rhodes studied the floor, his expression uneasy.

"What *is* it?" Dacey cried. "Please, tell me what's happened. Why was I released?" She stopped, hearing for the first time the sound of voices raised in the street. "Why are all those people outside the jail?"

Bella and Rhodes looked at each other. At last, Bella sighed, looking troubled.

"They are angry at your release, Dacey. Angry at the bargain we had to strike."

"What bargain?"

"Why, dearie, it was hopeless, you know. You would have gone to prison, there was no alternative, the evidence was far too overwhelming against you. It's almost impossible to fight a diamond charge. And that's why we had to do it."

Dacey felt a horrid prickling of the skin along her neck and back, a feeling of nightmare. "What, Bella? What did you have to do? Please tell me."

"Darling, your mining company, the Elizabeth Mining Company, is being confiscated by the Mining Board in lieu of your imprisonment. It's a sort of penance, a sacrifice on your part." Bella was weeping now, her face looking crumpled. "Oh, Dacey, don't you see? There was Elizabeth . . . and Jed. We had to do it, we hadn't any other choice!"

Dacey drew in a quick stabbing breath of shock. She looked at Bella's face, then at Rhodes, feeling as if this were all a dream. "Is it true?" she asked Rhodes. "Did they really take the mine?"

"Yes, I'm afraid so, Mrs. Donohue. It was unfortunate, but you must consider the fact that the alternative was far worse."

"I . . . I see."

The work, Dacey was thinking. The effort, Jed's dreams, her own, even Elizabeth's . . . Oh, God, Elizabeth had been so proud of the mine that had been named after her. And Jed . . . Jed had lived for the mine, it had been the one thing that could draw his interest even from the deepest depths of his despair. And now the mining company was no more . . .

"Now, Dacey." Bella's arms went around her again. "Eh, you know this isn't the end of the world. You're out of jail, aren't you? You still have your wonderful, beautiful Kimberley Flame, and all the money you've managed to save, you aren't exactly penniless. You'll be able to start over again. It's been done before. And you're free now, you can go home to Elizabeth and to your husband."

Yes. She could. Dacey swallowed over a tight, hard knot that filled her throat. "But I didn't do it," she whispered. "I *didn't* take that ten-carat diamond or any of the smaller ones they say I did. Why should I be punished when I didn't do it?"

"Ah, honey. This is Kimberley, where a fortune can grow in a single day," Bella soothed. "You can start again tomorrow. And now, come along, Dacey. We must get into the fine carriage I ordered up for us, and take you home."

Home. Numbly Dacey sat beside Bella on the seat of the buggy and tried not to look at the crowds who gawked at them as they drove by, who pointed and whispered. She was Dacey Donohue, owner of the fabulous Kimberley Flame, who had been caught with illicit stones in her possession. She had paid to be let off, but she was still guilty. . . .

Oh, Dacey heard what they said. Some didn't even trouble to whisper. Shame flooded her in wave after wave. Why had Bella and Rhodes done this thing without bothering to consult her? It would have been far better for her to have stayed in jail and fought to prove herself innocent.

But there *was* no proof, she reminded herself. There never was in illicit diamond cases. . . .

She sat rigidly as the buggy left the thronged Market Square for the Dutoitspan Road. *Quinn*. The thought cut into her mind with the clean pain of a knife. If Quinn had been here, this couldn't have happened. Quinn would have done something, she knew he would have. Even if he hated her, he still could not have stood by to see her destroyed. . . .

When Dacey walked into her house, the first smell to reach her nostrils was the warm, vanilla-fresh odor of baking cake. The furniture had been freshly polished with beeswax, the crystal and brass knickknacks rubbed to a burnished gleam. There were even masses of daisies from Bella's garden, an explosion of yellow and white blooms. Dacey thought her heart would turn over with the painful pleasure of being home again.

"Mama! Mama!" Elizabeth raced to meet her, her black curls flying. There was a smudge of sugar icing around her mouth.

Dacey knelt and embraced her daughter, drinking in the warm silk of her child's skin, the smells of sunlight and baking caught in her hair. She felt herself tremble. This, she thought, was why she'd had to give up the mining company. For Elizabeth, for her very life.

Weren't those things worth any sacrifice?

Bella lingered for a few minutes, then took her leave, promising to return the following day. Dacey hugged her friend, wishing she did not have to go, yet also wanting her to leave. Jed must be told about this. She would have to do it gently, kindly. . . .

Oh, where *was* Jed? Why hadn't he yet appeared to greet her?

She forced herself to listen to Elizabeth's story of how she had frosted the cake and sprinkled it with tinted granulated sugar.

"For sparkle, Mama—Bella taught me to do that, do you want to come and taste it? Mama, are you listening?"

"Of course I'm listening." Dacey forced a smile. What was Jed going to say when he learned what Bella and Rhodes had done? Would he explode in anger? Would he be able to understand? "Of course, darling, I'd love a piece of your cake," she went on. "Would you like to cut us some?"

"I see you are back." Jed came wheeling into the sitting room, a powerful-looking figure in his invalid chair. Over the years, it seemed as if Dacey had rarely looked directly at Jed. But today her eyes were drawn to her husband. Jed had aged. His brown beard was now mixed with gray, his skin leathery from the sun. His torso and upper body were heavily muscled from hours of working at the claims.

Yet there was something sullen about his eyes and a loose look to his mouth today. And she could smell whiskey on his breath, sour and rank.

"Hello, Jed," she said, her heart sinking.

"I've heard, dear wife, how you managed to get out of jail." Jed challenged her, his mouth twisting viciously.

Dacey glanced down at Elizabeth, whose face had begun to pucker as she sensed the anger in the air. "Elizabeth, darling, why don't you go back in the kitchen with Makema and the maids, and set the table for our cake? And you can cut pieces for all of us. I'll join you in a minute."

"Oh, but, Mama, I want—"

"Please, Elizabeth." Dacey was relieved to see the little girl trot reluctantly from the room. Surely Jed would not stage a scene in front of their daughter; surely he would realize that Dacey had not *wanted* this turn of events, had not engineered it herself.

As soon as the child's steps had faded, Dacey began to explain, to apologize. But Jed cut her off, a muscle in his jaw knotting.

"Sorry? Is that all you are, Dacey? Don't you realize what you've done? You've destroyed us—ruined everything we had!"

"But, Jed, I didn't do it, it was—"

"You bitch, that was *my* company, too. I worked, I put in hours of sweat labor in the sun. But you didn't care about that, you gave it all away just to buy your own freedom!"

"Jed, please, you must listen to me. It wasn't like that. I didn't know they were going to take the mine, I didn't ask them to, I had no idea—"

But even as she tried to explain, Dacey knew that it was useless. Jed didn't even want to listen. His eyes were wide, wild-looking. He was like an ignited firecracker that would soon explode; nothing could be done to stop it. Her heart sank as she thought of Elizabeth and the maids in the kitchen. She must contain Jed's fury here, in this room. She must deal with him somehow until he calmed down and could see reason again.

"Jed, could we talk about this? Talk quietly?"

It was like asking for reasonableness from a thunderstorm.

"Bitch! Bitch! Controlling bitch!" Jed's big hands, weathered from years of handling diamond earth, fumbled beneath his chair for the long stick he carried. Frightened, Dacey backed away from him.

"Jed . . . please put that stick away."

"What's the matter? Are you afraid?" he sneered.

"No—no, I'm not. Put the stick down, Jed."

As answer, Jed only brandished it at her. Was this the way he had looked when he had beaten the native women in the street? His face dark, glowering, distorted with fury? "This is *your* fault, Dacey—yours, do you hear me? Everything . . . you never loved me . . . if you hadn't driven me out of your bed . . . if you hadn't driven me into the arms of a Kaffir whore . . ."

"Jed! I *didn't* . . ."

Dacey's voice trailed away. Jed blamed her. Not just for the loss of the mine, but for the accident, for everything. She drew a quick, scared breath, taking another step backward, then another, until she was pressed up against the hard edge of a table near the window.

"Jed, please calm yourself," she managed to say. "The servants and Elizabeth are still in the house and you will alarm them—"

"The hell with 'em!" The stick whistled in the air, its sound terrifying. Jed's hands savaged the wheels of the chair, rolling it closer to Dacey.

"Jed—no, please . . ."

"You are a liar, Dacey, a thieving bitch!" Jed swung the stick in the air, bringing it down on Dacey's hip with a sharp, agonizing lash of pain.

Agony gripped her, followed by nausea. Gagging, swallowing a scream, Dacey darted behind the table, putting its bulk between her and her husband. Ugly pictures raced through her mind. Setenga, the black girl who had been so brutally beaten . . .

"Jed—"

"Kaffir whore! Bitch! I should have killed you years ago, damn you, but I'll do it now—yes, I'll get rid of you—"

It was a nightmare, Dacey thought feverishly. Was Jed talking to her, or to some unknown woman from the past? She heard the stick whistle through the air again, this time striking the tabletop with a loud crash, missing Dacey's hand by inches. A crystal vase smashed to the floor.

Blows, one after the other, rained down on the tabletop and on her hands, shattering china bric-a-brac into fragments, sending brass ornaments flying. "Bitch! Kaffir whore!" Jed cursed the woman he believed had caused his accident, a sour smell coming from him, the reek of anger and hatred and madness.

"You thief, you stole from me, you took the mine, you stole my legs, you Kaffir—"

Another blow smashed into Dacey's wrist, flaming pain up her arm. Was it broken? He had her trapped now, pressed against the wall, with only the teetering bulk of the table to protect her.

The table. Desperately Dacey grabbed for the edges of the table. She lifted it up, pointing the legs toward Jed, so that the top became a shield. Taken by surprise, Jed had to use one hand to push his chair backward. Wheels crunched on the broken china.

Dacey was beyond fear now, past anything but a wild, grim need to drive Jed back. She shoved the table toward him, ramming one of the legs into the middle of his chest. To her surprise, he uttered a grunt, the chair rolling farther back.

Dacey darted past him and ran out of the room, into the kitchen.

* * *

In the kitchen, she found chaos. Makema cowered in a corner with Elizabeth in her arms, the two other serving maids huddled with them. From the front of the house came bellows and the sounds of wild crashing as Jed smashed his stick in the sitting room, demolishing it. The sounds were raw, mad, violent.

"Missy, missy, oh—" Makema babbled. The maids, too, jabbered in Bantu, their eyes wide.

But before Dacey could do more than gather Elizabeth to her, the crashing noises stopped.

Makema let out a low, terrified cry, and Dacey, too, was frozen with dread. She gripped Elizabeth, wondering if Jed was now wheeling his way toward the kitchen. Would he burst in on them at any moment, smashing and shouting? Even in his chair, he was a man of fanatical strength, and the long stick made a vicious weapon.

Her eyes darted quickly around the kitchen, stopping on a large wooden bowl that sat on a shelf. It would make a weapon, if she needed one. She grasped the bowl with her throbbing hands and stood holding it, her heart slamming so wildly in her throat that she thought she would be sick.

So this was what her life, her marriage, had come to, she thought raggedly. She had been imprisoned, stripped of the mine that meant so much to her, beaten by her husband. Now Jed, maddened with rage, was loose in the house like some demented animal. And here she was, poised with a wooden bowl as a weapon, ready to defend herself and her child against him. It was all madness!

They heard the creak of chair wheels on glass. Makema uttered a sob, and one of the other girls, Boti, whimpered like a child.

"Hush," Dacey hissed, although she, too, was terrified. "Hush, and stay near me. We'll start toward the back door, and when we are outside, we can run. He won't be able to hurt us then."

But the black women seemed paralyzed, and it was only Elizabeth who rose obediently to her mother's command.

"Bitch! Kaffir bitch!" came Jed's cry from the depths of

the house. Then, like a miracle, they heard the creak of the front door. Wheels rattled on the ramp that had been built off the veranda.

Jed was going out. They had been reprieved. Dacey thought her knees would collapse with her relief. She stood holding the wooden bowl until she was sure that the invalid chair was safely in the street. Then, trembling, she put the bowl down.

"He's gone," Elizabeth said in a small voice.

"Yes, darling. Your poor father is . . . ill in his mind and heart, and it is a sad, terrible thing." But Dacey could say no more. She gathered Elizabeth into her arms once again, burying her face against her daughter's fragrant hair.

Her left hand was battered and bruised, swollen to twice its normal size. There were other welts on her hip, arm, and shoulder, all of which throbbed painfully. But, Dacey told herself grimly, she had been lucky, for nothing was broken. Her bruises would mend.

All that night, with Bokembi and Mubuto, the other male servant, beside her, Dacey sat up waiting for Jed to return. The sitting room was a shambles. The table had been broken, and shards of china, glass, and crystal littered the floor. A Japanese screen was in tatters, and the drapes hung from their rods in crazed disarray. But Dacey no longer cared about the house, or even about her bruises.

As the long night inched by, she wrestled with her feelings. Fear, pity, anger, guilt. Yes, guilt. Jed had been maddened, but were some of his accusations true? They *had* fought, long ago, over Jed's visits to the black quarters. She *had* denied her husband her bed, and throughout her marriage, she had loved another man. Had her love for Quinn stolen from the affection she might have been able to give to Jed?

Feeling sick, she remembered the time that she had threatened to bind Jed to his wheelchair, other occasions when she had used Jed's very helplessness to prevent him from harming others. She had hated herself for these things, but she had done them, and was this now the result? A Jed crazed by drink and anger, storming off into the town to wreak God only knew what kind of revenge?

For hours she sat watching the flickering shadows that the paraffin lamp made along the wall. Shadows growing larger and smaller, as fitful as her thoughts. Then, like a darker shadow, the realization came to her.

Jed had not been her anonymous informant. If he had been, he could not have raged at her as freely as he had done, for he would also have had a share in the loss of Elizabeth Mining Company. Besides, Jed's rages had always been open, violent. He had never been given to stealth.

Whatever Jed had done, whatever sins he had committed, at least he had not been her betrayer.

Comforted in some measure by that thought, Dacey at last dozed off into a restless sleep, Bokembi and Mubuto snoring on the floor beside her. She was awakened at dawn by a loud pounding on the door.

"Missy, missy!" a voice called. "Missy, open the door."

Dacey struggled to sit up, feeling the pain of battered muscles that had stiffened during sleep. She winced as she went to the door.

One of the mine workers stood on the veranda. Adowa was a youth of nineteen whose eyes were reddened from the miners' ophthalmia. His dark face looked agitated and his large lower lip was trembling.

"Mr. Jed, Mr. Jed, he go to the mine!"

"What?" Still groggy from sleep, Dacey could only stare at the youth.

"He go to the mine." Adowa mimed the operation of the wheels of Jed's chair. "He drinking the whiskey, he shouting and yelling. Then he wheel too close, wheel catch on rock, mebbe. Then he go over edge."

"*No*. Adowa, there must be a mistake . . ." Behind her, Dacey heard Bokembi struggling awake, yawning and stretching. Out on the street, a wagon rumbled by, its sound very ordinary, one that Dacey had heard a thousand times before. Yet at this moment the squeal of wheels seemed unbearably new and poignant.

"Oh, it true, missy, I tell you truth. Mr. Jed, he is dead. He fell into the mine hole."

The hole. That yawning, huge excavation that had been

scooped out of the earth like a gigantic crater, where deep
cliffs plunged many feet into the abyss . . .

"It's . . . a mistake," she repeated frantically. "Jed has
worked around that mine for years, he would never . . . he
would have been careful . . ."

Adowa's eyes gleamed at her, and Dacey remembered the
way Jed had smacked at the Africans' legs with his stick.

"It is no mistake, missy, it is real. He fell into the mine
hole, he fell very deep."

18

"HE FELL INTO THE MINE hole, he fell very deep." Adowa's horrifying words echoed in Dacey's mind as she stood at the grave site, Papa and Elizabeth at her side, to hear the brief, stark service.

"Man that is born of woman hath but a short time to live and is full of misery. He cometh up and is cut down like a flower . . ." Even as the words droned sonorously in the hot, dry air, Dacey felt the ache of the bruises that Jed had given her, the throb of her injured hand. The funeral service seemed brutal and final, and for Dacey, it did not bring comfort, but a terrible burden of guilt. She had been stunned and horrified at Jed's death, yes. But she had also felt relieved. That was the shameful truth; it was as if some heavy burden that she had carried for years had finally lifted, leaving her free.

And it wasn't right, she told herself in agony, that a man's wife should feel relief when he died. No matter what he had done. Hadn't Jed been helpless, caught in his own anger like a fly in amber? Hadn't he worked at her side for years, had not the Elizabeth Mining Company been purchased with his assets as well as hers? And Jed had loved Elizabeth. She must not forget that. There *had* been good things to his life.

As the service drew to an end and clumps of earth were being thrown into the open grave, Dacey heard a whisper behind her.

"They say it's all *her* fault, you know. He was despondent over her giving away their mine like that, to get herself off going to prison. And she didn't take care of the poor, crippled man properly, or he couldn't have got loose to go and fall into the mine hole like that. Smashed to death, poor thing . . ."

The cruel words lashed at Dacey like a whip. They blamed her for Jed's death. She whirled, trying to see who the gossips were, but they had already disappeared into the crowd of mourners. She stood, trembling.

"Well, he is gone." Royce came up behind her, appropriately dressed in black broadcloth and sober hat. But a diamond stickpin glittered in his cravat and his handsome actor's face seemed flushed. His eyes refused to meet hers.

Were you the one who betrayed me? Dacey wondered, looking at him. Do you hate me that much, Royce?

"What are you going to do now, Dacey?" he asked her.

"Do?" She stared at him.

"Yes, now that you are no longer a mine owner. I suppose you'll soon have to sell that fine big red diamond of yours, in order to live." Royce said this with satisfaction, as if he relished the picture of Dacey in poverty.

Dacey lifted her chin, glad to see Papa and Elizabeth coming toward them. "I haven't had time to make any decisions yet," she told him sharply.

"Dacia, my Dacia." Papa was with her now, guiding her adroitly away from Royce toward the buggy that they had hired to take them from the cemetery. "Is that half-brother of mine giving you trouble, Dacia?"

"No, Papa," she lied.

"He is a fox, that one, sly and self-serving. I never trusted him, even when he was a boy. That was why I let you run the troupe."

Other mourners, some of them staring at Dacey, others looking pointedly away, were dispersing. They whispered together, their voices a low hum of disapproval.

"I would watch out for Royce if I were you," Papa went on. "Yesterday I heard a rumor about him."

"Oh? What sort of rumor?"

Papa cleared his throat, rubbing at his mustache. "There are some who say he has a new woman, a stunningly beautiful colored woman who has him in her thrall. He has apparently given her a pair of diamond earrings and she has been flaunting them in the town."

But Dacey did not wish to hear about Royce's mistress, or indeed, Royce himself. She tightened her lips. "Well, that doesn't matter now, does it? The mine is gone and Royce McKinnon is no longer my employee. There is no reason I should ever have to deal with him again."

After Jed's burial, the town seemed to turn against her. Endlessly, the newspapers discussed the diamond offense, implying that Jed had committed suicide as a result of Dacey's turning over her company to the Mining Board.

She should have gone to prison and served her term, many believed. It had been unfair for her to buy her way out, and resentment ran high.

Shortly after the funeral, Lavinia paid a call on Dacey, ostensibly to offer her condolences.

"What happened here, Dacey?" Lavinia's eyes darted around the sitting room, fastening on the evidence of repairs hastily made, a table bare of ornaments. "Your prized china seems to be gone."

Lavinia gave a nervous giggle, smoothing the fabric of her biscuit-colored silk. Her large bosom was crisscrossed with rows of French lace, giving it a massive appearance.

"I have put everything away," Dacey lied. She wished that Lavinia would leave. It seemed years ago that they had been girls, young actresses together. Now Lavinia was a stranger, here for no better reason than to satisfy her curiosity.

"Ah, yes . . ." Lavinia's eyes gleamed. "I suppose you're already packing, aren't you? Do you plan to go back to England, now that you're a widow?"

Dacey shook her head. Why did people keep asking that? Did they think that leaving was her only recourse? That she didn't belong in Kimberley unless she had a man beside her? The truth was, she had no plans. She lived from day to day now, hour to hour. The future seemed like an impenetrable gray veil, separating her from what lay ahead.

"I hadn't thought, Lavinia," she said at last.

"Well, I suppose you should think, shouldn't you? You are branded here as a thief, Dacey. I know I can say this frankly to you. Some say you drove your husband to his death. I, of course, know better, but still . . ." Lavinia let her voice trail away delicately.

Dacey sat very still. Then she felt a rush of anger, the first real emotion she had felt in days. "Jed made his own death," she snapped. "I'm sorry to disappoint you and the town, but it's the truth. Now, Lavinia, if you'll excuse me, I have work to do."

"Work?" Lavinia looked offended. "What work, Dacey? Now that you have given up your mine, I don't see what there is for you to do."

With that, she rose and swept toward the door, her heavy skirts rustling grandly behind her.

Weeks passed, then months, marked off by the warming of the days to Kimberley's scorching summer. Each day the sun seemed to burn hotter, the sky to glare a more pitiless blue. Torrential summer thunderstorms would soon be on the way, Dacey knew, a violence of nature that, in previous years, she had rather enjoyed, despite flooding and other inconveniences.

But this year, she could not seem to care about anything. Jed's ghost seemed to wheel the chair through the house, an accusing presence that filled her with guilt. *Was* his death somehow her fault, as the town believed?

"Don't be a little fool," Bella snapped at her one day when she mentioned this to her friend. "That man harbored anger for years, it ate away at him like a cancer. He *beat* you, Dacey. Don't forget that. And it was anger that killed him in the end; that and his own carelessness, the fact that he was drunk."

"But—"

"Stop it, Dacey, stop blaming yourself! It happened, it's done with. Your only job now is to try to go on."

To go on: a task difficult to accomplish, Dacey found. She

seemed caught in a dulled lethargy, a depression that did not lift, despite her efforts. She tried to read, found that she could not concentrate. She wandered on the veld for long hours, trying to find solace in the vast, arid spaces, the harsh colors of earth and sky. Instead, she found herself thinking of Quinn, wondering where he was, what he was doing, if he had reconciled with his wife.

Did he lie at night in Janine's arms? Did he hold her tightly, passion flaring between them like a flame?

Then at other times she pushed him grimly from her mind, creating a tiny trapdoor at the back of her thoughts into which she pushed Quinn and every memory of him. He wasn't part of her life anymore. He would never be again.

Then one day Elizabeth caught a fever, probably from the poor drinking water, always one of Kimberley's problems. Dacey no longer had time for depression or for thinking about Quinn. She and Bella spent days nursing the child, cooking broth, sponging her hot skin, feeding her medicinal potions. Slowly, Elizabeth recovered, but she seemed quiet and listless, her glowing suntan faded by days spent indoors.

Dacey worried about her daughter, and then, shortly, she began to worry about money. The sum that she had saved had never been as large as Bella had assumed. Its total had been depleted when Dacey paid off her workers, who were not going to be kept on by the Mining Board. Jed had also left a number of gambling debts, which Dacey paid, and there was John McKinnon's upkeep at the genteel hotel where he lived.

Dacey would have no one in town saying that she did not pay her debts. . . .

One Friday morning she returned from a visit to Papa, in which he had offered his small gambling winnings in order to help pay expenses.

Touched, yet alarmed that he would have felt he had to offer, Dacey turned him down. "No, Papa, I can't take your money from you—I don't need it. Elizabeth and I are just fine, we have plenty of money, and you needn't worry about us, you old rogue."

"But I do worry, Dacia. In the town they are saying—"

Firmly she kissed him. "Don't listen to what *they* say,

aren't *they* always wrong? Papa . . . oh, Papa, I love you so . . .''

She went into his arms then and clung to him for long minutes, burrowing into the warmth of him, the feel and the smell that she remembered from her childhood. For a moment or two, she allowed herself to sink into the comfort of his embrace. Then she pulled away. Papa could not help her now. No one could, except herself.

After she left Papa, she walked listlessly along the street, not even bothering to adjust the rim of her bonnet so that it would shield her from the sun. What did a few freckles matter now? Who would see them, who would care?

Two women came out of the apothecary shop and stopped to gape at her, but Dacey ignored them. It was automatic for her now to hurry on past, her chin held proudly, her back straight.

"Butter won't melt in her mouth, will it?" one of the women whispered to the other. "What makes her so proud? She . . ."

A malicious giggle floated after her as she turned a corner, and Dacey felt her cheeks redden. Were the whispers, the accusations, ever going to stop? Even Elizabeth had been made to suffer . . .

"Hello, Dacey Donohue." The voice was low, sultry, female, and it brought Dacey up with a start.

Natala was dressed today European-style in a green silk with double flounces that revealed the lush, firm lines of her body. She carried a parcel, and in her ears, Dacey could not help noticing, glittered a pair of diamond earrings.

"Hello, Natala."

The two women stared at each other, and in the hostile silence that hung between them, Dacey seemed to hear the words that Natala had spoken to her long ago, on the day that she had delivered Elizabeth.

"You should leave Africa . . . If you do not, then a curse will fall on you. Your life will be as barren as the veld after many months without rain, as dry as a rock that has been scoured clean by the wind. . . ."

She shivered, hearing the mocking intonation again. How

strange that she should remember those words now. She
shuddered, turning away from Natala, almost running down
the walk in her haste to be rid of Quinn's mistress.

Finally she slowed to a walk, her heart pumping erratically.
It was almost as if Natala's curse had come true; she thought.
She was now a pariah in Kimberley, blamed for Jed's death,
for buying her way out of prison. Elizabeth had been sick and
Quinn was gone. Her money was running short and today
she had actually found Papa offering her his poor, pathetic
gambling winnings.

Had Natala somehow *known* all this would happen? Had
she even caused it, with the words she had spoken at Elizabeth's
birth like some evil witch? And then, with enormous effort,
Dacey pushed away the fancy. Was she no better than a
primitive tribesman, to believe such things? Witchcraft wasn't
real. Wishes and thoughts could not make events happen.

No, people made things happen. She was in control of her
own life; well, wasn't she? She was going to have to do
something about the apathy into which she had sunk, and take
advantage of the one asset that she still had left.

The Kimberley Flame, she thought feverishly. She would
have to sell it. She would take it to France and sell it to the
Empress Eugénie in person. Once she saw it, surely the vain
Eugénie would not be able to resist such a splendid gem. . . .

Two days later, John McKinnon sat in the Blue Post
Saloon, surrounded by a group of his cronies, mostly old men
like himself who had been drawn to the excitement of a
mining town and now eked out their existence with small
claims, businesses, or diamond dealing. This noon, he had
had luncheon with Dacey, and now he was bursting with the
astounding news. Dacey planned to sail to France and sell the
Kimberley Flame to the empress! With the money, she would
come back to Kimberley and start over again, building up a
new fortune.

He sat nursing a beer, watching as four men spun a roulette
wheel, gambling coins. Around him rose laughter and the
usual thick blue plumes of cigar smoke. What would these

men say if they knew that Dacia, his daughter, was going to have an audience with French royalty?

Dacey had been snubbed, of course, by Victoria in London. But the French were different, and surely no one could resist the splendor of the magnificent diamond that had made Dacey, Elizabeth, and himself famous in Kimberley. Even now, the regulars at the Blue Post pointed him out as "the father of that woman who owns that big red diamond."

"Eh, John, want to come and try your luck?" Yancy Cartwright, formerly of New York, now struggling to run a small auction house, came up to him, puffing on a long cheroot.

"Not today, I'm a bit short." John McKinnon patted his pockets in a casual way, as if to indicate that he wasn't really as poor as he claimed. Yancy Cartwright had been one of the worst in speaking out against Dacey, and for weeks he had harbored the desire to punch Cartwright in the nose.

"Surely *you* aren't short," Cartwright taunted. "Not when your daughter is flush with other people's diamonds. And doesn't she own a big red diamond with a fancy name? Kimberley Fire, or some such? I hear it isn't nearly as big as she lets on."

"It's big!" John McKinnon, goaded, burst out. "More than 140 carats, cut weight, that's large enough to heft in your palm or to wear in a crown, too. As a matter of fact, that's exactly where it's going to end up. With French royalty. My daughter is going to sell it to the Empress Eugénie!"

"Is she, old man? Or are you just talking from your beer?"

John McKinnon flushed. He had promised Dacey that he would not talk about her plans, and now he had revealed them to Yancy Cartwright, of all people. But his head felt warm, slightly fuzzy from the beer he had drunk, and Cartwright was laughing at him, not even believing what he said.

As if he was some poor, garrulous old man dependent on the saloon regulars for company, someone laughable and pathetic. He, John McKinnon, who had appeared thousands of times on the London stage, who had owned a great theatrical company!

"Oh, yes, she is, and you needn't laugh, you needn't poke

fun, because it's all true." His voice, deep and booming, was the one thing about him that hadn't aged, and it carried through the saloon, quieting conversations. Heads turned to hear whatever it was that John McKinnon was saying now.

"Yes, my daughter's leaving for the Cape tomorrow, she's taking the Kimberley Flame with her to sell to the empress. She's going to make her fortune, and when she does, she's going to come back to Kimberley and spit in your eye! My Dacia never stole any diamonds. She never hurt her husband, either. And anyone who says she did is a liar!"

Too late, Papa saw that Royce McKinnon had just come into the saloon. His half-brother stood at the back of the room, barely visible in the blue clouds of cigar smoke, a look of interest on his face.

She was ready. Dacey smoothed the folds of her traveling dress, a dove-gray faille with an elegant polonaise, which was a draped front trimmed with rich fringe. Faille sleeves, with striped cuffs, were finished with a double row of buttons, and her bonnet was a confection of ribbons and silk flowers.

Dacey leaned toward the mirror, feeling better than she had in months. She was pleased with the appearance she made. The soft gray set off the coppery glow of her hair and made her eyes look soft and large, full of hope. She was glad that she had put away her mourning clothes. She had been unable to bear their harsh black anymore, or the bleak thoughts that went with them.

Jed was gone, she had grieved, she had wallowed for months in depression, but now all of that was over. Soon she would be on a ship for France. She'd be *doing* something about her life, making things happen. That was the way things should be, and she'd wasted entirely too much time on feeling sorry for herself.

She glanced at her stacked-up trunks and tapped her foot impatiently, wishing that Bokembi would hurry with the cart. She planned to take the coach to Cape Town, and there book passage on a ship leaving for France. She had already dug up the Kimberley Flame from its hiding place under Elizabeth's playhouse, and now she wore both the Flame and its duplicate on her person, hidden in a leather sack that she wore around her waist, under her gown.

Or would it be better to separate the two stones, to wear one on her body and put one in her trunk? And which should go where? And what of Elizabeth . . . would her daughter be all right while she was gone? For she had felt that she must leave Elizabeth in Kimberley rather than risk her health this time on a choppy passage and damp air.

"Mama, Mama, are you ready yet? I don't want you to go!" Elizabeth rushed into the room, her face still pale from her recent fever.

Dacey knelt and hugged the little girl, feeling a sharp stab of guilt. "I know, darling, but you are going to stay at Bella's, and she is going to take such good care of you. And I won't be long in Europe—perhaps only a few months. Then I'll come back and we'll have lots of money again, and we can buy another mining company."

"Another?" Elizabeth brightened.

"Yes, darling, it will be even bigger, better than before." Dacey tried to smile. "And we can name it the Elizabeth II. Would you like that?"

"Oh, yes! And I want to help run it. Could I?"

"Of course, when you are old enough. But you can begin helping me just as soon as I get back. You can help keep the books, and I'll show you how to weigh diamonds and how to judge them."

"Oh—" Elizabeth danced around the room in a burst of her old enthusiasm. Then she stopped as they heard the rumble of the cart outside. "There's Bokembi, Mama, with the cart, and will I ride over to Bella's with you?"

"Of course you will. How else did you expect to get there, poppet?"

"And what are you going to do with the Kimberley Flame, Mama? Will you wear it?"

Dacey hesitated. "No, I don't think I should, in case anyone should see it and covet it for themselves."

"Then . . . here, Mama, you must take Kathryn along." Elizabeth darted out of the room and returned with Kathryn, the large doll that Lavinia had given her when she was born, now well-worn from years of cuddling and loving.

"But, Elizabeth, that's *Kathryn*. You love her." Dacey was touched by this offer, for she knew how much the doll meant to the child. "I can't take your doll."

"You have to, Mama. Kathryn has a little rip in her body, just at the stomach seam. It's a good place to hide things, I use it all the time. You must put the Kimberley Flame inside Kathryn. She'll keep it for you." The child's clear blue eyes, so like Quinn's, grew stormy. "I want Kathryn to wear the Flame—since I can't."

Tears looked imminent.

"Very well, then," Dacey agreed. She reached up under her skirt and extracted the leather bag and, loosening its drawstring, took out the large diamond.

The Kimberley Flame. Elizabeth, who had not seen the gem in months, suppressed an involuntary gasp at its beauty. The deep ruby-red diamond caught the light in its depths, exploding it outward in bursts of glittering fire. The stone seemed to shimmer and flame, a magical thing with a living presence of its own.

"I'll never see it again," Elizabeth mourned suddenly. "Will I? And *I* found it, and . . . oh, Mama . . ." Her eyes welled with tears.

Dacey, too, felt her eyes grow moist. "I know, darling, I know how much this hurts you. But maybe someday we'll travel to France together and we'll visit the empress and she will let us see the Flame again. Maybe it will be in her crown by then. And we'll know that it is a part of history and that it belongs to everyone, not just to us."

"I . . . I suppose . . ."

Bokembi was banging on the door, calling to them to hurry. Hastily, Dacey slid the diamond pendant inside the doll and smoothed down the long white dress.

"There," she said to the doll. "There you are, Kathryn. I hope you don't mind having a big diamond inside you."

The doll's china eyes stared at her blankly. Dacey smiled to herself and, opening the largest of her trunks, put Kathryn inside.

It was time to leave.

*   *   *

Quinn was returning to Kimberley. He leaned out of the
open coach window, gazing at the horizon where the town sat
like a mirage, iron roofs flashing in the sun. Smoke from
cookfires and dust from the mines hung over the settlement in
a gray pall. A few Australian blue gems and beefwoods,
newly planted, sent forth a shoot of greenery. But heaps of
bluish-gray mine refuse were visible, even from this distance.

This, Quinn thought, was the town he had conquered, from
which he had wrested diamonds that now meant exactly
nothing. He touched the lump in his jacket pocket—the diamond necklace that he had never even offered to Janine.
What was he going to do with it now? Sell it, he supposed. It
was glittering, ostentatious, and ugly, and in his mind it
would always stand for revenge.

Narrowing his eyes, he saw a cloud of dust. He watched
idly as a coach—one of the Gibson Brothers'—approached
along the well-rutted track, obviously headed west toward
Cape Town.

The coach grew nearer, its outline growing more distinct.
It was loaded with passengers, their trunks and valises strapped
to the top under a canvas tarpaulin, and pulled by a team of
four horses, "salted," or immune, as all South African horses
had to be, against horse disease.

More travelers, Quinn thought, watching it. Discouraged
miners leaving town, or speculators returning to the European
and American cities from which they had come. For some
reason, he thought of Dacey, and her face as he had last seen
it, her beauty pale, as carven as a cameo, her eyes flashing
with anger.

The coach rumbled past in a clatter of hooves and equipage,
the faces of its passengers blurred behind the dusty window.
Quinn sank back into his seat. As soon as he reached town,
he must seek out Dacey. He must try to explain. . . .

"What do you mean, she isn't here? How could she not be
here?"

Quinn stared at Bella Garvey, anger and alarm filling him.
Bella looked just as she always had, plump and comfortable,

clad today in a gray work gown, its nap strewn with raveled threads from her sewing. Her workroom hummed with the noises of two sewing machines operated by assistants, and flowers in tins were lined up along the windowsill, making bright splashes of color.

A day—a precious day—had been wasted since Quinn's arrival in Kimberley. When he had first called at the Donohue home, he had found no one there, and he supposed that Dacey and Jed were at the mine. But when he went to the Elizabeth Mining Company, he had found a strange man sitting at Dacey's desk.

"She doesn't own the place anymore," the clerk had informed him, not without a hint of satisfaction. He was in his mid-twenties, tall and weedy.

"Then who does? Did she sell? What happened?"

"You mean you haven't heard?"

"No," Quinn said savagely. "I've been in America, I haven't heard anything. Tell me."

"Why, she bargained away the Elizabeth Mine in exchange for her freedom—a poor bargain, some say, seeing as it caused the suicide of her husband."

"What? Jed Donohue is dead? What are you talking about?" Quinn lunged forward and grabbed the clerk by the collar, jerking him forward.

"I said—he died right here at the mine, he did, ran his chair over the edge and crashed down. Leave . . . leave me alone . . . I said he's dead, and *she* doesn't own this place anymore. They confiscated it."

"*Who* confiscated it?"

"Why, the Mining Board. She gave it to them for her freedom."

Quinn felt the blood leave his face. He let go of the clerk and stepped back, anger filling him like a poison. He watched as the man brushed at his collar nervously.

"Where is Dacey now?"

"I . . . I don't know. Go and talk to Bella Garvey, the seamstress. She's got the little girl, the child, she's taking care of her at the shop."

So that was why Quinn was here, and now he stared at

Bella, rocked to the core by the fantastic story she had just told him. Dacey, charged with illicit diamond possession. Jailed, her friends forced to strike a bargain in order to free her. Jed's death in the mine excavation, an apparent suicide, some said. The town's blame, the whispers and gossip. And now Dacey was on her way to France.

Quinn felt as if he were reeling from shock after shock.

"But, my God, how could it have happened?" He wiped a hand across his forehead, where beads of cold perspiration had begun to gather. "Dacey is honest, there's never been a whisper of scandal about her integrity, I'd stake my life on that."

"So would I." Bella said it grimly. "But I have my suspicions. Someone planted those diamonds in her office, and it was done deliberately."

Quinn focused his eyes on Bella, impaling her with his look. "By whom?"

When he saw Bella take a startled step backward, he realized that he had been glaring at her with the full force of his anger. He forced himself to relax. He must not allow himself to get out of control, not until he got to the bottom of this, realized clearly what he must do.

"All I know is that the diamonds were put in her office, probably smuggled in. Eh, Jed himself could have done it. But I keep thinking, why would he? He depended on Dacey, much as he was loath to admit it, and whatever his sins were—and they were many—at least he wasn't stealthy. No, I think that the blame for what happened can be laid at the door of someone else." Bella paused. "Royce McKinnon and his mistress."

"Royce's mistress?" Quinn gazed at Bella, puzzled.

Bella said nothing for a moment. She picked up a spool of thread and began to toy with it. "I'm sorry, Mr. Farris, but—well, you were gone a long time. While you were in America, Royce McKinnon took up with that woman of yours, Natala. He gave her diamonds and she wore them openly in the town, he was quite besotted with her."

"I see."

"Royce McKinnon is a weak man, Mr. Farris, easily

distracted. He wanted power, money, all of those things, but I don't think he wished to work for them. As for Natala, I suspect that she dislikes Dacey very intensely."

Bella raised brown eyes to meet Quinn's, their expression sober. "We both know why that is, don't we? I believe that Dacey has been in love with you for years, and you with her. Where were you when she needed you? Where, indeed?"

The first heat of Quinn's anger had gone, to be replaced by cold fury. "Where were you when she needed you?" Bella's accusation seemed to follow him down the path that led to Natala's hut, torturing him with its implications. Dacey, his sweet, loving Dacey, humiliated in front of the town, made to suffer. And Natala had done it. He felt convinced of it.

He felt sure it was no accident that her name should be mentioned in connection with Dacey's misfortune. Natala, he knew, never did anything without purpose, and once he had heard her express her derision for some of the overdressed diamond men like Royce.

Now apparently she had taken Royce as her lover. Why? Quinn could think of only one reason: to get close to Dacey, to use Royce McKinnon as another weapon in the quiet war that Natala had been waging on Dacey for years.

The thought made him feel sick.

Natala's hut stood as it always had, isolated on a small patch of veld, the dooryard garden growing in rank profusion, alive with bees, butterflies, and darting hawk moths. Natala herself knelt by a clump of plants, watering them with a gourd container. For a moment he did not think she saw him. Then, with a graceful movement, she rose.

"Quinn." She said his name with the faint, delicious accent that once had intrigued him. Her face was smooth, beautiful, sultry, just as it always had been. But why had he never seen it before, the willful cut of her lips, the arrogant flare of her nostrils, the mocking way her eyes regarded him? Natala did not love, he realized—she possessed. She swore promises, then broke them in a dozen subtle ways.

"Natala, I wish to talk with you. About Dacey Donohue."

"Ah?" He saw a slight, involuntary widening of the pupils

of her eyes, a quick flare of hatred that flamed, then disappeared in an instant.

"You destroyed her, didn't you? You were the one who drove her from town."

Natala said nothing. She reached down and plucked a leaf from a plant that she had been tending. It was thick, bulbous, some exotic form of aloe with an unpleasant, purplish color. She stared at the plant, her eyes stony.

"You were determined to have your revenge, and since I was no longer in Kimberley, you felt that you could do whatever you pleased. So you seduced Royce McKinnon. He is a man easily drawn to women, easily bent to a strong woman's will. And you used him to plant stolen diamonds in Dacey's mining office. Did you promise him that he could run the company? That he would get rich?"

Natala remained mutinously silent. Her hands squeezed the aloe convulsively, fluid dripping from between her fingers.

"You hated Dacey—you've hated her for years." Quinn felt the sickness rise in his gorge. "And I . . . I was the cause of it. I fostered your jealousy by being unable to commit myself either to one women or to the other. Always I was in the middle, torn by obligations . . . ."

He spoke more to himself than to her, feeling as if he had lifted a blindfold from his eyes, enabling him to see for the first time in years. And what he saw made him feel disgusted with himself. He had allowed himself to be blackmailed by Natala, because of the hold she possessed over their daughter, Lilah. He could have broken that hold by taking Lilah and leaving Africa—and yet he had not.

Why hadn't he? Quinn asked himself bitterly. Because he was obsessed by the need to collect a queen's fortune in diamonds, then to flaunt those diamonds before his mocking wife. Once, Janine had taunted him, made him feel less than a man. And he had daydreamed of the expression he would see on Janine's face when he placed the diamond-encrusted necklace around her throat.

But when the time had come, the moment had been nothing like he expected; it had been empty and hollow. The wish for revenge had slipped away from him, leaving him with nothing.

Now, as he looked at his former mistress, seeing her face twisted with anger and jealousy, Quinn realized the wrong that he had done her. Yes, Natala had been eaten by jealousy, but he, *he*, had caused that feeling. Didn't he stay with her for years when he had really loved another? Natala was no fool, she was sharply intuitive, she had sensed the division of his love, she *knew*. No wonder she was angry. Many another woman would have been angry also.

Yet hadn't he also warned her of what would happen if she ever harmed Dacey?

Quinn drew in sharp, painful breaths, until at last he had mastered his anger. "I'm sorry, Natala," he said at last, meaning it. "I have wronged you. In your way, you, too, have suffered, and almost, I could pity you."

"Pity!" Something flared in Natala's eyes, some fierce pride, and Quinn knew that he had said the wrong thing. Yet he forced himself to go on.

"There is no way to make amends, but I am sorry, truly I am, Natala, if I have ever hurt you." Quinn reached into his breast pocket and pulled out the packet that held Janine's necklace. He slid open the leather flaps and took out the diamonds.

The stones dripped from his fingers, their glare blinding in the direct sun, a startling contrast to the green plants in Natala's garden. Natala gasped.

"Here—" Quinn took the strand, crafted by the jeweler in Amsterdam, and savagely twisted it until two of the large pendants broke off in his fingers. "These are for you and your family. Take them into town and sell them; these are large stones and will bring you much money, enough to support you for the rest of your life. And this—" He ripped off a third pendant, then a fourth. Each contained a large central stone, pear-shaped, surrounded by smaller brilliants. "These are to compensate you for Lalah. I wish to take her to America with me, to rear her as my own."

With each diamond that Quinn tore from the necklace, Natala had drawn herself up taller, her fingers clenched on the crushed plant. Her face drained of color, her eyes darkening until she looked, Quinn thought, like a cobra about to strike.

"*No.*" She exploded the word as if it were a weapon. "No, Quinn, you will not take Lilah. She is *mine*, she will follow in my steps, she will carve out your heart if that is what I ask her to do. As for your little Englishwoman, your Dacey Donohue, I can possess her, too, if I wish."

"What do you mean? You speak in riddles, Natala."

"*Ai.*" She shrugged. "Who knows? Perhaps the spirits do not like her. Perhaps they wish her to go away, so they can take their revenge. Maybe they want to take the Kimberley Flame, with all its magic, away from her. And maybe they will succeed!"

Quinn felt a spurt of real alarm. For all that she spoke in parables, in puzzles, maybe there was something that Natala knew which he did not.

He moved forward and grasped her arm. "Is Dacey in danger?"

Again she shrugged, smiling.

"Is she? If you hurt her. . . ."

"*I* will not hurt her. Why should I have to, when the spirits will do it for me? The veld is full of the spirits of the dead and they do my bidding!"

Natala had become totally absorbed with the image of herself as witch, Quinn realized with a sinking twist of his heart. He thought of the girl he had met years ago at the Vaal diggings, the sensuous priestess who had saved his life. Then, Natala's belief in the spirits had been almost self-mocking. That Natala had been playful, vain, almost childlike.

Now she was bitter and vengeful. When had it happened? Had her transformation been due, in part, to him? One more burden of responsibility that he must bear?

Saddened, he released his hold on her arm, and that was when Natala jerked her hand up to his face, the movement as quick as that of a striking cat. He felt something damp and sticky touch his temple.

"*Ai—ai*—do you like that, Quinn?"

Quinn rubbed his face with revulsion, realizing that Natala

had smeared the crushed juice of the purplish aloe on him. Its smell was rank, sickening, like that of a rotted animal corpse.

"Wipe it off, Quinn, *ai*, wipe it away . . ." Natala's laughter rose to taunt him. At her feet, half buried in the dust, lay the diamonds that he had given her for Lilah.

A sense of urgency consumed him. Yet by the time Quinn had hired a pair of fast horses, he had lost nearly two days, and he knew that he would have to run the animals to their limit if he was to catch up with Dacey. Yet he knew he must—now, more than ever. She was in danger. He felt it with all of his instincts, honed from years in Africa.

"Perhaps the spirits do not like her. Perhaps they wish her to go away, so they can take their revenge. Maybe they want to take the Kimberley Flame . . . away from her. And maybe they will succeed!"

Natala's threat taunted him as he spurred the chestnut stallion to a gallop, leading a second mount, a mare, by a loose halter. Both were Boer horses, shaggy, sturdy, with great endurance. Fortunately, he was hurrying to catch up with a coach, which would be slowed by the needs of the passengers. And even if he could not catch up, Dacey would still have to wait several weeks in Cape Town for a ship.

He urged the horses at a steady gallop and by dark had covered forty miles. From now on, he would have to ride more slowly, offsaddling every hour to spare the horses, traveling by the light of the full moon that spilled light, like melted silver, onto the earth.

As he rode, hour after hour, the night began to seem to Quinn to take on an odd air of unreality. Hard black sky stretched overhead, flung with chips of diamond stars. Floods of moonlight washed the track with light. He heard the occasional cries of wild jackals and once the dry cough of a lion. It all began to seem like a dream, as if he rode and rode forward, but never made any progress.

The track on which he traveled was not really a road, but only a line across the veld cut deep by the wheels of many wagons. Trees and bushes had been removed when necessary, logs thrown over streambeds. After a heavy rain, Quinn knew, a stream might be impassable for days, and the dry stream channels were always hazardous. Like the washes in Arizona, these could fill with a wall of water at any time, flooding away everything in its path.

He rode, endlessly. He switched horses and rode again, his body aching from the hours in the saddle. Twice he stopped to drink from a canteen, slaking a thirst that seemed to grow with each hour. His skin had begun to hurt. Strangely, he could feel the pound of the blood in his temples and at his throat, a quick, erratic beat.

Near dawn, he met a wagon train. Each wagon was pulled by a span of twelve to eighteen oxen, slow vehicles that took up the entire track for a quarter of a mile, inching along at less than a mile per hour. If he waited for the wagons, he would be blocked for days; it was an ever-present annoyance on the trail, and at night, when the road was narrow or wound among trees, the wagon trains were hard to pass.

Impatiently, he spurred the stallion on, the mare following. He pulled out to the right, galloping among a clump of thorn scrub and dwarf mimosa trees. In the distance were low hills, everything painted with silver by the moon, given an eerie beauty.

Within minutes, he had passed the wagon train, with its rumble and bellowing of oxen, and was alone again on the veld. His skin was saturated with damp perspiration, his blood throbbed in his head like a drum.

Had he come down with some sort of fever? Quinn put a hand to his forehead to feel his own temperature, aware of the rhythmic rocking of the horse beneath him, its powerful muscles flexed in a steady gait.

And then that gait changed. The stallion's right foreleg struck a loose outcropping of shale and skidded, the hoof sinking into a hole made by some small animal. The horse wrenched and jerked in an effort to steady himself, then collapsed to his knees, throwing Quinn to the ground.

Pain shot through his rib as he landed roughly. He heard the stallion give a frightened whinny, then grunt as it staggered to its feet again. The mare had already bolted, her bridle dragging.

Quinn felt a wave of nausea. He closed his eyes, gritting his teeth as pain from a broken rib stabbed him. He heard the clatter of hooves against dirt and rock and knew that the horses were running away. His mind formed the word *Dacey*, and in his head he saw her as she had been long ago, when she had first come to Kimberley; eager, excited, beautiful, her eyes flashing with zest and adventure.

He struggled to sit up, fighting the stab of agony from his rib. Already his skin was hot from the fever.

Dacey took a room in a hotel in Cape Town to wait for the ship, the *Windhoek*, on which she had booked passage to Marseilles, France. She locked the Kimberley Flame and its duplicate in the hotel safe, which was guarded day and night by hotel staff, and tried to settle down for her enforced wait.

After the long, arid stretch of desert, Cape Town seemed incredibly lush to her, with its gracious oaks and Mediterranean climate. Adderley Street, its wide main street, branched out into a maze of narrow lanes, alleys, and dead-end streets. There were Cape Dutch-style houses, and whole streets occupied by Malays and by the brown-skinned, mixed-blood people called Cape Coloured. These streets were a thronging clamor of children, people, and animals, filled with exotic music and smells.

And over everything towered the majestic mass of Table Mountain. It rose to 3,600 feet; its steep, partly wooded slopes were capped by a line of sandstone precipices, flanked by bold, isolated peaks.

It was Table Mountain that drew Dacey's eyes when she rose in the morning to explore the streets restlessly. As she walked, she thought of Elizabeth, worrying that the child might have contracted another fever, that she might be lonely. In spite of her resolve not to, she also thought about Quinn. A picture haunted her. As her carriage had rolled out of Kimberley, passing an inbound coach, she had seen a man's face in the window of the passing coach.

Carven cheekbones, a shock of unruly black hair, deep-set eyes arched over by straight brows. Quinn. She was sure it had been he.

The sight of him had rocked her, striking to her heart like a sword. She had had to cling to the carriage seat, her heart slamming against the wall of her chest as if it would explode from her. Quinn was back in Kimberley.

For an instant she had had the impulse to batter on the window of the coach, to beg the driver to stop and let her off, so that she could run to him. But, grimly, she had quelled the urge. Behind Quinn she had glimpsed the faces of other passengers, women as well as men. He had gone to America to take the necklace to his wife, and Janine was undoubtedly with him now, seated beside him in the coach. Did Dacey wish to make a fool of herself, chasing after a man who no longer wanted her?

No. She was too proud for that. Quinn belonged to Janine now; it was hopeless, hopeless . . .

So she had done her best to put him out of her mind. But now that she was in Cape Town, with little to do but to wait for her ship, her mind played tricks on her. Once, walking a steep, cobbled street, she thought she saw him standing at the top of a hill, his black hair ruffled by the wind. Another time, she fancied that she glimpsed him at the prow of a boat in the harbor, his eyes narrowed into the sun.

She even thought she saw Natala in the Malay section of the town, dressed in native garb, and once she wondered if her room had been searched, for when she came back from her walk, there was the heavy, sweet scent of flowers in the room.

The vultures that had been swooping in the air over his head were now getting braver and had begun to dive down to inspect his progress toward death. Ants and other insects had begun to investigate him, too, and Quinn sometimes remembered to brush them off. He turned and writhed in his fever, fumbling for the canteen, only to find that it was empty. He had drunk his last water yesterday.

He was stranded off the track, in the empty veld; he would probably die here, of thirst and fever. A part of

Quinn's mind knew this and tried to accept it. Another part—the stronger part—raged against his fate. Dacey. His lips repeated her name, over and over. Dacey . . . It seemed the only thing he could cling to, the only truth.

There were times when he lifted himself to his hands and knees and tried to crawl along the bare rock, closer to where the wagon trail snaked across the veld. Twice, in the distance, he had heard the unmistakable bellow of oxen and rattle of iron wheels. He had crawled, enduring the agonizing pain in his rib, finally staggering to his feet to strip off his shirt and wave it, signaling for help.

But he had still been too far away and no one had seen him. The fever consumed him again, and finally he drifted into semiconsciousness, lying where he fell. He had awakened hours later to find that it was night again. The wagon train, if there had really been one, if it had not been merely an illusion, was gone.

Now a huge vulture, crawling with lice, its head naked, its body thickened with black feathers, hopped closer to him. It pecked experimentally at Quinn's leg. Quinn kicked at it and watched it flutter away to stand at a safe distance.

He tried to moisten his lips, an almost impossible task, for his mouth and tongue were leathery, swollen from thirst. Again he forced himself to crawl to his knees. Pain ripped at his rib, forcing his mind in and out of reality. Natala's eyes burning with anger at him. Her hand, smearing his face with the sickening fluid from the aloe plant . . .

Almost he thought he could hear her laughter, high and mocking.

He shook his head, thrusting away the hallucinatory sound. More vultures circled overhead, gliding and dipping, and Quinn closed his eyes, gasped for air, and pushed himself to his feet. He stood swaying, his broken rib knifing at him savagely. He felt nauseated and thought he would faint from the pain. Dimly he was aware that the waiting vulture had shifted its position, fluttering a greater distance away.

He focused his eyes on the veld to the east, where a dark ridge of rock thrust up from the sand like the spine of some prehistoric beast, scraggly thorn trees softening its lines. Over the ridge, he thought he saw another cloud of dust.

He narrowed his eyes. Was it another wagon train, plodding over the horizon, surrounded by the dust kicked up by the hooves of a hundred oxen? Quinn felt his legs wobble and begin to buckle, but with grim effort he steadied himself.

Yes. He squinted again at the dust cloud, experiencing the first dull throb of hope. Yes, it was another wagon, it had to be, and if he could only intercept it . . .

Staggering, moving with unutterable agony, each step more a lunge than an actual step, he began to move in the direction of the cloud of dust.

19

THE SUN BURNED OVERHEAD, FILLING all the sky, all of Quinn's head, with the flaming enormity of its heat. He staggered on, no longer aware of the direction in which he walked, knowing only that he must keep going. If he collapsed, he would die . . .

The vultures swooped downward, again and again, but he no longer saw them. Dacey. Dacey, my darling . . . Her name repeated in his mind, over and over, until it became the strength that sustained him, that pushed him on. . . .

"My God, what is this? What have we here?" The voice spoke in Afrikaans, startled with surprise. Quinn heard the words, but they sounded very far away and did not make any sense to him. He was barely aware when a hand slid around his shoulders, supporting him to the canvas-shaded interior of a bullock wagon.

"Dacey . . ." Quinn muttered through cracked lips. A face leaned toward him, fading in and out of focus. "Must . . . must get to Cape Town . . ."

"And you'll get there, man," the voice said, this time in English. "But best to do it alive, eh? Here, have some water. What happened to you? Have you been bait for the vultures?"

Quill felt metal touch his lips, and then water poured into his throat, cool, *wet,* the most beautiful, welcome, incredibly wonderful drink he had ever had. He tilted back the canteen and drank greedily, until water spilled down his face and neck.

"Well, at least you can drink," the voice approved.

Quinn swallowed again and again and finally put the canteen down. He tried to speak, found the words stuck in his throat, and managed to moisten his lips and try again.

"How . . . how far from Cape Town?"

His rescuer, a Boer wagon driver, had skin browned a deep mahogany from the sun and hair sunbleached almost white. "Four days on a good horse. But, man, you're in no condition to go anywhere, you're half-dead, from the look of you."

Quinn drew a deep, hurting breath. "I must get to Cape Town. I have a broken rib, but if you can strap it, I'll manage. Do you have any horses? If you do, I'll pay for them. I'll pay well."

The water had revived him temporarily; he sensed that his fever had abated, but he knew he was still near collapse. He needed rest. Food and water and hours of deep sleep. And he knew that he was not going to get them. For something had occurred to him, drifting into his mind as he staggered along the veld, the revelation made vivid by the curious state of detachment in which his mind floated.

Dacey's danger was real, and it wasn't from spirits or from any unspecified men who might be after the Kimberley Flame. It was from Natala herself . . . and from Royce McKinnon.

After ten days of waiting, Dacey finally boarded the *Windhoek*, an iron-hulled screw steamer with a capacity for 150 passengers. By oceangoing standards, this made it a small ship, but passengers would have a deck on which to stroll, comfortable quarters, well-cooked meals, and facilities for deck games and sports.

To Dacey, the ship seemed ugly, with its squat masts equipped with auxiliary sails, its black smokestacks. Nervously she waited in the line of passengers crowded near the gangplank to board. There were men in dark suits, a pair of women who chattered in Dutch, a British family with red-cheeked children, several wealthy-looking women. Accompanying one of these well-to-do women was a brown-skinned maidservant. The maid's hair was pulled tightly to the nape of her neck, and she wore a sober white cap. But her face, with its full-carved lips and flashing eyes, looked anything but servile.

Was it Natala? Was her mind playing more tricks on her, seeing Quinn, or things associated with him, everywhere? But as soon as she noticed Dacey's glance, the maidservant looked sullenly downward, and soon her face was blotted out as the line of people moved forward.

No, Dacey decided, it had not been Natala. Why should it have been? She was being foolish and imaginative. When her turn came, she approached the steward, who was consulting the passenger list.

"I'm Mrs. Donohue."

"Yes, of course, we have you in Cabin Seventeen-A. Since the passenger roster is not full, you will have the cabin to yourself. I trust that meets with your approval, Mrs. Donohue?" The steward spoke in a clipped British accent, for this was a British ship.

"Yes, that will be fine."

"Yours will be the second seating for dinner, madam, and you will be at table two."

"Thank you."

Overhead, the sky was a deep blue scudded with fluffy white clouds that turned to dirty gray as they massed over Table Mountain. The mountain itself looked grim and gloomy. After looking at it for a moment, feeling the dark pull of its mood, Dacey gathered up her reticule and descended below to her cabin.

Abruptly she felt tired, her anticipation of the journey quite gone. It would be a long voyage and she knew she would spend some of it ill with seasickness. She decided to unpack her cabin trunk and hide both Kimberley Flames—the real one and the replica. After that, she would lie down, rather than return to the deck with the other passengers to watch as the ship slowly pulled out of the harbor.

Table Mountain, with its masses of brooding rock, had put her in an uneasy mood.

*   *   *

It was dusk, and the fishing boats were coming in, unloading their catches, rich with rotting fish smells. Gulls squawked and swooped, hoping for a share, while gangs of black laborers thronged home after a punishing day's work on the breakwater.

Quinn Farris had just come from the shipping office of the White Star Line, and what he had learned there chilled him to the marrow. Dacey had sailed at noon: he had missed her by only hours.

"I don't usually let anyone look at the passenger list . . ." the shipping master had begun tentatively.

"Will this change your mind?" Quinn had handed the man a small diamond.

"In that case . . . ah, I suppose . . ."

Quinn had nearly snatched the list from the man's hand. He had seen Dacey's name, of course. But something had drawn his eye farther down the list, and that was when he had seen the name of the Reverend Royce McKinnon.

Royce McKinnon, aboard the *Windhoek* as a preacher? A chill gripped Quinn as he remembered that Royce had been an actor, a very competent one. Somehow, he felt sure now, Royce hoped to acquire the Kimberley Flame for himself. Perhaps he had tried to get it while Dacey was en route to Cape Town, only to find that she was surrounded by too many people. Perhaps at her hotel there had been other obstacles, or cowardice had stopped him.

But this was his last chance. Dacey was aboard the *Windhoek,* the diamond had to be somewhere about her person or cabin, and within the confined space of the ship, she would be vulnerable. At sea, accidents sometimes happened. People fell overboard, the tragedy a result of carelessness, infirmity, or force . . .

If I were planning to steal that diamond, Quinn thought grimly, I would first take it, and then I would dispose of Dacey so that she would not be able to tell what happened. That way, no one would ever know about the Flame and I could simply continue on the journey to Marseilles . . .

Now, tamping down his anger and fear, Quinn faced a dark-skinned Portuguese whose tangled, curly hair and bushy beard and salt-stained clothing made him look like a pirate. Which was practically what he was, Quinn had learned.

"What do you want with me?" Joe Fuguero asked suspiciously.

"I am Quinn Farris and I need to catch a ship, the *Windhoek*, which sailed eight hours ago. I heard your cutter is fast enough to do it."

The Portuguese stroked his beard, in which salt spray had dried. "Ah, my ship, she is light and she go by sail power, not coal." He spat contemptuously onto the quay. "She go fast, *fast*. She catch anything that floats—for money, eh?" He rubbed his fingers together in the universal gesture.

Quinn scowled. He had searched the docks for an hour, striding like a madman despite the pain in his ribs, looking for this very Joe Fuguero, reputed to be a fanatical sailor, with skills verging on the supernatural—if he hoped to gain something.

"Gold," the Portuguese repeated. "Or British pounds, I will take those, too." His grin revealed a missing tooth. "But only if you give me plenty, and it must be in advance—"

Quinn eyed the man coldly. "I'll pay you well, never fear."

He reached into his pocket for the remnants of Janine's necklace. As the Portuguese stared, Quinn twisted off another of the huge pendants. The diamonds flashed and glittered, catching the light.

"*Madre!*" Fuguero crossed himself, gawking at the diamonds. Then, greedily, he reached out and closed his fingers over them.

"Very well, you've accepted your pay, now let's go." Quinn stared into the eyes of the Portuguese. "I want you to understand something, Fuguero—a woman's life is at stake. I'll do anything, *anything* to reach her. I'll smash those diamonds to bits if I have to—or I'll smash you. But I'll reach the *Windhoek* by morning."

Dacey lay on the narrow bunk in her cabin, smelling the deep odors of rubbed mahogany, brass polish, and engine oil. Distantly, she could hear the rumble of the ship's screws and erratic creakings and other noises deep within the ship. A constant swaying motion of the bunk kept her awake.

She had placed Kathryn, the doll, on a shelf that was guarded by a brass rail to prevent objects from slipping. But at the last moment, she had traded the real Kimberley Flame for the replica. She had felt safer wearing the real diamond on her person, somehow. It was in a soft chamois sack suspended by a thong around her neck.

Now she lay staring up at the darkness. Somewhere stays and timbers snapped, and overhead she heard the swift patter of a seaman's steps as he went to relieve a watch. It was very dark and she began to feel as if she were being pressed down by that utter blackness, carried helpless in the maw of the ship, at its mercy.

Anything could happen to her here, on board the *Windhoek* . . .

Shaking away the odd feeling of alarm, she rose quickly and fumbled for the gown that she had worn during the day. She dressed in the dark and slipped up the narrow companionway outside her cabin and went on deck.

She passed one lone sailor, perhaps the one whose footsteps she had heard. Other than that, she saw no one.

For a while, Dacey simply paced the deck, breathing in the moist sea air with its mist of fine spray. But at last she stopped to stare over the rail at the sea. Instantly the sight gripped her, sweeping her up in its spell. Enormous rolling combers stretched out as far as she could see, surging and reforming, each capped with silver jewels of foam. Overhead, an enormous moon spilled its light down on the water, creating phosphorescent gleam and shadow. She could hear water smash rhythmically against the hull of the ship, giving her a sense of its enormous, relentless power.

For perhaps an hour, Dacey leaned over the rail, drinking in the night, the feel of the sea, the sense of its eternalness. After a while, it seemed as if the waves beat fiercely in tune with the rhythms of her heart.

She was leaving Africa, she mused, taking the Kimberley Flame with her, the big, coveted stone that Elizabeth had found and that had brought nothing but ill luck. Imprisonment. Shame. The loss of love.

Dacey gave a rueful, sad smile as she remembered the day, so long ago, when the McKinnon Troupe had first arrived in Kimberley. Then, anything had seemed possible, and when she met Quinn, she had been captured in the powerful, electric intimacy of his look, her heart instantly lost to him.

Papa had thought it an omen. Instead, her love for Quinn had turned out to be only heartbreak, longing, a few encounters over the years, lovemaking poignant with loss. She had loved Quinn. Yet what had the purpose been, the meaning of that love? She felt her throat tighten. She had been given only a glimpse of a happiness that could never be fulfilled. She had yearned, intensely and hopelessly, for something that could never happen.

Yet would you give up what you did have? a voice whispered softly in her head.

Dacey stared downward at swirling, tumbling sea foam and tried to answer the question honestly. Would she? Would she erase Quinn from her life if she could, so that it was as if he had never been? Erase the pain he had caused her, the helpless longing?

She felt her chest grow tight, constricting her breathing like a band of tears. For long moments she stood rigidly, gripping the rail with every muscle of her body clenched. Then, slowly, one muscle at a time, she relaxed. She allowed the grief, the anger, the pain, to flow out of her, to merge with the rolling breakers and the silver floods of moonlight.

I'll never have you, my darling, she whispered to the night. Not to love, not to hold you in the darkness and know that you are mine. But there is a part of you in me, and there always will be. I can't make it go away, God knows I've tried. So I will accept that you're part of me. I don't have any other choice. Oh, Quinn, I do love you so . . .

She turned, brushing at her face, which was damp with sea spray and tears. Then she went below.

She fell asleep immediately, feeling relaxed and cleansed, made free somehow, as if she had come to some momentous decision about herself, some turning and changing of her life. She slept soundly for hours, dreaming of the day the desert had flowered, when she had walked in the field of Namaqualand daisies. Orange blooms had stretched out for miles, wild, lush, their profuse beauty dependent on nothing except rain . . .

A sound interrupted her dream, a noise like that of a cabin door opening and closing softly. Dacey moaned lightly in her sleep and turned beneath the blanket.

Then she felt a presence looming over her bunk. Something touched her shoulder and she started violently awake, a scream clogging in her throat.

"Where is it?" a man's voice demanded, inexplicably.

Dacey's heart slammed as she struggled awake, trying to make sense of what was happening. Was someone in her cabin? She could feel fingers grip her upper arm, squeezing like iron into her flesh.

"Where is it? Tell me, where did you put it?" the voice demanded.

"I . . . I don't know . . . I don't . . ."

Dacey shook her head, wondering if she was still dreaming. It was Royce's voice she heard. *Royce.* And yet how could that be? Royce was in Kimberley, hundreds of miles away.

"Royce?" she whispered.

"Shut up, Dacey." Royce slapped at her face with contemptuous smacks. "And try to get yourself awake, because you are going to tell us where you've stowed that famous red diamond that you're so proud of."

Royce. It *was* Royce, dear God, it was; this wasn't a nightmare at all, but real. She thought she would sob with her fear. Somewhere in the cabin she heard movement, a noise as something fell from a shelf. Then a match was struck, and in its flash of yellow she saw a second shadow, a smaller figure that moved about the cabin, searching it. She could also smell perfume, thick and musky, like crushed flowers.

It was the same scent she had detected earlier in her hotel room.

"Where is it?" Royce demanded again.

"It isn't with me," she managed to say.

"Liar!" He slapped her again, this time harder, a blow that

jerked her head to one side. Pain rocketed through her nose, spilling into her head. On the other side of the cabin she was dimly aware that someone had lit a candle. The flickering yellow light revealed Natala, wearing the maid's uniform, her hair skinned back into a bun.

"*Natala.*" Dacey felt more and more incredulous. "It *was* you, it was you I saw . . ."

"Never mind that." Royce leaned over her. "Do you think that I'm a fool, Dacey, that we both are fools? The Kimberley Flame is in your cabin. Why else are you going to France but to sell it to the empress? Oh, I heard everything, your talkative father was kind enough to reveal all. Only this is one diamond that the empress won't wear, after all. Do you have it in a trunk? Is it in your luggage?"

"No!" Through the thick glue of fright, she fought to think. "I . . . the captain has it . . . I gave it to him to keep . . ."

"I don't believe that. No, I think you've stowed our beautiful red diamond very close to yourself—maybe even on your body."

Suddenly Royce reached out and grasped the neck of Dacey's nightgown, ripping it viciously downward. Dacey screamed as the fabric split apart nearly to her waist, cutting cruelly into her skin, baring her breasts.

They were going to search her. To plunder her body as if she were nothing more than pirate's booty. The realization came instantaneously, and it filled her with horror and revulsion. With all her strength, she began to kick, striking out wildly at Royce and Natala, feeling her heel strike the soft part of Royce's belly. She had the satisfaction of hearing his surprised grunt.

She kicked again viciously, but this time Royce dodged. "You bitch—you proud little bitch!"

"Leave . . . leave me alone!"

Now they were on her again, one of them holding her legs, the other ripping at the chamois sack, yanking it off her. Dacey screamed and fought, only to feel Royce push her aside.

He fumbled at the sack.

"Ah . . ." Royce expelled his breath in a sigh. "My God, look at it, look . . ."

In the palm of Royce's hand, the Kimberley Flame caught the candlelight, gleaming almost evilly, its ruby color like a drop of dark blood. Seeing it, Dacey remembered the stories Papa had told her, of the Koh-i-noor, the Great Blue Diamond, others. Diamonds whose history had been written in suffering . . .

She pulled her torn nightgown back up over her breasts, her fear leaving her, to be replaced by icy anger. On the shelf overhead, the doll, Kathryn, sat calmly regarding the scene, her china eyes inscrutable.

"*You* are the fools." Dacey heard the words pop out of her mouth with a sense of dim wonderment. "Did you think that I would carry such a rare diamond on my own body?" She pointed toward the doll, knowing only that she had to do *something* to gain a little time. The Kimberley Flame was her only chance of starting over again.

"But that is only a doll," Natala said.

"Is it? Tear her open."

Natala snatched down the doll from its shelf and pulled up the long, flowing white dress to reveal the doll's soft cloth body. Neat stitching closed up the seam in the bottom of the torso. Feverishly Natala ripped open the seam and thrust her hand inside.

Stuffing fell to the cabin floor. In a moment Natala held a second Kimberley Flame. She stared down at it, her nostrils flaring.

"Another diamond?"

"What, there are two of them?" Royce, too, looked bewildered.

Seizing her chance, Dacey edged off the bunk and started toward the cabin door, holding the torn cloth to her body.

Instantly Natala was before her, blocking her way. "No, Dacey, you won't get out, not now. You see, it is the spirits of the sea who want you now, Englishwoman. They want to take you to them, they do not want you to talk."

"What . . . what do you mean?"

But Natala's only response was a strange, triumphant smile.

*   *   *

Desperately, Dacey fought. She flung her body from side to side, kicking, scratching, and clawing, caught in the wild struggle for her own survival. She screamed and grunted, she even sank her teeth into Royce's hand, drawing hot, salty blood.

But it was no use. Royce and Natala, between them, clubbed her into submission. A hand pressed cruelly into her mouth as they dragged her out of the cabin and up the narrow companionway. She felt herself being slammed into brass railings, buffeted against a bulkhead. And then they were on deck. She could hear waves, smell sea spray. Again she tried to scream, but her cry was stifled by Royce's hand.

"No . . ." She thought she heard Royce say. "No, Natala, this . . . this has gone too far. I didn't think . . . I didn't plan on this . . ."

"You will do it, fool."

Were they arguing? Had Royce changed his mind? Was he going to help her? But before Dacey could try to twist out of his arms, she felt another pair of arms go around her from behind. Natala dragged her away from Royce and shoved her toward the rail, which was tilted downward now with the movement of the ship.

A white canvas life preserver printed with the name of the *Windhoek* had been tied to the rail. Desperately Dacey clutched at it, felt it rip away in her fingers. Then she was falling.

Her scream was drowned out by the sudden, horrifying smash of water in her face.

She was in the sea. Choking, gagging, struggling to stay afloat, to clutch at the life ring which, miraculously, had fallen into the water with her. Huge breakers rolled toward her, capped with evil, bubbling diamonds of foam. They towered over her, looking as if they would dump tons of water directly on her head.

Then, just as Dacey cried in horror, each wave would somehow lift her up with it. She would bob on its surface, water splashing her face, invading her mouth, stinging her eyes.

She didn't know how much time had passed. Surely it could have been only minutes. But already the *Windhoek* had moved farther away. It grew smaller and smaller as it churned away from her, apparently unaware that she was missing.

Dacey screamed after it, shrieking until she was hoarse. But the surge and crash of the big waves was surprisingly loud, drowning out her voice. The *Windhoek* drew farther away, fading into the night as if it had never been there at all.

She was alone.

Alone on the surface of the sea in the dark.

She gripped the life preserver, assuring herself that it wasn't as bad as it seemed, it couldn't be. Royce . . . he had regretted what he and Natala did. He would tell the captain, they'd turn the ship around and come back for her. Or someone else would notice her missing, perhaps the steward. Or. . . . or dawn would come and one of the lookouts would spot her floating on the waves . . .

Stubbornly she clung to hope. She refused to admit that this could last longer than a few minutes, an hour or so. It was impossible, *impossible*, that she could die out here! She could swim a little, she'd learned when Papa had taken her for holidays to Brighton, years ago. She had the life preserver. As long as she held on to it, didn't let it slip away from her, and didn't lose her courage, she'd be fine. All she had to do was wait . . .

Waiting. It grew very hard. Minutes passed and the ship did not turn back. Dacey kept choking on sea spray, fighting the urge to vomit out the taste of the awful salt water. Apprehensively she realized that her cotton nightgown was heavy, weighting her body down with the sag of its water-logged fabric and strips of lace. And what if the life preserver itself grew waterlogged and stopped holding her up?

Horror!

But before she could contemplate this fear, she saw another wave, huge, twice as large as any of the others, roll toward her. Glittering silver in the moonlight, it loomed over her head.

Dacey gasped and waited for the tons of lethal water to crash down on her.

Then the wave surged under her, lifting her. It sucked at her with unbelievable force, almost jerking her life ring away from her. But she was bobbing on top of it, not being pulled beneath.

In a moment the wave had rolled on past, and she was being lifted again by smaller waves, ordinary ones. She spat out sea water and this time she did vomit. Bile pushed out of her throat, and she gave herself up to retching, too exhausted and frightened to worry about the heavy nightgown, or another big wave, or the fact that her preserver might grow waterlogged and sink her . . .

After a time, she recovered herself enough to rip off strips from the bottom of her nightgown and bind herself to the preserver.

Richard Chapman, the captain of the *Windhoek*, was British, a man of spit-and-polish rectitude. His clipped beard was immaculate, his eyes blue chips of sky that gazed at Quinn with unconcealed disapproval.

"What is the meaning of this? You come sailing out of nowhere on that—that *pirate* ship—" He gestured toward Fuguero's cutter, which had already turned and was heading back toward Cape Town, although Quinn had paid him to wait. "You have yourself dumped aboard like a rogue. Well, I want you to know that you will be required to pay your full passage to Marseilles. Or you'll work your passage, and I warn you, I expect hard work from my men and I get it."

"Captain Chapman, that isn't important right now. You have a woman aboard named Dacey Donohue. I have reason to believe she is in great danger."

The captain looked affronted. "Danger? I don't see how she can be, she is aboard a ship of the White Star Line."

"She is in danger, I assure you. Please, there isn't any time to waste. Take me to her cabin."

Quinn's urgent expression and commanding tone of voice at last had an effect. After a hesitation, Captain Chapman turned and led Quinn down a companionway to a lower passage. It was nearly dawn, and somewhere in the ship, bells clanged for a watch.

As soon as Quinn saw Dacey's cabin, his heart sank. The tiny space was a shambles. The bedding was in disarray, and several ragged strips of lace, apparently torn from some garment, had fallen to the floor. A candle still guttered, perilously close to tipping over. Objects had been thrown to the floor, among them a doll that Quinn realized must belong to Elizabeth. Stripped of its dress, its cotton stuffing strewn on the floor, its limbs sprawled askew, the doll was an eerie replica of a battered human woman.

Quinn stared at the doll, nausea racing through him, harsh and metallic. He swallowed it back, the fear twisting in him like a living thing.

Captain Chapman, too, had been affected by the grisly sight of the broken doll. "My God! What happened here?"

Quinn spoke grimly. "I don't know, but I suggest you launch a search at once for Mrs. Donohue. I can't tell you how urgent this is."

"But—" The captain frowned at the doll. "But how . . . who?"

"Never mind that now," Quinn groaned. "For God's sake, man, let's just look for her!"

Somehow, she lasted through the rest of the night. To her horror, in the long hours of darkness she had slumped over in a half-sleep and her hands had loosened on the slippery canvas. But the rags had held her, and she had awakened to find herself being drawn into the vortex of another huge wave.

But she had fought it. She had kicked and struggled to stay on top, and she had survived. Now her throat was raw from salt water and from gagging. Her fingertips had wrinkled from long submersion, her lips burned, her body shivered convulsively. But at least she was alive. And it was near dawn now; she could tell by the faint, soft glow on the horizon, softening the darkness to gray.

Her hope grew. In an hour or so, the sun would begin to rise overhead and she could strip off the remnants of her nightgown and wave it in the air, use it for a signal.

She waited impatiently for the light to intensify. Once, beyond the series of heaving, foam-capped breakers, she thought she glimpsed something black. A piece of driftwood? A bit of garbage thrown off a ship? A dolphin? Or—her breath caught with sick terror—a *shark?*

But she had pushed sharks from her mind all night and she rejected the ugly fear now. Perhaps if she stayed very still, she would not attract their attention. Meanwhile, there was nothing else she could do about them, so it was no use to torture herself.

Slowly, imperceptibly, the sky pinkened. Dacey tried to occupy her mind with calm thoughts. Dawn. This was the hour of the horns, Chaka once had told her. It was the time, he had explained, when a man, by kneeling on one knee, could see the horns of his sleeping oxen black against the graying sky.

Chaka. Her eyes blurred with tears. It had been months since she had thought of him, that loyal and kind man who had lost his life in the Kimberley Mine. He had been her friend. And Bella, Bella was her friend, too . . . What would she have done without Bella to comfort her when she was sad or depressed, her salty wisdom brightening many a grim day?

Dacey's throat tightened as she thought of those she had loved. Quinn. Elizabeth. Even Jed, in a way . . .

How much longer could she last out here? A day, two days? Already she was thirsty, her mouth and throat burning. Her body felt numb, she could barely feel the movement of her feet or hands. She was going to die, a small piece of human flotsam drifting wherever the waves wished to take her . . .

Another wave lifted her. The foam on its crest made a rippling noise, *ssssing* and evil, like watery snakes. Dacey automatically gripped the life preserver. Quinn, she thought as the water fell toward her.

Quinn was in a rage, a fury formed of frustration and a sick horror. Dacey was overboard. She had to be, for they had searched the *Windhoek* from galley to saloon, from cargo hold to engine room. Quinn had found Royce McKinnon cowering in his cabin, one hand marked as if by teeth. He had beaten the man against the bulkhead, pounding at him in shameful loss of temper until the captain and two of his crewmen had to pull him away.

"What did you do with her?"

"Now, sir, now, Mr. Farris—" Captain Chapman tried to remonstrate, but savagely Quinn struck away the restraining hands, ignoring the knifelike pain in his injured rib.

"Tell me, Royce, tell me where she is or I swear I'll kill you—"

Royce slumped against mahogany paneling, his handsome actor's face now wobbly and weak, the pockmarks on his skin showing up clearly. His eyes shone with fear. "I . . . I don't know, I swear it! I didn't see her, I didn't even k-know she was aboard . . ."

"You're lying!"

"No . . . No, I'm not, I'm really not, I'm not lying, I . . ."

Quinn gripped the man's collar, tearing the clerical garb away. "If you're not lying, then why are you wearing this? A preacher! You've never preached a sermon in your life. You wouldn't know what to do with God if He spoke to you in tongues."

"I . . . really . . ." Royce's mouth opened and shut like a fish, as if he feared something—or someone—even more than Quinn.

"Really, Mr. Farris," Captain Chapman said. "I doubt there is anything more we can do with this man right now, and we haven't time. I'll put him in the brig. Meanwhile, I suggest we interview the crew again. One of them may have seen something."

"Very well." Quinn narrowed his eyes at Royce McKinnon. "I'll leave—for now. But I'll tell you this, McKinnon: I think you had a part in this and I'm going to find out what it was. And when I do . . ." He let the threat hang.

"Please . . . please . . . I didn't . . . I didn't know—"

They slammed the door on Royce's pleading and went on deck again, where Captain Chapman had called the entire ship's crew together near the forecastle. A bandy-legged seaman whom they had not questioned before said that he had seen a woman on deck near midnight. Her windblown hair had possibly been red.

Dacey. Who else could it have been?

"What are you going to do?" Quinn demanded of Captain Chapman. "You must turn the ship at once and search for her—she's obviously overboard. My God, she could be dead out there!"

Chapman nodded. "I prefer to operate under the hope that she isn't. Men have been known to survive in the sea for days, and there are even stories of lost seamen being carried along on the backs of giant sea turtles."

As Quinn gave a short, angry exclamation, the captain hurried on. "Meanwhile, we'll try something more practical than that. We now have the time she was last seen. That will help with my calculations. I can return to our latitude at that time, and then we'll move in widening circles to search the area."

Quinn tried to speak and found that he could not. Dacey, he thought. Was she already drowned, her beautiful soft body sinking effortlessly to the sea bottom, to be eaten by fish? Or was she still alive, desperate, and scared, fighting to stay afloat?

He didn't even know if she could swim.

Please, he thought. Please, God . . . He choked out a prayer, meaning it more than he had ever meant anything in his life. Dacey had to be alive. She had to be.

For Dacey, the world had become no more than water and sun glare, tossing spray, waves, the constant effort to signal, knowing that her efforts were all futile.

Hours had gone by, hours . . .

At first she did not see the *Windhoek*, for it blended with the noon sun and seemed only another spot in front of her eyes. Then, as the waves tossed her high again, she saw the familiar long black hull. The ship! It steamed toward her through the waves, a flag of black smoke waving from its smokestack.

Dacey had never seen anything so beautiful. She waved her signal rag. She screamed and waved the cloth again and again; she cried and splashed up water, shouting until she was hoarse.

Then, like a miracle, she saw the small boat being lowered. Three men got in it, small specks in the distance, but they gradually grew larger, more real. Would they ever reach her? Dacey clung to the sodden life preserver with the last of her strength, feeling herself blur in and out of consciousness.

The boat splashed up beside her, maneuvering with difficulty because of the heavy sea. Its hull smashed down on the water again and again, narrowly missing hitting her. But at last arms reached for her to haul her aboard.

"Dacey!" someone choked. "Oh, my God, my darling . . ."

It was Quinn. Quinn. Dacey decided that she was dreaming, that it was all an illusion after all, some tormented figment of her mind. Quinn leaned toward her, holding a blanket with which to wrap her nakedness. His face was burnished with sunburn, his hair rumpled by the wind, his eyes fixed on hers with the most tender expression of love that Dacey had ever seen.

"Quinn . . ." She managed to croak through her dry, burning lips. "It isn't you, is it? You're only a dream . . ."

His arms enfolded her. "No, I'm real." She felt him lift her, giving a slight wince, and then the wool nap of the blanket warmed her skin. "And you're real, too. You're alive . . . oh, Dacey . . ."

She tried to look at him again out of the black wave of sleep that flowed toward her, heavier than the water, compelling her toward its depths. "I didn't think . . . ever see you again . . ."

She thought she heard him say something, but she couldn't hear what it was; she was sinking down fast now, into exhaustion that dragged at her, and then she knew no more.

Dark, unclear, memories . . .

Herself shivering, her teeth chattering so violently that she bit her tongue and felt tears spring to her eyes. She was being carried on board, wrapped in layers of blankets, swaddled so tightly that she could not move. She shivered and moaned, drifting in and out of awareness, helpless against the darkness.

For a while, she slept. Then she floated awake, aware that

Quinn's arms cradled her. His voice murmured to her, unutterably tender.

"Dacey, you have to drink . . . you must try to take something . . ."

She stirred and tried to talk, the words coming out as a sort of mixed-up garble. "The hand . . . I bit down on his hand . . . Royce! He took it, he took the Flame—"

"I know, darling. The captain has Royce in the brig now, and everything's all right."

"No! No—" She struggled to talk. It all seemed a thousand years ago, a nightmare that had happened to someone else. "I woke up . . . his hands . . . and Natala, the Kimberley Flame . . . in the doll . . ."

"Hush, now. There'll be plenty of time to talk later when you've recuperated. The captain is turning the ship and taking us both back to Cape Town. As for the diamond, we've set up a search of Royce's quarters, although he claims to have thrown it overboard. Drink now, darling, try to swallow this. It's chicken broth, and I've also some of the cook's best oolong tea . . ."

Obediently, for her head was thick and fuzzy and she could not seem to concentrate on anything, Dacey did as Quinn asked. The broth was hot, tasting of chicken and thyme, and the tea slipped down her throat, warming her. Within seconds, she felt drowsy again. Thick, liquid waves of sleep flowed toward her like a tide.

Natala stood at the rail, respectfully to the rear of Mrs. Godivan, the British dowager who had hired her to accompany her to France as a ladies' maid. The *Windhoek* was again docking at Cape Town, being nudged into the harbor by a small tug. Its passengers crowded at the rail, laughing and chattering, intrigued by this variance in their voyage.

Natala listened coolly to their chatter. Why, everyone wanted to know, were they returning? Who was the mysterious woman who lay unconscious in her cabin below, and who was the big, dark-haired, grim-faced man who was at her side constantly? Another man—a preacher!—was apparently locked in the brig and would be offloaded in Cape Town, questioned for some crime he was supposed to have committed. It was all very exciting.

Let them talk, Natala thought angrily, thinking that they were like a flock of secretary birds, jabbering endlessly. She had taken care of everything. She had put a sleeping drug in the tea brought to Dacey's cabin. She had managed to slip near the door of the brig, where Royce waited despondently, and had whispered a threat beneath the crack of the door. If Royce told . . . if he revealed one thing that had happened on the night that Dacey Donohue fell overboard, she would kill him.

She would do it slowly, pegging him out beside an anthill, smearing honey on his face and hands and genitals, as the Bushmen did to punish their enemies. Then, at a last touch, she would slice off his eyelids so that he was forced to stare directly at the sun as he was being eaten alive by ants.

It was a horrible threat, and inside the metal-studded door of the brig, she was satisfied to hear Royce choke and gag on his fear. She had smiled to herself. He would not talk. Not now, not ever. There was nothing those soft Englishmen could do to him that would outweigh what *she* could do.

To the annoyance of her employer, Natala had also faked an attack of seasickness so that she could remain in her cabin, out of sight of Quinn, who would, of course, have recognized her at once.

So she was safe. She had used Royce, he had served her well. Now she must depend on herself again, and on her family, six members of whom had accompanied her to Cape Town, blending into the narrow streets as if they belonged there.

Nearby, her employer, Mrs. Godivan, spoke in commanding tones to the steward. The two Dutchwomen giggled and pointed to Table Mountain just as if they had not left it the day before. Let them laugh, Natala told herself. Let them stare curiously when Dacey was brought up from below on a stretcher and taken off the ship.

What did it matter?

She would try again. Later, when there was time to plan. Were not the spirits angry with Dacey? Did they not covet her? Besides . . . Natala touched the apron pocket of her black uniform, in which rested a chamois bag. It sagged against her thigh, heavy with the weight of the two diamond pendants. *Two!* Gleaming, shining heavily with their fire, the inner flame that consumed them.

With the diamonds, she intended to make powerful magic, enough to reduce Dacey Donohue to ashes, and Quinn along with her. Yes, Quinn, whom she now hated as powerfully as she did Dacey.

Ten minutes later, when the ship docked at the quay, Natala was among the first to slip down the gangplank. With her graceful walk, she disappeared into the town. . . .

20

DACEY AND QUINN SPENT THREE weeks in Cape Town, recuperating from their ordeal and sharing with each other the months and years that they had been apart.

Quinn told her about Janine, and how he had never even taken the diamond necklace out of his pocket, but had turned on his heel and walked away.

He had also broken with Natala and now planned to return to Kimberley to get Lilah, his daughter, and to rear the girl in his own world. Dacey listened, and commented, and agreed, all the while feeling as if her face were enclosed in a glass mask that would shatter at the slightest touch.

Slowly, Quinn's rib healed, and he was able to walk and breathe without the pain that had plagued him when he had first taken Dacey out of the sea.

But Dacey was slower to mend. She had spent twelve hours in the water. The terror, the struggle to survive, had left her physically weakened. But she knew that her mind was also battered. Seeing Quinn's face, feeling his arms about her, knowing that he had come for her . . . this had been the most joyous moment of her life.

But it was also the most bitter.

Over the years, they had had to give each other up again and again. Why should it be any different now? Could Quinn really be hers now, his love burning as steadily, as fiercely, as the sun? Was happiness now within her grasp, the first real, sustaining joy that she had dared to anticipate in years? It seemed almost too perfect to be real.

Maybe it *wasn't* real. Something, she thought, would happen to spoil it. . . .

They took adjoining rooms in a small British hotel on Adderley Street, and Quinn hired a nurse to care for Dacey's personal needs. Mrs. Cootze was cozy, pleasant, and gossipy, a plump Dutchwoman who assumed that Quinn and Dacey were married. She worried about the failure of her charge to grow better.

"You nearly drown, *ja;* it was terrible, terrible shock," she said in her broken English. "But you live and now you be happy. You might lose your jewels, a few strings of beads, eh? But what are they when you have your husband to love you and care for you? Such a handsome man! So now you must not grow too skinny to please him. Eat and grow strong!"

Obediently, Dacey tried. Quinn paid the hotel chef extra money to concoct delicious meals to tempt her flagging appetite. Yet Dacey could not eat much, and she knew it was fear that crippled her, that she seemed powerless to deal with. A fear that she would lose Quinn again . . .

"What's wrong, my darling?" he would ask in the gentle voice he used with her.

She would shake her head, feeling miserable and shrewish. "Nothing."

He smiled, although a line of worry quirked at his forehead and more worry lines bracketed the full, humorous mouth that she had come to love.

"Nothing? Is it nothing that has taken away your appetite, Dacey, and made you so tense?"

She felt the blood sweep to her cheeks, turning them bright red. But she could not look at him, could not force herself to say what was on her mind.

For several more days she rested, trying to read the novels that Quinn brought her or start the knitting project for which Mrs. Cootze brought her yarn. Then, abruptly, her moodiness took a new tack. The hotel room suddenly began to feel too small. Like a cramped ship's cabin, its walls seemed to close in on her, and Dacey felt anxious and claustrophobic. She couldn't read the novels and made so many mistakes in the sweater she was knitting for Elizabeth that she threw it down in disgust.

She wondered what was the matter with her and was afraid to think about it too deeply.

"Let's hire a carriage and take a drive outside Cape Town," she suggested to Quinn one brilliantly sunny day. "I haven't seen the villages of Rondebosch and Wynberg, and Mrs. Cootze says they are very Dutch and charming."

"But, darling, do you think you're strong enough yet for—"

"I am strong, I am!"

"You're not, Dacey, you've barely moved from this room since we got to Cape Town. You won't even come for walks with me. You'll barely eat your supper, you're as skinny as a little antelope, you haven't any life, Dacey—"

She felt offended that he should say such things about her. Tears, new, easy tears of exhaustion, filled her eyes, causing Quinn's face to become a blur.

"Well, now I *do* want to walk," she pouted. "I want to get out and about, I want to go for a ride! Do you wish me to remain forever helpless, an invalid?"

She knew she was being contradictory, but couldn't seem to stop. It was maddening to see the frown that appeared on Quinn's brow, the worried look that touched his mouth.

"Of course I don't. You know that, Dacey."

"Then let's go into the country! I want to get out of this room, it's—it's too small, I can't breathe in here!"

"Darling." He covered her hand with his own. The feel of his skin was soft and warm, causing an electric tingle to jolt through her. He leaned close to plant a soft kiss on her cheek. She trembled feeling vulnerable to him, open and weak.

"I want you to grow better, I *care*. But I didn't virtually commandeer two ships and nearly get eaten alive by vultures in order to watch you become sick from overdoing. From trying to do too much, too soon."

"I . . . I know," she choked. "It's just that . . ."

Again the tears welled. She dashed angrily at them, bewildered at these moods that seemed to rule her now. "Why do I feel like this, Quinn? Why? I cry at nothing. You are concerned about me and I'm angry at you. What a shrew I am. I wouldn't blame you if you decided to leave me in Kimberley and then—"

"Leave you?" Quinn's eyes fastened on her intently. "So that's it! That's what's been the trouble. No, Dacey, I'm not going to leave you. Not now and not ever, I couldn't. Didn't I tell you everything that happened when I visited Janine? I told you, I made a mistake. A terrible, terrible mistake that cost us years. And now I'm going to rectify that mistake if it takes me the rest of my life. My whole lifetime spent loving you wouldn't be nearly enough, Dacey; it could only be a beginning."

"*Oh* . . ." She felt strange, as if the mask that had enclosed her was beginning to crack apart, one shard of glass at a time, splitting open to free her.

"I love you, Dacey. I always will." Quinn said it huskily. He moved forward and pulled her gently into his arms.

Dacey melted against him, feeling the hard lines of muscles that rippled beneath Quinn's clothing, the strength in the arms that gripped her, the gentleness. Hot tears stung her eyes. She felt Quinn tilt her chin and gently wipe the moisture away, the gesture one of infinite love.

"Darling, I think I know what's the matter with you . . . and I know it is the matter with me, too. Ah, God, I want to touch you, hold you, feel you close to me . . ." Quinn's breathing had quickened and he uttered a soft, urgent moan. His fingers began to release the buttons that fastened the back of Dacey's dress, until he slid a hand between the fabric and her skin. The feel of his touch on her flesh was so electrifying, so sensuous, that Dacey thought she would faint.

Her knees actually did start to buckle; she felt utterly weak, suffused with a burgeoning excitement that flowed upward from her feet to her heart. Their bodies, their skins, the feel of him, the way he pulled her dress from her, gently at first, then with mounting urgency. . . .

Feverishly she began to help him. She slid out of the gown and pulled at the camisole and corset and petticoats, stripping out of them as if she had lived her whole life waiting to do just this, to reveal herself before the man she loved.

Quinn tore off his own clothes, and in a moment they were on the bed, embracing full-length, the full lean lines of him pressed against her with potent desire. Dacey wrapped her arms around him; she arched herself into him, shamelessly, joyously, unable to get close enough to him, to love him deeply enough.

Quinn breathed deeply, groaning with desire, the sounds so powerful, an aphrodisiac of love, that they drove Dacey wild with pent-up desire. She shivered and trembled, forgetting herself in this wild transport of touching and warm physical sensation.

Quinn planted small, light kisses on Dacey's neck, tonguing the hollow of her throat, her collarbone, then running his tongue down the curve of her breastbone to the softness of her breasts. He licked her nipples until they became hard, delicious nubs of pleasure.

He kissed her navel, her flat belly, he kissed the line just above her soft, silky triangle, he stroked the soft flesh of her inner thighs and kissed her there, the feel of his breath on her skin like warm bursts of heat.

Finally Dacey could bear it no longer. She gasped and cried out, and they rolled together in a paroxysm of desire, their flesh exquisitely sensitive, striving ever closer. Finally Quinn lowered himself above her, his bulk strong, hard. Dacey opened herself wide to receive him, and felt the first long, smooth penetration, releasing a violent flood of feeling that grew, slowly, with each sure stroke.

Quinn rode her, guided her, gave to her, pulling her with him, upward, upward, to a peak of pleasure so blindingly powerful that Dacey screamed out her wild, fulfilling joy.

She cried out again and felt him shudder with her as he, too, mounted the rivers of pleasure and flowed with her, forever hers.

Later she lay within the circle of Quinn's arms, sheltering her head on his chest, utterly at peace, content with herself and with him. It was then that the knock came on the door.

"What the . . .?" Annoyed at the interruption, Quinn rose

and pulled on his clothes. He strode to the door and opened it a crack, so as not to reveal Dacey still in the bed. "Who is it? What do you want?"

"Message," an African voice said. "For Missy Donohue."

"A message? From whom?" Impatiently Quinn took a folded paper from the man's hand, found a coin, and handed it to him. He shut the door. "I believe this must be for you, Dacey."

Dacey felt an odd surge of apprehension as she sat up in bed and took the folded paper from Quinn. Her hands shaking slightly, she unfolded it.

ELIZABETH HAS FEVER. URGENT YOU COME AT ONCE BEFORE IT IS TOO LATE. SORRY. BELLA.

The message hit her like a hammer blow. Dacey felt her heart give a horrid, squeezing jerk into her throat. Her eyes fastened on the note again, numbly rereading it. But the message was burned into her mind. Elizabeth was sick, perhaps dying—oh, God, *God*—and Bella wanted her to come. She should never have left Kimberley at all, she'd been selfish and foolish. . . .

She sat rigidly, all of the joy she had felt at Quinn's lovemaking flowing out of her body like water leaving a sieve. Elizabeth. Her little girl, *their* child . . . And she had allowed Elizabeth to wear the Kimberley Flame. At the unveiling . . . My God, had wearing the diamond somehow brought the child bad luck, brought her this sickness?

"Darling? What's wrong?" Quinn's voice was sharp.

Dacey handed him the note. She slid off the bed and reached for her dress, pulling it on with jerky, trembling motions, getting half of the buttons in the wrong holes. She had to get back to Kimberley—the urgency swept over her.

Somehow, she had to get to Elizabeth.

Their horses were hobbled nearby, and Quinn had cut down thorn bushes and ranged them in a circle around their camp, in order to protect the animals from lions that might be in the vicinity. They had also brought two Boer hounds, huge, lanky dogs that would warn them by barking.

It was two days later, and they were on their way back to

Kimberley, riding long hours, camping only briefly, pushing the horses to their limit. Dacey had ridden doggedly, clinging to the saddle horn until she swayed with exhaustion. Finally, Quinn had insisted that they camp.

"You are a valiant woman, Dacey, but it won't benefit Elizabeth if you have to be carried into Kimberley half-dead."

"But I'm delaying us!" she wailed.

"No, you aren't, darling. The horses need the rest, too. We can't allow them to founder."

For that, Dacey could find no answer, and when Quinn lifted her out of the saddle, she wearily acquiesced. Now they were camped in a grove of camel-thorn trees, their bedrolls spread on the bare, dry earth. Overhead, the moon glowed like a coin. Its etched face seemed to stare down at them mockingly.

Despite her exhaustion, Dacey could not sleep. She lay looking upward at the sky, hearing Quinn's deep breathing beside her and the restless movements of the dogs. Both hounds had been uneasy all day, barking frequently, cowering close to the horses. The air had felt different, too, Dacey thought. Tonight, on the horizon over the low range of mountain peaks to the south, she had thought she glimpsed the fitful flicker of heat lightning.

Now she gazed up at the moon, almost hating it. That full, African moon—how inscrutable it was, how uncaring of human beings and their concerns. If she and Quinn were to die tonight, here on the veld, the moon would go on shining exactly as before. It wouldn't care.

She shivered, wondering why such a thought had occurred to her. But it was true that something uneasy had been bothering her ever since they left Cape Town. As they rode, she had been trying to think of what it could be.

The veld, as always, was gaunt and forbidding, disconcertingly in keeping with her mood. They had seen masses of shale and sandstone, the flat-topped hills called *koppies*. There were great dykes of rock thrown up in rugged, irregular shapes. Wind-scoured land barren of vegetation except for the sporadic thorny trees and bushes

This desolation, however, had been relieved by the sight of

a herd of springbok, graceful antelope that moved across their line of vision in an unending flow. Fawn-colored, the springbok had white manes down the center of their backs and a dark streak on their flanks, their horns lyre-shaped. At the moment of death, Quinn told her, the animals exuded a sweet perfume from a gland located on their backs.

Hearing this, Dacey had shuddered. Now, as she watched a cloud move across the face of the moon, obscuring part of its glow, she tried to think again of what was bothering her.

It had something to do with . . . yes, with the note she had received from Bella. Breathing shallowly, Dacey squeezed her eyes shut and tried to picture the message again. The large, slightly uneven printing, as if the writer had once learned how to write well, but got little practice.

She tried to remember if she had ever read any note that Bella had written before. She decided that she had not. Then she remembered the note Bella had sent to the jail. Bella had had only a few years of schooling, and even to do her accounts was a matter of perspiring labor for her. So, she supposed, the printing could have been Bella's.

Still . . .

Stop it. Of course Bella wrote the message, she told herself, feeling beads of perspiration spring out on her face, although a damp, cool breeze was blowing from somewhere. Bella had dispatched the message, probably with one of the drivers headed for the Cape. She had known that—

And then Dacey's thoughts froze.

Bella thought Dacey was on a ship bound for France! How could she have known that Dacey and Quinn were staying at the Bradley Hotel?

For an instant Dacey lay very still, her heart pounding so thickly that she thought she would be ill. Then she threw aside her blankets and began to shake Quinn.

"Quinn—Quinn—the note! It wasn't from Bella, it couldn't have been! There's something wrong!"

"Mmmm . . . darling . . ." Sleepily Quinn reached for her, running his hand over her warm swell of her breasts. In frustration, Dacey pounded at his arm.

"Quinn! Wake up! That message couldn't have been from

Bella because no one knew we were in Cape Town and it was delivered to our *hotel* . . .''

Quinn sat up, waking quickly and alertly. ''My God. I think you're right, Dacey. Damn, we've been lured out here on the veld.''

''Lured?'' Dacey's mouth trembled over the word.

''That's right. Elizabeth isn't sick at all—she never was.''

Dacey looked at Quinn's grim face, relief and alarm filling her in equal measure. ''Then . . . then that means—''

''That means, my darling, that we had better return to Cape Town at once and travel to Kimberley only by coach, or in a large and well-armed party. We're out here on the veld alone, and I have a strong feeling that that's exactly where someone wishes us to be.''

Spirits. Figments of the mind, of the dark imagination, roaming the rocks and the sand, weeping and crying out . . . Odd, how Natala's talk seemed to come alive in Dacey's mind as they packed up and began moving immediately, back the way they had come.

Quinn kept his pistol ready, his posture alert. Dacey rode numbly, so weary that it seemed an enormous effort just to hang on to the horn of her saddle. Yet she knew that she must. Quinn seemed full of grim purpose, and once, when they heard a distant, menacing rumble, he pulled up his horse to listen warily.

''What was that noise?'' Dacey asked, pushing aside images of spirits, malevolent creatures of the night.

''Thunder. This is the summer season, Dacey, it may rain.''

''Oh!'' So it was only nature after all. ''Then I suppose we'll get wet, won't we?''

They rode on, changing horses frequently, and Dacey tried to occupy herself with normal, ordinary thoughts, pushing away her apprehension. Since Elizabeth wasn't sick, what was she doing at this very moment? Dacey supposed that her daughter was asleep, her hands tucked underneath her cheek as she usually slept. If only she could be there, to lean over the bed and kiss Elizabeth lightly on the forehead . . .

By dawn they had gone twenty miles. They were approaching one of the large spines of rock that bisected the land,
looming up raggedly in the purpling dawn shadows. On the
horizon the line of mountain peaks was still a dim lavender,
gradually being revealed by the rising sun. Quinn pulled up
his horse and gazed ahead, shading his eyes.

"Those rocks . . . I don't like it, Dacey."

"Is something wrong?"

"I don't know. I hope not. Still . . ."

It happened without warning. One of the dogs gave a low
growl that turned into a high, yipping scream as an assegai
flew through the air and buried itself up to the hilt on its side.
The other hound plunged forward, only to have blood gush
out of its neck from another spear.

Dacey was too horrified to scream or to do anything more
than try to control her mount, which had begun to plunge and
buck in terror. She heard a pistol shot and Quinn's angry
shout.

Then a human figure melted out of the shadow of the rock
and ran gracefully toward them. Ostrich plumes bobbed and
bead ornaments on arms and legs lent a barbaric splendor to
brown skin.

Hatred, like a poison, a strong, surging flow of virulence,
filled Natala as she ran forward, delighting in the strong
plunge of her muscles, the power of her body. Around her
wrist she wore the lioness claws, and under her tongue she
had placed a dried fragment of lion heart.

She felt totally aware, totally alive, and when she saw
Quinn's hand raising the pistol, when she heard the frightened whinny of the horses, she did not even have to command her body what to do. Swiftly her arm went back. In one
long smooth motion she threw the assegai . . .

Nightmare: of what did it consist? Shouts, wild animal cries,
pistol shots, Dacey's own scream of terror. It all seemed to
happen so quickly, within the space of a single shriek. The
assegai, flying through the air, piercing the fleshy part of
Quinn's arm, so that he was forced to drop his pistol.

He had shouted at her to run, to flee, but there hadn't been time; she had been surrounded almost at once by painted figures, wild embodiments of spirits that roped her with rawhide thongs and dragged her behind them, pulling her toward the looming shadow of the rock.

Now they had been taken to a tent, erected in a sloping depression at the base of a large thorn tree. Quinn and Dacey were bound to its trunk, their hands tied with rawhide thongs. Blood seeped from Quinn's wound, staining the ropes that bound them and his clothing.

It had gone past reality, Dacey thought, past anything that made sense and into a world of animal terror. Natala and the other women—for these were all women, dressed in the feathers, ornaments, and proud paint of the Zulu—had taken them captive. Now they were apparently deeply engrossed in some private ceremony.

Again Dacey had to push away the panic-stricken image of night spirits. All of this was human-made. There was music, made with drums and with some metal instrument that Dacey had heard called a Kaffir piano. In Kimberley, the sounds had been clattery, dissonant, oddly hypnotic. Here on the veld the music seemed to beat eerily in tune with the terrified pump of Dacey's blood. This effect was augmented by the singing of the women. Their voices soared and moaned and keened, the sound totally primitive, savage.

Some wore animal masks, and Dacey could not distinguish their faces, although Quinn pointed out several that he thought he recognized, including Teki, Lilah's nurse. *Her* mask, Dacey saw with horror, seemed to be partly constructed with human hair.

"What . . . what is happening?" she whispered to Quinn through stiff lips. She was terrified by the strange sounds, the thick reek of animal fat, musk, and perspiration, the smoke from the fire that had been built from animal dung, its flames snapping sullenly.

"Magic." He said it grimly. "Apparently this is Natala's idea of revenge—to work a spell on us."

"A spell!"

"I'm afraid, Dacey, that she has become quite unhinged

with her jealousy and her preoccupation with the spirits.''
Quinn sounded weary and Dacey knew that it was a struggle
for him to talk. He had lost much blood from his wound.
''She is quite unpredictable now, and we must only try to
wait for—''

But he was not able to finish his sentence. The chanting,
the drumbeats, and the wild music grew louder, building to a
dissonant climax that seemed to clang and buzz in Dacey's
ears, assaulting her senses.

Then—abruptly—all music stopped.

In the utter, terrifying silence, Natala entered the tent.

Dacey suppressed a gasp, for this was a Natala who was
sinuously beautiful. She was entirely naked, except for a
small loincloth that covered her thighs. Her skin had been
painted with red and ocher symbols, and eerie red stripes
marred her face.

In Kimberley, Dacey had seen Quinn's mistress in native
garb and in European dress that pointed up her exotic beauty.
But this . . . It was as if Natala had flung all of the normality
of that life behind her. She was now entirely a physical
creature. Glorying, exulting in her own body.

Dancing, whirling, Natala approached them. Her glisten-
ing body was magnificent. Her full breasts, tipped with dark
nipples, were daubed with paint; her thighs were strong and
proud. The curves of her form reminded Dacey of a priestess,
a goddess. Or perhaps a spirit, one of the very entities what
she worshiped . . .

''*You.*'' Natala stopped in front of Dacey as the music and
chanting resumed again, a low tapestry of sound. A thick
smell of musk and herbs came from her. ''You don't belong
here. *Ai*, the spirits wish you gone, and I will help them.''

Dacey felt a twist of fear. Was there any way of reaching
this proud woman, of appealing to the Natala who had once
delivered Dacey's child, given her herbs for child-bed fever,
preened herself in a dress made of Japanese silk?

''Natala,'' Dacey began. ''Please, let us go. Quinn has
been injured and needs to have his wound washed and
bandaged. I suppose you have the Kimberley Flame now, but

you are welcome to it. Keep it, do as you wish with it. But let us go. You don't need us, and—''

''*No.*'' In the glow from the fire, Natala's expression was venomous.

Beside her, Dacey saw that Quinn had slumped against the ropes and was attempting to staunch the bleeding of his arm by pressing it against the ropes that held them. But his face was pale and she knew that it was only by the greatest of efforts that he held himself upright.

She narrowed her eyes at Natala, returning her look, praying that her own terror did not show. What was going to happen to them? How could this possibly end?

For an instant, Natala held Dacey's glance, her eyes smoky, defiant. Then, with a gesture of contempt, she broke the look and resumed her dancing. She whirled around the tent, flashing, beautiful, deadly. Then, with instinctive drama, she turned her back and lifted something high.

When she turned, Dacey saw that Natala had put on the Kimberley Flame. The ruby diamond gleamed at her throat, firelight burning off the stone's facets, reflecting shards of dark fire.

''Diamonds,'' Papa had said once, ''whose history has been written in blood . . .''

''Keep calm,'' Quinn whispered beside her. ''This is ceremony, Dacey, symbolism. Don't show your fear, no matter what happens.''

No matter what happens. Dacey supposed that Quinn was trying to be reassuring, but for her that phrase sounded sickeningly ominous. She could not stop thinking of the young son of Napoleon III and Eugénie, who had been massacred by the Zulu, left naked and mutilated. She sagged against the support of the tree trunk, her knees weak and shaky. She had a sudden, powerful need to urinate. They were going to be killed . . . Suddenly she felt sure of it.

The other women joined the dancing again, their voices rising. One of them took a handful of dried herb and threw it onto the fire. Acrid smoke immediately rose, thick and choking. Yet its stench was oddly stimulating.

"That is dagga," Quinn whispered. "It is a hallucinatory herb, it can stir them to a frenzy . . ."

On and on it went, growing wilder, more frightening. At some point a small animal was split apart with an assegai. The red, grisly gore was thrust into Dacey's face, and she fought not to show her terror and revulsion. Teki, the woman who brandished the dead animal toward her, gave a sharp laugh, clearly audible against the backdrop of the singing.

"Something's going to happen soon," Quinn warned. "I want you to be ready."

"Ready . . . but what can we do? Oh, Quinn—"

"Wait, that's all. Perhaps nature will help us, darling. I am sure it is going to—"

The music rose, ebbed, and then there was silence again. A new kind of silence, stark and commanding. In the dramatic space, another figure entered the tent.

Dacey heard Quinn draw a sharp, agonized breath. *"Lilah."*

The new dancer was smaller than the others, her frame delicate, yet regal, her slim body draped with the pelt of a lioness. Around her neck, glittering in red flashes, was a second Kimberley Flame. She wore it with calm majesty.

"Quinn, is that— Can that be your *daughter?*" Dacey gasped, aware that Quinn's face had turned cold, grimly angry.

"Yes, it's Lilah, and they are apparently using her. I think this is part of her initiation into magic, and I believe that Natala wants her to watch me die. Maybe even kill me herself as proof that she is worthy of being initiated."

"Oh . . . my God . . . ."

Dacey fought a scream, swallowing back her shock and horror. She felt more and more as if this was some horrible nightmare, in which they were stuck, unable to awake. She had never met Lilah. But Quinn had told her of the girl's striking beauty, her eager interest in the world, her bright, quick mind.

Now she watched the girl move into the tent, her steps an even glide. It was as if she were an atomaton, a puppet. Dacey could see no trace of that other Lilah in this young priestess.

Lilah moved gracefully in the ritual dance. She even bent

near the fire with the others, to breathe deeply of the halluci-
nogenic smoke. Her eyes were fixed and blank, hard coals of
savagery.

Dacey was filled with despair at the evil of it all, the cruel
waste. That a child should be forced into this . . .

But apparently Lilah *wanted* to be here. Was only doing
what she had been taught to do, was fulfilling the destiny that
had been planned for her. Again the singing intensified, and
now Lilah was at its center, a small figure dwarfed by the
adult dancers, yet somehow dominating them. With each of
her movements, the huge diamond that hung at her throat
moved, its prisms flashing red light.

Fear. Raw, aching fear coiled like a serpent inside Dacey's
belly, flicking its tongue into her heart. She saw Natala hand
some object to Lilah, something that gleamed silver.

An assegai. A long Zulu sword, its handle crudely set with
dozens of topazes and rough diamonds, its blade gleaming
An assegai . . . meant to be thrust into a human body . . .

Was the terror never going to end? How much more could
she take? Dacey felt her mind twist and retreat, fright transfix-
ing her. She fought the urge to scream and scream.

"She's going to kill me," Quinn said hoarsely. "This is
her moment, this is what it's all been about. If she dispatches
me coolly and with courage, if she cuts out my heart . . ."

"Your— No. Stop it!" Dacey thought she was going
to lose her mind. "Quinn, we have to do something. We've
got to—"

"There is nothing we can do."

Like a small puppet, Lilah approached them, holding the
assegai out in front of her so that its point was aimed directly
at the center of Quinn's breastbone. Dacey felt her heart
slam, the blood beating in her ears, the moment stretching out
endlessly, stretched beyond bearing.

The child paced toward them, her eyes full of purpose. She
did not seem to recognize her father.

"I love you, Dacey—above all else, remember that,"
Quinn whispered. "And no matter what happens to me, don't
show your fear. Maybe that way it will go easier for you. Oh,
God, my darling—"

Outside the tent, there was a sudden clap of thunder and then it began to rain. Water sluiced down on the tent and huge booms of thunder split the air, a giant and abrupt cataclysm of nature. It was the rain that Quinn had expected.

And it's also the end, Dacey thought feverishly. This isn't happening, it isn't, it can't be. In a moment I'll wake up . . .

Lilah thrust the assegai toward Quinn.

But instead of stabbing him, she twisted the blade downward and cut away the thongs that held her father to the tree trunk. Instantly Quinn kicked away the ropes and sprang forward. As Natala shrieked, her reactions made slow by the dagga smoke, Quinn lunged forward. He grabbed his daughter by the arm, and with his injured hand, he gripped Dacey.

Together they ran out of the tent into the rain.

"Look," Lilah said, transfixed. "It is gone. Everything . . . there is nothing there anymore." The girl's voice was high, small, and frightened.

It was about twenty minutes later. The rain had stopped as abruptly as it had begun, and the air was thick and wet, redolent of earth smells, ozone, and life. The sun was rising, spilling its light over the veld, touching the rock, the sparse thorn trees, the bare earth with its golden brush.

The three of them stood on a spur of rock and gazed downward at the place where, only minutes ago, Natala's tent had stood around the trunk of a thorn tree. Now nothing remained. Not the tent, not the prancing, half-naked dancers, not even the tree itself. All had been swept away by the torrential rush of a wall of water that had come racing down the dry streambed. Its source had been somewhere in the wall of mountains on the horizon.

"My God," Dacey whispered. She clung to Quinn, her left arm protectively around Lilah, who trembled with shock. "It happened so fast, I can scarcely believe it. One minute we were running, and the next . . . the next . . ."

She stopped, unable to find words. Death. So sudden that it seemed a mirage, a prank of nature. Natala dead, gone forever, the Kimberley Flame still around her neck like a curse.

"I knew that she had erected her tent in the wash," Quinn said at last, heavily. "She has lived in Africa all her life, I don't know why she did it. But she did. I'm afraid that Africa is a continent of violence—not only in nature, but in her people. I only hope that Natala has found some sort of peace at last. If only—"

He stopped, his face twisted with regret.

For long moments they stood in silence, watching the last remnants of the swirling floodwater flow away. Somewhere a hyena gave its gibbering, mocking cry. Dacey shuddered, drawing closer to Quinn, her arms automically tightening around the little girl who had saved both of their lives.

"My mother made magic," Lilah said abruptly. "But I still have some of it with me." She reached under her animal skin she wore and pulled out the red diamond, handing it to Dacey. "This belongs to you now."

Trembling, Dacey took the pendant. The stone glinted in the sun, dark with suppressed fire. Slowly she turned it over and searched for the tiny scratch that had been made by the jeweler months ago, in Amsterdam, to distinguish the replica.

It was the fake. The paste duplicate that she held in her hands.

She looked up and saw that Quinn's eyes were fastened on her intently. "Once," she whispered, "I thought that the Kimberley Flame was going to be the answer to my dreams. I suppose that I was like Natala; I thought that it held some kind of magic, something that was going to change my life forever."

Quinn's smile was gentle. "But there isn't any magic, is there?"

"No. I don't think there is." She said it with a feeling almost of relief, as if something in her had been freed. "A diamond in only a piece of hard carbon, no more."

Quinn smiled, his eyes kindling as he slid his arm around Dacey, pulling her to him. "People are what's important, my darling—you and I, and the ones we love. And we *can* make our own magic, Dacey—if we want to do it, if we try."

Dacey nodded. She felt her eyes mist with hot, happy tears as Quinn tightened his embrace around her. She savored the warmth of him, the strength, the feeling of security that she knew she would always feel near him.

And she knew what Quinn had meant, in speaking of magic. They would return to Kimberley now, with Lilah. They would rear her as their own daughter, a sister to Elizabeth; they would start over again. And their love would be the magic that cemented them together, the joy that bound their hearts.

Overhead, the African sun looked down on them. Later in the day, it would burn down upon the veld, its light harsh. But for now it glowed in a nimbus of haze, warm and soft, a promise of happiness to come. . . .